FLOWERTOWN

Text copyright © 2012 S. G. Redling

Published by Thomas & Mercer
P.O. Box 400818
Las Vegas, NV 89140

ISBN-13: 9781612183022
ISBN-10: 1612183026

FLOWERTOWN

S. G. REDLING

This book is dedicated to my parents,
Matthew and Isabel Redling, who
always believed I could do it.

CHAPTER ONE

"Water's brown."

"Shit." Ellie Cauley ground her cigarette out on the hallway floor, her leg rattling her shower bucket. She had to be at work in less than half an hour. She could pull her hair back into a ponytail; the grease would just make the blonde look darker. The problem was she still stank of sex with Guy, that peculiar smell somewhere between copper and chlorine that sweated out of his skin from the protection meds. She also reeked of weed, but that was nothing new. "Shit." It was all she could think to say as she turned back toward her room. Anything would smell better than the water when it was brown, even actual shit.

"Water's brown." She repeated the message to a young mother herding her children down the hall toward the showers and heard the exact same response from the harried woman. The word spread quickly up and down the hallway, and all around her doors slammed and expletives flew. She squeezed past a couple arguing in front of the toilet closets and could hear, behind one of the thin doors, the sound of vomiting. Probably Rachel, she thought. Her roommate was hell-bent on getting to Vegas.

Inside their small room, Ellie tossed the shower bucket onto the crowded shelf over the hotplate and fished around for her hairbrush. The mirror over the sink was filthy, neither she nor Rachel being overly inclined to keep things tidy. It was just as well. She knew what she looked like as she dragged the brush through her straight, oily hair, then fastened it with a rubber band at the nape of her neck. Dropping her bathrobe onto the floor, she bent over and picked through the pile of clothes beside her bed, catching a whiff of her own scent. Flowertown, indeed, she thought. Shittiest smelling flowers I've ever heard of.

Flowertown was the derogatory, and therefore customary, term for the PennCo Containment Area. It used to be the west end of Dalesbrook, Iowa, in the northeast corner of Penn County, until six years ago when Feno Chemical spilled an experimental and highly dangerous pesticide along the interstate and into Furman Creek, which ran directly to the reservoir that served the area. At first the county had issued a shelter-in-place order and Ellie, along with all the other unsuspecting residents of the area, complied. It wasn't the first time a truck had wrecked on the highway and at the time didn't seem nearly as interesting as when the truck full of live turkeys had overturned out near Brunswick. It got a lot more interesting when the United States Army showed up and barricaded the town while men dressed in space suits poured from unmarked trucks to round up the open-mouthed Iowans like the terrified and stupid turkeys from the summer before.

Contamination and containment became the buzzwords, replaced quickly with quarantine and treatment, all to the musical backdrop of international media and outrage as the world demanded to know who was responsible for the poisoning of seven and a half square miles of America's heartland. There were Senate hearings and criminal investigations. Some people died and many more people suffered, but as weeks turned into months, most outside of the Penn County spill zone went back to their jobs and their newscasts and their horror at the other atrocities available on every continent, on every channel. But the people of Penn County, Iowa, now the PennCo Containment Area, stayed where they were. They pissed into cups and took fistfuls of pills and, as the insidious chemical leeched into their systems, noticed their skin put off a sickeningly sweet smell, like the smell of too many flowers in too small a room. That's when PennCo became Flowertown, and when seven and a half square miles became a world unto itself.

Rachel left the door open when she came into the room, not bothering to notice Ellie standing naked, examining a shirt for stains. Rachel spit into the sink, resting her head against the cool metal. "Tell me again how cool Las Vegas is."

"Not that cool."

"Wrong answer." Rachel pulled a jug of iced tea from the small refrigerator and began to chug. When she'd finished and wiped her mouth with the back of her hand, she said, "You're supposed to talk about the outrageous clubs and the fabulous shows and all the hot guys. And the buffets. Don't forget the buffets where filet mignon is only a dollar and baked potatoes are the size of a dog's head."

Ellie decided the shirt was clean enough and pulled it over her head. "If I were you, I wouldn't plan too much on

3

enjoying the buffets. You'll be lucky to swallow toast by the time you're done with your detox."

Rachel flopped down on her bed, kicking away a pile of clean laundry. "It's all your fault. You're the one who told me about that sick bachelorette party you went to, where the cop turned out to be a stripper and you puked hurricanes all over your bridesmaid dress."

"Yeah, well that was back in the glory days when we could still use public toilets and actually get in our cars and go wherever we wanted."

"Fogey." It was Rachel's nickname for Ellie whenever the conversation turned to life before the spill. Rachel was only twenty-two, ten years younger than her roommate, and determined to survive the four-week detox regimen required to leave the containment area for a weekend. The meds brutalized the body and the mandatory enemas shattered the dignity, but for the young farm girl who had only seen Sin City on the small screen, any amount of sacrifice was worth it to meet up with her family for her sister's wedding. "Nice bruises."

Ellie looked down and saw the dark purple marks coming out on her thighs. They'd match nicely the brick scrapes on the small of her back. "Guy's a romantic."

"Yeah, where was it this time? The dumpster?"

"The back stairwell." She pulled on a pair of jeans, not bothering with underwear. "He let me touch his gun."

Rachel laughed as she lit up a fat joint, blowing the timing and coughing up a lungful of smoke. "I bet he did. Did he at least kiss you on the lips?"

Ellie took the joint and hit it. "Depends on what lips you're talking about." She bit back a cough, holding in the smoke, as Rachel made gagging sounds. "Here, take the rest of this. I smoked up before I thought I was going to get a shower."

"I don't know how you go to work high, Ellie."

"I work in the records office. Trust me. I'm not splitting the atom."

The PennCo Records Office took up two-thirds of the second floor of what had been a tractor supply store. Out of habit, Ellie flashed her badge to the guard, who didn't look at it, and cut through the front corridor of cubicles to get to the stairs. Human resources took up the entire first floor, each cubicle filled with the clicking of keyboards trying to keep up with the tsunami of bureaucracy the long quarantine had created. Ellie peeked over the sea of beige walls, looking for Bing, her friend in export/travel. At first she couldn't see him, but as she turned the final corner for the steps, she saw his skinny back slumped over his desk, his fist pounding the side of his leg. He was on the phone, and whatever he was being told was clearly not what he wanted to hear. He popped up just before Ellie cleared his area and held the phone out to her. Over the din of the office, she couldn't make out any sound but easily understood the one-fingered hand gesture Bing was making at the receiver. She laughed and waved and flipped off the caller in his honor before heading up to her office.

Bing had once told her she was lucky to work upstairs away from all the noise and telephones. The records office was hushed, but she had tried to explain that the silence he heard was the last sighing breath of despair. There was no rush in records. Once your file made it here, whatever you had been fighting for or fighting against had been resolved. This was the evidence graveyard of Flowertown, where petitions and complaints and suggestions came to die, the red rubber-stamped "Closed" their only epitaphs. It was a job made bearable only by being very high, which worked out well for Ellie, who preferred to stay that way.

She threaded her way through file cabinets and piles of document boxes to her desk in the back of the room. She could hear Big Martha, her boss, trying not to lose her cool with a young woman up front. Ellie couldn't think of the girl's name. She knew she had transferred up from HR and had big ideas on how to update and streamline the records process. From the first day, Ellie had ignored her completely, but Big Martha had no choice but to try to explain to the ardent young woman that expediency was not a high priority in records—it was more a game of outwaiting and outlasting—but the girl wanted none of it. She fancied herself quite the firecracker, Ellie wagered, flopping into her crooked office chair and turning on her computer, letting her hazy thoughts play with images of firecrackers and the endless boxes of paper. She liked the image—the sight of all of this going up in flames, burning hot and smoky and acrid enough to cut through the putrid smell of flowers that she still had not gotten used to after all these years.

A short stack of envelopes sat in her inbox. The first she recognized from the much-wrinkled, worn, and marked interoffice envelope. Flowertown was probably the last place in the industrialized world to use these things. Like so many other things in the zone, Internet access was so spectacularly unreliable that most people had pretty much given up on it. Messages were sent the old-fashioned way, on paper, which made them no harder to ignore. Her bosses expected her to attend a mandatory staff meeting that Thursday. It amazed her that anyone within the confines of Flowertown thought that anything could be mandatory anymore, anything other than meds, tests, and check-ins. What were they going to do if she didn't attend the meeting? Fire her? Kick her out? Regardless of her state of employment, she would still receive her quarantine stipend check. It went without saying that her medical was covered, and she had been grandfathered into her living quarters. The only purpose this shadow of a job served was to put some sort of artificial shape to the hours of her day. She showed up, she moved some papers around, she went back to the shoebox she shared with Rachel. And occasionally, if Guy was MP on her floor that night, she slipped off with him for a diversion of the hip-banging kind. It was a freedom that the outside world could never understand and, like her job, was better appreciated very, very high.

The next envelope contained a badly printed flyer from VolCorp, one of the many charitable groups that had crossed the quarantine barrier in the early years to help the contaminated. The message was the usual lamenting and threatening and impassioned plea for resources and volunteers. Ellie didn't know why these messages kept coming to her or who had put her name out there as somebody who could or did give a shit about it. The only involvement she'd ever had with VolCorp was when they were giving away lemonade to anyone who would help repaint the community center. The lemonade had tasted like iodine, and Ellie hadn't painted a thing. She tossed the paper into the recycling bin.

The third envelope stood out from the rest. It was a real envelope, an actual U.S. Postal Service delivery, stamp and all. From the mashed-up look of it, the delivery had been rough, but that wasn't what made her hesitate to open it. It was from her sister, Bev, in Hershey. Ellie ripped open the envelope before she had time to know she didn't want to read it, and confetti showered to her desk. The message invited everyone to a surprise birthday party for their mother three weeks from today at a community park Ellie had never heard of. There would be a pig roast and kegs, and for those family members coming in from out of town, a block of rooms at the Best Western were being held at a special rate but they were going fast because everybody was planning on coming in for Rosalind Seaton Cauley's big sixtieth birthday party! Bev had even inserted maps with directions to the party from every compass point, but Ellie closed the invitation without reading them. She felt pretty certain nobody had mapped out the path from Flowertown to Hershey, and even if she had thought of going, three weeks was not enough time to detox and get the paperwork to leave the site. She also felt pretty certain that Bev knew this and tried not to think of what her sister's motivations might be for sending the festive little note. She dangled the invitation over the recycling bin, wanting to drop it, to make it disappear, but couldn't. Instead she shoved it in a drawer and reached for the final envelope.

She didn't recognize the fourth envelope. The writing on the front was just a series of jumbled letters and numbers. It didn't even have her name on it, but Ellie thought even a brochure for another volunteer rally was better than ending on her sister's message. She unfolded the crisp white paper, seeing nothing but two lines of type:

All You Want.

Arm yourself.

Beneath the message, a cartoon clock danced on the margin. Ellie flipped the paper over, but the rest of the page was white. With a laugh, she scribbled Bing's name on the envelope, tagging it "New Staff Meeting Agenda," and put it in her outbox. Feeling lucky, she tried to open her Internet connection. The screen went white for a long moment and Ellie kicked back in her chair. The odds of getting online were slim to none, but what the hell? She contemplated bumming a cigarette from Big Martha while she waited, but her morning high had just reached that point where time got sort of stretchy, so she just closed her eyes and waited for the screen to come to life.

She drifted, the warmth of the office and the whispers of papers settling over her like a soft throw. She crossed her feet on an open drawer and crossed her arms over her head, once again catching her unwashed scent. This time it didn't remind her of the broken water system or the daily irritations of quarantine. This time her thoughts wandered back to Guy, to the thick twist of muscles in his biceps, etched with a tribal tattoo, to the cut of that muscle that led down to his pelvis. God, she loved that cut. The first time she had seen him, he had been unloading crates outside of her building. His army-issued T-shirt had come loose from his fatigues, and when he reached up to grab a heavy crate from the truck, she had seen those muscles in his stomach. She hadn't even bothered to pretend to not watch him. Guy was short and thick and dark, nothing like her usual type, especially in army clothes. But he wore those clothes and those muscles like he had something dirty on his mind, which, she happily learned, he did. She rubbed her hands over her face, fully prepared to let her mind wander as far afield as it wanted until a voice boomed out before her.

"In Flowertown, secrets can KILL you!"

"Fuck!" Ellie tipped forward in her seat, scrambling for the knob to turn down her speakers. A preview of a new cop drama filled the screen, flashes of a gorgeous starlet, a hail of gunfire, and serious-looking men flickering in and out of sight. Ellie clicked and clicked on the little "x" in the corner, swearing all the while.

"Why don't you just kick the screen in?" She hadn't noticed Bing come up behind her.

Finally the commercial ended, but the image of the show's logo remained frozen on the screen. "Seriously?" Ellie threw the mouse in disgust. "I don't have enough juice to download Championship Sudoku but this shit will play? And stay? I can't get this crap off my screen."

"That's because they want you to see it."

"Of course they do, Bing."

"They want us to see it and they want the folks outside to see it. And they want us to know the folks outside have seen it. They want us to know what we look like to them."

"Obviously. It makes perfect sense. The same people who can't keep the water on in two buildings at the same time have a master plan to hijack the web. They can't keep track of how many paperclips to order, but they can link up satellites and brainwash TV producers."

"It's all part of the plan, Ellie. Trust me." Bing pushed her empty inbox to the side and sat on the corner of her desk, pulling out a pack of cigarettes. "You smoking?"

"I'm in a room full of dry boxes of paper and no ventilation. Of course I'm smoking."

She led her friend toward the back of the office, where the metal sheeting of the walls lay exposed, covered only with thin sheets of plastic nailed to framework. The floor around the area was marked off in scuffed red paint, a warning to anyone up here that this area was for Feno Chemical paperwork only. Document boxes sealed with red tape and mismatched file cabinets that someone had once carefully organized were now rearranged into a functional if uncomfortable sitting area. Ellie hopped up onto a pale gray three-drawer cabinet set perpendicular to a tall, six-drawer tower. The arrangement suited her needs perfectly, giving her room to stretch her legs while leaning back comfortably. It should suit her; she was the one who had rearranged the boxes and cartons into a mazelike warren.

Bing settled down on a low, square cardboard box against the wall. Had he been even twenty pounds heavier, the box would have collapsed under his weight, but it suited him perfectly, and he referred to it as his beanbag. Beside him, the handhold opening of a sealed file box provided a perfect ashtray. A teetering wall of matching sealed file boxes cut the area off from the rest of the office. He lit a cigarette and tossed the pack and lighter to Ellie.

"What would happen if we just burned this whole place to the ground?"

Ellie laughed, blowing out a smoke ring as she tossed the pack back to Bing. "Funny you should say that. I was just thinking that very thing. Maybe it's that new weed you're growing."

"Unlike you, young lady, I don't get high before I come to work." He flicked a long ash into the file box. "Like other respectable Flowertownians, I wait until lunchtime to get wasted."

"See? That's the problem with you HR drones. You never take the initiative." She rested the back of her head against the cool file cabinet, hearing the familiar ka-thunk of the thin metal bending under the weight of her skull. "I got a letter from Bev. They're having a surprise party for Mom. Kegs and everything."

"You going?"

"I was thinking about it. Oh, no, wait!" Ellie smacked her hand against her forehead. "I forgot. I'm in quarantine! Shit! I better call them back."

Bing said nothing, only shaped his ash against the red security tape.

"It's in three weeks. There isn't time to get out even if I wanted to."

"When did you get it?"

"This morning."

"Ouch."

"Yeah." She held the ember of her cigarette against the edge of the cabinet she sat on, adding to a long line of scorch marks. "You're gonna get a little something in the mail from me today too."

"I try not to check my mail at work, knowing what's coming. It's not from that stupid missionary group, is it? I swear to God, those crazy bastards have given me a new religion, the Church of I'm Gonna Kick Your Ass. If they request one more Kirk Cameron video—"

"Whenever I get those I send them to that bitch in the front office. She loves crushing people's hopes and dreams." Ellie ground out her cigarette and wedged it into a dent in the back of the cabinet. "No, this was weird. The address looked like code. You know, R four two two six Alpha Dogstar kind of crap. Like mail from a Klingon."

Bing fished another cigarette from his pack and talked around the smoke. "Maybe you have family in Nigeria who need help getting their money out of the country. I've heard that's been happening a lot lately. Sounds lucrative."

"I wish. All this had was this little dancing clock and this totally cryptic message, like 'You're doomed' or something."

"It actually said 'doomed'? Who says 'doomed'?"

"It was something like that." Ellie rubbed her eyes, trying to think through her morning buzz for the exact message. "Wait, I remember. It was 'All you want.' I remember thinking 'You don't even want to know what I want right now' because I had just read Bev's—"

"You didn't send it to me, did you?"

"What?" She laughed at his sharp tone. "Yeah, why?"

"Shit, don't you ever pay attention to anything? All You Want? That doesn't ring any bells for you? You haven't seen those words plastered all over buildings everywhere you look?"

"Oh please, Bing, don't. Don't start with your crazy government master plan shit. You know I love you. You are my best friend, but I swear I cannot take another second of—"

"This isn't Area 51 crap, Ellie. This isn't a bunch of geeks looking to get off—"

"You of all people should know the innate ineffectiveness of government and bureaucracy and political pork. It's ludicrous—"

"I'm not the only one who thinks this, Ellie!" He finally succeeded in shouting her down. She rolled her eyes but let him speak. "This isn't about a government master plan. This isn't the censorship that is going on right under our noses, even though it's a fact that every word of our correspondence, digital and paper, is filtered before entering or leaving—"

"Bing..."

"Okay, okay, let's just put that totally off to the side." He leaned forward on his box, threatening the strength of the sealing tape. "This is something totally different. This is simple economics: supply and demand, widgets and gadgets."

"Garbage in, garbage out."

"Exactly." He pointed his finger at her, and Ellie tried not to smile at how much he looked like a bird at this moment, a big pissed-off bird. "The problem is there is no garbage out. There is only garbage in and the system is overloaded. PennCo was designed to accommodate a limited number of residents for a limited amount of time. Not seven years, I can guaran-fucking-tee you that."

"No argument here, brother. What's your point?"

"Yeah, well not only has the time frame been stretched way too long, so has the population matrix."

"Population matrix?" Ellie asked. "I'm outta here."

"This was supposed to be a quarantine zone for a potentially fatal chemical, but instead of the population shrinking, it has grown. And continues to grow. Rescue workers, military, civil engineers..."

"Racketeers, extortionists—Walmart, for the love of Pete." This part of the argument Ellie knew well and agreed with. Flowertown had become a high-risk/high-pay zone for a number of ambitious and ruthless businesses hoping to make a quick buck on the sudden need for infrastructure. For those healthy and greedy enough to give it a try, the lucrative contracts, whether from Feno or the government, made the sickening prevention meds worth the trouble. The problem was that infrastructures don't pop up overnight and they don't maintain themselves, so the seven and a half miles of restricted space became more congested by the month.

"So what happens when we outgrow our resources?" Bing had worked himself into a state, perched on the edge of the box. "What happens when our contained water and waste supply breaks down? When our food storage systems can't meet safety regulations and food ration lines turn into riots? What happens when the power grid fails from yet another amateur entrepreneur overtaxing it to put up another third-rate rat trap of apartments?"

Ellie knew better than to try to interrupt her friend when he was on a tear, so she simply shook her head and waited.

"I'll tell you what's not going to happen: the government is not going to step in and save us. PennCo bleeds millions of dollars from the American taxpayers every year, and if it looks like there's a chance to ease that burden, don't think for a second this administration or the next will hesitate to plug that hole. And the beauty of it is they won't even have to do anything. All they'll have to do is withdraw the troops, recall the security forces, and let natural human entropy work its magic. Think about it, Ellie: no law, no power grid, no communication. Just Flowertown. The only people left standing would be those who thought ahead and armed themselves now while there's still time."

"Oh my God, I never thought of it like that. If what you say is true, if that's really what's going to happen, then it can only mean one thing." Ellie put her hand to her forehead. "It would mean that...Soylent Green...is...*people.*"

"Fuck you, Ellie!" Bing leapt from his seat, kicking at the file box between them.

"Sorry. My Charlton Heston's a bit rusty, but I thought it was okay."

"Yeah, sure, you know what?" Bing jammed his hand in his pocket and pulled out a baggie of weed. "Get fucking high. Just get high and hide out here and bang your little soldier boy while you can, and then when the shit goes down, you can sit there like all the other sheep and go 'Somebody help us! Somebody save us!' Except there's not going to be anybody. Nobody's coming to save you, Ellie. Nobody. Let me hear you say it."

"Nobody's coming to save me."

"Fuck you, Ellie. I don't know why I waste my time on you."

"Because you want to bang my roommate."

Bing's face flushed deep red, but he bit back whatever nasty retort threatened to escape. Ellie could hear the breath tearing through his large nose as he struggled to contain his temper, and then he stomped out of the office and down the stairs. She reached into the baggie and pulled out a half-smoked joint. As she coughed back the harsh smoke, she could hear the alarm going off on her cell phone on her desk. Eleven thirty, time for her meds appointment.

She held in the smoke so long she began to get light-headed. There was no need for her to hurry to her appointment. She hadn't bothered to share the news with her friends, but after last month's checkup she had received her new medical status—blue tag. It meant she wouldn't have to stand in line with the other hundred people at the dispensary getting their handfuls of maintenance medications. Nope, now she could swipe the crisp new keychain tag under the scanner and be let into the hallway to the left of registration, to the blue tag lounge. It wasn't as crowded in there, and last month there had even been snacks on the table. It seemed a nice perk for finding out her liver had betrayed her.

When HF-16 had first been spilled, thousands had been contaminated. The actual numbers were never released, but statistics snuck out to the press. Approximately 17 percent of those contaminated died within two months, including her boyfriend, Josh. Six percent showed no signs of chemical absorption and were released. That left 73 percent of the population required to undertake a maintenance/rehabilitation medication regimen that killed 12 percent of participants in the first year. Adjustments were made to the medications, and if the reports could be believed, as contamination levels slowly receded, the health of Flowertownians remained steady. Mostly steady, that is. One small sector of the population remained resistant to the medications, their livers choosing instead to throw in the towel and leave the rest of the organs to a slow and miserable death. Those residents were switched from the sickening maintenance medications to simply "quality of life" treatments. And their medical records were transferred to the blue folders. These residents were known as blue tags.

Ellie finally exhaled.

"Nobody's coming to save me."

CHAPTER TWO

Ellie picked through the tray of Twinkies and granola bars until she found the Little Debbie snack cakes she'd been looking for. She grabbed a Nutty Bar for herself, slipping an extra Swiss Roll into her purse on her way to the examination room. Her cottonmouth had not receded with her morning high and she considered turning back for some coffee, but the doctor was already waiting for her. The blue tag lounge had that to recommend it: the service was certainly prompt.

"Good morning. I'm Dr. Lavange. Please have a seat."

Ellie nodded, trying to suck the dry chocolate off her teeth as she allowed the tall woman to hold the door open for her. Dr. Lavange had that skinny, thin-haired look that could have put her anywhere between an unhealthy thirty and a fantastic sixty, and her tendency to talk with her head cocked in permanent sympathy irritated Ellie.

"Why don't I get you set up with your sample cups, and as soon as you get back—"

"I can do it here." Ellie snatched the urine sample cup from the doctor's hands and, before the older woman could protest, dropped her pants and squatted. Six years of urine samples on demand had turned most Flowertown residents into pissing sharpshooters.

Ellie handed the warm cup back to her, not a drop out of place. Dr. Lavange succeeded in hiding her discomfort, and Ellie tried not to grin as the doctor got her fingers damp snapping the plastic lid back on. "I keep telling my roommate that'll be quite a party trick when we get out of quarantine."

"I'm sure it will be." The doctor put the sample on a sliding tray in the wall. In the older woman's eyes she saw the certainty that, urinating abilities aside, Ellie would never be leaving quarantine. "We will also need a blood sample before you leave. Or can you do that too?"

Ellie tried to smirk, but felt that familiar smothering sensation of panic trying to overwhelm her. She shook her head and hopped up on the paper-covered examining table. Dr. Lavange opened her file and began to read.

"It says here you are an admittedly heavy user of marijuana. Is that still the case?"

"More than ever."

She tilted her head even farther to the side. "Ms. Cauley," her eyes flickered to the file then back up, "Ellie, I know the laws regarding illegal drug use within the containment area have been relaxed a great deal. After all, security certainly has enough on their hands, don't they?" Ellie sighed, wondering if Dr. Lavange could actually touch her ear to her shoulder. "But just because there are few criminal consequences for marijuana use, it doesn't mean there are no medical repercussions."

"You mean like liver failure?"

Dr. Lavange's face puckered into a sympathetic mess that made Ellie want to smack it back and forth. "It certainly doesn't help."

"Yeah, well, I'm thinking your HF-sixteen did a lot more damage to my liver than a few dank buds, and with a lot less fun attached."

"It wasn't my HF-sixteen."

"You work for Feno Chemical."

Ellie liked the way the doctor's head jerked. "No, sorry. Not me. I work with Barlay Pharmaceuticals. As an independent contractor."

"Who signs your check?"

"Who signs yours?" As soon as the words left her mouth, Ellie could see the doctor's regret at having allowed herself to be baited so. Lavange turned back to the file, her fingernail tapping out her irritation. Everyone knew Barlay Pharma was a subsidiary of the multinational that also owned Feno Chemical. It made sense, at least to Ellie. Feno had made the mess; their parent company had to clean it up. Why everyone acted like it was some dirty little secret was beyond her. It came in handy, though, when one of the med-techs needed to be put back a step.

Speaking to Ellie's file, the doctor said, "I suppose it would be a waste of both of our times to suggest that you reduce, if not completely stop, your use of marijuana."

"I suspect that is true."

The doctor kept her eyes on the paper. "Have you been informed of the comprehensive counseling services we offer for quality of life treatment?"

"They sound very comprehensive."

She flipped through several pages of the file, searching for something, then closed the folder, clutched it to her chest, and looked at Ellie. "I don't see any mention of family within the containment area. Are our records accurate?"

"They are." Ellie sat very still, promising herself that if Lavange tilted her head so much as a centimeter, she would kick her. Lavange did not move. "I'm not from Iowa."

"May I ask how you came to be in this area?"

"You mean in the spill zone? You can call it that, Doctor. We all do. We all know why we're here." This time, the older woman did not take the bait. Ellie wished she could eat that other Little Debbie in her purse so she wouldn't have to keep talking. "I'm from Pennsylvania, near Hershey."

"Is your family still there?"

"Yes. My parents rented a place in Iowa City for a while, in the early days. They and my sisters took turns living there, visiting me, back when they had the suits and all. Well, my mom never did. Visit, I mean. She couldn't handle the suit and the rest of it."

Lavange nodded, still clutching the file. "And do they still come visit? The clean rooms have gotten much better in the last two years." When Ellie was quiet, Lavange asked, "Do you keep in touch?"

Ellie could feel her throat closing as that gray hairy panic descended once more. "Yeah, you know, they've all got kids and stuff. We e-mail when it's working." She tapped her foot against the table leg, rhythmically soothing herself. Lavange said nothing, just let her tap-tap-tap until Ellie found herself speaking without thinking.

"I wasn't supposed to be here. I quit my job. Advertising. I had a big job in Chicago and I hated it, so my boyfriend, Josh, and I decided to save up our money and take a summer off and go to Spain. My parents were furious. They said I was wasting my education and destroying my career, but when I looked ahead, I just couldn't see myself spending the next forty years churning out demographic reports and test-marketing jingles." The words spilled out so fast, Ellie had to gasp to catch her breath but could not stop her thoughts.

"I was packed. I was packed." Her foot pounded against the table. "I had all my stuff packed in my trunk and we were staying with Josh's parents for a month before we left, out on Blair's Branch Road on the edge of the county. They had the nicest little farm. And you know what's funny? I remember thinking, 'God, it's so beautiful here, why don't we just stay here and skip Spain?' Isn't that funny?" Ellie dragged in a ragged breath and then crossed her feet at the ankles to stop her nervous pounding. She had to tuck her hands under her thighs to keep her fingers from fluttering. Another deep breath, this one smoother, and her tone returned to normal. "So long story short, no, I have no family here."

"And your boyfriend, Josh, and his family?"

Ellie found her sneer once more. "You must not be familiar with the area. Blair's Branch Road is right off Furman Creek. What your people like to call the epicenter of the incident."

The tech Lavange had turned her over to jabbed Ellie's finger like it was personal, but Ellie didn't flinch. All they needed was a drop of blood and her finger complied. Bing had told her once that the maintenance meds contained a blood thinner to make the constant blood samples easier to obtain. She hadn't cared then; she cared less now. Everyone in Flowertown bore the constant bruises and prick marks of needles on their arms and hands and feet. The tech signed off on the blue form and handed it back to Ellie, waving her off to the dispensary window. Lavange had checked off several boxes on the preprinted form for the first tier of quality of life meds.

Ellie leaned against the wall outside the dispensary, waiting behind an older couple leaning on each other. The woman steadied herself by placing her blue-veined hand against a framed sign. The sign was behind thick plastic, protected, and Ellie thought it must be some sort of collector's item by now, at least within the confines of Flowertown. It was a large, soft-focus photograph of a young man swinging his daughter over his head, the sun making both of them glow on the edge of a field of sunflowers. Behind them, laughing and smiling, stood a small crowd, family presumably, with a picnic laid out behind them, complete with a healthy jumping dog. Beneath the photo, in understated type, was the caption "Bringing families together." And beneath that, nearly hidden in the green, green grass, was the Barlay Pharma logo.

Someone with stunningly bad judgment had decided years ago to place those ads around Flowertown, and the graffiti that covered them was both instantaneous and obscene. A couple of times, Ellie had even had to look up what some of the words meant, and she and Bing never tired of seeing the new vulgarities. After a while, Barlay and/or Feno decided to save the PR for the outside world. Now the only place to see the Barlay logo was behind Plexiglas in the heavily guarded dispensary. She couldn't tell if it was an accident or intentional, but when the old woman pulled her hand away from the sign, she left a greasy smear over the center of the photo.

As soon as she made it to the corner, Ellie fished out the roach she had snubbed before going into the med center. Not caring who was watching, she pinched the brown bunch between her fingernails and noisily sucked the lighter's flame to the tip. A few deep hits and nothing remained but a scorched twist of rolling paper that Ellie flicked into the shrubs. Her slow exhale was interrupted by the sound of shattering glass, followed by sirens and the sound of a voice on a bullhorn. Ellie followed the sounds down the block and joined a growing crowd at the corner where a string of military trucks formed a barrier around an apartment building.

"Stand down!"

Ellie couldn't find the owner of the bullhorn. She figured he was probably hiding in one of the trucks, letting the security forces do the actual enforcing. The soldiers were certainly ready. They had riot shields and batons and helmets with thick eye guards. They seemed more than a match for the dozen or so elderly women who were throwing rocks and pieces of broken pavement both up at the building and across the yard toward the trucks. None of them seemed to have the strength to hurl the missiles far enough to be any real danger to the soldiers, but they found a good bit of success smashing out the windows on the lower floors. Around her, people were laughing and cheering the women on.

"Come on over here and arrest us, you little chicken shit!" A short woman in her early seventies brandished half a brick like a hand grenade, threatening a trio of heavily armed soldiers nearest the building. "Come on! Arrest us! Your country club jail is better than this rattrap shit hole you've got us stuck in! What's the matter, boy? You scared of an old lady?"

The men looked back to whomever was in command and, either by order or by instinct, stepped away from the woman as a group. The crowd cheered and the woman held her brick up in triumph. "These are the living conditions we're supposed to accept!" The woman's voice was strong, despite her age and small size. "They put us in this building, this 'senior center,' because they claim it's the safest place for women of our age to live on our own. I had a house!" The crowd yelled back, encouraging her. "A lot of us had houses, and we had to give them up, and for what? For safety? For convenience? How convenient do you think it is to have sixteen old women living in a building where the toilets don't flush half the time?"

Beside her, a larger, older woman hefting a heavy chunk of asphalt chimed in. "Hell, we're lucky to make it to the toilet half the time, so it's not like we're overtaxing the system!" The crowd roared out a laugh, and the smaller woman continued.

"We're not asking for special treatment. We're just asking for safe and hygienic conditions and some goddamn air-conditioning before the catchall trenches start to stink!"

All around the building, people yelled and clapped, everyone dreading the days coming up soon when the spring rain runoff that was caught in containment trenches around the city would begin to stink with the cleansing agents. Somebody, somewhere behind Ellie, started the chant, "All you want! All you want!" and soon the sidewalk was rocking with the words. A young man beside her put his arm around Ellie, trying to get her to sway with him, but she pushed her way back through the throng. Orchestrated demonstrations were never her thing.

As she cleared the thickest part of the crowd, the chorus broke down into boos and catcalls. Looking over her shoulder she saw a soldier in riot gear step up to the ringleader of the rock-throwing. He didn't flinch when she held her brick high in her hands. Instead he flipped up his visor and came even closer. Everything about his posture was relaxed. With all the gear he looked like a catcher for a strange baseball team heading out to the mound for a conference with the pitcher. The woman lowered her brick and her friend put the hunk of asphalt down on the ground. The three huddled together, other women on the lawn coming in closer to listen in. The crowd quieted down and even the military radios stopped squawking. Nobody could hear anything of the conversation until the soldier pointed with his thumb over his shoulder to a fat and sweating soldier perched on top of a jeep and the smaller woman threw back her head and cackled.

All of the women were laughing and the lead soldier shrugged. He turned to face the crowd, and the women put down their bricks and rocks and headed back toward the building. Ellie watched, as curious as the rest of the crowd, as he unstrapped his helmet and tucked it under his arm. It was Guy. She was surprised she hadn't noticed the swagger. Guy headed back toward the convoy, speaking loud enough for the crowd to hear his Boston accent.

"Crisis averted, sir. I promised them we'd have services come out immediately and fix their plumbing. Of course, they wouldn't take my word for it, so I had to up the ante." His eyes slid to the side to see if he still had his audience. "I told them the good news was if it didn't get done, one of our guys would give them a lap dance. The bad news was I told them it would be from Fletcher." He gestured to the fat soldier he had pointed to during the powwow, and even the soldiers laughed. Fletcher flipped him off and the convoy began to disband. Guy, along with a few others still in riot gear, moved through the crowd, shooing people away from the scene.

"C'mon, c'mon, let's go." Guy waved his arms as he walked along the sidewalk. Ellie stayed where she was, watching the crowd obey him as they stepped back into the streets. He started to turn back and then noticed her standing there. He grinned and tucked the helmet farther up under his arm. "Don't you have anything better to do than watch a bunch of old women throw rocks?"

"Not really."

Guy moved in closer, his heavy gear not impeding his grace at all. "I guess we can't all have those cushy office jobs, huh?"

"Guess not."

She stood still as he stepped in close enough for her to feel the heat coming off the black vest and gear. His face shone with sweat, and she could smell a fresh version of

27

the aroma that lingered on her body from last night. He tossed his helmet into the open back of a covered truck and stripped off his flak vest.

"That's a lot of gear for a bunch of old women."

"Yeah, well, you know when we get the call, dispatch doesn't specify."

"Just sends in the big guns."

Ellie let her eyes drift over the damp T-shirt that clung to his chest, sweaty from the riot gear. He stepped in closer—too close, as he always did—and her hand drifted up to rest on his chest. On the edges of her vision she could see a wicked smile on his lips, but her focus remained on the blossom of dampness beneath his collarbone and the two-tone of the drab shirt, wet against dry. Her cottonmouth was back in force, and she licked her lips pointlessly. At the sight of her tongue, Guy pulled her by the hips into him, his mouth stopping less than a whisper away from her own. His lips just grazed hers and his tongue darted out in the lightest touch. She knew he knew what that did to her, and even his arrogant chuckle at her response didn't put her off.

He pushed forward, between her legs, walking her backward until he pressed her against the rough canvas of the truck. Less than an inch taller than she, Guy seemed to Ellie to be a wall, a hot, breathing wall that she wanted to throw herself against again and again. Around them, soldiers reloaded the trucks and cleared away bystanders. Pressed deep into the canvas and using the flak vest that hung from his wrist to shield them from sight, Guy took her hand and slid it down to his groin.

"I thought you didn't like my riot gear." He ground himself against her hand, whispering into her ear.

"I don't." Ellie felt him harden in her hand. "I like it when you take it off."

Guy laughed and took a quick look around for his superiors. "Don't you have to work?"

"Don't you?"

He reached around and grabbed her ass and squeezed. "I think you're probably worth a good disciplinary hearing."

"You could talk your way out of anything." Ellie let her head fall back against the truck, the canvas pulling at her ponytail, as Guy kissed her neck. "You talked those women down."

"What can I say?" He spoke into her skin. "I have a way with the ladies."

"What if you didn't?"

He bit down on her earlobe. "Then I guess I'd be getting a hand job from Fletcher."

Ellie pulled her head to the side. "I mean what if you weren't able to talk those women into surrendering today?" Guy cocked his eyebrow and laughed at the question. "I'm serious. What if they hadn't put down their bricks? Would you have shot them?"

He sighed, putting his hand over hers on his crotch to resume her massage. "It never would have come to that."

"What if it did?"

"It wouldn't." He pulled away and Ellie resisted, pulling him back to her. "What do you want me to say, Ellie? That we'd mow down a bunch of old women for being upset that they have no water? That we'd take our batons to them to shut them up? Is that what you think?"

"No."

29

"No. That's not what we're here for. We're the ones keeping those women safe. We're the ones making sure nobody tampers with the water or the food or the power stations. We're the good guys, Ellie. Or don't you believe that?"

She sighed and nodded, and he leaned back into her again.

"Good girl." His hands tugged at the belt loops of her jeans, banging her softly against his pelvis. His mouth went back to her ear and his breath was hot on her skin. "Now why don't you tell me exactly where, when, and how you're gonna thank me for my services? And use all the dirty words."

Ellie had to laugh as his hands slid inside the waistband of her jeans and his fingers played softly on the small of her back. "It's an awfully big debt to repay. We may actually have to break with protocol and find a bed."

"Ooh, kinky. Go on. Remember, I'm the good guy. A really good guy."

She felt him getting harder against her, and her hands grabbed at the thick plane of muscles in his back. She let her eyes drift up from his neck and saw the broken windows.

"What if they told you to withdraw?"

"Hmm, baby?" Guy purred into her neck.

Ellie hooked her hands around his back, clinging to him, unable to look away from the shattered glass and the damaged building. "What if they told you to withdraw from Flowertown?"

"Why would they do that?"

"What if they did?"

She felt him tense beneath her hands.

"Why would they tell us to withdraw, Ellie? We're the good guys, remember?"

"I know." She felt a draft as his damp skin pulled back from hers. "You're the good guys. If they told you to withdraw, who would protect us?"

Guy stepped back from her, holding her out at arm's length. "What's with you today?"

Before she could answer, a rash of obscenities broke out on the other side of the jeep.

"Roman! Goddamit, Roman! Fletcher!"

Guy swore and stepped toward the rear of the truck, letting her fingers slide free of his. "Roman here, sir. What's the problem?"

Ellie couldn't see the man shouting, but he sounded very pissed off. "The problem is, Roman, that while you're giving lap dances to the old broads here, someone vandalized the goddamn trucks!"

"Aw shit." Guy ran off, leaving her resting against the unmarked side of the truck. "I'm on it, sir." She heard orders being barked and bystanders being warned to keep back and decided it would be a good time to head back to work. Pushing herself off the rough canvas, she traced her fingers along the rope webbing holding the canopy in place and tipped her head around the corner of the truck to see the damage. Three trucks were lined up along the sidewalk, each one spray painted in bright orange, one word per truck:

ALL YOU WANT.

CHAPTER THREE

Bing wasn't at his desk when she returned, so she stuck a sticky note to the Little Debbie with a smiley face and the words "Forgive me yet?" Just to be sure, she scribbled a few bubble hearts around the words. Of course Bing would forgive her; these little dustups were nothing new. She was a little surprised he hadn't waited for her to get back before taking his lunch, but then Bing's supervisors were a bit more strict than hers about break times. Or maybe Bing just paid more attention to them. She perched the snack cake on the buttons of his telephone just as a page buzzed out of the speakers.

"Ellie Cauley, if you are in the building, Ellie Cauley report to your office immediately." Big Martha's voice sounded extra strident, as if she had been making the page for a while. Ellie didn't hurry—med appointments trumped all else in the magical world of Flowertown—but as she made her way down the corridor, more than one worried face looked up at her. At the last cubicle, Ellie heard a woman whisper into the phone, "She's on her way up right now."

Part of her wanted to spin on the woman and call her a tattletale or snitchy-pants or some other ridiculous childhood taunt, but she thought better of it. Until, that is, she heard that same woman whispering over the cubicle walls. God, she didn't know how Bing stood it down here. At the steps, knowing she had the eyes of a gaggle of HR drones on her, she spun back and glared. "Do you get paid extra for that? Some kind of suck-up bonus?"

"They've been paging you for, like, an hour." With her oversprayed hair and oversized glasses, the woman looked exactly like every cranky librarian Ellie had ever known.

"I've been gone for, like, my meds. Like, it's the law."

All of her coworkers had ducked back into their cubicles, but the woman was undaunted. "Like you're so concerned with the law. I guess that's why the suits are here."

Ellie headed up the steps. Some people would let anything clench their asses. "The suits" were either Feds or Fenos, authority figures who liked to think they still had some ability to intimidate the population, and judging by the way some people still danced to their tune, she guessed they did. She put on her best game face, which looked very much like her "I don't care" face and her "I wish I were higher" face, and took her time heading up the steps. There was nobody in the front of the office—not a good sign.

"She's here." The new girl, perched as lookout, announced her arrival. Ellie could hear Big Martha swear under her breath and, as she turned the final corner to her little desk crammed as far back in the office as possible, saw that her boss was physically shielding her desk from two men and a woman in matching suits. They didn't call her Big Martha for nothing. Ellie felt reasonably sure that all three suits, with the new girl in tow, couldn't have moved the heavyset woman. Once Ellie was in sight, however, Big

Martha sighed and, with some reluctance, took a step away from the desk.

"Something I should know?" Ellie asked.

Big Martha shot her a warning glance, telling her with overgrown eyebrows that the situation was serious. "It took you long enough."

"Meds." Ellie addressed the answer to the three unsmiling suits.

The new girl spoke quickly. "Your appointment was marked for eleven thirty." She held out her watch. "It's after one now."

Ellie leveled her gaze at the girl, no expression on her face. The girl stood her ground for a moment, then another moment, but as long seconds ticked past, her face flushed red. Nobody jumped in to save her, and Ellie let her twist a while before speaking.

"Don't get a wet spot just yet. The job is still mine."

"I...that's not...you were supposed to..."

Ellie dismissed her with a roll of her eyes and turned back to the people in the room who still thought they mattered. "Is there some sort of problem?"

The shorter of the two men tapped a manila envelope against his palm. "Are you Eleanor Marie Cauley?"

"Seriously?" Ellie asked. "Don't you think we're past that by now?"

"Please answer the question. Are you Eleanor Marie Cauley?"

Big Martha nodded at her to answer. "Yes. I am Eleanor Marie Cauley. But my friends call me Lady Esmeralda of Wainright."

The man smiled at that, still tapping the envelope. "Hello, Ellie."

"Or some people call me Ellie. Whichever you're more comfortable with, Agent...?"

"Mister. My name is Mr. Carpenter."

"Ah, Mr. Carpenter." Ellie nodded, mimicking the false friendly body language of the man before her. "No Federales here, eh? Just working people. Feno Chemical getting down and dirty with the proletariat. Little PR stunt?"

"Hardly."

Something about the man's easy smile put Ellie on her guard. Maybe it was the way he tapped that envelope like it held the golden ticket or the way his coworkers tracked him from the corners of their eyes, making sure to stand just slightly behind him. This man held himself as the dominant force in the room, and Ellie understood that, although late to the party, she was being lured to conversion. She wouldn't go easily.

"Now that the niceties are out of the way, Mr. Carpenter, why don't you tell me what exactly it is that I can do for you?"

"Do you know what that red paint on the floor over there means, Ellie?"

A thousand inappropriate answers rushed to her tongue, but Ellie took a deep breath to contain them. "Yes sir."

"Do you?" He held the envelope in mid-tap, feigning surprise at her answer. "Well now, that makes my job a little more complicated then. You see, that red paint is a clear indicator of where public files end and Feno Chemical confidential files begin. Everything on the red paint is to be handled by authorized Feno Chemical employees only. I don't suppose you've picked up classified authorization over the past few weeks, have you, Ellie?"

"No sir. Haven't been able to pass the written test."

He took a sudden step toward her, and had she not been close to a small pile of file boxes, she might have jumped back. "Do you want to tell me then who has been in the classified area moving boxes around?" His voice cracked with anger, and she could see him struggling to rein it in. It was such a ridiculous thing to be furious about, Ellie almost laughed.

"I have, Mr. Carpenter. I have moved those boxes around."

His eyes shone, as if the fact of this outrage brought tears to his eyes. "Would you care to explain to myself and my associates why?"

"Rats."

Big Martha snorted a laugh and quickly covered it with a dry cough.

"Rats."

"Rats, Mr. Carpenter. Big Norway rats. I'm afraid it's a terrible problem. I saw a pair of the little bastards scampering around back there and, well, I guess I just lost my head." Ellie sighed. "I got a broom and I charged back there with no thought to my personal safety. All I could think was what those buck-toothed little demons would do to classified Feno property."

Mr. Carpenter went back to tapping his envelope, his eyes down, and his associates held themselves in a tense posture of anxiety and anticipation. When he looked back up, he was composed. "Do you know what this is?" He waved the envelope before him.

"A toaster?"

Mr. Carpenter laughed. "That's funny. I'll tell you what it's not. It's not a joke. You must be one hell of an employee, Ellie, because your boss was adamant about keeping us out of your desk. She physically blocked us until we had a signed warrant."

Ellie shook her head. "Oh, you know Martha. Give her a constitution and she's like a dog with a bone. She just won't let it go. Imagine that."

Mr. Carpenter looked down at the envelope like he was reading from it. "According to the search and seizure of property policy within the PennCo Containment Area, authorities cannot begin process until the owner or holder of the property is present."

Ellie felt a cold spot form in her stomach. "Kind of makes you want to salute, doesn't it?"

"It's a good law." Mr. Carpenter smiled. He would have been handsome if he weren't scaring the crap out of her. "You know what else is a good law? The law that says that illegal drugs cannot be in restricted areas. Rumor has it you're quite the pothead, Ellie."

"Gee, if only there were some blood and urine samples you could check with."

He laughed again, seeming to really enjoy himself. "Now we both know what you do in your own time is your own business. But what you do here at work? Well, that's another kettle of fish." He held the envelope up once more. "This warrant gives my associates permission to take your desk apart, inch by inch. I sure hope we don't find any illegal substances."

"You've got to be kidding me," Ellie said. "What are you going to do if you find it? Arrest me? Keep me in Flowertown with no chance of parole?"

"I will put you in the detention center." Mr. Carpenter stepped up closer to her. "It will be my pleasure. You think you've got it tough living in the East Fifth Towers? Try bunking with a couple dozen women in a room half the size."

"Oh no," Ellie said. "You mean I'd have to share a toilet with twenty people instead of eighteen? The electric only works two days a week instead of three? Oh the humanity!" She put her hands on her hips, faking more confidence than she felt. "Knock yourself out, shithead."

Mr. Carpenter snapped his fingers at his associates, who leapt into action. They rifled through every box and tray on the top of the desk, tossing everything onto the floor as they went. Then came the drawers, which they ripped out of the desk with pleased fury. Pens, pads, clips, folders, scissors, the debris of office life went flying with each drawer. Ellie felt that cold spot within her growing. In the bottom drawer, the file drawer, in the back, was a Tinkerbell lunch box full of fresh, green buds and several pipes and packs of rolling papers. It was the biggest drawer in the desk and the most logical place to hide any sort of stash, and so, of course, the goons saved that drawer for last. The woman got the pleasure of discovery, and she slapped the metal box on the desktop with satisfaction.

"What's this?" Mr. Carpenter asked.

"My lunch."

"I'm hungry." He smiled and flicked the metal latches. "Let's see what you've brought."

Ellie couldn't bear to look and instead turned to Big Martha for a moment of consolation. Her boss shook her head, disgusted, until she looked back at the desk. Her eyes widened and once again she bit back a laugh.

"What the…" Mr. Carpenter began emptying the lunch box, pulling out handfuls of Twinkies. "What is this?" He ripped open a package and squeezed it in his fist. He held the yellow and white mess under her nose. "What the hell is this? Some kind of joke?"

"No, Mr. Carpenter. That's a Twinkie."

"You think this is funny?"

"No, I think it's delicious."

He threw the snack cake on the ground. Before he could let loose another tirade, Big Martha stepped in. Easily six feet tall, she didn't need actual physical contact to make her presence felt.

"I'll tell you what this is, Mr. Carpenter. This is over. You got your warrant. You did your search. You found out who moved the boxes and why. I think your visit is over."

Mr. Carpenter spun on her, too angry to be aware of anything but his failed search. "I don't really give a good goddamn what you think. I don't know who tipped you off to our visit today, but you're on my radar now, both of you." The warning would have been slightly more ominous if he hadn't chosen to turn sharply on his heel. In his rage he had failed to notice the smashed Twinkie beneath his feet and nearly fell on his back. Everyone in the room had the good sense not to laugh, but Big Martha and Ellie both suffered from the effort.

Swearing, Mr. Carpenter stomped out of the office, followed by his associates and a diminishing trail of cake and cream. Only when the last footstep sounded down the stairs did Big Martha and Ellie dare let out the breaths they held, which immediately led to near-hysterical laughter. They leaned against each other, laughing and gasping, both suddenly damp with delayed flop-sweat. The new girl, who had stayed well out of sight during the exchange, crouched down and began picking up the office supplies around the desk.

"What the hell are you doing?" Ellie asked.

"Cleaning up. I can't believe the way they just—"

"Get the fuck away from me."

The young girl clutched a stack of tabbed folders to her chest like a shield. "What?"

"You heard me." Ellie pointed to the front of the office. "Get the fuck away from me, you little suck-up." Her voice skipped up to a comically nasal tone. "'It's after one o'clock. Your meds were at eleven thirty.'"

"Well, they were!"

Big Martha laughed and shook her head. "Honey, go up front. Just go." The girl threw down the folders, big tears in her eyes, and stomped off. They watched her go, and Ellie let out a sigh that held the last of her tension. She felt like she had been running on stilts. Big Martha stared at the mess before her.

"Twinkies? Where the hell did you get Twinkies?"

Ellie picked up the Tinkerbell box as if it were actually magic. "I have no idea."

She didn't see Bing again until the end of the day. Big Martha kept the new girl busy in the front of the office and left Ellie to spend the day organizing and cleaning up her ransacked desk. She wanted to leave the smashed Twinkie on the ground as a badge of victory, but both she and Martha knew the rat story would get a lot more believable if they left open treats like that around. She didn't need three and a half hours to rearrange her paperclips and scissors, but that's how long she took. With every paid minute spent stacking sticky notes in neat little columns, Ellie felt more vindicated. Granted, it was true she wasn't supposed to have moved any boxes within the red-painted floor space, but really, Mr. Carpenter's little storm trooper routine seemed a bit much.

When Bing finally peeked his head around the corner to her workspace, she sat with her chin propped up on her palms, staring at the once again organized classified space.

"You're still here. That's a good sign."

"I guess you heard about all the excitement."

"Didn't you get my text?" Bing dropped his voice in standard Bing excitement style. "I knew it. I told you they're filtering everything."

Ellie pulled her phone out and checked the screen. "No texts."

"See? See?" Bing took his usual spot on the corner of her desk. "They were looking for you and so they blocked your phone."

"I doubt that, Bing. We just have really shitty service." Just then, her phone chirped twice. Two messages had arrived. "Oh look, here you are. 'U r being paged.' That was your big warning? Thanks, man. So much for your filter theory."

"On the contrary." Bing folded his arms. "They were looking for you. They blocked your phone. They're done with you, so now your texts go through. Once they've been cleared through their security filter."

"Well, I can see why they'd block this text, Bing. That's an explosive message you sent."

"What did you want me to say? 'Suits are imminent. Hide the weed.'"

"That would have been nice. And hey," she leaned forward and hit his leg, "where *is* my weed?"

Bing laughed. "I took it. You took mine."

"No, you threw yours at me during your hissy fit. And what's with all the Twinkies? You know I hate them."

"I know." Bing kicked her chair. "That's why I left them, to teach you a lesson."

"You taught me a lesson, all right. Find a better place to hide my weed at work." Ellie shook her head. "You should have seen this guy, Bing. Talk about a teeny tiny little power suck. He had every intention of dragging me out of here by my hair and throwing me in a hole. And all just because I moved some of those stupid Feno boxes."

Bing looked over at the neatly arranged area. "How did he know you had moved them?"

"Big Martha said a messenger delivered two new boxes and, I guess when he saw our living room, ran back and tattled." Ellie put her chin back in her palm and squinted at the boxes. "I know I'm not what you'd call a model citizen or even an especially law-abiding one, but doesn't that seem a little excessive to you? I mean, they're just boxes. They're all sealed. The file cabinets are locked. If they're that classified, why aren't they locked up somewhere? Somewhere guarded?"

"Uh, Ellie, they are locked up somewhere. The records office is supposed to be secure. Remember that badge you're wearing?"

"Yeah, but nobody ever looks at it. If these boxes are so freaking precious, so tip-top secret, why don't they keep them away from stoner drones like me? For that matter, why aren't they on a computer? Who the hell prints all their records?" Ellie rose from her chair and headed toward the red zone. "What's in these boxes that's so freaking important I can't sit on them?"

"Ellie, what are you doing?" Bing jumped up and stepped behind her. "You almost got arrested for playing around with those boxes."

"No, I almost got arrested for moving these boxes. Now I'm just looking at them."

Bing's eyes darted all around the area. "How do you know they haven't installed sensors or cameras in here?"

"In an afternoon? With Big Martha watching? Are you serious?" She folded her arms and stared at Bing. "Are you telling me that you, Ian Billingsly, the King of All Conspiracies, is afraid to step onto the dreaded red zone?"

"I'm telling you that..." Bing's mouth moved, trying to decide exactly what he was telling her. "What I'm telling you is that I don't want to be arrested."

"Well, neither do I, and I damn near was because of these stupid piles of cardboard." Ellie turned back to the red zone. "I think I should at least know what nearly incarcerated me." She hesitated before putting her foot over the red paint, the idea of sensors and cameras never having occurred to her before Bing suggested it. While it was highly unlikely Feno could have had them installed, she figured nothing was impossible. Not wanting Bing to think she took his paranoid fantasies seriously, she stomped onto the red paint and walked quickly between the columns of boxes.

"See?" She turned back to Bing. "No sirens."

"At least none we can hear."

"Oh shut up and help me look at these." Bing took a deep breath and jumped onto the red paint as if it were a platform. Still no alarms sounded and nobody came running, so the two of them scanned the labels on the sides of the boxes and the cards in the pockets on the front of the filing cabinets.

"Well," Ellie sighed, "that was a huge anticlimax. It's nothing but codes."

Bing squinted and read from a box at eye level. "B seven six eight Hv four to B nine seven zero Hv four. Any ideas?"

"Besides a sneaking suspicion that Feno Chemical is run by androids? No," Ellie said. "They sure do love their alphanumeric codes though, don't they? What's the whole name of the stuff that spilled? HF-sixteen Lj four something something."

Bing continued to scan the boxes while he spoke. "HF-sixteen LjR four two nine three."

"How do you remember that?"

"How do you not?" Bing asked. "It's the chemical compound that's kept us prisoner in a military superstate for almost seven years."

Ellie supposed he had a point, and he looked too tired for her to rib him about the military superstate comment. Plus, after the shakedown today, her faith in the apathy of authority had been shaken a bit. "Do you think these codes could be other chemicals?"

Bing rubbed his eyes. "I don't know. That seems kind of hard to believe."

"Even for you?"

He laughed. "Yeah, even for me. It just doesn't make any sense. Surely they keep their chemical records on a highly guarded computer. These really can't be that important if they're just boxed up like this."

"Well, they were important enough to threaten me with jail." Ellie fished her beeping phone from her pocket. "And they cost the life of an innocent Twinkie." She glanced at the screen and shoved the phone back into her jeans.

"Anything interesting?" Bing asked. Ellie didn't have many friends and therefore didn't get many texts. "Let me guess. Action Star Guy Roman wants you to watch him bench press a school bus full of children." Ellie laughed but said nothing. "You know as well as I do that nobody's real name is Guy Roman. He's totally making that up."

"It's his name, Bing. I saw his ID."

"Oh, and the military never uses fake names."

"Guy Roman? You think the army's going to make up a name like that?" She headed back toward her desk and Bing followed.

"See? Even you think it's a ridiculous name!"

"Unlike Bing."

"Hey, that's a nickname. Guy Roman is a porn name."

Ellie dropped into her chair and put her feet on the desk. "Well then, I guess that suits him, doesn't it?"

"Oh, gross." Bing perched on a low file cabinet near the desk. "So where's he whisking you off to tonight? The water tower? A quickie behind the barracks?"

"Why is everybody so worried about where I fuck Guy?" Her tone was nastier than she meant it to be, but the stress of the day was starting to settle on her. She softened her tone and shot a rubber band at Bing. "Why don't you be a hero and take some soup over to Rachel? She's only a few days from clearance and she's as sick as a dog."

"I bet she still looks hot."

"Oh yeah, green is really her color. And I'm sure her breath's a real treat."

"I bet it smells like honeysuckle." Bing sighed dramatically and laughed with Ellie. "I don't think I'm going to have any luck finding any soup, though. I looked a couple days ago and even Walmart was out. Something about a breakdown on the barrier road last week. The trucks didn't get through."

"You managed to get Twinkies, though."

"Well, of course." He got to his feet and dusted off his jeans. "I've got my standards. I want those back too, by the way. Maybe Rachel can keep down some creamy vanilla goodness."

Ellie groaned. "Now who's being gross?"

"Hey hey hey!" Bing wagged his finger at her. "Keep it clean. My intentions for the lovely Rachel are pure. Nothing but good clean fun. If it happens to involve occasional nudity, well, so be it."

"Go on, get outta here." Ellie waved him down the corridor. "Go save your damsel."

"All right," Bing shouted over his shoulder. "Have fun fornicating!"

"I will!" Ellie waited until she heard his footsteps heading down the stairs. She pulled her phone from her pocket once more and read the message again. It wasn't from Guy. It was from Med Services. Since quality of life treatment medications could not be taken in weekly doses, each blue tag patient was required to take their various pills at regular intervals throughout the day.

"For her convenience" the pharmacist had explained that each blue tag patient was enrolled in an automated med-alert phone system that would text when a dosage was due. Ellie had already ignored the first alert, the one that had come in after Bing's message had finally gotten through. Pulling two small red pills from her pocket, she wondered what would happen if what Bing suspected were true, if text messages around Flowertown could actually be blocked and filtered. Would they block the medical alerts for someone in need of medications? Was she already behind on her quality of life treatments? Figured. She swallowed both pills.

CHAPTER FOUR

"Well, that was a bad plan," Ellie said to herself as she passed through security outside the records office. It had occurred to her that if Bing was headed to soothe the ailing Rachel, that meant her room would be too crowded by one. She knew Bing had absolutely no shot at winning her young roommate's heart or favors, but she saw no need to dash his hopes. Rachel liked Bing's flirting, and Bing didn't seem to mind the constant, if friendly, rebuffs. Whatever it took to pass the time, she figured. But while another fruitless attempt was underway, Ellie would just be an interloper, so she had to find somewhere else to go. Plus, Bing and Rachel both figured she'd heard from Guy. Ellie had no intention of revealing the true texts she had received.

She headed down Avenue Four. The heart of Flowertown had originally been mostly farmland, and as quarantine and treatment facilities had sprung up, the military had laid them out with military precision. Starting from the few blocks of already present structures, Flowertown had blossomed out in a near-perfect grid, the names of the streets showing the same imagination as their shape. North-south lines were avenues, east-west were streets, and everything was numbered.

For the most part, there were no real sidewalks because there were very few cars to dodge. After the initial chaos of containment, all roadways were closed to everything except military and rescue vehicles. Personal vehicles within the spill zone were impounded along the barrier zone for disinfection, and as centrally located living quarters became permanent, few residents bothered to reclaim their vehicles. There was really no place to drive anyway.

What made HF-16 so dangerous was what would have made it such an effective pesticide, had the testing been allowed to continue. Targeted for a specific strain of grain-eating beetle, the chemical was intended to not only eradicate a large segment of the parasite population, but to remain inert within those birds and bugs that ate the remaining survivors. It was hoped that those predators would then continue to excrete the pesticide, the chemical having attached itself to the animal's cellular structure, and therefore ensure the eternal extinction of the grain-eating beetle.

In a horrible sense, HF-16 worked. It did attach itself at a cellular level, and any organism that absorbed it did continue to secrete the chemical through any form of elimination, from bodily waste to fallen hair to saliva-soaked chewing gum. Unfortunately, it proved toxic to a large number of organisms, including people, farm animals, and most of the bird population. It also proved to be quite resistant to decontamination, which was why the water system of Flowertown had been completely contained. City and county water mains were diverted, sewage lines internalized. A ring three miles wide around Flowertown had been completely burned and sterilized with a combination of herbicides and decontaminants as well as high-frequency jamming waves, to prevent any wildlife from sneaking out with the dangerous chemical. Anything that made it to Flowertown had a very difficult time getting out.

This included any type of pollution. Open burning within the confines of the spill zone was prohibited, and containment engineers had even tried to enforce a no-smoking ban for the first six months before they realized there were limits to human cooperation. Litter was strictly controlled, hundreds of people employed simply to pick up scraps of paper and wads of gum, lest they blow out of the containment field. Recycling was mandatory, and packaging on incoming supplies was legally required to be kept at an absolute minimum. The end result of all this containment and legislation was that Flowertown, the most contaminated place on earth, was also the most environmentally progressive. It was an irony that was only amusing for the first year or two.

A tall, skinny kid with bad skin was scraping peeling paint off the yellow curb Ellie walked along. She wouldn't have noticed him if he hadn't stuck his arm out before her.

"Hey, Ellie, right? You carrying?" She shook her head. He was looking to buy some pot and must have met her sometime she was with Bing. "I heard Bing's got some good stuff right now. Tell him to call me, okay?"

"Yeah, I will." Ellie kept walking, not bothering to get the kid's name, much less his number. Bing knew everyone in Flowertown, at least all the pot smokers, whose numbers had grown exponentially over the years. Boredom, anxiety, and the nausea-inducing maintenance medications made marijuana a household staple, and since none of it could leave the spill zone anyway, the law turned a blind eye to its commerce. As Bing had wisely crooned one night, "The opiate of the masses has finally become an actual opiate." She patted her pocket, feeling the bag Bing had thrown at her earlier still tucked away there. It was strange, she thought as she pulled open the door to an unmarked bar, that Mr. Carpenter hadn't insisted on patting her down.

The noise within the bar blew her thoughts from her head. Some basketball game was on the big screen behind the bar, and whoever was playing mattered a great deal to the gang gathered before it. Ellie groaned, the sounds within the small room seeming louder than usual. She made her way to the far corner of the bar and waved to the bartender for a tall draft. The girl behind the bar nodded and held up an empty shot glass, silently asking Ellie if she also wanted her customary shot of bourbon. Ellie shook her head. She was getting a headache and could feel the two pills she had swallowed on an empty stomach turning into something bitter and foul. It looked like the quality of life meds, or QOL, as they were labeled, were going to be as hard to get used to as the maintenance meds, assuming she had long enough to worry about it. The bartender reached across the bar and traded Ellie the tall glass of beer for a debit card. She swiped the card and handed it back to Ellie, along with a bowl of saltines.

Ellie took a bite of a cracker. "What, no American cheese slices to go on them?"

The bartender shook her head in disgust. "Can't get peanuts or even potato chips. Larry wanted me to start charging for the bowls so we wouldn't go through them so fast. Can you imagine trying that in this monkey house?"

"Why can't you get peanuts?" The crowd watching the game had begun to chant, so Ellie had to shout to be heard.

"That truck wreck." The bartender was now at a full shout. "On the barrier. Won't get anything until next week!" Someone must have made a basket because the bedlam at the other end of the bar got even louder. The bartender, knowing where her money came from, headed back into the fray as Ellie waved her off. First Bing's soup, now the bar's snacks. Word around the zone was that only one tractor-trailer rig had overturned on the secure highway through the barrier zone, but it seemed it had been carrying an awful lot of supplies.

The beer bounced around in Ellie's stomach, and she was grateful for the crackers. She rubbed her hands over her face, and it felt like her eyeballs were too big for their sockets. Was this how it would be, she wondered? Would she just begin to feel progressively worse every day, every minute? Her phone buzzed in her pocket and she didn't want to answer it. She hadn't paid attention when the pharmacist had told her how often she would need to take her QOL meds. If this was another dosage reminder, she wanted to ignore it, but curiosity got the better of her. She pulled out her phone and tapped the screen. It was from Guy.

"PS1 til 10. Alone."

Ellie tipped back the glass and drank the beer down in a few deep swallows. PS1 was power station one, less than six blocks from the bar. If memory served, it had a decent-sized living area for the guards and workers, including a shower that almost always worked, to say nothing of a decent-sized cot. She belched and grabbed a few saltines for the road. Meds aside, she still had some say over the quality of her life.

Before she made it to the door, the crowd at the bar erupted again, this time in angry shouts and some creative obscenities. Ellie glanced over her shoulder, expecting to see some referee getting the business from fans, but instead the screen was full of a trailer for a new action film coming out. She had seen flashes of ads online, but this was the first actual trailer, and judging by the sea of middle fingers jabbed at the screen, her opinion of the film was the popular one. The movie was called *Leak,* and from what she could gather, it was about a band of terrorists who escaped Flowertown to infect Chicago or New York or some other place more important than Iowa for whatever reasons the jackasses in Hollywood thought people would buy. It was an outrageous concept and hugely insulting to all the people who had had their lives restricted for so many years through no fault of their own. Containment and contamination weren't just buzzwords in Flowertown. Everyone had lost someone after the spill, and nobody endured the maintenance medications lightly. When Ellie thought of the implications of suggesting that anyone in Flowertown would willingly subject the rest of the country to what they had been put through—

The crowd cheered again. The screen was black, as if bending to their collective will. People high-fived each other, glad to see the odious trailer gone, replaced by a black screen, then a blue screen, then a scroll of technical jargon before freezing on the network logo. Someone had cut the trailer short. In the middle of the college basketball playoffs. Ellie knew how much it cost to run a TV ad during the playoffs. That was a mighty expensive mistake on someone's part. She turned and headed out of the bar, remembering the ass-chewing days of advertising. She didn't think she'd want to trade places with whoever would be paying for that mistake. Then she stepped out onto the street and the smell of the rainwater decontaminants struck her. She'd trade places with that fuck-up in a heartbeat. In a heartbeat.

On the walk to the power station, Ellie decided that even more than Guy's body, what she really wanted was a shower. Her skin felt slick with oil and old fear, and she burped up traces of the vile medication. Nobody would ever call her a stickler for hygiene, but even Ellie had her limits. She pushed the buzzer and stuck her tongue out at the closed-circuit camera above the panel, and the latch on the chain-link gate opened.

"There's my girl." Guy sat with his feet propped up on the front desk of the small station. "I see you got all dolled up for me."

"Don't start. Are we alone?"

"Just you, me, and cable TV."

"Good." Ellie peeled her shirt off and stepped out of her jeans as she headed for the shower. "Tell me you have water."

"It's the power station. Of course we have water. Is that the only reason you're here?"

"Not the only reason." Ellie spoke loudly enough to be heard over the running water. "But if you could smell me, you'd know it's for the best." She pulled the flimsy plastic curtain across the small stall, but Guy pulled it back. Grinning, he sat back on the toilet, folded his hands behind his head, and watched her.

"Consider it the cover charge."

Ellie smiled and turned her face up to the water. It stank of chlorine and was only barely tepid, but it washed the smell of anxiety off of her skin. She rolled the bar of hard government-issue soap between her hands until a pathetic lather formed, and she ran her hands over her body, not bothering to see if Guy was watching. She knew he was. She would love to luxuriate in the moment, or maybe invite Guy to join her, but they both knew that even water for military facilities could only hold out so long. A quick lather of medicated shampoo and Ellie felt clean once more, the smell of flowers overcome for the moment by the smell of chemicals.

She turned off the water and leaned back naked against the cool tile. "Seems a shame to get back into those dirty clothes now that I'm all nice and clean." Ellie expected Guy to join her in the stall, making one of his usual comments about getting dirty. Instead he tossed her a towel.

"We've got to talk."

She stared at the scratchy white cloth. "This can't be good."

"It's not all bad."

"Okay." She made no move to cover herself. "Let's hear it."

"Get dried off. I'll get you a drink."

She tipped her head back, the fluorescent light making her eyes hurt again. Guy stepped out into the office and she followed him, dripping water and leaving sopping prints behind her.

"You want a beer?" He turned to her with an open bottle. "And do you think you could put something on?"

Ellie took the bottle. "I never thought I'd hear those words out of your mouth. This day is just full of surprises." She took a deep drink. "I don't suppose you have anything clean around here that I could borrow for a little while. I wasn't kidding about not wanting to put on filthy clothes."

Guy poked around in a cupboard and pulled out an army-green T-shirt. "I don't know whose it is, but it's clean." He tossed it to her and turned his back, leaning on his fists at the desk.

"Wow, thanks for the privacy." Ellie pulled the shirt over her head. "I'm decent now. I think it's okay to look." When he still didn't look up, she took another drink from the bottle. "You know, Guy, this is still a drama-free zone, remember? I thought we were both cool with that. If you're seeing somebody else and you don't want to—"

"I signed the papers."

"What?"

He straightened up and turned to her, holding a thick sheaf of paper. "I signed them. Today. After I saw you."

Her mouth hung open, waiting to hear something that would make sense of what he was saying. "I thought you weren't...you said you'd never...you love the army."

"Yeah, well, I thought about it." Guy leaned against the back of the office chair, his feet crossed casually, but the fingers that gripped the pages were white. "I changed my mind."

"You changed your mind."

"Yeah, I changed my mind. You know, it's a good offer. A really good offer." Ellie stepped backward unsteadily, reaching behind her for the cot she knew was close. She sat down hard on the edge of it, not caring that she was naked beneath the shirt. Guy tapped the rolled-up papers against his palm. "I thought maybe you'd be, you know, happy about it."

"I'm just…shocked. You said you'd never sign those. You said those guys were toy soldiers. What did you call them? White-collar mercs?"

"What, are you wearing a fucking wire or something?" Guy hurled the pages at her, his anger making his Boston accent thicker, and Ellie jumped at the sudden rage. "You recording every word I say? I don't need a goddamn transcription of what I said before. I changed my mind. If you don't like it, get the fuck out. Is that what you want? Huh?"

He turned around and slammed his fists down on the desk, hanging his head and breathing deeply. At her feet the pages unfolded themselves and Ellie could make out the large type portions of the contract that Guy had signed. The easiest part to read was the red Feno Chemical letterhead. She didn't need to read any more. She waited until Guy turned back to face her, leaning once more against the desk, composed. She chose her words carefully.

"Can you tell me what made you change your mind?"

He shrugged, looking down at the ground. "It's a good deal. I get my full army pension, full retirement benefits. It would take me another fifteen years of service to get that. There's a signing bonus, and then, on top of that, I'll be making a shitpot full of money. For doing the exact same thing I'm doing now."

"Only now you'll be doing it for Feno, not the army."

"Same shit, different uniform, right?"

Ellie nodded. He sighed and pushed off the desk, coming to sit next to her on the bed. He rested his elbows on his thighs and stared down at the floor. "It's not just the money, you know? My nephew Tommy wants to go to Boston College, got a scholarship and everything, but it's not enough.

My sister can't afford the rest, and this money will go a long way to helping him out. I don't want him to have to do what I did—join the army to pay for school." He laughed and shook his head. "Join the army and see the world."

Ellie leaned against him. "You saw Iowa."

"Yeah." Guy leaned back into her. "Seven and a half miles of it."

They sat that way in silence for a long time, touching but apart in their thoughts. Ellie couldn't understand what had prompted Guy to sign the contract with Feno. He had always been adamant in his disdain for the private security forces of the chemical company. He had called them amateurs and implied more than once that it was only the U.S. Army that was really protecting the residents of Flowertown, that nobody should expect the criminals to guard the prisons. He had called Feno's enormous salary offerings proof that they had something to hide, and once, when they'd both been very drunk, he had said they were trying to buy a get-out-of-jail-free card, should criminal charges ever arise from the spill. And now, with less than two months left on his tour of duty, he had signed with Feno.

Guy broke the silence, squeezing her thigh. "I guess you're stuck with me. If you want me, that is." Ellie still could not wrap her head around what she was hearing and said nothing. "Don't worry. It's still a drama-free zone. It's not like I'm going to move in with you."

Ellie rubbed his back, feeling the muscles and tension there. Her throat closed as she finally found the words she had to say. "You were so close. You were out. Two months and you were out." She blinked back tears and choked back the scream that wanted to tear from her chest. "Why would you stay? If you could get out, why would you stay?"

He looked up at her and she was startled at the tears she saw in his eyes. His mouth twitched, fighting for control, and when he spoke his voice was a hoarse whisper. "You've got to promise me. Promise me you won't say anything. To anyone, not even Bing. Especially not Bing, that fucking nutcase."

"I promise." Ellie's stomach cramped and the words were just air. She wasn't sure she was ready for one more surprise today. Guy pulled in a ragged breath.

"I'm contaminated."

"What?"

He dropped his head into his hands and scrubbed his face hard.

"Are you sure? How did it happen? You guys are on all those meds."

"Nobody's sure. Not yet." He took her hand in his. "But there are signs, you know? Fletcher and Porter, they're both showing more than me. They signed yesterday. You got to swear you're not going to tell anybody, anybody, because if word gets out…"

"Geez, Guy, they're going to know. You think you're going to keep it a secret?"

"For now, yeah, I've got to." He squeezed her hand tight between his own. "Ellie, you've got to listen to me. Nobody can know this. I don't have a med check for two weeks, and if they even think I'm contaminated, I lose everything. I'm in here forever, and I've got nothing."

"They won't kick you out of the army." She turned his face up to look at her. "There are tons of contaminated soldiers here, all the first responders, everybody."

"Yeah, and they got shit to show for it. They got no choice, no hazard pay, nothing. They get their army pay and that's it. It's no different from any other fucking job in here. If I can sign with Feno, the money goes in the bank. I got a contract for two years. My family doesn't have to know, nobody at home has to know."

"Why don't you want your family to know?"

"That I'm stained?" He couldn't catch the word before he said it and saw the insult hit home with Ellie. Stained was the outside term for the contaminated, with all the unclean implications that came with it. "I'm sorry. I didn't mean to say it like that. I don't want them to worry. You know, my mom, she's not doing so well, and if she thinks I'm sick... This way Mary Catherine can use the money to pay Tommy's tuition and nobody has to worry."

Ellie wrapped her fingers up in his. "Have you told them you're staying?"

"Yeah. They were pissed. My mom told me to stop being a stupid fucking hero."

"Your mom said fucking?"

"Like I said, she was pissed." Guy let out a deep breath and his body relaxed. Ellie freed her hands from his and swung herself onto him, wrapping her arms around his shoulders, her bare legs around his waist. He put his head down on her shoulder and let her hold him, and when he spoke, his lips brushed her throat.

"What are those flowers called?"

"Which ones?" Ellie asked, breathing in the smell of his hair.

"The ones in the funeral bouquets, that everyone smells like. Some kind of lily."

"Stargazers."

Guy sighed. "It's a pretty name for such a stinking flower. I guess I'm going to have to get used to a whole new set of meds now. Can't be that bad, right? They don't seem to bother you much."

"No, they don't bother me much." Ellie rubbed his back. "But then I'm tough. You're kind of a pussy."

He laughed and wrapped his arms around her more tightly. "Is that right? I guess I'll have to man up a little bit."

"I guess you will." She leaned back and rested her forehead against his. He kissed her once and then again.

"Do you think I could wait until tomorrow to man up? Tonight, I'd kind of like to just lay here. Is that okay?"

"Yeah." She slid off him, lay back on the bed, and held her arms open. "That'll be okay." He lowered himself beside her, draping his arm and his leg over hers, pressing his face into her neck. They lay still for a long moment, their breathing falling into the same relaxed rhythm. Guy snored softly and Ellie was just beginning to dream when the explosions started.

CHAPTER FIVE

The iron grating rattled in the windows as the glass absorbed the shock of the nearest blast. Guy was out of bed in an instant, reaching for the radio that came alive in between the second and third explosions. It sounded like gibberish to Ellie, but Guy barked back a series of answers as he grabbed a set of riot gear stowed behind the door. He was holstering his weapon by the time Ellie could think.

"What's happening? Why do you need a gun?"

"You've got to get out of here." He snapped his vest in place and then stopped. "No, stay here. Ellie, listen to me. I don't know what's going on out there, but you've got to stay inside. Lock the door. Don't touch anything. Don't let anyone in. Don't answer the phone or the radio, do you understand me?"

Ellie nodded, the sounds of sirens growing, only barely drowning out the rising sound of people screaming. Guy yelled into the radio once more and headed out into the night. Not thinking about his orders or the fact that she had no pants on, Ellie followed him as far as the top step of the power station. The night burned red with harsh black ribbons of smoke that tore into her throat and made her eyes tear up. Sirens wailed so loud and so close her eardrums vibrated and she could just hear Guy swearing as he fought his way through a panicked crowd that was rushing to get away from the blaze shooting from the building at the end of the street. He made a point of fastening the power station gate, although Ellie doubted any of those fleeing the explosion would want to linger so close to the blast. A terrible sound, like a monster exhaling, rolled down the street, and Ellie saw the fire trucks had gotten the first wall of water onto the flames.

It was a storage depot for the maintenance division. Whatever had exploded hadn't taken out much of the building, and the steady stream from the fire hoses replaced the red and yellow flames with a puffing cloud of vapor and chemical stink. Someone had the sense to turn the sirens off, but the throbbing still lingered in Ellie's ears. From where she stood, she could make out flashes of emergency lights pulsing through columns of smoke coming up from across Flowertown. People stopped rushing and herding and began milling about outside the power station gates, trying to see the rescue workers at work. Realizing she was half naked, Ellie ducked back inside the station and fished around the floor to find the cell phone in her pocket.

She dialed Bing but heard only a busy tone. On the screen flashed the message "Network Unavailable." Just her luck. She tried dialing twice more. If one of those explosions had interrupted the relay tower that serviced the spill zone, it would wreak havoc on all communications. Ellie searched around the desktop for the remote to the flat-screen TV mounted on the wall. The cable was on. ESPN, of course.

One time she had come in on Guy and Fletcher watching *Golden Girls* and had never let them live it down.

She flipped through the channels, looking for the local news channel to see if they would break in with a story about the explosions. Dalesbrook was not a large city, and although technically Flowertown existed separately, surely the news of an explosion in the contaminated zone would raise some eyebrows. She flipped through channel after channel, seeing nothing but TV dramas and sitcoms. On one station she caught sight of the containment fence around the east end of Flowertown and stopped, hoping for a news bulletin, but it was only another cop show using the threat of contamination for some artificial thrills.

She thought of trying to reach Bing on the power station's landline. Maybe her friend's paranoia was getting to her, maybe she just didn't want to get Guy in trouble for leaving a civilian in a secure area, but she couldn't bring herself to pick up the receiver, much less dial her friend's number. Police sirens started up outside the window, and the red and blue flashing lights illuminated the room enough for her to pull her pants on and make sure she was leaving nothing behind. Guy would no doubt be pissed that she had disobeyed his order to stay put, but locked in a power station twenty feet from an explosion didn't strike Ellie as an evening well spent. Plus she wanted to find Bing. If anyone knew what was going on tonight, he would.

Rumors flew as people shouted to each other on the smoke-filled street. Ellie ducked her head and pushed through the crowds. From what she could gather, it sounded like nobody had been hurt in the depot blast. No ambulances had arrived, although one angry cluster on the corner of Sixth Street insisted that the ambulances had all been called to a different blast, that the people on "the low end" of Flowertown were somehow less important than those injured on "the high end." Ellie didn't bother to correct them. There were only three ambulances in Flowertown. With three blasts in the zone, odds were all three trucks were busy. She knew that the rescue workers and military personnel were all trained EMTs. It was the sort of multitasking required for work in the quarantine zone.

A military blockade stopped Ellie at the corner of her block. Two army soldiers with gas masks and guns stopped her and everyone around her, while a bullhorn ordered everyone within earshot to stay where they were with their hands in plain sight. Yellow emergency lights flashing from a Feno security truck were the only illumination; the streetlights and all the windows on the surrounding blocks were dark. The smell of smoke and burning rubber put a bitter taste in her mouth, and Ellie had to blink back tears from the noxious fumes. All around her people shouted up to the darkened windows above, ignoring the orders from the soldiers to remain quiet. Three times Ellie got jostled hard enough to make her stumble, and it wasn't until she felt her shoulder being jerked hard enough to bring her to her knees did she realize a soldier was screaming at her.

"What is your business here?" It was hard to make out his words behind the gas mask, and the flashing yellow lights created a surreal strobe effect in the reflection of his goggles. "Tell me your business here!"

Ellie pulled her arm free of his grasp and tried to tell him that she lived on the block he had barricaded, but as she spoke, the bullhorn voice announced an immediate

curfew for all residents. Every time she tried to speak over
the sirens and the shouting, the bullhorn would cut her off,
repeating the command for all residents to return to their
apartments. People surged around her, trying to push past
her, past the soldiers, past the barricades in both directions.
There seemed to be no consensus of direction. People were
just moving. The soldier grabbed Ellie's elbow once more,
squeezing it hard enough to hurt, as if she were the ringleader of the chaos. It seemed he believed if he could control her, he could control the madness around him. Finally
Ellie leaned in close enough to shout in his ear.

"My apartment!" She pointed past him to East Fifth Towers and then back to herself.

He shouted something back at her, his grip on her
elbow making her fingers ache, but all she could make out
was "identification." It was absurd. The only proof of her
address was on her medical tags, and those would have to
be scanned electronically. If this joker thought he was going
to whip out a hand scanner and leisurely read through her
personal information in the middle of this bedlam, he had
obviously gotten his gas mask on too late.

She shook her head at him, but before she could argue,
glass shattered somewhere very close, as if a bottle had been
thrown. The soldier spun around, whipping Ellie with him,
and she used the momentum of his turn to break free from
his grasp and run. She didn't check to see if he pursued her.
She brought her elbows up high before her and crashed
her way through the senseless crowd until she made it to the
steps of East Fifth. People pounded on the metal doors and
shouted obscenities at the guards, but when Ellie pulled the
handle, the doors swung open and none of those pounding

followed her in. She slammed the door behind her and took the stairs two at a time.

When she made it to the eighth and top floor, Ellie bent at the waist, gasping for air and praying her legs would hold out. It didn't occur to her until she threw herself against Bing's door that he might not be home, but as she pounded, fear at the thought flushed through her body. Panic hung in the air like a smell. As she pounded she heard the dead bolt being thrown, but the door remained shut.

"Bing! Bing!" She pounded harder. "It's me. It's Ellie!" Before she could repeat herself, the door flew open and she was yanked into the room. Bing slammed the door behind her and threw the bolt once more. "What the hell is going on?"

"Be quiet!" Bing dragged her farther into the room, toward the windows, over which thick drapes hung. "Nobody knows I'm here. How did you know I was here?"

"You live here."

Bing held her by the shoulders, staring into her wild eyes, until they both realized the absurdity of their conversation. Bing blew out a sigh so hard it whistled as he let his head fall back. "I don't know what the hell is going on out there. All I know is I was halfway up the stairs when the power went off and then there were these explosions and people just started running everywhere. All I could think was 'save the weed,' so I ran up here and locked the door."

Ellie looked around the cramped room, full of planters with lush marijuana plants and half-melted candles. Every surface had something growing or glowing on it. As the adrenaline ebbed, she began to giggle. "You thought they were blowing up your weed?"

"Hey, don't judge." Bing tried not to laugh. "It was chaos. It was a gut reaction."

"Maybe we'd better test a few plants to make sure nobody tampered with them in all the hubbub." She pointed to the carved wooden box he used to store his personal stash.

"That's probably a wise idea."

He made certain the door was bolted. Two bowls full and a heavy coughing fit later, Ellie could feel that familiar looseness in her neck and spine. Bing always saved the best weed for himself. They moved a heavy plastic planter away from the window, pulled the curtains apart, and watched the simmering chaos on the street below. The barricade had fallen apart, and the soldiers, both army and Feno security, moved through the crowd uselessly. With no electricity, the buildings were getting stuffy, and people hung out open windows and shouted down to friends on the ground. The energy of the situation seemed to be ebbing, transforming the crowd from a panicked mass to bored party guests. The yellow emergency lights still flashed from security vehicles, but the bullhorn blowers had long given up on clearing the crowds.

"Why did they block off the street?" Ellie asked, leaning out over the sill.

"I don't know." Bing pulled out his cell phone. "Probably just a gut reaction. You know how the military is—when in doubt, shut it down."

"Was one of the explosions close?"

"What do you mean one of them? How many were there?"

Ellie waved her hand out over the darkened skyline. Patches of darker than dark could be seen in the sky. "I think

at least three. That's what it sounded like. Don't bother trying to call out. I think that one of the explosions knocked
out the cell tower." Bing swore as his phone buzzed the busy
signal. "Let's check the news. Maybe's there's something on
by now."

"If the phones are down, the cable is too."

"No." Ellie shook her head. "The cable was on at the
power station. I checked before I left. All the channels were
on."

"That's impossible." Bing tossed his useless phone onto
a nearby table. "The phones and the cable run on the same
power relay. If one goes down, they both do."

"Well, the cable was on when I left and my phone wasn't
working. There was nothing on the news, but that was just a
few minutes after the explosion at the supply depot. Besides,
how do you know what 'power relay' the phones and cable
are on? What does that even mean?" When Bing said nothing, just shrugged and lit a cigarette, Ellie laughed. The
weed was making her lips feel fat and soft. "Let me guess.
You've downloaded the schematics for the resistance, right?"

"Think that's funny?" Bing leaned far out the window.
"Look around you, Ellie. What do you think is happening
out here?" The smell of bitter smoke still drifted by in waves.
"You think it's a coincidence that buildings just start blowing up? That the military is losing control of Flowertown?
That supplies have been cut off and the government is turning a blind eye to us?"

His bird image had returned, which always made Ellie
struggle not to laugh. She was tired and she was very high.
"Maybe you're right, Bing. Maybe this is it, but to tell you the
truth, after a day like this, I don't really give a shit." When he

reared up for the obligatory impassioned Bing retort, she waved him down. "No, don't. Please, not tonight. I'm too high and way too tired to fight with you."

"The fight's not with me, Ellie. Look out there. What do you see?"

Night was fully upon them, and with the fires almost extinguished and the emergency vehicles shutting off their lights, there was very little to see. Rather than put her mind at ease, the darkness, the invisibility of the small world of Flowertown, sent a new wave of anxiety and disorientation over her, and she had to steady herself against the window frame.

"There's not much to see out there."

"No, but there's plenty going on. Trust me."

Ellie sighed and closed her eyes, trying to stop a building sensation of dizziness. "What's the endgame, Bing? I mean, what's the point of it all? If someone inside really did blow up the buildings, what are they trying to achieve? To get the army to withdraw? And leave us with no supplies? It doesn't make any sense."

"It's complicated, Ellie. There are a lot of factors at play."

"Well, who's controlling it all?" She snatched a cigarette from the pack in Bing's pocket, as much to bring more light to the darkness as to keep her awake. She could see Bing gnawing on a fingernail, staring out into the night. "You keep telling me that some kind of shit is going down, but whose shit? And why? The army? Why would the army blow up Feno buildings? Why would Feno? Why would anyone living here blow up the only buildings we have access to?" She could feel the logic of her argument evaporating as fatigue and weed weighed down on her mind. Bing reached across the sill in the darkness and took her free hand.

"We live in a world where I can legally sell weed but I'll be put in detention if I litter. Are you really looking for logic here?" They both knew the answer and sat together in silence until the last flashing light went out.

Ellie woke with a jolt when her leg cramped from its bent position in the easy chair. Swearing before her eyes were open, she threw herself to the floor trying to straighten out her suffering limb. The power was still out, the candles long burned out, and the room was black, but Ellie knew Bing's space well enough to maneuver. She forced herself to stand, the cramp ripping through her calf muscle, her brain demanding her body put its weight evenly on both feet, knowing it would alleviate the spasm. It did, but it took several tooth-grinding moments before Ellie could breathe easily.

She couldn't remember how she had wound up in the easy chair or how long she and Bing had sat up, looking out into nothing, talking about nothing. She could just make out Bing's white socks sticking out from beside the plant-covered coffee table. Her mouth was so dry it hurt to swallow and her eyes felt swollen and hot. She wanted something to drink and knew Bing would have nothing in his apartment. He was like an air fern. Ellie sometimes wondered if he actually lived purely on pot.

Pulling her cell phone from her pocket, she unlocked the screen to use the light as a flashlight to navigate her way through the crowded living room. No sooner had she pointed the screen ahead of her than the phone beeped. She had a text message.

"Are the phones working?" Bing said, his voice strong in the dark.

"Shit, Bing, you almost gave me a heart attack. Have you been awake this whole time?"

"No." She saw him sit up between two small pot plants, his hair sticking up in every direction. "I was dreaming. I was dreaming the phones were working. Are they?"

"Mine is. Got a message." She wasn't going to tell him it was another dosage reminder.

"Is it for me?" Now Ellie could hear the sleep in her friend's voice.

"Yeah, it's from Santa Claus. He's not coming this year."

"Oh, okay." He lay back down between the plants, even in sleep mindful of his cash crop. "I'll check mine in a little bit."

"Okay, Bing. Sleep tight."

The emergency lights in the hallway were fading, their batteries unable to keep up with the regular usage from the power outages. Nobody seemed to be moving, and the only sounds Ellie could make out as she headed for the stairwell were the sounds of snores and coughs. The chaos of the night had faded, at least for the residents of her building. The stairs were pitch black and Ellie's phone spilled light in a stingy little pool at her feet, but after the second flight, her body picked up the rhythm of the steps and she trotted down them without worry, all the way to the third floor. Silence greeted her in her hallway as well, and she didn't bother looking at her feet as she felt her way by memory down the corridor. She smelled the bathrooms to her right and knew that it was just a few paces, three doorways on her left, and she would be at her room. Her fingers trailed against the walls, feeling the doorjambs ticking off under her touch, but before she cleared the third and final doorway, she tripped over something in the hallway.

Ellie swore as she pitched forward and landed on the floor in front of her roommate. "What the hell are you doing out here?" Rachel drew her legs up to her chest, rubbing the shins Ellie had trampled. The emergency light down the hall flickered on, and even in the faint light, Ellie could see Rachel was in bad shape. She knelt down beside the girl and held her face between her hands. "Rachel? Can you hear me?"

"Yeah, yeah, I'm okay." Rachel's face was cool and damp, her hair stuck in greasy clumps to her cheeks, and her breath was unspeakable. "I fell asleep out here. It was so hot in the room and I kept having to puke. I sat in the bathrooms for a while, but they're so nasty."

"Do you want to come back inside now? There'll be more air inside than out here." Rachel nodded and let Ellie pull her to her feet. Her clothes were damp to the touch, and a sour smell of copper and sweat wafted off of her with every move. Ellie led her to her bed and then hurried to open the window, wondering if she would ever get used to the smells of Flowertown. She wanted to light a cigarette; she wanted to set the mattress on fire—anything to combat the smell of sweat and vomit that filled the room. She shuddered to think what she would find when the lights came back on.

"Sorry about the smell. I didn't make it to the bathroom the first time."

Ellie took a deep breath of outside air before turning back to the room. "Any place I shouldn't step before the lights come back on?"

"Nah, I hit the garbage can. Bing cleaned it up for me."

"Bing?" Ellie could imagine her friend doing a great number of things. Emptying a vomit bucket was not one of them.

"Yeah, he was really sweet to me." The bed creaked as Rachel settled herself in, sitting up with her back against the wall. "He put a cold cloth on my head and everything."

"You certainly have a way with him. All he does is leave Twinkies on my desk."

Rachel laughed and groaned at the same time. "Oh please don't talk about food. He brought me a whole box of Twinkies. Ugh. I almost threw up in his hands. At least it was better than that weird Japanese soup he was bringing me."

"Oh, now that stuff is nasty." Ellie sat back on her bed, facing her roommate. The sun was just thinking about coming up, and she could make out Rachel's shape across the room. "First of all, the only thing Japanese about that crap is that it makes you want to lop off your own head with a samurai sword. He gets it off the dollar shelf, and he buys it by the case."

"I know!" Rachel laughed again, and Ellie could see she held her stomach in pain but kept on laughing. "He keeps bringing it to me, and I swear it smells just like vomit."

"I wish it smelled like vomit. He keeps a drawer full of it at work, and every time he heats it up, we have to evacuate the building." Rachel's laugh turned into a gagging cough that lasted long enough to make Ellie sit up straighter. "Rachel? Are you okay?"

"Yeah." The word rasped in her throat and set off another round of choking. "I'm fine. It's just these meds make my throat so dry and I can't swallow anything."

Ellie listened to her struggle to get her breath. "Are you sure it's worth all this?"

"Absolutely." Rachel sounded sure. "You have to see what I got in the mail today. I wish the lights would come on." And like a wish granted, the electricity surged and the overhead fluorescents flickered to life. Rachel gasped in delight, as if she had made the magic happen, but Ellie, seeing her roommate's face in the harsh light, gasped for a different reason. Rachel was gray. Her skin, her lips, even the flash of her gums and tongue when she smiled—she looked like a puppet made of dull putty. The only color on her face was the angry red blood in her eyes. She looked to Ellie like a dead thing, a giggling, smiling dead thing, and Ellie had to struggle not to react. If Rachel saw her effort, she made no sign of it. Instead she clapped and lunged forward on the bed to pull up a box from the floor.

"Look! Come over here. Aren't these great?"

Ellie moved to sit beside Rachel, breathing through her mouth to avoid the swirl of odors around her. Rachel forgot her nausea as she pawed through the box and pulled out what looked like a big sequined sock. Laughing, she put her hands inside the elastic and drew them apart.

"See? It's to go over my hairnet. Isn't that funny? And look, there's more."

Ellie could only stare as Rachel pulled out a bedazzled face mask, ankle bracelet, and a rhinestone-studded box of bleach wipes. It would have been horrible if it hadn't been making Rachel giggle like a little girl.

"And here's the best part. Look at this picture!"

She pulled out a glossy eight-by-ten photo of a group of women, or at least Ellie guessed they were women, dressed in a grotesque and colorful version of the containment garb that was the final step to get a pass out of Flowertown.

In the first year of containment, everyone was hopeful when word got out it was possible to get a pass out of the zone. Once people realized what was involved to get that pass and saw what it actually entailed, the list to leave dropped dramatically. First you had to complete a medical check to prove your contamination levels were within acceptable limits. Then you had to undergo a minimum of four weeks of grueling chemical decontamination to lower the levels of HF-16 as much as possible. These levels would only hold, or more accurately the meds would only be tolerated, for forty-eight to seventy-two hours maximum. Even then, you had to wear protective garb to prevent as much skin and hair shedding as possible.

The medical teams of Barlay Pharma assured Congress that the measures were sufficient, but after three reported, and baseless, contamination claims, seventeen states completely banned the admission of any Flowertown émigrés. Strict measures were put in place to monitor the location and containment of anyone with a pass, and as the years went on and rumors grew, more and more cities closed their doors to admission. Many states claimed economic hardship, since special chemical toilets and showers had to be installed, as well as electronic monitoring devices to ensure a Flowertownian didn't, as Bing put it, "go on a killer pee spree." Even if family members were willing to shoulder the financial burden to install the precautions in their own

homes, state governments across the country produced legislation to block it. At this point, anyone willing to undergo
the horror of temporary decontamination had few choices.
San Francisco had three hotels with accommodations. Chicago had one. Both Disney parks had a limited area, and of
course Las Vegas opened its arms with seven casinos that
met the Nevada EPA safety restrictions. That's why Rachel's
sister had opted to get married in Las Vegas.

Rachel laughed as she slipped on the paper respirator
mask that someone had decorated with full red lips. Her death
pallor only made the cartoon grin more ghastly, and Ellie had
to dig deep not to recoil. Rachel pulled the spangled hairnet
on and slipped the sparkly ankle bracelet over her wrist.

"I told Mom I wouldn't be able to take these out with
me, but she said they made two dozen of them. And they've
all got different colored paper suits too. Mine is pink, since
that's my favorite color. Abby's is white since she's the bride.
They're all going to wear them so I don't stand out. Isn't
that sweet?"

It was all Ellie could do not to scream. She knew Rachel's
family hadn't seen her in the clean rooms since she started
the detox. The webcam on her computer hadn't worked in
months, and Ellie could only imagine what Rachel's mother
and sisters would say when they saw her, even in her contamination suit. Bing had told her two weeks ago to keep
her mouth shut on the topic. Rachel wanted to see her sisters more than anything in the world, and for her, the decon
process was worth any agony. For Rachel, the silly sparkly
versions of the ugly containment garb showed playful cama-
raderie with her family. To Ellie, it was a scene from a nightmare.

Rachel was laughing under her mask, waving the brace-let around under the lights trying to make it sparkle. "Only three more days, Ellie. Three more days and I'll be in Las Vega—" She bent over, choking on her words and covering her mask with her hands. Ellie thought she was getting sick again until she saw the blood dripping through her fingers. Rachel coughed, still covering her face.

"Rachel. Rachel? What's happening?" She tried to get the girl to turn, but Rachel curled up tight on the bed, clutching the mask. "Are you throwing up blood?" Rachel shook her head and looked up at Ellie with wide, frightened eyes. The mask had turned completely red, making the car-toon lips black behind her fingers. Ellie grabbed a T-shirt from the floor and held it under Rachel's mouth. "Let me see. Move your hands."

Keeping her head down so the blood dripped into the mask, Rachel peeled the paper off her face. Blood and saliva dripped in a thick ribbon into her hands and Rachel stared into the wet mess. With her free hand, she poked a finger into the gore, then looked up at Ellie with tears in her eyes. "How bad does it look?"

She pulled back her lips in a terrible smile, revealing a bloody gap where a front tooth had been. Ellie wiped blood off her chin with the shirt, not wanting to look into those desperate eyes. "Well, honey, tell your mom to make you a mask with a big toothy grin." Something between a laugh and a sob blew out of Rachel's mouth, showering Ellie in blood and spit. Horrified, Rachel moved to wipe it off but had her hands full of the bloody mask and couldn't figure out what to do.

"It's okay, honey. Just...it's okay." She put her arms around the filthy, bloody girl and let the tears and spit and blood soak her shirt. It didn't matter, she told herself. It was an army shirt, and she didn't know anyone in the army anymore.

CHAPTER SIX

Ellie waited until she heard Rachel's breathing even out before she lit her cigarette. The blood-soaked clothes and pillowcase were balled up in the corner by the door, Ellie promising to launder them, which she knew meant pitching them in the dumpster behind the building. Rachel had held the tooth in her palm for a long moment, afraid and willing to let Ellie decide its fate. Ellie had palmed the tooth and focused on getting the girl into bed to hopefully sleep off even a shade of her dreadful pallor. Rachel had sighed on her way to sleep, her breath raspy, her muscles twitching, but she finally lay quiet.

Climbing onto her bed, back against the wall once more, Ellie lit her cigarette and watched color return to the room as the sun made its way over the building. She didn't unclench her left fist, the tooth scraping and sliding against her sweating palm. Of course she would throw the tooth away. What else was she going to do with it? Put it under the pillow and give Rachel a quarter? Make a necklace out of it? It was nothing but a dead ganglion of enamel and useless calcium, but somehow the thought of tossing it into the same garbage can as old cigarette butts and tampon wrappers seemed indecent.

Her phone buzzed in her pocket, and still unwilling to let loose the tooth, Ellie tucked the cigarette in her mouth and reached awkwardly across her body to fish the phone from her left pocket with her right hand. Smoke from the cigarette drifted into Ellie's tired eyes so that by the time she got to the phone, she was swearing. When she saw the text, she nearly threw the damn thing out the window.

Med check. 11 a.m.

"Fuck you," Ellie whispered to the phone. Another med check? She thought the whole idea of quality of life treatment was to let her die in peace, not drag her in and out of the med center every day. It wasn't going to be easy keeping this a secret if she was constantly being paged. At the very least, she wanted to make sure Rachel got her pass out of Flowertown before telling her the bad news. If there was one thing Rachel did not need, it was anyone vying for her share of sympathy. Ellie blew out a thick ribbon of smoke that caught a sunbeam, sparkling over her roommate's face. Rachel had turned over, fetal position, facing Ellie, her hair greasy against her cheek. The sunlight did little to improve her color, and Ellie very much wanted to get high at that moment to keep from imagining that color on her own face in the coming months. She had a vague memory of leaving her weed at Bing's last night and swore once more.

There was nothing to do but head to work. She didn't want to wake Bing; she only wanted to get high to not have to do any of the things she wasted her days with. The sharp edge of Rachel's perfect white tooth lodged itself in a wrinkle in her palm. Ellie wanted to squeeze it and crush it to

dust and fling that dust in the face of everyone and everything that had made such a fucking mess of her life. Her
life and Rachel's and Bing's and all of Iowa's. She wanted
to load the tooth into a gun and shoot it into the face of
the next person who walked by her in a Feno uniform. She
wanted the tooth to explode like the buildings last night,
leaving a crater of waste and destruction in the heart of the
earth itself.

She wanted to get high. She wanted to not want anything.

Rachel muttered in her sleep, her hand struggling under
the pillowcase, so Ellie slipped off the bed and pulled on
her sneakers. Of all the things she did not want, she did not
want to see Rachel's face when the lost tooth was remembered in the mirror. Slipping the tooth into her pocket, she
grabbed her cigarettes, badge, and phone and headed out
the door.

Flowertown was silent at this hour. Even the damage
from the night before didn't prompt anyone to get an early
start to the day. Ellie thought she could still smell traces of
the wet burned wood, but over the stench of the decontaminants in the runoff gutters, it was hard to tell. She had
learned long ago not to take too many deep breaths in the
spill zone. It didn't matter what the source was, odds were
good it stank, so Ellie lit a cigarette and wandered down
the empty streets toward the records office. It wasn't even
seven yet and the offices wouldn't open until eight, but Ellie
felt a prickling in her spine and nervousness in her muscles
that made walking better than sitting. If this were her old
life, this would have been her body's signal to her to run.
She would have put on her sports bra and her expensive

Nikes and run along the lake in Chicago. She would have
let the heat and the breath and pounding clear her head
and refresh her body, feeding her lungs and muscles, sweat
cleansing her skin. Now the hardest work her lungs did was
dragging in the heavy clouds of a variety of smokes; the fast-
est her legs pumped was on ambling strolls like this one. She
felt like a perpetually cocked gun that had begun to rust.

Turning the corner onto Avenue Four, Ellie saw a line of
army trucks in front of a storage facility, back flaps open, soldiers humping cartons from the building into their holds.
Instinctively she searched the men for Guy, then wondered
if he would still be reporting for duty. Would the explosions
last night hold up his transfer to Feno? Would they change
his mind about his decision, if such a change of heart were
allowed? She hadn't bothered to worry about his safety last
night. Guy was the sort of man who always charged into the
center of a fray and came swaggering out with just enough
scars to look cool.

Ellie stood in the middle of the street and lit a cigarette.
The soldiers ignored her, if they saw her at all, and she wondered if any of the men she watched had learned, like Guy,
they were infected. She wondered if any of them even suspected such a thing was possible. As her fingers once again
found the tooth in her pocket, she tried to imagine the fury
and the shock these men, these boys, would feel learning
the sacred protection meds they so worshipped had for-
saken them, razing their haven and bringing them down
to the unclean level of the stained Flowertownians they so
nobly protected.

"Fuck." Ellie pulled her finger from her pocket. She
had squeezed the tooth so tightly a jagged corner had bro-

ken the skin on the pad of her thumb. Ignoring the long-neglected instinct of hygiene and sanitary concern, she stuck her thumb in her mouth and sucked off the blood. At this point, infection from Rachel's tooth was the least of her problems. She knew she should pitch it, but again, tossing away a piece of young Rachel's body like trash disturbed her.

For the first time in years, Ellie wanted to run. She couldn't remember feeling so agitated and restless. Then she remembered this was the first morning she could recall she hadn't smoked weed upon waking. It was a mistake she didn't plan on making again, because awake and hyper at seven in the morning in Flowertown was an abysmal state to be in. The bar on Sixth and Eighth would be open; there were no blue laws around here. But even as she headed in that direction, she knew she wouldn't drink. The more she woke up, the louder the sounds of the soldiers working around her, the danker the smell of the runoff channels, the clearer Ellie felt her mind becoming.

She passed the soldiers on the corner, meeting each of their stares. They didn't interrupt their work but followed her with their eyes. She made a wide berth of the trucks but stopped at the corner, watching. They were loading unmarked plastic tubs from the storage building into the trucks. At first Ellie couldn't think what seemed so strange about the activity until she realized that, in all the time she had watched soldiers working around storage facilities, she had never seen tubs loaded *out* of buildings. She supposed they had to be moved out at some point, for distribution or trash removal or something, but this was the first time she had seen soldiers stacking tubs in trucks rather than tossing them out.

She almost walked up and asked the nearest soldier what they were doing, but caught herself. This sober-in-the-morning thing was making her feel like she had in high school the first time she had snuck a bottle of wine. It was tampering with her decision-making ability. Nobody talked to the soldiers in Flowertown. And not just when they were on duty. There were unofficially segregated bars, diners, even picnic tables where the stained and the clean never met. Ellie supposed there were other pairings like her and Guy and nobody came right out and pronounced a division, but for the residents of Flowertown, the coppery smell of protection meds could not be separated from the drab green or bright red of security force uniforms. Those penny-scented greens and reds were the only ones allowed to own and carry guns, and for the hundreds of country people imprisoned within the zone, giving up their weapons had been a sore spot indeed.

A soldier noticed how long Ellie had been standing and staring and headed her way. She held his stare, taking a deep drag off her cigarette as he approached. There was nothing illegal about standing on the corner, but it was obviously making the men uncomfortable. She waited until he was within five feet of her, his hand resting on his sidearm. Just as he opened his mouth to speak, she flicked her cigarette at his feet and laughed, turning her back on him. She could hear his breath and imagined the glances his fellow soldiers gave her. Just another nut job wandering the streets, they were probably saying. Or maybe not. Maybe those explosions last night had put their nerves on high alert. Ellie made a point of not turning to look back, knowing without a doubt she was being watched until she turned the corner on the next block.

Dingle's Market was open, of course. Annabeth Dingle never slept a night and so never bothered to close her little market. Ellie knew lots of people who claimed to have trouble sleeping since the spill, but she believed Annabeth when she said she never slept more than fifteen minutes at a time. Ellie had witnessed more than once Annabeth propped up on her padded stool in front of the curtain to the market's office, her black and silver hair slipping like a visor over her eyes as her head nodded in quick rabbit dreams. Fifteen, maybe twenty minutes at the most, and Annabeth would raise her head refreshed and alert. Well into her seventies, Annabeth often said it was a cruel irony that now that she no longer needed sleep, she was stuck in Flowertown with nothing to do.

Ellie wasn't certain if she was catching Annabeth in one of her naps or if the old woman was reading the magazine folded in her lap. Either way, she kept her steps quiet, liking the feel of Dingle's Market. Of all the markets in the zone, Dingle's still felt like outside. The shelves held nothing the other markets didn't carry, and today they were even barer than usual, but there was something about the way the shelves huddled together and the handwritten signs popped up like subtitles that maintained the illusion of a small-town market. She didn't want anything, although she could feel her stomach growling, but ran her fingers along a row of cereal boxes, waiting to see if Annabeth would awaken.

Ellie turned the corner, past a nearly empty display of oyster crackers, and continued her stroll down the canned food aisle. Great gaps in the selection made the wall of shelves look like a giant checkerboard, small piles of canned spinach and sauerkraut separated by open spaces that had once held more desirable vegetables. Demand for canned hominy had obviously tapered off long before the run on canned corn, despite the two-for-one special advertised on the sign. Ellie did grab two cans of chili with beans, knowing they wouldn't last long. She didn't know how Annabeth always managed to keep it in stock, but when it came to canned chili, Dingle's was often the only game in town. Seeing even more gaps in the shelves before her, Ellie grabbed two more cans, tucking them up under her arm.

She headed to the front of the store to grab a basket, deciding to try to find something that Rachel might be able to keep down later, when she heard voices coming from within the curtained office. Ellie peered around a pile of toilet paper value packs. It was early for anyone to be in Dingle's, even with Annabeth's famous round-the-clock service, and Ellie paused when she saw that the old woman still had not moved from her napping position. The voices were low, whispering, and Ellie could hear something being slid across the floor and the sound of cabinets being latched. It was probably just deliverymen bringing in some much-needed stock, she told herself. And it was probably just the novelty of sobriety that was making her stand perfectly still, eclipsed by the toilet paper, not daring to breathe. So much for weed making you paranoid, she thought.

The voices quieted down and Ellie listened for the sound of the back door opening, but as she stared at the unmoving curtain, Annabeth raised her head, looking for all the world as if they had been in the middle of a conversation.

"You're up early, Ellie. Got the munchies?"

Ellie dropped the cans into the plastic basket and headed toward the counter in the back. "Couldn't sleep. You know how that is." Whoever was in the back room had fallen silent. Annabeth took the basket from Ellie and began punching in numbers on the old-fashioned cash register.

"Oh, I know all right. How's Rachel doing? Did she get her pass yet?" A small metallic clink sounded behind the curtain, but the older woman made no sign of hearing it. Ellie tried not to stare at the curtain.

"Not doing so well. Can't keep anything down."

"Well now, why don't you grab one of those boxes of oyster crackers and take them back to her? My treat." Ellie turned and grabbed a box and, as she turned back, noticed the curtain flutter then fall still. Annabeth smiled and put the crackers in the bag. "Poor little thing can't afford to lose any weight. She must want to get to that wedding awful bad."

"I think it's as much Vegas as anything else." Ellie handed her the debit card. "That and getting out of Flowertown."

Annabeth's mouth twitched as she swiped the card, but it came up a smile when she looked up. "I can see why a girl would want that. Who wouldn't?"

Ellie took her card and her groceries and headed back out into the street. She kept reminding herself that she was not high. She was awake and clear minded so there was no doubt about what she knew she had seen. Behind Annabeth, under the curtain, peeking out near the doorframe, had been a box of bullets.

Walking on autopilot, Ellie found herself at the records office before she had even decided where to go. The office didn't open for another fifteen minutes, but there were a few early arrivals floating around and she could hear the distinctive ting-ting-ting of the overworked industrial coffee pot coming to life. She flipped her badge to the guard and headed in and almost didn't stop when he called to her.

"Are you talking to me?" Ellie turned to the guard who had shouted to her, wondering if everyone who didn't get high had mornings this complicated. "What do you want?"

"I need to see your badge." The guard was big, and Ellie couldn't tell if his army crew cut was blond or gray. For the life of her, she couldn't remember if he was new or the same guy she passed every day. She came back to his post and held up her badge.

"Is there some kind of problem?"

The soldier compared her face to her badge but didn't look her in the eye. "You are to show proper identification upon entering all government buildings."

"Yeah, I did. Nobody ever looks."

Finally he met her gaze. "Well, we're looking now."

"Oooh." She snatched the badge back. "I bet you've been waiting all morning to use that line. Did you practice in the mirror while you shaved?" She spoke over her shoulder as she moved on. "You might try curling your lip a little bit and maybe reaching for your weapon. Or maybe throw in the word 'punk' once in a while."

She looked back when she reached the stairs and saw that he was still watching her, his face unmoving. This crap she did not need. She paused on the bottom step, knowing she was under surveillance, and turned back. As she cut down the cubicle aisle for Bing's desk, she saw the guard perk up and head her way. Grinning, she waved her badge in the air, the bold red type visible from across the room, and mouthed the word "clearance." Her clearance for the records office gave her clearance for the entire building, a little detail that occasionally irked Bing, who did not have the same badge. Why anyone in charge thought she was more responsible than Bing was a mystery to anyone who bothered to think of such things, but at the moment her presence irked the army guard enough. She took her time sauntering down the aisle, swinging her hair in her best impression of a pageant walk, and just before she sat down at Bing's desk, blew the staring guard a kiss.

She let out a breath as she disappeared from his sight. It had to be the explosions last night that were putting the soldiers on edge. Now more than ever this was no place to be without smoking a nice fatty, and Ellie knew Bing had to keep at least one emergency bag somewhere in his cubicle. She sat back in his seat, ignoring its trademark screech of protest, pulled up to his desk, and tried to think like her paranoid and complicated friend.

Corporate cubicles were strange places, even within government quarantine chemical spill zones. Ellie remembered her days in the cubicles in Chicago and the pleasure she used to take in piecing together the secrets of her coworkers by the things they did and did not display in their little white work spaces. She had never sat in Bing's chair before, had never been in this space without him, and if it hadn't been for the personnel label on his inbox, she wouldn't have been entirely sure this was his space at all. There were thick binders of government forms and protocols, requisition records, manuals, and other mind-numbing bureaucratic paperwork present on nearly every desk in the room. A computer sat sleeping in the corner; stapler, tape dispenser, sticky notes, cup of pens. A little yellow monster made of silicone crouched beside the mouse holding a sign that read "Bite me," and on the installed bulletin board, amid the forms and phone lists, Ellie saw one photo of a grinning black Labrador wearing a bandanna.

As far as Ellie knew, Bing did not now nor had he ever owned a dog. She was pretty sure he was allergic to most animals; she smiled at the picture. It was so like Bing to put up a fake picture of a pet. Even at work—hell, especially at work—she knew her friend's paranoia never rested, and it was typical Bing style to try to mislead any snoopers to a false impression, even about something as unimportant as a pet dog. The squishy little stress ball monster too, she knew, was a misdirection. Bing was not one for stress balls or whimsical toys. To the un-Bing-trained eye, this was the desk of a happy, functioning employee, but Ellie had spent enough time with him to know better. He thought she never paid attention. *She* thought she never paid attention, but this morning Ellie found herself examining the desk like a puzzle to be solved.

"I don't want to know your secrets, Bing," she whispered to herself. "I just want to find your weed." If it were her work space, she would have intentionally hidden a baggie in the thick binder marked "Laws and Regulations" just to be contrary, but she knew Bing would think of the possibility that someone would at some point borrow that binder. No, his weed and whatever other little secrets he might be keeping were hidden someplace more clever, certainly not in a Tinkerbell lunch box in the file drawer.

She pulled open the center drawer. She knew none of them would be locked. Bing thought locks were for amateurs and said they only raised suspicion. The center drawer held the usual office paraphernalia as well as some breath mints and a bottle of eye drops. Bing got the red-eye when he smoked too much. Ellie poked around a bit, knowing she wouldn't find anything here, but she sort of enjoyed the scavenger hunt. She turned to the set of drawers on the left, and the chair let out a gruesome screech. Some bolt or spring complained at her motion and Ellie had to laugh. It was probably an intentional sabotage Bing had rigged in his seat so he would know if anyone were sneaking into his cubicle. Laughing at her own paranoia, she could imagine him sawing through an I-bolt in such a way that he was the only person in the office who could sit here silently.

Nobody came at the sound of the chair screeching, and Ellie continued her search. She started with the large file drawer on the bottom. The front of the drawer was filled with the usual hanging files with the usual indecipherable labels used for government work. She flipped through the files, knowing nothing would be found in them. At the last file, she pushed the collection forward, opening a gap in the back of the drawer where a stack of books lay. Bing was a huge reader, she knew, and felt more than justified hiding in his cubicle reading on the government's dime. She pulled out the first three books in the stack: *The Illusion of Thought: How Stimulus Dictates Mass Action*; *Paranoia for the Aware*; and *When Bad Things Happen to Bad People—Great Retributions in History*. Guess I'm not going to find a bodice-ripper in here, she thought. She had also still not found the weed.

She put the books back and pulled open the shallow drawer above the file drawer. Rows of a variety of rubber and box stamps filled the space. There were date stamps, classified stamps, rejected and accepted stamps, even a notary public. Who knew? Bing, a notary public. Ellie scanned her fingers over the stamp handles and box tops, reading through their contents, and noticed there were two notary stamps. The one in the front was current; the one in the back of the drawer had expired two years earlier. Both stamps were large plastic box stamps, and both were still in their white boxes with the windows on top. Peeking around to be sure nobody was watching, Ellie pulled out the expired stamp and took it out of the box. The plastic lid, under which an imprint of the stamp had been set, had a tiny crack in the corner. Jackpot.

She grabbed a staple remover and pried off the top of the stamp. The simple mechanism inside fell apart and she had to quickly grab it to keep the rubber stamp at the bottom from falling out. Other than the plastic and spring, the stamp was empty. She had been so certain he would have hidden some weed there. Before she put the plastic lid back on, she sniffed the little case and smiled. Oh yeah, she was right. There had definitely been pot in here, but where was it now? Maybe he had cleared it out after her little run-in with Feno's Mr. Carpenter. She slipped the stamp back into its box and back into its slot in the drawer and was leaning in to continue her search when a hand grabbed her shoulder.

"What the fuck are you doing?"

Ellie jumped. Bing's face was red as he leaned into her face. She tucked her hands under her thighs innocently. "Nothing." She laughed, knowing she was busted. "Rummaging through your desk."

"Why?"

"Looking for your weed."

Bing snorted, his anger gone. "Good luck with that. You'll never find it."

"Oh really?" Ellie leaned back in the chair. "You so sure about that?"

"I am one hundred percent sure. Trust me. You're out of your league."

Ellie swung her feet back and forth, making the chair squeak rhythmically. "Wanna bet?"

Bing leaned against the cubicle wall and looked her up and down. "Okay. Let's make it something worthwhile. Judging from your customary style of dress this morning—what is that on your shirt? Gravy?—let's bet a load of laundry."

"Let's bet two."

Bing narrowed his eyes at her cockiness. Ellie was probably the only person to hate the laundry facilities more than he did, but he also knew her to be an excellent bluffer. He decided to call her on it. "You have three minutes."

"I only need ten seconds."

His face fell as he saw her hands behind her back, peeling up the seam of the worn-out pad of his chair, pulling out a tightly packed baggie of marijuana. "Fuck."

Ellie laughed and took a deep sniff of the dark green herb. "Mmm. Tasty. And now with a fresh laundry scent! Oh, I'd like my whites bleached, please."

"How did you find it? Did you feel it?"

"Nope. Smelled it."

"Bullshit."

Ellie laughed again and waved the bag under his face. "I've told you before, I can smell a dank bud from a hundred paces. Never underestimate the nose."

"You did not smell that bag."

She got to her feet and repeated her entrance prance back down the corridor. Bing called out after her but she ignored him, taunting him with the sight of his weed being taken away. That was the smallest part of the torment, she knew. It would drive him mad wondering how she had found it. Of course she hadn't smelled the pot; even her sensitive nose was not that good. It was when Bing had surprised her and she'd jumped back in the seat that she'd figured it out. The office chair was broken down. The springs were loose and the casters were off balance. There were a dozen chairs all around him that were in better shape. Bing knew that anyone might rifle through his desk looking for any sort of office supply to pilfer, but nobody who spent their day in a cubicle would steal an uncomfortable chair. It was better than a locked safe. Unless someone knew how you thought.

Ellie hurried up the steps, wanting to get a joint rolled, knowing Bing would be up shortly, unable to stand not knowing how she had figured him out. She tossed the bag in the air, catching it as she waved to Big Martha, who was just turning on her computer. Martha didn't see her and so couldn't warn her that just around the corner of the tall stack of file cabinets, hidden from view of the door, stood a heavily armed guard in Feno red.

CHAPTER SEVEN

Ellie nearly dropped the baggie when she and guard surprised each other. As she stuffed the bundle deep into her left pocket, he grabbed the machine gun slung around his neck in readiness. All things considered, it seemed to Ellie he had a distinct advantage. She held her hands up slowly and saw the young guard trying to get his breath under control. It didn't look like that gun made him any more comfortable than it made her.

"Is something wrong?"

"What is your business in this area?" He snapped out his words with the clipped precision of a drill sergeant, and from the tension in his grip and posture, Ellie suspected he was not only nervous, he was new. She couldn't decide if that made him more or less dangerous.

"That's my desk." She pointed to her left, to the area past their standoff, and his eyes flickered between her and the workspace. Apparently this was as far as his dialogue training had taken him because he neither moved nor spoke, only looked at Ellie, ascertaining her threat level. She saw dark circles of dampness under his arms and along the front of his shirt where his arms pressed with the gun, and bright pearls of sweat on his light brown skin. She relaxed even as he readjusted his grip on his gun. "What is it exactly you're here to guard? Me?"

"No ma'am." He straightened his stance, relaxing his gun grip, and stared past her. "Go on about your business." Ellie chuckled when she caught him peeking down at his shoes to be certain his feet were on the edge of the red-painted section of the floor. This had to be Mr. Carpenter's doing, sending a newbie guard to protect his precious red-zone files. Shaking her head, she strolled past the nervous guard and dropped into her seat as her phone buzzed a text.

"Thanks for the chili." It was Bing. She had left her groceries in his cubicle.

"Don't you dare!" she typed back. "Those crackers are for Rachel."

"But the chili is for me!!! Unless you want to trade..."

Ellie laughed as she typed and saw the guard eyeing her from his position. "Afraid it's gonna have to wait. I've got company up here."

"???" Bing typed.

"Come see for yourself, but make sure you have ID. He's nervous & armed." She knew that would be enough to make Bing scale the side of the building if he had to. Once he saw the guard was a private Feno guard, he would freak. Bing hated Feno security even more than Guy did. Ellie didn't look forward to breaking the news that Guy had changed sides.

"Give me 15," Bing typed. "Staff meeting."

Ellie kept her eye on the guard, who tried to keep her in his vision without turning his head. A stack of files had come in with the morning delivery, and she piled them high in her inbox to eclipse her from his sight. She wasn't hiding anything. She just liked making him nervous. As she waited for her computer to come on, she let her gaze drift over to the closest boxes stacked on the red paint near her desk. It had been so long since she and Bing had rearranged them for their convenience, she had forgotten how close the red paint came to her desk and boxes of files nearby.

As a test, she strolled to a pile of file boxes on the safe side of the red paint and opened the top one. She could see her guard jump to attention, ready to stop her if she breached the secure zone. It would have made her laugh if he hadn't been so nervous with that gun in his hand. Instead, like a six-year-old who had discovered wrapped Christmas presents, it made her all the more determined to know what those red-taped boxes contained.

The guard relaxed a bit when she returned to her seat, an unnecessary file in her hand. His head turned even less when she returned the file to the open box, and he looked away, relaxed, when she pulled a file box out from the pile and scattered the boxes on the floor. She wasn't looking for anything. Despite the business of her appearance, she was doing nothing more than removing and returning files unopened to their original boxes. She was also putting her guard at ease while she figured out how to put her plan in motion.

She was going to get a box out of the red zone. She wasn't sure how exactly she would do it, but when she saw the guard wipe sweat from his upper lip, her plan became a little clearer. It wasn't that hot in the records office and the guard wasn't that nervous. She hauled a few more boxes of files down from the shelf behind her, stacking them two and three high in groupings big enough to block line of sight, but not big enough to make it seem as if she was hiding anything. She pawed through the boxes, muttering and cursing as if she were looking for something she couldn't find, all the while creating a cluttered line that came very near the red paint. She knew her guard was keeping that red line in sight, and as long as she showed no interest in crossing it, he showed no interest in her. Besides, judging from the way he kept licking his dry lips, she suspected he had something else on his mind.

Ellie rose to her feet and put her hands on her hips, staring around her as if disgusted at the mess and her failure. She grabbed a file and headed to a file cabinet closer to the guard. Once there, she set the file on top of the cabinet and began pawing through a drawer. He was really sweating, his red Feno security shirt turning a dark maroon against his skin. She could see a sheen on the tight black curls on his head, and she could hear him trying to quietly take deep breaths. She knew those signs. Either his protection meds had been upped or he was new to Flowertown. Either way, his skin advertised the nausea he was trying to hide, and Ellie knew just what she needed to do.

First, a cigarette. She pulled a file from an open drawer and opened it, laying it across the other files, and lit a cigarette while she pretended to read. She made a point of blowing the smoke over her shoulder toward the guard. Pulling a thick file from the drawer, she pretended to read while she walked slowly back toward her desk, puffing hard on the cigarette. She paused close enough to the guard to be sure the smoke would hit him square in the face and feigned being engrossed in her reading. She could hear the guard struggling to keep his breathing steady.

Those early days in Flowertown were not easily forgotten. HF-16 had made everyone sick, some sick enough to not recover. Those lucky enough to survive the first contamination then had to suffer through the first generations of decontamination meds. If she lived to be a hundred, Ellie knew she would never forget the swirling, wracking nausea and vomiting that had afflicted her and everyone around her. As Flowertown residents had gotten as accustomed as possible to the meds, they had taken a dark pleasure in watching the incoming military, treatment, and business workers adjusting to their own gruesome protection regimens. It wasn't unusual for people to place bets on which soldier or missionary or construction worker would vomit first with the proper stimulus. Like peeing in a cup, tipping a newbie's nausea to vomiting had become a skill highly prized among many of the long-term residents.

The soldier fanned away the smoke, and Ellie looked up as though startled. "Oh, I'm sorry, is this smoke bothering you?"

"Smoking isn't allowed in the records office." He wouldn't meet her eyes, and she could see the droplets of sweat on his temples had banded together into a steady stream.

"Oh, I know." She blew another long plume of smoke out before her. "Nobody really pays any attention to it, though. I mean, there are so many rules, the little ones slip through the cracks, you know?" With the poor ventilation, the smoke hung in wisps before him, and she saw him swallow hard. "But if this is bothering you, I won't smoke anymore."

"I'd appreciate it, ma'am."

"Do you mind if I just finish this one?" She inhaled deeply, letting the ember of the cigarette burn into the filter, a smell she knew was revolting. As she let loose the last thick load of smoke, she fanned her hand around his face, before his eyes, driving the smoke in closer. She didn't figure the back and forth motion was especially pleasant either. Finally she dropped the cigarette at his feet but didn't crush it, so it continued to smolder.

"There you go, all finished. I'll take my smokes outside now since it's obvious it bothers you." Thin tendrils of smoke drifted up, and she knew he wanted to crush the butt but didn't want to look weak. Ellie leaned in closer to him, close enough he had to smell her cigarette breath. "You don't look like you feel so good. Are you on new meds? Aren't they the worst? The way they just make your stomach flip-flop and churn." He narrowed his eyes, both from the drifting smoke and trying not to focus on her words. Ellie let her voice drop to a sympathetic whisper. "The worst is the shits. Have you gotten those yet? Oh God, those are horrible. Your stomach just turns into lava and you dare not sneeze or shit just pours out of you. And the smell of it, oh it's revolting. Feels like your O-ring's just gonna melt away. I hope you haven't started that. I mean, the puking is bad enough, the way your mouth sweats and those chunks just come pouring out and get stuck in your nose." She paused. "This probably isn't helping any, is it?"

He didn't move or answer. He never turned his eyes to her. He had no doubt been warned about this unpleasant hobby of the locals and had readied himself. Or thought he had.

Ellie sighed as if defeated. "Well, it looks like you're going to be tough enough for those meds. Good for you. I hate when people puke up here. It stinks up the whole place. That's one of the reasons we smoke up here, to hide the smell of newbies puking. Oh look, that butt's still smoking. I'll go ahead and put it out."

He relaxed a hair, no doubt happy the test was over. Rather than grind the smoldering cigarette out with her shoe, however, Ellie pulled out a trick Rachel had taught her when they had first moved in together. It was tough this morning because she was so dehydrated, but she knew her lack of saliva would make it that much more effective. With a growling sound deep in her throat, Ellie used every drop of spit she could muster to work up a thick and sticky wad of phlegm and let it drop slowly and heavily from her lips onto the smoldering butt. The loogey hit the ground with a satisfying splat, and Ellie embellished the effort with a little gagging of her own, followed by some final drops of spit.

"Bull's-eye." She grinned at the soldier who, while sweating more than ever, was holding up admirably. "There you go. No more smoke. Hope you feel better." She headed back to her desk, whistling, waiting.

Ellie hadn't expected the soldier to throw up just at that. Even though that was her goal, she would have been a little disappointed if it had been that easy. Part of the fun of tummy tipping was watching the mind struggle that ensued within the nauseated after a stunt. She knew he wouldn't look at the sooty, lumpy, and yellowish clump of slime. He wouldn't even want to think about it, but that was exactly what he would do until the front of his mind was nothing but cigarette-filled pockets of dripping snot and slime. She tried not to laugh, imagining how revolting it must look. If she were in a position to give a shit about him, she would have felt bad.

While she waited for his mind to betray him, she planned on the best way to get a box out of the red paint zone. Since she didn't know what she was looking for or what the boxes contained, it didn't really matter which one she took. It was a crapshoot, so she might just as well get the easiest one she could get her hands on. The boxes that held her files were exactly the same as the classified files, except for the bright red tape that secured the latter. She couldn't be sure she would get more than one chance to sneak into the red paint zone, so she had to be sure whatever box she took stayed hidden and whatever gap she left wasn't noticed.

Ellie knelt on the floor behind the boxes she had stacked up around her workstation. The soldier completely ignored her, his mind no doubt busy disciplining itself against visions of foul sputum. She studied the stacks of Feno boxes closest to her. They were stacked three high, three deep, three across; the file cabinets were now neatly lined up against the walls. Tidy little fuckers, she thought. Her cozy maze of boxes was gone, as was her private sitting area. Hell, it seemed like half the boxes back here had been removed. Those that remained were stacked in such neat little bundles throughout the red-painted area, it was going to be a bitch to swap them out unnoticed. All those red-taped seals were prominently displayed. If she was going to switch out one of her unsealed boxes, she was going to have to tuck it into the middle of a stack. Great. So all she had to do was somehow get enough time to lift, haul, drop, switch, hide, and restack. She hoped her guard had had a nice big dinner last night.

Ellie returned to her desk to wait. The secret to tummy tipping was timing. Throw too much at the target too fast and your efforts were just the distraction that could keep them from focusing on their nausea; take too long between stunts and they could get control of their focus. Ellie knew she had to wait until the heat, the smoke, and the idea of snot at his feet became the white elephant in the corner he could not stop thinking about. Judging from the way he swayed just slightly, she knew it was time for phase two.

She picked up her office phone and dialed Bing's extension. "Hey buddy, how about an early lunch? Or would it be brunch?"

"I'm not giving you your chili back until you tell me how you found my stash." She could hear the chatter of Bing's officemates returning from their staff meeting.

"That sounds great! You having your soup?"

"You mean what you call my Ass Soup? Oh…" Bing dropped his voice to a whisper. "Let me guess. Your new visitor isn't feeling so good? Who is it? Can you say?"

"Nah." Ellie leaned forward on her elbows, doodling on her desk blotter. "I think I'll have chili. Why don't you heat yours up downstairs and just bring the can to me? Our microwave's a little stronger up here. Plus that will give your soup plenty of time to develop its flavors while my chili gets nice and bubbly."

"On my way. But you'd better warn Big Martha. She threatened to beat me to death if I ever brought that soup upstairs again."

"Will do. See you in two."

"Please tell me you're not going to keep rhyming everything."

Ellie laughed. "What can I say? It's my way." She hung up the phone on his curses. Big Martha would need a heads-up if Bing was going to bring the foul-smelling soup upstairs. Ellie very rarely got nauseated anymore, but if anything could do it, it was the odor of that concoction. As she headed to the front of the office, Ellie stopped and looked at the guard.

"Do you feel okay? Oh my God, you are really green." Keeping the potential for vomit forefront in the mind was crucial to success. Symptom lists helped. "You're sweating so much. Can I get you something? A drink? A towel? Your lips are absolutely gray."

"I'm fine, ma'am. Please step away from the secure zone." His nostrils flared as he tried not to gulp air. His lips were papery dry, and Ellie knew he would die before he would lick them in front of her. For now.

"Okay, if you're sure. I'll be happy to get you a Coke or something. Something cold." As she spoke, she made a point of swinging her hair and swaying from side to side, knowing the motion would make his stomach roll. "So I'm going over there," big hand gesture toward Martha, "and I've got crackers in my desk," another big hand swing in the opposite direction, and the young guard closed his eyes and blew out a breath. He reopened his eyes quickly and focused over her shoulder.

"Just let me know if you need anything. Believe me, we've all been through it." Ellie started walking again and then turned quickly, getting very close to the guard. "But if you puke, you have to clean it up. Every chunky drop.

Remember that." Without waiting to see his response, she made her way to Big Martha's desk and hopped up on the corner. The smaller desk across from her was empty.

"Where's Little Miss Can't Be Wrong?" Ellie asked, referring to the missing new girl.

"Asked for another transfer. Said the conditions were hostile."

"Waaaah. Speaking of hostile, Bing is bringing up his Japanese soup."

"No, he is not." Big Martha looked up at her with a glare that brooked no question. "I told him the last time he brought it up that I would beat him so badly he'd fit inside the can. And then I'd run it over with an army truck."

"I know, but..."

"And another thing." Big Martha waved a pen at Ellie. "This may come as a huge surprise to you, but there is actually work that does need to be done around here. You didn't happen to notice that big stack of folders that showed up on your desk, did you? Ever wonder what's supposed to happen to those?"

"I know, Martha, I know." Ellie bumped her feet against her boss's desk. "It's just that it's really hard to work with company. Especially when that company doesn't feel so good."

Big Martha leaned back in her chair. "You mean our new guest?" Ellie nodded. "Do you know that he told me that you and I were to sign in with him every morning and sign out at night before we left?"

"I didn't sign in with him."

"Because I set him straight on that matter." Big Martha needed to say no more. Getting set straight by Big Martha was something nobody needed to experience twice. "So do you and Bing have a puke pool going on this guy?"

"Sort of. Want in?"

Big Martha rose from her chair to see the suffering young man standing across the room. "Aw shit, that's a sucker's bet. He won't last another fifteen. Especially if that nasty soup fouls up the air."

"Who's criticizing my soup?" The smell preceded Bing into the office, and both Ellie and Big Martha blew out disgusted breaths.

"Jesus, Bing." Ellie fanned under her nose. "That would be the smell salt would have if it could have body odor."

"And a dead mouse in its pocket," Big Martha said.

Bing sipped from his oversized mug. "I'm telling you guys, you should try it. It's really delicious, and Walmart had it three for a dollar."

"You were robbed. Did you bring my chili?"

Bing held up the grocery bag. "First I want to know who, what, and why."

Ellie shrugged over her shoulder. "Remember the delightful Mr. Carpenter who threatened to arrest me for stepping onto the red paint zone? Well, he has decided to enforce his will with an armed guard."

"Feno?"

"Of course. Newbie. Sweating like a whore in church."

Big Martha laughed. "I hope you didn't bet anything on this tummy-tip, Bing, because this kid is going down fast."

"I've got no money on it, Martha. This sounds like it's personal for Ellie."

"It is." Ellie folded her arms and scowled. "I don't like people coming in here and trying to throw their weight

S. G. REDLING

around. I have never given half a shit what was in those boxes, and now they're treating me like I'm a security threat." She almost spilled the beans on her plan to steal a box of files but didn't want to take a chance of implicating her friends if she got caught. She doubted very seriously if there was anything worth getting in trouble for in those boxes, but if she got caught, she wouldn't take her friends down with her. "I just think we should make it clear that Feno authority is no stronger than their weakest stomach."

"What do you want me to do?"

Ellie and Big Martha spoke as one. "Eat your soup."

"I'm going to go heat up this chili and do a little splash and dash." Ellie grabbed a can from the grocery bag in Bing's hand and headed for the little kitchenette off the center of the office, on the other side of the bathrooms from where the guard stood.

She dumped the can into a big mug like Bing's and waited for the old microwave to heat it up enough to smell. Of course even if the chili were rancid it couldn't smell worse than her friend's soup, but she also needed the meaty chili warm enough to be runny. If this worked, she hoped her friends would stay at the front of the office long enough for her to make the box switch. From the small alcove she couldn't see anyone else in the room. One advantage of the clutter in the records office was that there was no clear line of sight from one end to the other. She would have to be fast, though.

She nearly dropped the hot cup of chili as she pulled it from the microwave when Big Martha popped her head into the kitchenette. "All set, Ellie?"

Ellie scooped up a spoonful of the chili and let it splatter back into the mug. "It seems a shame to waste perfectly good chili on this guy, but a girl's got to do what a girl's got to do."

"How about a little insurance policy?" Big Martha held up her thick fist. "If you're up to it, this is a trick I learned from Clancy down at the maintenance depot. I warn you, it's not pretty, but it's ninety-nine point nine-nine percent effective if used orally." Ellie nodded, and the other woman opened her hand, revealing her fail-safe secret weapon. Just the sight of it, much less the idea of it, almost made Ellie gag and she immediately agreed.

"Martha, I have never known a sicker and more disturbed individual."

"You're welcome."

"You might want to keep your distance."

Ellie took the cup of chili and headed back toward her desk. She had to steel herself for what she was about to do. It really wouldn't help if she threw up too, and only six years of contamination gave her the gastric fortitude to pull this off. The smell of Bing's soup hovered in the air like nuclear fallout, and Ellie could see the young Feno guard struggling mightily to control his body. Good luck with that, buddy, she thought as she stirred her chili, keeping track of Big Martha's secret weapon within it.

"How you feeling?" Ellie asked. "You still don't look so good. Sure you don't want a cold drink or something?" The guard said nothing, just clamped his lips together, forcing him to breathe through his nose. "Oh, you might not want to breathe too deeply in here. My buddy's eating this soup

that smells so foul. Can you smell it? It smells like decompos-
ing flesh. Like bloated, green rot, doesn't it? Can you smell
it?"

She stirred her chili, making loud squishing sounds
within the mug. "See, that's why I'm eating this chili. I had
it left over from last night. Left it in the fridge. Want some?"
She held the mug out for him to take a peek, which he
refused. "I sure hope nobody screwed with it. You know how
people are, always fucking with other people's stuff." She
wished the kid would just vomit already so she wouldn't have
to take the next step, but she gave him credit. He was hanging tough. With a sigh, she scooped up her bowl's secret and
shoved it in her mouth.

"Mmm." Ellie fought her own gag reflex then let out
a cry. "What the fuck?" Reaching into her mouth with two
fingers, Ellie began to draw out the matted clump of hair
Big Martha had slipped her. Long strands tangled up with
clumps of meat and tomato skins, and she tried not to think
of what she was doing as she let the greasy, matted hair slip
out from between her lips. With a flick of her wrist, she
hurled the chili-soaked clump of hair onto the arm of the
security guard as she threw the cup to the floor to shatter in
a red, chunky splatter.

It was almost enough to make *her* vomit. The young
guard didn't stand a chance.

He clamped his hands over his mouth as vomit sprayed
between his fingers. Ellie pointed him toward the bathrooms, and as he ran, he slipped in the chili and vomit flew
from his lips like wet confetti. She could hear Big Martha
and Bing laughing their asses off in the front of the office as
she jumped over boxes to get to her desk. Not waiting to see

if it was safe, Ellie grabbed the closest unmarked file box, dashed onto the red paint and pulled off the top center box from the secure pile, and then slid out the one beneath it. She pitched her own file box in that one's place, returned a red-taped box to the top, and shoved the swiped box under her desk just as Bing's heavy footsteps and applause approached.

"Would you like to make the announcement or shall I?" He planted his elbows on the nearest file cabinet, his chin in his hands.

"Why don't you?" Ellie handed him her office phone receiver and punched "Page."

Bing cleared his throat and got on the all-call. "Maintenance. Maintenance. Could we get maintenance to the records office for a cleanup? We have a digestive disturbance in records. Thank you." He hung up the phone. "Wait for it."

A few seconds ticked off and someone got on the all-call system. "Newbie pussy!" Applause could be heard coming from the offices downstairs. Ellie laughed and clapped and kicked back in her seat, her feet resting on a hidden box sealed with red tape.

CHAPTER EIGHT

Ellie couldn't pull her feet down from the box beneath her desk. It wasn't like it was full of live puppies, but somehow she thought it would give its presence away to the guard, to Bing, to anyone who might be interested, and the thought of getting caught doing something so stupid made Ellie's fingers tingle. She pulled her chair in close, her knees bumping the crooked middle drawer, and laughed along with Bing. The guard didn't stay in the bathroom long and beat the maintenance crew to the scene of the crime by a good ten minutes. The office smelled horrific, and even though they laughed, Ellie and her coworkers gave unspoken respect to the ailing guard for not only returning, but dropping a load of paper towels down over his mess. They knew what the smell and the sight were doing to his stomach; they were all long-term residents of Flowertown. It showed grit to face your own sick mess, especially under the teasing gaze of those who'd brought it on.

He couldn't make himself pick up the wet towels. As soon as the liquid began soaking into the brown paper, he righted himself and stepped several feet away from the site.

Big Martha had returned to her desk, and Bing and Ellie turned away from the young guard. Ellie knew he wanted to come over to the desk and threaten her with that gun he still had slung over his back. She could see him fighting that urge as much as he fought his own vomit, but whoever had trained him in Flowertown ways had obviously done a good job. Everyone knew that the only thing funnier to the jaded long-termers than making a newbie puke was watching said newbie then throw a hissy fit afterward. It was considered something of a comic encore, and the young guard struggled mightily to control his temper.

He marched the perimeter of the red paint zone. Bing bit back a laugh as the heavy footsteps stomped beside Ellie's desk, the guard eyeing and measuring every inch of the secure zone. She hoped she looked convincing as she rolled her eyes at the guard's attentiveness, praying she didn't seem too obvious with almost half her body shoved into the cubby beneath her desk, trying to obscure even a glimpse of the stolen property. The guard walked the red paint line and then, keeping the giggling workers in his peripheral vision, marched between the stacks of boxes and file cabinets. Ellie tasted blood in her mouth from biting the inside of her cheek as the guard stopped at the stack of file boxes she had just disturbed. Had she gotten them lined up correctly? Had she missed some sort of secure marking only trained guards would spot?

Bing watched the guard watch them from the other side of the pile of boxes. He leaned in close to whisper to Ellie. "Do you think he's taking a leak?" Ellie laughed so fast and so hard she snorted, and the guard stepped quickly out from behind the stack and resumed his post. Bing rapped his knuckles on her desk in salute and good-bye and rose to leave, mouthing something about getting his weed back. Ellie waved him off and watched as he made a joke with the janitors who arrived to clean up the stinking mess. She couldn't hear what they said, but when the three men burst out in loud laughter, she could see the gray face of the guard flush. It was a simple truth in Flowertown: it didn't matter how big your gun was; you were always overshadowed by your puddle of vomit.

Ellie tried to concentrate on the folders in her inbox. She had made such a mess in her attempt to distract the guard that her desk was now littered with random folders from the boxes scattered around her desk. She knew she would have to pull her seat out of the cubbyhole eventually, and so, with a deep breath, she pushed off the box with both feet and rolled her chair back. The guard didn't look her way. She doubted he ever would again. But if he glanced at her desk from the right angle when she was away from it, the game was up.

Taking a deep breath and a handful of files, Ellie began putting the files back in the proper boxes. The mindlessness of the task made her relax a bit, although she still desperately wanted to roll a short joint and smoke up at her desk. A bad idea, she knew, but in comparison to her last stunt, child's play. The thought made her laugh out loud, and she caught the tension in the guard's jaw. He thought she was still laughing at him, and Ellie reasoned that probably wasn't the smartest psychological ploy. If ever there was a time to play nice, the moments after stealing classified documents was probably it. Ellie rose from the stack of boxes she was working in and headed toward the kitchenette, not looking at the guard as she passed.

She grabbed a can of no-name ginger ale from the refrigerator, paused for a moment, and grabbed a second. The guard watched her approach, doubtless dreading what she might have planned, and refused to meet her eye when she stopped in front of him. She held out both cans.

"It's ginger ale. It will help."

"Step away from the secure zone, ma'am."

Ellie sighed and kept the cans held out before her. "Really. It is just ginger ale, and I haven't opened either can. Your choice. I'll drink the other."

"You put a hairball in your mouth." The guard swallowed hard just saying the words. "I don't think I want to picnic with you again."

"Funny." Ellie popped the top of one can and took a drink. She read the sweat-soaked name tag sewn onto his shirt. "Cooper. It was nothing personal, you know."

He shifted his eyes to her, not turning his head. "That's a real comfort."

"You know, I've been sitting next to those boxes for years and I've never once given a shit what was in them. Why are you here?"

He started to shrug but caught himself. "I go where they send me."

Ellie was beginning to realize how unaccustomed she was to conversations in which she wasn't high. She couldn't seem to keep her mouth shut. "How do you know I didn't rifle through your precious boxes while you were hurling chunks in the can? How do you know this wasn't all an elaborate plan to thwart the dreaded Feno Red Guards?"

Cooper finally looked at her, from head to toe. "Because you don't look that smart."

"Why Cooper, was that a joke?"

"No." He went back to staring into space over her shoulder, and she couldn't tell if he was fighting off a smile.

"You didn't call for backup. Why not?"

"Because I'm gonna take enough shit from you. I don't need it from my coworkers."

"That's probably true." She held out the unopened can. "So you might as well take a peace offering too. Trust me. I'll make you pay for it later."

He watched her for a long moment and then reached for the can. He took a small sip, probably expecting it to explode or taste like urine or some other horror, but when Ellie continued to drink hers as she headed back toward her desk, he relaxed and drank more deeply.

"This gonna kill me later?"

"Only time will tell." Ellie pulled back up to her desk. "Guess you're going to have to trust me." The guard shook his head and continued sipping at his drink.

His attention diverted once more, Ellie felt less nervous reaching down to her feet for the box hidden there. Obviously she wouldn't be able to carry the whole box out, so she was going to have to sneak a few files out at a time. She also knew she had to strip the box of its red security tape, and that wouldn't be easy. For one thing, the sound would be very noticeable. Most of the boxes in the unsecure area simply had lids or were closed with the old-fashioned string and button closures. Only the Feno boxes were taped shut. Plus the tape itself was a bright, unmistakable shade of red. A big wad of tangled red tape would be noticed in a garbage can. If it was found wadded up in her desk, well, it wouldn't take Sherlock Holmes to piece the story together.

Ellie pulled a letter opener from the center drawer. In the six year she had worked in this office—actually, in the ten years she had worked in *any* office—she had never once used a letter opener to open an envelope of any type. She never really understood why she always seemed to have one in her desk. Now she knew. Letter openers were the modern equivalent of hairpins in the old film noirs she and Bing liked to watch—they were innocent-looking weapons of crime. Slipping the sharp silver blade down between her legs, she kept the guard in sight between the stacks of paper baskets on her desk while she felt for the tape. Trying to muffle the sound, she jammed the blade into the tape and split the seal. There was no turning back now. She had officially broken into Feno property.

When her phone buzzed, she jumped so high her arms and knees knocked against the shallow drawer above the cubby. The letter opener flew from her fingers and skittered across the top of the opened box, teetering for just a moment before sliding the wrong way off the cardboard, down to the floor and out from underneath the desk. She didn't dare breathe as she peered over her inbox at Cooper, who ignored the ruckus. Ellie decided at that moment that she was going to kill whoever had texted her.

Med Center reminder—bloodwork 11am

A stream of filth flew from her lips as she righted herself in her chair, causing Cooper to glance her way quickly, then look away when he saw the dark expression on her face. There couldn't be a worse time to have to go to the med center. That would mean leaving the box exposed, uncovered. She couldn't get the tape off. She had nothing to drape over the carton. If Cooper or Big Martha or even Bing thought of a reason to come back into her little corner, she would have some very tough questions to answer. But if she missed a med check, she knew the guards who would come for her would not be newbies like Cooper or even charming tough guys like Guy. The lesson had been well learned in the early days of contamination that Feno saved medical security duty for the hardest, coldest, and roughest of their forces. Nobody resisted med checks twice; nobody even argued with them. Feno and Barlay Pharma claimed it was all for the health of the residents, but nobody in Flowertown would forget the brutality the med force had shown in the early days. Nobody dared risk it now.

If she was going to get busted for stealing the box, she was at least going to see what was inside those files. Not caring if her guard watched, Ellie reached into the box and grabbed three folders from its center. A quick glance told her they were labeled with that same indecipherable alphanumeric code on the outside of the box, so she figured any file was as good as the next. She couldn't just walk out with files under her arm, she knew. Even the non-Feno files were under security watch. If it had been winter she could have shoved them up under the many layers of sweaters she would be wearing in the always-freezing office, but today all she had on was an old Cheap Trick T-shirt that wouldn't hide a pack of cigarettes.

Then she saw the bag of groceries Bing had dropped beside her desk. God bless you, Annabeth Dingle, she thought, for sending Rachel those oyster crackers. The box wasn't big enough to hide three manila folders, no matter

how tightly she tried to roll them, but if she slid the folders between the cracker box and her body, Ellie thought
she would be able to stroll out of the building without
attracting any undue attention. As far as she could see, it
was her only choice. Tucking the bag between her feet,
Ellie placed the folders carefully, being sure not to rip the
cheap bag. Both the folders and the crackers left no room
for the three remaining cans of chili, so Ellie tucked them
into her large file drawer. She hoped Bing wouldn't steal
them. They could well turn out to be the last meal of a
condemned woman.

When she stood up and pulled the bag to her side, she
realized what a terrible hiding place she had chosen. The
files were longer and taller than the oyster cracker box, and
the bag strained at the seams. Still, Cooper had noticed her
rise, and she couldn't think of any other options. All she
had to do was get past the guard and she was confident she
could rush her way out the door. It was time once again to
go on the offensive.

She grabbed her cigarettes as she cleared the corner of
the desk and, shifting the bag to her right hand, the oyster
crackers against her leg, she lit a cigarette and puffed hard
as she walked. Cooper smelled her before he turned to her
and didn't pretend to disguise his disgust.

"I thought you weren't going to smoke in here. I thought
you made a peace offering."

"Relax, Cooper." Ellie blew out another thick cloud as
she passed, keeping herself in the middle of his line of sight
of the bag. "I'm taking it outside. If I get any calls, take a
message." The guard coughed and fanned the offensive
smoke away, not bothering to watch her go. Ellie swung the

bag on her wrist, turning the folders against her, the cracker box on the outside, and hurried to the stairs.

"Where the hell are you going?" Big Martha leaned on heavy forearms across her desk.

"Med check." Ellie froze, thinking quickly of the best way to turn around without exposing the bag.

"Bullshit. You had one yesterday."

Ellie let anger be her disguise. "Well, I've got another one today. What do you want me to do? Bring you a note?" She could hardly hear her own words over the pounding of blood in her ears as she watched Big Martha's gaze drift to the bag she half hid behind her leg. Her boss quickly lifted her gaze, her mouth set in a hard line, and it felt like hours before she spoke.

"I've never known you to eat oyster crackers before."

Ellie could only blink several times, trying to wrap her mind around what her boss saw. Nobody chose to eat oyster crackers. They were a last resort when nothing else would stay down, and Ellie felt a twinge of guilt at misleading her boss. People got sick in Flowertown. It was a fact of life, just like the fact that many of them didn't get better. In this new bizarre world of chemical containment, etiquette demanded that one never, ever ask the question, "Are you okay?" when issues of wellness arose. If Ellie had two med checks in one week and she carried around a box of oyster crackers, that was her business. If she wanted to share it, Big Martha would have listened, but until then, the topic was off-limits.

"Don't make a day of it." Big Martha turned back toward her computer. "Those files are piling up."

Ellie nodded, trying not to gasp out her relief. She was sick, she told herself, so technically she hadn't misled her boss. That would have to do as far as comfort went, and Ellie took the stairs two at a time.

She didn't trust herself to exhale until she turned the second corner on her way to the med center. She'd made it from the building with the files. Trying to slow her pounding heart, she cut across the street to the newsstand. Ellie didn't know what kind of files she had in her bag, but she didn't want to go strolling into the med center and have someone there recognize them. A newspaper would be just the right size to wrap around the bulky manila folders.

Ellie scanned the nearly empty rack of newspapers. There was a small stack of week-old *New York Times,* one three-day-old *Sioux City Journal,* and a few two-day-old *USA Today*s. Flowertown never got the news the day it happened. Folks inside often referred to the "USA Yesterday," but usually the national paper made it a day late. Not today, though, and judging from the scowl on Mr. MacDonald's face, the proprietor was none too happy about it. Well, she wasn't here to read. Ellie grabbed the Davenport paper.

"What the hell are you doing that for?" MacDonald's voice roared from his small stand.

"Uh, what? Buying a newspaper?"

"That's not a newspaper!" The old man slammed his veiny hand down. "Newspapers carry news! News as in new, not day-old, not two-day-old. That's not news in there. That's history. Why don't you go to the library and check out a history book?"

Ellie waited out his tirade. She liked Mr. MacDonald. She liked the bourbon she smelled on his breath and the way he yelled at everybody, especially his customers. Bing had told her he had been a professor at Northwestern

121

before the spill, and she thought he would have been the kind of professor she would have enjoyed.

"I want to buy the paper."

"You want to piss your money away?"

"Why not?" Ellie shrugged. "I'm just going to drink it away otherwise. Or maybe I'll use this paper to hide a bomb."

MacDonald leaned over the counter and lowered his voice. "Talk like that can get you arrested, young lady."

"Oh, I sure would hate to be confined in a small area with no chance of escape." She held MacDonald's hard gaze until his eyes crinkled up in a smile. He loved a smart-ass. "And if I do go down, old man, I'm taking you with me."

"Yeah, yeah, yeah, promises, promises." He swiped her debit card. "Did you pick up 'the local' today? It's got some interesting tidbits." "The local" was a newsletter residents of Flowertown put out on random days, from random outlets, with a random selection of topics. It read like a badly printed church bulletin. MacDonald stuffed one in the fold of her paper.

"Thank you, sir. I'll check it out."

"Liar."

The med center was crowded as always, the eleven o'clock line for meds filing all the way out the glass doors into the lobby. Ellie elbowed her way through the bored-looking mob and flashed the keychain tag that she had hooked to her work badge under the scanner. The door to the left buzzed, and she let herself into the blue tag lounge. That wasn't really the name on the door, but Ellie never bothered to read the words on the sign. Leaning on the ledge under an unmarked window, Ellie waiting for the heavily made-up clerk to acknowledge her.

"Hello." Ellie rapped her knuckles on the glass after a solid minute.

The woman continued to type and kept her eyes glued to the screen before her.

"I have a med check at eleven."

The woman typed some more and then made a great show of craning her neck to see the large clock behind her before turning back to Ellie with leaden eyes. "It's ten fifty-two."

Ellie waved her medical tag under the opening in the glass. "Yeah, well, considering the fact that I'm a blue tag, you might say time is of the essence. Plus I have a job to get back to."

The woman curled her lip, cracking the shellac of foundation around her mouth, and Ellie could see she was older than she first appeared. Perhaps a steady diet of being a bitch had aged her prematurely. In any case, her sneer made her face that much more unpleasant as she leaned forward on her elbows.

"I have a job to do too, ma'am." She looked Ellie over with much the same look Ellie had given Martha's hairball. "And my job is to make sure appointments are kept on schedule. Your appointment is for eleven o'clock. Not ten fifty, not eleven oh one."

"You've got to be fucking kidding me."

"Please take a seat," she tapped on the glass with long, pink, flowered nails, "and I will call you at your proper appointment time."

Ellie knew it was pointless to argue, so instead she pressed her forehead against the glass. "I bet you win employee of the month every month." The woman pursed her lips in an ugly semblance of triumph. Then she saw the greasy spot Ellie's skin had left on the glass. Ellie ran her finger through the stain, spreading it. "You might want to clean that up, honey. I bet that's part of your job too."

She flopped into a chair out of sight from the bitch behind the glass. In truth, she was glad for the moment to sit down. It gave her a chance to slip the files from the bag and into the fold of the newspaper. Ellie desperately wanted to peek into the files, but she knew every inch of the med center was under camera surveillance at all times. Bending from the waist, she did her best to block the camera's view of her bag until the folders were well out of sight. Just as she was straightening up, the door to the examining rooms opened and the She-Nightmare from the reception desk stood, holding a clipboard.

"Cauley?" She spoke loudly as she scanned the empty room. "Eleanor Cauley?" Ellie rose and headed her way, and still she paged the empty room. "Eleanor Cauley."

"I'm right here."

The woman checked the clipboard and then looked up at Ellie. "Eleanor Cauley?"

"Yes."

"You had an eleven o'clock med check?"

If the bag had not contained stolen classified files, Ellie would have given in to the temptation to beat the woman to death with it. "Yes."

The woman scribbled on the clipboard, then held open the door. "You're late."

Ellie bit her tongue as she passed her, then stopped and turned. "You know, I think it's really heartwarming that Barlay hires the mentally handicapped."

"Room three." As Ellie turned away, the woman shot her a syrupy smile. "Hope you feel better." Then, pretending to notice the blue files on her clipboard, made a show of covering her mouth in fake surprise as she walked off. "Oh, wait. That's right. My bad."

Ellie was certain, as she forced herself to sit on the stool next to the med tech, that if she looked she would see her heart beating out of her chest. The receptionist's remarks played over and over in her mind. Her fists were clenched and the plastic handles of the bag cut into her white fingers. Her face felt hot with rage, and while she could hear the tech's voice speaking to her, the part of her brain that understood words had been eclipsed by something far more primal. It wasn't until a hand touched her arm that she could break the spell of the anger consuming her.

"I need your tag." The woman touching her wore the pale blue coat of all Barlay med techs. Her brown hair was pulled up in a loose bun, revealing a large strawberry birthmark on her smooth neck. Ellie stared at the red mark, trying to gain control of herself.

"It's on my badge." The words scraped out of her tight throat. She handed her badge over to the tech, who scanned it and studied the computer screen. Ellie worked on taking the deep breaths she had learned would control her temper, and by the time the tech handed her badge back, Ellie felt in control once more.

"Have you taken your meds this morning?" the tech asked, studying the screen. When Ellie didn't answer right away, she cocked an eyebrow at her. "Don't lie. It's going to show up on the blood test anyway."

"No, I haven't. I forgot them at home." The truth was she had no idea where the bottle of red pills was. They could have fallen out of her pocket at any point last night. "If I were to lose them or something..."

"You can get a refill. Your QOLs are unlimited."

"That's reassuring." Ellie watched the young woman type. Apparently terminal diagnoses were no big thing in the blue tag lounge, but Ellie wouldn't have minded a little less offhandedness. "Can you sign for a refill for me?"

The tech rolled her chair closer to Ellie and tied a piece of rubber tubing above her elbow. As she wiped Ellie's bulging vein with an iodine swab, she laughed under her breath. "You mean you don't want to deal with Miss America out front?"

"What a bitch."

"Tell me about it. Try being stuck in here all day with her." The tech jabbed a needle into Ellie's arm and started to withdraw blood. Rather than look, Ellie watched the woman, seeing the name tag stitched to her lapel.

"Olivia. That's pretty."

"Yeah, I was named after a pig."

Ellie laughed, remembering the children's books with the pig named Olivia. "You must be a local."

Olivia nodded, gently pulling back with the needle. She didn't meet Ellie's eyes, so Ellie took the conversation no further. Nobody liked to talk about how they wound up here.

"I need to take a pretty big sample."

"I'm not using it," Ellie said. "Take all you want." Olivia looked up quickly at her, and Ellie felt a sharp pinch at the site of the blood draw. "Ouch!"

"Sorry." Olivia pressed her gloved fingers over the injection site and put the full syringe back on the desk. She replaced her fingers with a thick wad of gauze and pulled Ellie's arm up over her head. "Put pressure on this for a minute. I'll get some tape."

Olivia turned her back on Ellie, pulling off a length of medical tape and sticking it to the edge of the desk. Rather than put the tape over the gauze, however, she picked up the phone and tapped a flashing button. Ellie couldn't hear what she said and wasn't interested. Instead she held her arm up, pressing on the gauze. With her luck, she would bleed out. Her fingers began to tingle as she heard the tech playing with the tape and laughing into the phone. It would do no good to complain, she knew. In the med center, all you could do was wait.

Finally Olivia turned back to her, lengths of tape stuck to several fingers, and told her to lower her arm. Quickly she taped the gauze in place and began reciting the medical instructions required by law within Flowertown. Ellie had heard them hundreds of times: medications were to be taken upon instruction with no exception; any complications or difficulties were to be reported immediately; no medications were to be shared or disposed of in any way, blah blah blah. But just because Olivia and her coworkers were obligated to say it didn't mean Ellie was obligated to listen. She smoothed out a loose piece of tape as she gathered her bag of contraband and waited for Olivia to finish her spiel.

Olivia finished chanting the words she had to say no less than twenty times a day and then picked up a pen. "You need a refill?" Ellie nodded and took the blue scrip from her. "Keep an eye on that arm. No heavy lifting. You can peel off some of the tape if you need to."

There was no line at the dispensary on this side of the building. As she waited for her pills, she pulled out her phone and punched in Guy's number. She wasn't really worried about him. She just wanted to hear his voice. Twice she misdialed, her fingers trembling, maybe from the blood loss, maybe from the ebbing rage she had felt inside, or maybe just from not being high. The pharmacist slid her pills across the counter, and Ellie dropped them in the bag, still trying to dial as she headed back out onto the street.

This is ridiculous, she thought, and plopped down on the curb in front of the med center shrubbery. She took the bag off her arm and focused all her attention on her fumbling fingers. At last she got the number correct. It rang several times, and while she waited, she tried once more to smooth out the dangling tape on her arm. She swore when Guy's message began to play. What a fucking day. The operator began the unnecessary instruction on how to leave a voice mail, and Ellie swore again as the tape on her arm refused to stick.

"Hey, Guy," she said after the beep. "Just seeing how you did last night. I'm heading back to work and—" She let the phone slip from between her shoulder and her ear. In her frustration she had pulled the uncooperative tape from her bandage. The gauze hadn't fallen off because there was another piece of tape underneath the first. On the lower piece, in small handwritten letters, were the words, "Don't take the red pills."

Ellie could only stare at the words. She heard the phone at her feet beep that her message was over and still she didn't move. Bing. She knew she had to find Bing. Grabbing the bag, Ellie leapt to her feet and began to run. All the tension from the night before, all the rage from this morning, all the years she had refused to run melted out of her as her muscles pounded to life. She felt her lungs burning but didn't stop, couldn't stop until she found Bing. He would know what those words meant. He would tell her some conspiracy theory and they would get high and she would tell him he was crazy, that the words were just a practical joke.

But she didn't believe it.

She was gasping for breath as she turned the final corner to the records office, the bag banging painfully against her aching legs. Bing would tell her what to think and help her make sense out of this. Bing always knew what to do. Bing always knew everything. Ellie stopped. Bending from the waist to catch her breath, she realized that Bing knew nothing about the red pills. He didn't know because she hadn't told him. After all they had been through together, she had kept the most important information of her life a secret from him and for the life of her couldn't predict how he would take the news.

Ellie stood there on the street, staring at her office, trying to corral her thoughts that were flying in a million directions. Her hair clung to her face with sweat and her breath was loud and raspy, but all she could think about was how she was going to tell Bing that she had kept a secret from him. She had to face him. He had to forgive her. She needed him. Nodding to herself, she took a step toward the records office just as the upper floor exploded.

CHAPTER NINE

The first thing Ellie thought was that her face had somehow fallen asleep. It tingled and burned. When she tried to open her eyes, she realized it was tiny shards of glass and wood raining down on her where she lay face-up on the sidewalk. The blast had blown her off her feet, or maybe she had just stumbled, but she lay on her back watching her office burn.

She couldn't have been out more than a few seconds because the chaos was only beginning. Sirens could be heard in the distance, and she was on her feet before people started running out of the front door. Soon the street was packed with people pushing and running in every direction as thick, black smoke poured from the hole that had been a vent on the upper floor of the records office. She knew that vent. It was the vent beside the bathroom, the vent she and Bing used to drag their smoke from the room. The vent in the red zone.

Ellie let the crowd push her as she scanned faces, looking for Bing and Big Martha. Within the smoke-filled building people shouted for help, barking orders and dragging people out behind them. The sirens ripped into the madness as firefighters parted the crowd, rushing in with their gear, ordering people to step back. A young man Ellie recognized from personnel bumped into her, bleeding heavily from his forehead. He slammed his shoulder into hers, spinning her around and nearly costing her the plastic bag with the stolen files. She clutched the bag to her chest, the mob's confusion infusing her, making it difficult to think.

"Bing!" She screamed his name at the tallest head she could see over the crowd and cried out when he spun around. Jumping up and down, she fought to keep sight of him through the smoke and the madness. She saw his arm pointing away from the flames, and she rushed to follow his direction. The sound of something within the building collapsing roared behind her, but all Ellie could think was to keep sight of Bing's skinny neck and messy hair as they both pushed their way through the panicked crowd.

"Ellie, my God!" Bing finally got to her, pulling her to him through a cluster of women. She stumbled over someone's foot and heard people everywhere screaming but buried her own cries in her best friend's sweaty T-shirt. Bing held her close, dragging her along through the crowd until they found an open space past the corner. Neither spoke. They held each other and watched their building burn.

"Did you see Big Martha?" Ellie asked. "Did she get out okay?"

"Didn't you see her?" Bing rubbed her shoulder. "I thought you would have gotten out with her. Oh shit, Ellie, I thought you were dead. There was that huge blast upstairs, and when the ceiling came down, all I could think was 'Where's Ellie?' I tried to get up there, but then all that smoke came pouring down. How did you get out?"

"I wasn't in there."

"What do you mean?" Bing looked down at her. "Where were you?"

The tone of his voice made the ebbing panic rise again. "I had a med check. I just ran out for little bit. What? Why are you looking at me like that?"

Bing chewed on his lip for a moment, scanning the crowd as the Feno security forces arrived and began cordoning off the area. Even as ambulances cut through the crowds, voices on bullhorns were ordering people to remain where they were, to remain calm and to make no attempt to leave the area. Bing pulled her along by her arm to the edge of the crowd, but a pair of men in red shirts ran yellow crime tape across their path, keeping the frightened crowd contained. Bing squeezed Ellie's hand.

"Listen to me." He turned her to face him. "You can't tell anybody you were out of the building when the bomb went off."

"But I was." Ellie felt herself shaking so hard she was having trouble thinking. "I was at med check. They're going to know. There's going to be a record. Besides, why would I lie?"

"Why would you lie? Ellie, you've got to start thinking." Bing glared at two young men standing too close to them and lowered his voice. "How do you think it's going to look when they find out that you just happened to be out of the building the exact moment the bomb goes off in the exact area you have been reprimanded for tampering with? The bomb that kills the guard assigned to keep an eye on you?"

"Cooper?" Ellie staggered back a step.

"Who?"

"Cooper. That's his name."

Bing started talking again, but Ellie could only think about the young guard struggling so hard to maintain his composure as she threw every cruel nausea-inducing trick at him. He'd had grit; she had admired his grit.

"How do you know he's dead?"

"What?" Bing grabbed her by the shoulders. "Ellie, are you even listening to me?"

"How do you know Cooper's dead?"

Bing worked to find the right words. "He...when the ceiling came down...he was burning. We couldn't...he was screaming and then...he was quiet. You're bleeding."

Ellie swayed on her feet, not wanting to hear her friend's words. Bing grabbed her arm, where a thin stream of blood trickled. She had lost her bandage.

"Oh no. Oh no." Ellie spun in a circle, looking down at the ground, hoping without reason to find the gauze pad and, more importantly, the tape with the cryptic message. "I've lost my bandage. I've got to find it. I've got to show it to you."

"Ellie, listen to me." He grabbed her once more. "Don't worry about the bandage."

"I had a med check. They took blood. Bing, I've got to tell you something."

"There isn't time. You've got to lie about that med check. Maybe they won't...aw shit."

Ellie couldn't hear those last words as all sound was drowned out by the roar of Feno security vehicles rolling in one after another, surrounding the blast site. The trucks and jeeps formed a tight barricade outside the crime tape, and dozens of armed guards piled from the vehicles, their weapons trained on the frantic crowd penned within.

"Please remain calm," a bullhorn voice blared over the noise. "Everyone stay where you are." Unlike the early commands, this voice had the security force to back it up and the crowd quieted down, the sense of relief palpable in the air. In the chaos and terror of the blast, even Feno security was a welcome sight, anything that could make sense of the madness. Several guards climbed on top of their vehicles, resuming their weapon-ready stances; some stood shoulder to shoulder, filling in the gaps the vehicles couldn't cover, while the rest returned their weapons to the vehicles and began to move through the crowd, breaking them into manageable, smaller groups. Bing held tight to Ellie's hand as they got herded into a group with a dozen others.

Fire trucks continued to spray the building with water while ambulance lights flashed and radios cackled. As the first two ambulances pulled away from the scene, the crowd parting silently to watch them go, Flowertown's final ambulance pulled in. It seemed rescue was going to work on relay today. Peering between huddled masses, Ellie could make out rescue workers treating people on blankets on the ground throughout the barricaded area. Mumbling something to Bing about looking for Big Martha, she cut through the crowd and spied a runoff grate. Hoping nobody was watching her in the chaos, she pulled back the drain and shoved the bag of files into the dark, narrow crevice. Finally able to catch her breath, Ellie stood on tiptoe and surveyed the area, then hurried back to her friend.

"Do you notice anything weird about this, Bing?"

"You're kidding, right? Besides our building being blown sky-high?"

"That's what I mean. Our building just got blown sky-high." Ellie kept her voice low. "Look around you. Where's the army?"

"They're..." Bing craned his neck, looking over the crowd in every direction. "I don't know. They're not here."

"No, they're not. I saw a truck loading up this morning, packing up supplies from a depot. It didn't look like they were leaving much behind."

A woman bumped into Ellie from behind, her face covered in soot, her eyes wild. "What did you say? The army's not coming? What do you mean?" The crowd picked up her panicked questions and a brushfire of rumor and speculation whipped through the crowd, spreading from their little cluster to the entire area in seconds. The calm that had settled burned off quickly as people began shouting and demanding to know where the army was. If they knew, the Feno forces weren't telling. Instead, the guards within the barricade used their strength, their authority, and their nightsticks when necessary to pack the clusters in more tightly. The voice on the bullhorn rang out once more.

"Stay where you are! Remain calm. Do not force us to take preventative measures against you!" People booed and shook their fists while more guards climbed atop the surrounding vehicles and pointed their weapons directly at the crowd. "Please do not make this more difficult than necessary. You are going to be evacuated to a secure location until the nature of the attack has been ascertained. Remain calm. You will be instructed on how to proceed."

All around them the crowd jeered and complained, but Bing grew silent. He pulled his cell phone from his pocket and then shook his head. He held his phone up for her to see the "network busy" message. "This building is nowhere near the tower or the power relay for cell service."

"What does that mean?" Ellie asked.

"They're jamming us."

For once Ellie didn't think her friend was being paranoid. "What do you think they mean by evacuating us to a secure location? Do you think there's another bomb?"

"I doubt it." Bing scanned the serious faces of the guards surrounding them and saw one of the large security trucks open its rear panel doors. "I think they're going to interrogate us."

Before she could ask him anything else, the radios on the guards' belts squawked to life. Codes and commands were relayed down the line, and like a practiced dance troupe, the guards moved into action. A group of fifteen people that was clustered closest to the end of the barricade was herded into the back of the waiting truck. The guns trained on the people from every direction left little room for arguing, and after locking the panel doors behind them, a guard pounded on the truck, signaling to the driver to pull away. As the truck left the barricade line, the rest of the convoy inched forward to keep the line intact.

"Where are they taking them?" It was the soot-covered woman who had eavesdropped earlier. "Are they being arrested? They haven't done anything!" She grabbed at one of the guards surrounding their group and received a sharp elbow to the face for her troubles. The crowd surged around her, cries of outrage shouted down by the harsh bark of another guard.

"Stand down!" He and his comrades held their batons up in practiced formation. "Do not approach the guards. Do not attempt to leave your group!"

"She was just asking a question." A man held the injured woman, whose mouth was now filled with blood. "You piece of shit—" Several people around him pulled him back before the nearest guard used his weapon in earnest.

The guard who had spoken, the leader of the team, warned them again. "You will be evacuated in due course. You are to follow our orders exactly. Failure to do so will result in detention and containment by force, if necessary. Do I make myself clear?"

Muttered obscenities drifted from the small pack as they turned their backs on the guards, drawing in closer together. Around them, the other isolated packs watched the exchange and followed suit. Throughout the area, the guards passed glances and messages on the radios as group by group, truck by truck, the barricaded area was evacuated.

The evacuation worked from the outer ring in, groups exiting in three directions, the now smoldering building blocking the fourth. It was impossible to tell who would be next, so Bing and Ellie huddled together, within but apart from their little pack.

"What do you think they're going to ask us?" she asked.

"The usual, I'd guess." Bing studied the faces around him. "Where we were, what we do there, did we see anything unusual? You know, for all their commandeering of the scene, I don't get the feeling that these guys really know what they're doing."

Ellie saw one of the guards burning a hole in her with his angry gaze. "I don't know about that, Bing. They seem pretty sure to me."

"No. Evacuating everybody? Containing the area like this? They're panicking. They didn't see this coming and they don't have a suspect, or they would have handled this much differently. This is a PR nightmare. They've scared these people more than the bomb did. It's going to take a lot to whitewash this in the news."

"Who says it's going to make the news?" Ellie stared up at Bing. "Maybe they don't care about PR anymore."

Bing put his hands on his head, a sure sign of worry. The tension in his face made him look more bird-like than ever, but this time it didn't make Ellie laugh. It was a hell of a way to bring it about, but she had finally become as paranoid as her friend.

"Fuck it," Bing said, dropping his arms and digging into his pocket. "Let's burn one."

"What? Now?"

He held up a thick joint. "You got something better to do? I don't know about you, but I don't think the jitters are going to help anybody during our interrogations." He lit the tip and breathed in deeply. The smell made Ellie's body come alive with longing, and she took the joint from Bing and inhaled until her lungs ached. They faced each other, holding in lungfuls of smoke until they both smiled and exhaled together.

"Good call, Bing." She could feel the rage and fear trickling down her spine, evaporating in the smoke of Bing's excellent weed. She hit it again as a man behind Bing leaned in.

"Mind if I hit that too?" He was nearly as tall as Bing and had a tattoo curling up around his neck. "Can't see any reason to talk to these dirtbags straight."

Bing nodded, and Ellie passed the joint over. He took a hit and gestured over his shoulder to the rest of the pack. Bing nodded again. "The more the merrier, man. Let's smoke up."

Nobody in their group refused the joint, so it burned out quickly. Without hesitation, Bing pulled another fat one from the bag in his pocket and passed it back. The tattooed man shook his hand, introducing himself as Torrez.

"I really appreciate the smoke, man. That's mighty decent of you."

Bing shrugged. "Times like these, you know, we've got to stick together."

"I'll tell you what." Torrez glanced around to keep an eye on the guards. "When this is over, we'll get together and I'll repay you with weed of my own."

"That's not necessary."

"No, but it's the right thing to do. Repayment in kind, you know what I'm saying? Come to my place and smoke my weed." He held Bing's gaze and lowered his voice. "All you want."

Bing stood very still, considering the man before him, then nodded. "All you want." Torrez bumped his knuckles against Bing's, then turned back to continue smoking with the rest of the group. Ellie watched the exchange, feeling the familiar softness of her high thoughts. All you want. Those words again. Bing lit another joint—how many did he keep in there?—and Ellie repeated the words again and again in her mind. When had she heard them recently? It had been recently.

She had said them. In the med center, when Olivia had been taking her blood, she had said those very words. Take all you want. That was when the needle had pricked her. That was when the tech wrote the note on the tape.

"Bing, I have to tell you something." Before she could finish, the guards around them shouted as a team and began herding them toward an awaiting truck. Bing grabbed Ellie's hand and she could feel the sweat in his palm.

"Don't tell them anything, Ellie." He spoke from the corner of his mouth. "Don't tell them you were out of the building. There's too many people to check. They won't catch it." The guards shouted again, and one by one they climbed into the back of a windowless paneled truck with benches lining the sides. There wasn't enough room for everyone to sit, so Bing and Torrez sat on the floor of the truck, their backs to the drivers. As the truck pulled out, Ellie could see the two men whispering to each other.

The drive was short, less than twenty minutes, but the lack of air and windows made Ellie feel shaky and sweaty by the time the truck came to a stop. The guards opened the doors and shouted at everyone to get out and proceed into the dining hall. Ellie squinted in the bright sunlight as she tried to figure out where they were.

"It's the Feno personnel compound," Bing whispered to her, sidling up beside her. The guards here were armed, lining the walkway the group followed into the dining hall.

"How do you know?" Was there nothing Bing was not privy to?

He pointed to a sign over the dining hall door. Feno Personnel Dining.

"Oh."

"Keep your eyes open, Ellie," he whispered to her as a guard directed them to a line of tables stretching the length of the room. "And keep your mouth shut. Don't tell them anything they don't need to know."

"I don't know, Bing. If they catch me lying about that med check..."

"Next in line!" A short, thick woman with a clipboard shouted at the new group. "Please step forward in an orderly fashion to the next available reporting clerk to make your statement. Ladies and gentlemen, you are not in trouble." From the singsong way she made her announcement, Ellie guessed she had made it several times already today. "This is not an arrest. We are trying to gather as much information as possible. Please answer the questions honestly and clearly so we can return you to your quarters as quickly as possible. Next in line! Please step forward in an orderly fashion..."

Ellie and Bing stepped together to the waiting clerk four stations down the line, who informed them the interviews were one-on-one only. Ellie took a seat and Bing moved to the next available clerk, looking back at Ellie with an encouraging nod.

The interview took less than ten minutes. Name, ID tag scan, and all the questions Bing had predicted. Against her better judgment, Ellie decided to lie about being out of the building during the blast. Bing was probably right; this was a routine cover-your-ass show Feno had pulled together in a panic to make it look like they were doing something. Still, Ellie faltered for a moment when the woman asked her where she was at the time of the blast. Considering the fact that Cooper had died and he had stood between her and the exit, she couldn't very well say she had been at her desk. Instead she said she was on her way to bring files to her boss in the front of the office.

"How did you get out of the building?"

A veteran liar, Ellie knew to keep it simple. "I don't remember. The blast threw me and then the next thing I knew I was falling down the stairs. I was on the street. Everyone was screaming." The clerk nodded, writing notes on her clipboard. She glanced up at Ellie, then reached under the table and came up with a tissue.

"You have blood on your face."

"I do?" She wiped at her face with the tissue. It must have been blood from her arm. The clerk signed off on the report, tore the sheet off the clipboard, and dropped it into a file box behind her. She grabbed a rubber stamp, pressed it in ink, and asked for Ellie's right hand.

"Go to the doors at the rear of the building to your left. Show the stamp to the guard and he will instruct you on how to return to your quarters."

"That's it? That's all you need?"

The clerk dismissed her with a nod, sighing at the line of incoming people that stretched out the door. Ellie rose, trying not to look too relieved. Her legs trembled as she walked, and she fought the temptation to look over her shoulder for Bing.

At the rear doors, a guard checked the stamp on her hand and pointed her in the direction of a group of picnic tables where two dozen people waited for a truck to return them to the center of Flowertown. Ellie couldn't sit, her nerves were too high, so she paced the area waiting for Bing to come out. It seemed to take forever. Typical Bing, she thought, always giving too much information. Finally she saw him walk stiffly through the door and she had to laugh. If this corporate military shit was freaking her out, she could only imagine the effect it was having on her paranoid friend.

Bing didn't exhale until he got to her side. They slapped palms and stood side by side, touching, as they waited to be called to the truck.

"Thanks for the advice," Ellie said. "You were right. They didn't blink an eye."

"Thank God." Bing stuffed his hands in his pockets. "Let's get the hell out of here."

Ellie knew it was a long shot but had to ask. "You didn't happen to see Big Martha anywhere, did you? In the crowd? Was she there?"

Bing shook his head. "I didn't see her, but that doesn't mean anything. We could have just missed her, or she could have been taken out in an ambulance. Try not to worry."

Ellie laughed out loud. "I can't believe I just heard those words come out of your mouth."

Bing grinned. "Yeah, well, I mean, don't worry about *that*. There's plenty of other shit you can worry about. I'll make you a list."

"They're calling us." She grabbed Bing by the arm and headed toward the trucks. Two guards stood at the rear of the trucks, far more relaxed than their coworkers in the front of the building. Each man held a scanner, and as people got to the truck, their ID tags were scanned. For just a second, Ellie felt a twinge of fear the scan would reveal her blue tag status, and she reminded herself that she had to tell

Bing the truth at the next available moment. In the back of
a Feno paneled truck, however, was not that moment.

Bing got to a guard first and, after his tag was scanned,
climbed into the truck. Ellie handed her badge over to the
other guard. "Save me a seat," she mouthed to Bing as the
guard scanned her tag. The guard stared at his scanner for
another several moments and Ellie rolled her eyes. Figures,
she thought. I get here and the scanners break down.

"Eleanor Cauley?" the guard asked, his relaxed stance
gone.

"Yes."

"Please step to the side of the vehicle."

"What?" She looked at Bing, whose eyes were wide. The
guard grabbed her by the elbow until two armed guards
stepped forward and took her under both arms. "What the
hell are you doing? Let me go! Bing!" she shouted over her
shoulder as the tall men lifted her nearly off her feet. She
could see Bing being held back from climbing out of the
truck until she and her escort turned the corner around the
barracks.

"What are you doing?" She tried to struggle against their
grip but couldn't even get her feet all the way on the ground.

"Remain calm, ma'am." The guard on her right never
looked at her as he and his comrade marched in step. "You
are wanted for additional questioning."

"About what?" she asked, already knowing the truth.
The fucking med check.

"Please, ma'am, cooperate and this will be a lot more
pleasant."

Ellie struggled once more in their grip. "Well, why don't
you let me walk, you meathead? You don't have to drag me.

I have legs." With that, they dropped her at the door of a squat, unmarked building. It looked like the kind of cinder block buildings she used to see at little league fields, although she seriously doubted there would be any popcorn or hotdogs inside this one.

The guard on her left stepped forward and held open the door. In the bright sunlight, it was impossible to make out any details of the room inside, and the guard on her right pushed her forward blindly. Ellie stumbled over a loose piece of linoleum inside the door and had to catch herself to keep from falling on her face. The guards slipped out the door behind her, closing it as they went, and Ellie could just make out a figure standing by a lamp at a small wooden table.

"Aw shit," she said, putting her hands on her hips. "Who are you, the inquisitor? Gonna take a rubber hose to me? Fuck you." She wanted a cigarette at that moment almost as much as she wanted to get away. "I don't suppose I get a lawyer or an advocate or anything, huh, tough guy? The laws of the United States suspended on this little acre of hell?"

"Why don't you take a seat?"

"Why don't you kiss my ass?"

The figure pointed to a chair at the table. "Take a seat, Ellie."

Ellie considered taking that seat and bashing him over the head with it. She stepped closer to the table and the figure stepped into the lamplight.

It was Guy.

CHAPTER TEN

Ellie could not have been more surprised had Santa Claus been standing there. Her brain struggled to sort through the confusion, finally deciding that Guy's presence was a good thing, a better thing at least than being interrogated by some Feno goon. He must have seen the revelation on her face and quickly shifted his eyes to an armed guard who stood posted in the shadows. Ellie picked up on his cue and stopped herself from running to Guy. She was so happy to see him, though, that she had a hard time keeping herself from grinning in relief.

She took a seat at the table, and Guy ordered the guard to leave them. The man, and his machine gun, stopped for a whispered conference with Guy out of earshot of Ellie, and Ellie assumed Guy had convinced him of the wisdom of leaving them alone. The guard eyed her with an unattractive smirk that suggested he was pleased with her situation. It was all she could do to not flip him off.

When the door closed behind him, Ellie let out a loud sigh. "Are you trying to kill me? You couldn't just call me?"

Guy remained standing behind the other chair, leaning on the solid wooden back. "Believe me, this isn't my doing."

"What do you mean? I thought you asked for me. That you saw my name come up."

"I didn't know it was you until you walked through the door."

"Then what am I doing here?"

He rubbed his eyes. "Shit, this has been the longest forty-eight hours of my life. I haven't slept since...shit, I can't remember the last time I slept."

Ellie could feel her relief at Guy's presence evaporating under the burn of something far less pleasant. "That's a real shame. Why don't you knock off early and let's get out of here."

"I wish we could."

"Uh-huh. And we can't because?"

"Because you're in a lot of trouble, Ellie." He finally looked at her. "Want to tell me about it?" When she said nothing, he dropped a folder on the table. "We know you lied on your statement about where you were."

"Shit. Fucking Bing and his big ideas."

Guy sat down and leaned in close. "Ellie, tell me Bing hasn't gotten you involved in anything stupid. I've told you that guy is a nut job. If he convinced you to do something..."

"He told me to lie about my med check." It sounded ridiculous as she said it, and saying it to Guy made it that much worse. "I know it was a dumb idea. He's just super paranoid. He thought he was helping me avoid a scene like this and now he's caused it. I believe that's known as irony."

Guy didn't smile; he stared at her as if deciding whether to believe her. "Tell me where you were when the bomb went off."

"I just told you. I had a med check."

"That was yesterday."

Jesus, did everyone keep track of her calendar? "I had another one today."

"Listen to me, Ellie, and listen very carefully. I want to help you, but you can't lie to me. Lie to anyone else, but don't lie to me." He brought his hands close to hers and Ellie pulled back.

"I told you. I had a med check at eleven a.m. A blood test."

"Two med checks back to back. That's your story?"

"It's not a story, Guy. It's the truth. I got called in today for another blood test."

"No explanation."

That wasn't exactly true. She didn't doubt it was directly related to her new blue tag status, and she could add Guy to the list of people she had kept this information from. "It's complicated." She pulled her badge out and showed him the plastic tag. "See how nice and new my tag is? I didn't get a new one because I'd been such a good girl." Her throat tightened as she tried to say aloud the truth she didn't want to face. "Interesting trivia for you. When you become a blue tag your tag isn't actually blue. Who knew?"

"I knew."

"Yeah, well," she sighed, "it was news to me."

"No, I mean I knew about you being blue-tagged. I read it last night in your file."

Ellie felt that same floor-dropping sensation she had felt when she first saw Guy in the room, only this time her brain opted for a different opinion of the situation. She felt her face redden as familiar rage rose through her body. "You read my file?"

Guy nodded. "I read a lot of files last night."

Her fingertips tingled with adrenaline and her teeth scraped together as Ellie used all her strength not to grab the chair and smash it over Guy's head. "Looks like you are quite the busy boy. Taking to your new job like a duck to water, I see. What's up for next week—installing listening devices in people's houses? Midnight knocks on the door?"

"You knew I was taking this job, Ellie."

"Yeah, I didn't know you'd be taking to it quite so enthusiastically."

"At least you knew," Guy said. "I told you about it. I didn't keep it a secret."

"I don't recall you mentioning anything about joining the secret police, about reading files on private citizens. What happened to being one of the good guys, huh? Or are you going to tell me the sad story of getting little Tommy into college again?"

"Hey, fuck you, Ellie." Guy leaned in, his voice a harsh whisper. "I trusted you."

"Good thing I didn't trust you, eh?" She met his face over the table. "Not that I need to. Why waste my time confiding secrets when you can just look it up? And tell me, Mr. Roman, were you in my file? Did it mention my lurid trysts with one of the army's bright boys? Or did that get redacted for national security reasons?"

"I'm not having this conversation with you." He flipped open the folder before him. "You should be less worried about what's in your file and more worried about why it was flagged the day before the explosion."

Ellie faltered at that. "What do you mean flagged?"

Guy held up a sheet of paper. "I got a list. My first assignment as a Feno agent was to ascertain the threat level of individuals who had been identified as people of interest."

"And I'm on there? Let me see that list."

Guy pulled the sheet back from her. "Yeah, that's going to happen. It's a long list and people are on it for a variety of reasons."

Ellie snorted. "I can imagine the variety of reasons Feno could come up with. Paranoid fuckers. What did I do to make the list? Let me guess, does the name Carpenter show up anywhere on my file? He considers me quite the threat."

"Getting pissed isn't going to fix this, Ellie." Guy folded his hands over the file and looked into her eyes.

"Getting pissed is what I do."

"I know."

He let the words sit there until a horrible truth dawned red on Ellie's cheeks. He'd read her file. He knew it all. Her throat tightened again so quickly her breath whistled through her lips and she once again felt her chair was falling through the floor. And now she wished it would. Her gaze drifted around the room, unwilling to see the gentle pity on Guy's face.

"Fuck you."

"Ellie, it's nothing to be ashamed of."

"Fuck you." Her voice was low, rasping through her ever-tightening throat. "You have no idea what it was like. You and your little army buddies rolling in with your protection meds and your private quarters—"

"It's not the only reason you were flagged—"

"You didn't see the bodies. You didn't lose people."

"Ellie—" He reached for her hand, but she pushed her chair back, gripping her knees with white fingers.

The words tumbled out through her clenched teeth. "You didn't know what it was like puking and shitting and praying to die. And then when the person next to you did, you'd thank God it wasn't you and then you'd go back to wishing it was. And all the while those Feno sons of bitches were pumping us with shots and pills and leaving us twisted and fainting in our own filth and nobody came. Nobody came for us. We'd lie there for hours, trying to help each other, each one of us dropping and fainting—"

"I know it was a terrible time…"

"You don't know shit, Guy." Ellie wanted to pace, she wanted to run, but her legs remembered the weakness and the cramping of those early days of contamination and her mind was powerless to overcome the memory. "When Mrs. McClusky died, when she was dying, she was choking so hard. She couldn't swallow; her tongue was swollen and she was crying out but couldn't make any noise, and I remember thinking, if I could just get her a drink of water, just a sip of water, maybe she'd stop that awful gasping. I couldn't even stand, my stomach was all balled up." She grabbed her stomach, remembering the pain. "But I got all the way to the end of the med tent, walked through puddles of vomit, deep puddles, but I got all the way to the door where the water was. It was just a bottle of water, for fuck's sake, and I never even saw him. I just saw that elbow, that white-suited elbow when it came down on my face. He could have knocked me over with a goddamn pencil and had to smash my face like that."

"Ellie, you don't have to—"

"Is that in my file, Guy?" Ellie focused on him for the first time since she fell into the memory. "Does it mention that I was crawling out of the med tent to get a dying woman a drink of water? No, I bet it doesn't. I bet it has all kinds of neat stories in it, about my 'recalcitrance,' at least that's the word they used at the time."

"You killed a man, Ellie."

"No, I didn't," she said. "He was already dead. We all were." Guy sighed and looked down at the file. She knew Feno had painted a different picture for their security team. "Do you want to know what happened?"

"I read what happened."

"No, you read what they told you. Do you want to know what really happened? Will you believe me if I tell you the truth?" Guy thought for a long moment and then nodded. Maybe she was as insane as they said she was, but she believed he would believe her.

"When he hit me, he broke my nose. My face just exploded, blood went everywhere. I couldn't think. I didn't even really know what had happened. We were all as weak as kittens; I'd been puking for days. I was just lying there, trying to figure out what I was tasting when these big arms grabbed me and pulled me up. I thought I was going to pass out when he pulled me up to my feet, and I guess I started to fall because I reached out to him, to the shelf next to him, hell, I don't know. I was going down and I just reached out. I couldn't see anything because of the tears in my eyes from my nose breaking, and my hand landed on something, something metal."

"A box cutter." Guy had read the file carefully.

"Was that what it was? I never did see it." Ellie closed her eyes, her body once again lost in the memory of the pain. "I just know I was falling and he grabbed me. I thought he was going to help me, but instead I felt this…this stinging sensation and everything started spinning and I realized he was hitting me. He was just slapping me and he was yelling something through that mask. All I wanted was for the spinning to stop and I swung my arm and I felt it hit something. Then there was screaming. It seemed like everybody was screaming. The last thing I remembered seeing was blood, my blood. It was running from my nose like a watering can, and when he fell he pulled me down on top of him and the blood started running into this cut in the suit, this space where the white suit had torn away. He was screaming and pushing me, but when I reached out for him, he just kept punching and screaming. I don't remember anything after that."

"You contaminated him."

"He punched me."

"He didn't survive the contamination."

"Neither did Mrs. McClusky. Neither did a lot of people." She could see Guy struggling with the truth of her story. "I never even saw him. I never saw his face. I didn't know what had happened until I woke up in restraints in East Fifth."

Guy sighed, looking down at the file. She imagined it was quite a surprise to learn that the apartment building where you banged your latest conquest had previously been a locked-down security ward and that said conquest had been a star occupant. It was common knowledge to the original occupants of Flowertown; many established buildings had been commandeered for all sorts of unpleasant duties, and East Fifth, formerly the Wiltshire Arms, had been the easiest building to retrofit with the necessary security measures to contain the crisis zone's more dangerous occupants. After the chaotic early days, a true detention center had been built, but back then, East Fifth was the closest to a prison/asylum Flowertown had. And Ellie had been there so long that when the restrictions were removed, she was allowed to keep her room.

"According to your file, there were other incidents."

"According to my file." Ellie stared up at the ceiling. "I never thought I'd become so familiar with that phrase. And I certainly never thought I'd hear it from you. How did you get this gig, Guy? Did you request it?"

"We're not here to talk about me."

"Humor me," she said. "I feel at a distinct information disadvantage. I'm sure my file mentions that I have a problem with being at a disadvantage."

"It's what I was recruited for. It was what I was trained for in the army."

Ellie folded her arms and stared at him. "You're going to have to be a little more specific. Use small words. I'm not too bright."

"Interrogation and information retrieval in hostile conditions. Those words small enough for you?"

"Well, I guess it doesn't get much more hostile than Flowertown."

"You know what?" Guy leaned forward once more. "Let's cut the crap. I answered your question. Now you answer mine. Where were you when the bomb went off?"

"I told you. I had a med check. A blood test. See?" She held out her arm where the puncture mark still shone red.

"You're telling me you were in the medical center between eleven and eleven thirty giving blood." Ellie nodded, not understanding why Guy was having such a hard time accepting this. He opened the laptop on the side of the table and clicked through several screens, never meeting her eye. "You were paged to the treatment center for a blood test. Today."

"How many ways do you want me to say this, Guy? I. Had. A. Med. Check."

"Who was your tech? Did you catch his name?"

The name Olivia was about to escape her lips when she remembered the cryptic message the girl had written on her medical tape, the message that had made her run hard back to Bing, the message that had put her squarely on site just in time for the explosion.

"I didn't catch it," she said. She hoped she sounded casual. "I didn't pay attention."

She didn't know what the message meant or if it was even just a badly timed joke, but until she had a chance to talk it over with Bing, Ellie was keeping the story to herself. If Olivia was actually trying to help her in some way, the last thing she wanted to do was tip off Feno.

Guy rubbed his eyes again. "Did you get a text telling you about your appointment?"

"No, Guy, they shot a flaming arrow into my room last night—"

"Goddamn it, Ellie!" He pounded his fists on the desk, bouncing the laptop onto the file. "You're in a lot of trouble, don't you get that? You're lying to a security officer about your whereabouts during a terrorist attack."

"I'm not lying!"

"It's Tuesday, Ellie. You are a QOL patient." He gripped the edges of the table as if he were going to flip it. "The med center doesn't take quality of life patients on Tuesday. The QOL center is closed for administrative maintenance. Every Tuesday. Every single Tuesday. If you had been at the med center for a QOL blood test, you would have been standing outside a locked room." He took in a deep breath and let it out slowly. "Now, do you want to change your story about where you were when that bomb went off?"

Rage evaporated from her body. Ellie slumped down in the chair, her jaw slack, her breaths coming in shallow rasps. She wanted to answer; she wanted to tell Guy the truth. She had been at the med center. She had seen the message on the tape; she could picture Olivia as clearly as she could see Guy sitting before her. A confusion washed over that she hadn't experienced since those early days of contamination, and part of her wondered if she was simply remembering a scene from those horrible months in East Fifth's lockdown. She'd been talking about it with Guy, hadn't she? Maybe she was just mixing up her memories. But she wasn't. She knew it. She knew she couldn't hide from the truth even if nobody else could see it.

Ellie bent forward in the chair, pressing her fingers against her eyelids until she saw stars. She could hear the words of the counselors from years ago instructing her in the deep-breathing techniques they wanted her to use to control her violent temper. She pulled in one breath, then another, and on the third she straightened up and faced Guy, her whole body trembling.

156

"I had a med check."

Guy shook his head and took a moment before speaking. "Do you still have the appointment text on your phone?"

"Yes." Hope flared up for a second as she reached into her pocket, then burned out with sickening speed. She could hardly say the words. "I lost my phone."

"You lost your phone."

She could hear the accusation in his voice. Ellie, like most residents of the modern world, rarely went anywhere without her phone. And as a QOL patient, Guy knew her medical reminders were sent via text. She would not have lost her phone. He stared at her and she could feel herself shrinking under his gaze. When he spoke, his voice was soft.

"We can run a trace on your phone's GPS. We will find it, and when we do, we're going to check to see if there is any record of a med check appointment. Do you understand what I'm saying to you?"

Ellie nodded, unable to speak, unable to swallow. She knew if they found her phone, they would find the text message confirming her med check. It would clear her name. What made her hands go cold, what made the pit of her stomach twist in a painful knot, was that she wasn't sure where her phone was. She had dropped it when she had seen the message written on her bandage, so the phone was one of two places. Either it was on the street in front of the med center, further strengthening her defense, or it had fallen into the bag with the oyster crackers and the stolen Feno files that was now hidden in a runoff drain less than thirty feet from the explosion site.

CHAPTER ELEVEN

The guards locked her in a small classroom. "Aren't you afraid I'm going to steal the chalk?" She banged on the door they locked behind them, then turned back to the overly lit room. On one wall hung a large, detailed map of Flowertown, marked with Feno logos and notations. Ellie rubbed her wrists, which were bruising from being pulled by the guards.

"You are here." She read aloud the words on the arrow pointing to a highlighted area on the map at the south end of Flowertown, the Feno personnel compound. "Yes, I am. And I am fucked."

Guy had called the guards in to take her away when she had refused to say anything else. It wasn't like she could incriminate herself. The Fifth Amendment was the least of Feno's concerns. There was simply nothing else to say. Above her head, the air-conditioning vent opened and a blast of cold air blew down over her skin. She could smell the chemical filter and stepped away from the draft, deciding the smell of her own fear-sweat was preferable.

Bolted high on the wall, a flat-screen TV was on, the audio muted. Ellie stared at the images flashing before her, hoping they would drag her mind out of the vortex of anxiety. Silent and slack-jawed, Ellie stood and watched a young woman bury her face in a fluffy towel and inhale ecstatically over the scent of her fabric softener. Without thinking, Ellie fingered the hem of her filthy Cheap Trick T-shirt, feeling the crust of some old food stain. Maybe it was the chili she had used to torment Cooper. Horror threatened to wash over her, so she clamped her teeth together and shut her eyes hard enough to see bolts of blue light. One, two, three breaths and she opened her eyes once more, emptying her mind.

Children lined up to get onto a school bus, clean and laughing. Ellie watched scene after scene flash of swimming pools and baseball fields, cutting in with shots of mothers holding their children and fathers frowning with loving concern. It was a well-made ad, Ellie knew from her days designing advertising campaigns. The people were attractive and real, the lighting soft and inviting. She didn't know what they were selling, but she imagined people bought it. The camera shot closed in on a wide-eyed child clinging to his mother's leg, then the screen went to gray with soft white letters: "It's your job to protect them. It's our job to give you the tools. EcciVac, pediatric vaccines." Half a second before the commercial ended, the Barlay Pharma logo glowed from the bottom of the screen. Ellie turned her back.

There wasn't much in the room, just some long tables, uncomfortable chairs, and some display tools. It obviously didn't take much equipment to indoctrinate the Feno staff. People willing to risk contamination for a paycheck were

probably on board for just about anything. A dented gray
file cabinet leaned against the wall and Ellie couldn't help
herself. She pulled open a drawer and shouted to the guards
she assumed were posted outside.

"I'm touching your stuff!"

Nobody came charging through the door. The drawers
held nothing but blank requisition forms, maps of Flowertown, and other useless generic forms. Ellie slammed the
drawer shut and turned to the bank of windows. They were
double-paned and well sealed. She figured, paycheck be
damned, nobody at Feno yearned for what passed for fresh
air around here. Ellie pressed her forehead to the glass and
looked out over the fog of her breath.

She couldn't remember ever being this close to the barrier zone. In all the years she had been here, and she'd been
here since the beginning, it had never occurred to her to
come to the barrier. Of course, Feno and the army preferred
it that way. Those who came close to the security perimeter
tended to get a lot of guns trained on them very quickly.
Here she stood now, though, less than fifteen feet from the
first line of chain-link fencing that separated the compound
from the void beyond.

The fence had to be twelve feet high, not including
the enormous roll of razor wire that decorated the top for
another three or four feet. She peered to both sides but
couldn't see any gates along this length of fencing. Beyond
the fence for several yards was a lane of large, sharp gravel,
and past that another tall razor fence. Ellie knew that
beneath the gravel lay the largest of the drainage pipes and
runoff culverts. It was essentially a service alley. Beyond that,
however, was the actual barrier zone proper. Ellie wasn't

sure she believed in hell, but as she stared over the burned ground, she imagined if it existed it would look a lot like this.

The ground was charcoal gray, almost like asphalt but with less firmness. Nothing grew in it; nothing broke from its dull surface. And from where she stood, nothing limited its vast expanse. Bing had told her the ring stretched for as far as three miles in some directions, sometimes narrowing down to a mile, depending on the terrain. She knew she could refer to the map on the wall to see if this was a wide stretch of the ribbon, but one mile or three, it was far enough that Ellie could not see what lay beyond it. All she could see was death, or at least the absence of life.

A tamping drone rolled slowly into her line of vision, far out in the barrier zone. Like a short, fat steamroller, the machine rolled along its programmed course. Ellie had seen the reports on the tamping drones when she had been too sick to get out of her cot, during the first round of maintenance medications that had nearly killed her. It's funny, she thought, that she would remember what they were called after all this time. Nobody ever talked about them; she couldn't remember ever seeing one in real life, but she remembered what she had learned when she had been too sick to get up and shut off the television. She knew it was the kind of thing Bing would have been able to draw from memory, complete with schematics and specs. All she knew were the basics.

The tamping drones never stopped. The machines were in constant rotation throughout the barrier zone around Flowertown. The front of the machine carried a tank of powerful herbicides and pesticides that it blew out in a fine, low mist. The back of the machine consisted of an enormous steel barrel that rolled over the moisture, packing the ground down hard, ensuring no dust could rise and get picked up by an errant breeze. Twenty-four hours a day, seven days a week, for almost seven years, the tamping drones rolled their prescribed acreage, ensuring a lethal barrier between Flowertown and the rest of the world. She wondered if anyone on the other side of the barrier could ever smell the chemicals and stenches of the spill zone. Probably not. She doubted anyone could or would live close enough.

Ellie pressed her face against the glass, smashing her nose and lips painfully into the smooth surface. What did it matter if she got arrested for the bomb? What were they going to do? Kill her? She was already as good as dead. Her liver had failed her. She would never get out of Flowertown; she doubted any of them ever would. All she had was a shitty room in a shitty building where she banged a shitty guy who ratted her out to his shitty bosses. She had shit clothes, shit food, a shit job, and decent weed. Ellie ground her face into the glass, hearing the squeak of friction. She jammed her hands hard into her pockets to keep from punching them through the glass, and when her fingers hit something hard, her sob would not be held in.

Rachel's tooth. After all this she still had Rachel's tooth in her pocket. Ellie gripped the sharp white tooth, feeling her tears and her harsh breaths heating up the glass beneath her skin. She didn't have much, she had almost nothing, but she wanted it. It was hers. She had a right to it. She had a right to her shitty clothes and her dirty mirror and the nasty filth in the little refrigerator she shared with that sweet, stupid country girl who still believed she was going to survive her detox and finally get to see Las Vegas. She had a right to get high with Bing and stare at his ugly white socks when he sprawled out under his coffee table and yelled at her for not caring about his crazy conspiracies. She had a right to eat shitty chili and not read the newspaper and smoke cigarettes with Big Martha.

"Agh." No other sound would come out as she pushed off the glass and turned her back to the void. "Agh!" She grunted louder, trying to close her eyes and take her breaths, but her body and mind would not cooperate. Instead she kicked out before her, high and hard, and sent the nearest table skittering across the room. That felt a hell of a lot better than deep breaths, so she kicked again, this time a chair, then another, then a third. She was clearing quite a space for herself, kicking and grunting and breathing only when whatever she kicked clattered and fell. If kicking felt good, throwing felt even better, and Ellie found she could toss the cheap plastic chairs hard enough to make a satisfying crash against the walls. She didn't just throw them, she swung them up over her head and hurled them, sometimes sideways, sometimes straight on, but always hard enough to make enough noise to let her breathe.

She had to climb over a toppled table to free the closest chair. Her hands were slick from the sweat pouring down her arms, but she knew her grip would hold. She didn't care if the guards shot her; all she wanted to do was throw and smash and scream. She hoisted the chair over her head and decided the television was far too smug on its little wall-mounted stand and she took aim. And she stopped.

Unrest in PennCo Containment Area. The words crawled across the screen over the heads of two somber newscasters. Behind them, the image of dark clouds of smoke rising in the distance played in an inset screen. Ellie had to squint to read the scrawl.

Four confirmed explosions in last forty-eight hours, two dozen confirmed dead, death toll expected to rise, stay tuned to this channel for live coverage of press conference with General Admont of U.S. Army PennCo Special Command. President expected to make statement. Authorities insist containment "secure."

"Two dozen dead?" Ellie asked the television. "There weren't two dozen dead. There weren't." She dropped the chair behind her and ran to the set, trying to find a volume button to hear what the reporters were saying. On the screen a young man in a windbreaker stood against a chain-link fence, an army truck to his left, and gestured into the space behind him. There was nothing to see, only the expanse of the barrier zone, but from his gestures it looked like he was describing the plume of smoke that had been witnessed.

"That's not what happened!" Ellie banged against the bottom of the set, looking for a button that wasn't there. "That's not right! That's not what happened!" Desperate to hear the story, she looked around the toppled tables and chairs for a remote that would adjust the volume. She found one. It lay in pieces underneath the second table she had kicked over. Ellie swore again and went back to watching the television, holding the bottom of the set as if it would get the reporter's attention and she could tell her story.

The reporter vanished as the cameras cut back to one of the newscasters, who had been joined by an elderly man with an ugly bowtie and long eyebrows. Between them hovered a map of the United States on what looked like some sort of space-age bulletin board. The newscaster seemed pleased with the high-tech toy, touching and pointing to it, lighting up sections of the map with every move. The old man nodded and put his finger on Iowa, lighting up a small area in bright red that Ellie knew all too well to be Flowertown.

Ellie swore again and again. Did America really need a map to remind them where the disaster had occurred? Had they already forgotten the corner of hell that had popped up in the middle of their safe little world? She was ready again to smash the screen in when the graphic changed. Instead of just one small red dot where Penn County was, a dozen pinpricks of red appeared scattered throughout the middle of the country. Ellie dropped her arms and stared as the old man pointed to several of the dots and spoke with short bursts of hand movements. He was angry; periodically he looked into the camera. Whatever he was telling America, he intended it to scare them.

The old man touched the screen again and Georgia, Florida, and South Dakota turned pale red, while several others glowed a flashing yellow. The newscaster nodded with a television-friendly scowl and motioned for a new graphic. A list filled the screen.

Sites of Contaminee Apprehension:
Georgia (confirmed)
Florida (confirmed X2 locations)
Oklahoma (unconfirmed)
South Dakota (X5, lockdown in place)
(All contaminees deceased. NO CONTAMINATION RECORDED.)

Ellie staggered back, feeling behind her for a place to sit, but she had thrown every chair against the walls. Unable to keep her feet, she let herself fall backward, landing hard on her bottom, and kept watching the news. The screen filled with photographs of men and women, like mug shots. She recognized those photos. They were too small to make out the faces, but she recognized the background and the tags superimposed on the bottom of each picture. Those were Flowertown identification photos.

Had people escaped?

Chairs clattered as two guards swung open the door. "What the hell?" Seeing the chaos around them, they lifted their guns and trained them on Ellie, who sat on the floor clutching her knees.

"On the ground!" the second guard screamed, jabbing the air with his gun.

"I'm on the ground," Ellie said, not moving. "How much more on the ground can I be?"

The two men kept their guns trained on her as they came into the room and circled her, careful not to trip over the debris. The one in front of her shouted to someone in the hallway. "The room is not secure, sir. I repeat: the room is not secure." Ellie started to protest, and he turned his full attention and his weapon on her. "Put your hands behind your head."

Ellie stared at him. "No."

"Put your hands behind your head."

"No." She was too tired to be angry. "You want to keep going? I'm free all night."

"Stand down, gentlemen." Guy stood in the doorway. The two guards hesitated until Guy nodded at them. "Put the weapons down. The room is secure."

"Mr. Roman," the guard behind Ellie lowered his voice, "someone has been searching this room. If the suspect has an accomplice on the premises—"

"Hey, Gomer," Ellie said, "I can hear you. You know that, right? I mean, I'm sitting four feet away from you."

The guard looked like he wanted to kick her where she sat, but Guy put his hand out to stop him. "Nobody's been searching the room. It's been trashed. There's a difference. I'll handle it." Both guards looked unhappy with the decision, but a look from Guy kept them quiet. Ellie saw resentment on their faces as they holstered their weapons and headed out the door. Guy had been at Feno for less than forty-eight hours and already he seemed to wield a great deal of authority.

When they were alone, Guy pulled the door shut and leaned against it. He pointed to the heap of toppled chairs. "Love what you've done with the place."

"I was feeling a little penned in."

"Want to tell me about it?"

Ellie shook her head. "A couple of years in here, you'll figure it out."

Guy nodded, his eyes moving over the damage around him. "Found your phone."

Her mouth went dry and Ellie was very glad to be sitting at that moment. She said nothing, only held onto her knees and waited. "I've sent someone out to retrieve it."

"Be sure to tip him for me." Her voice wasn't as steady as she'd hoped.

"Aren't you going to ask where it was?" Ellie could only shrug. "Someone turned it in at the med center, said they found it on the street just past the stairs."

Ellie struggled to hide her relief, but when she looked up she could see Guy examining her face. He nodded at something he saw there.

"So I guess that means you're free to go. The last truck is loading witnesses now." He turned and opened the door. "You might want to hurry. It's a long walk back to town."

Ellie sat for another moment, trying to read Guy, trying to get her thoughts together. This wasn't the place. She didn't know if she'd ever have another clear thought. Without another look, she got to her feet and headed out the door. She hurried to the end of the hall, and by the time she made it around the building and saw the line of people climbing into the truck, she was at a full run.

The truck dropped them off at the still-smoldering ruins of the records office. Again the ride in the closed truck had made her shaky and woozy; Ellie knew she had to get something to eat soon or she would faint. Blue explosions blossomed before her eyes and she had to lean against a Feno truck to steady herself. The stench here at the cordoned-off area was worse than anything she had ever smelled. Water puddled around oil stains and charred debris, and she wondered if the bag she'd hidden was still intact within the runoff drain. Maintenance crews were hauling debris away in dump trucks under the gaze of armed guards. There was no way she could get the bag out today. Ellie headed toward her apartment, putting the bag and the stolen files on the ever-increasing list of things she would have to worry about tomorrow. Tonight she wanted to sleep.

As she headed down the hallway toward her room, she smelled chili and seriously considered finding the source and falling to her knees to beg for some. Her stomach groaned, and when she pushed open the door to her room and saw Bing and Rachel huddled over bowls, she let out a sound somewhere between a sigh and a cheer.

Bing dropped his bowl and ran to her, holding her by the shoulders and guiding her to the bed. "Oh my God, Ellie, what happened? How are you here?"

"I'll tell you anything you want, Bing, but please, can I have some chili?" He passed her the bowl and then returned to his spot beside Rachel on the other bed. Ellie put down two large spoonfuls in no time and then took a closer look at her much-improved roommate. "What are you doing eating chili? Eating *anything*?"

"I know, right?" Rachel grinned at her, showing the gap where her front tooth had been. "I went for another round of detox and they gave me this shot that made me feel so much better. I mean, like, a hundred times better." She turned her smile to Bing. "And Bing showed up looking for you and totally saved my life by making chili. I'm absolutely starving."

"No doubt." Ellie scooped the last bits out of her bowl. "I can't believe how much better you look."

Rachel laughed. She could even make a missing tooth look cute. "I can't believe how much better I feel. Two days. In two days I am outta here! I'm still super tired, but at least I can eat something. And I got a shower." Ellie noticed Bing's face redden. "Of course Bing here had to help me. It was so embarrassing. I was too tired to stand up, and you know how nasty the floors are in there. He brought me a chair and helped lather my hair. He was so sweet. And a perfect gentleman."

Bing leaned back on the bed out of Rachel's line of sight. Ellie licked the spoon to keep from laughing when he looked heavenward and mouthed "Oh my God." She could imagine what a perfect gentleman he had been in his mind. "Yeah, he's a real champ."

Bing grimaced. "I guess it was a bad idea lying about the med check."

"You could say that."

"They checked, huh? Sorry."

"They didn't…they knew I wasn't in the building and then…" The enormity of the explanation was more than she could face at that moment, and the chili seemed to be heading directly to her eyelids. "It's a long story. But hey, guess who interrogated me? Guy."

"What?" Rachel threw her spoon in surprise. "That little prick."

Bing looked surprised at the profanity from the girl. "So the army was there."

"No. He's not in the army anymore. He signed with Feno." Ellie could see Bing's curiosity firing up and she shook her head. "It's another long story. It's nothing but one long story after another, and I really don't have it in me." She put the empty bowl on the floor and fell back into the bed. "There are so many things I have to tell you, Bing, but I just can't tonight." Her speech grew thick as she sank into the sagging bed.

"Go to sleep, Ellie." Bing stood up and pulled back the covers of Rachel's bed. "You too, young lady. And I don't want to hear that you were dreaming about me in the shower." Rachel giggled as she let Bing tuck the blanket in around her. "I'm going to stay here until both of you are asleep. You know you're both killing me. I'm not built for worrying like this."

"Our hero," Rachel said.

Ellie watched Bing settle in on the floor between the beds and pull out a paperback. "Amen to that, Rachel." She was asleep before he could answer.

She was dreaming she was sorting through enormous boxes of laundry when she felt someone touch her cheek. Her eyelids refused to part as she came up from sleep. "Bing?"

"No."

That whispered voice brought her out of her dream. She opened her eyes and saw Guy sitting on the edge of the bed, leaning over her. Even in the near darkness, she could see his eyes were bloodshot and he needed a shave. Without a thought, she lifted her hand and caressed his cheek.

He leaned into her palm and closed his eyes. "I brought your phone back."

"Yourself? Don't you have underlings that can run errands like that?"

"I wanted to see you. I didn't know where you'd be tomorrow, and it's not like I could call you." He kissed her palm. "I'm so sorry about today. About all of it. Your file and detaining you and those goons. It never should have gotten to that."

Ellie put her fingers over his mouth to quiet him. "You look exhausted."

"There aren't words to describe what I am right now." He let her pull him down across her body, and Ellie wrapped her arms around him. Earlier today she would have beaten him to death, but now, in the quiet and the dark, she couldn't think of anything that had ever felt better than his body against hers. She felt his lips on her neck as he twisted himself fully onto the flimsy bed, and she wished she could rip away the clothes and blankets that wrinkled between them. Before she could get to his skin, Rachel cleared her throat from her bed with a theatrical "ahem."

Guy pulled back, putting his feet back on the floor and pulling the thin sheet back up around Ellie's shoulders. She kept her hands on his arms, stroking the muscles there. "I'm going to go." She nodded and he leaned in once more to kiss her. He let his mouth slide to her ear. "Be careful, Ellie. Really careful."

She clung to his neck, but he pulled away, shaking his head as Rachel once again made her presence known.

Guy looked over to the other bed. "You can relax. I'm going."

"Good," Rachel said from her dark corner.

He traced his fingers over Ellie's cheek before rising and slipping out the door. As the light from the hallway disappeared and the room grew dark, Ellie rolled onto her side and faced the wall.

"You are kidding me," Rachel huffed. "He arrests you and interrogates you and then expects you to keep banging him?"

"It's not like that." Ellie sighed. "You weren't there. You don't know him."

"Don't even think about it, Ellie."

But that's exactly what she did.

CHAPTER TWELVE

The sun warmed her face. Ellie stretched long in the small bed, feeling stiffness before she even knew she was awake. Her mouth tasted like paste, but she felt more relaxed than she could ever remember feeling. She didn't want to open her eyes, lost in the softness of deep sleep. She heard Rachel moving around the room and decided to ignore her in the hope she would go away and let her sleep all day.

"I know you're awake." It was Bing.

"No, I'm not," Ellie said, keeping her eyes shut.

"Yeah, you are. I know because you've stopped snoring."

"I don't snore."

"Okay, then you've stopped trying to catch gnats in your epiglottis."

Ellie laughed, putting her arm over her eyes to keep out the sun. "Leave me alone."

"I have two words for you." She could feel Bing's breath on her face. "Crispin's Diner."

"You bastard."

"I know. C'mon. My treat."

Ellie pulled herself up to sit on the edge of the bed. "Good lord, I didn't even take off my shoes. How come you gave Rachel a shower and you wouldn't even take my shoes off?"

"Because your feet, even bare, look nothing like Rachel dripping in honeysuckle lather."

"Bigot." Ellie kicked around in the pile of clothes by the bed. "Just because I'm older and meaner, you judge me." She pulled a shirt out from underneath the bed and sniffed it. Deciding it would do, she pulled at the hem of the wrinkled shirt she wore. "Keep your eyes peeled, buddy, and I'll show you what you're missing."

"I'll try to contain myself." Bing sat back on Rachel's bed and began to roll a joint. He had seen Ellie dress plenty of times. "Holy shit! Did they do that to you?"

"What?" Ellie yanked the clean shirt down. "Do what?"

"Bruises. You've got them all over your arms."

She held her arms out to inspect them. Ugly purple marks spread all along the backs of her arms, up near her shoulders. Her wrists, too, had turned a greenish blue from being dragged by the guards. "I guess it got a little rough in there yesterday."

"Tell me you didn't resist armed guards."

"There was no resisting, trust me. They had me off the ground half the time. But I might have thrown a little temper tantrum. Just plastic chairs. And a few tables."

Bing shook his head and laughed as he lit up the joint. "Leave it to you to pick a fight in a roomful of goons. It sure looks like they did a number on you. That or you bruise easily."

Ellie busied herself throwing her incredibly filthy jeans into the corner on top of Rachel's bloody shirt and pulling on a slightly less filthy pair that hung from the doorknob. Bing didn't seem to notice her silence, and when she sat back down on the bed, she waved off his offer of a smoke. "I've got to tell you something."

"Don't try to tell me you're a man." Bing took another deep hit and winked at her. "I confess. Sometimes I peek when you dress."

"No, this is something else. It's about the bruises."

Bing leaned forward on the bed. "If you tell me that son of a bitch Guy hit you—"

"No, stop. It's nothing like that. Geez." She pulled her hair hard off her face. "And lean back. This is hard enough to say. I don't need you in Full Bing Alert Mode." He leaned back a little, but Ellie knew she had his undivided attention. She swallowed hard. "I think the bruises are because I have…um…I've been blue-tagged."

His lips moved like he was practicing words before he said them. Other than that, Bing did not move at all. They stared at each other, Ellie terrified he would say something to comfort her or, God forbid, start to cry.

"How long have you known?"

"About a month."

Bing stared out the window, smoke slipping through his open mouth. "Have you told anyone else? Rachel? Captain America?"

"No, just you. Although Guy knows. He had my file."

Bing clamped his lips shut, and Ellie could imagine the things he was trying not to say. Finally he settled on, "Is that what you were trying to tell me yesterday?"

"Yesterday?" She had to think to remember. She thought of the stolen files, the cryptic message, the news broadcast, even the bullets she had seen in Dingle's Market. "God, it's like we haven't spoken in weeks. There are so many things I've got to tell you."

Bing slapped his knee with his free hand and extended the joint with the other. "Well, there's no point in telling it in this dump when the dump down the street is making pancakes. Let's go to Crispin's. Why aren't you smoking?"

"I don't know." Ellie laughed as she pulled on her sneakers. "I just feel all relaxed and rested. I guess that's what sleep will do for you." Bing held out his hand to pull her up, and she scowled at the softness in his eyes. "Don't stare at me with mushy eyes."

"Can I send you a Hallmark card with puppies and roses on it? Add you to my prayer chain?" Ellie laughed and pushed him away as he spoke. "I could knit you a shawl. Or slippers."

"Shut up!" She pulled him back to her and he wrapped his arm around her shoulder. "Save your style points for Rachel. Maybe someday she'll fall for that crap."

"Did I mention that I saw her naked yesterday? And that I touched her?"

"Yeah, I think that came up. Lunatic."

Bing grabbed a table near the window of the little diner, keeping his back to the corner as was his practice. Ellie sat beside him so the sun wouldn't hit her directly in the face. In Flowertown, window seats had lost a great deal of their appeal. She was just glad she couldn't see the work trucks that continued to dismantle the records office. Peg, Crispin's only waitress, turned over their coffee cups and poured them each a cup.

"Thank God you've come, Peg," Bing said. "We're starving and we want everything on the menu."

Peg sighed. "Well, you might want to stop wanting eggs. Or sausage. Or whole wheat toast. And the only cereal we have left is Frosted Flakes."

"You didn't get any supplies either?" Ellie asked. "How big was that truck that overturned? For crying out loud, can't they send another?"

"Oh, they sent one," Peg said. "From what I understand it was turned back on the barrier once those explosions started. Something about it being a security risk. Like starving to death isn't." She set the hot pot down on the table and pulled out her pad. "In better news, we're having a great deal on pancakes. While they last, of course."

Bing tapped his finger against his coffee cup. "How many can we have?"

Peg glanced out the window and then back toward the kitchen. "All you want."

"Sounds good to me," Bing said. "We'll pay you in kind."

Peg nodded and turned back toward the kitchen. Ellie watched her go and then grabbed Bing's arm. "What does that mean? Why did she say that?"

He blew out a nervous breath. "I'm not entirely sure. But it means something."

"Holy crap, you're faking it? Why did you say that about paying in kind?"

"Because that's what Torrez said to me, remember?" Bing lowered his voice. "It's like some kind of signal."

Ellie leaned back in her chair and shook her head. "You mean to tell me all this time that you have been yammering on about conspiracies and underground movements, you didn't even know for sure they were happening?"

"I know plenty. Trust me. It's just that this is different. And keep your voice down."

Bing looked around the empty diner. "We don't know who to trust."

"For what?" Ellie laughed. "Pancakes? Weed? I know who to trust for both of them. Shit, this is what I get for staying high all the time. Yesterday I was sure the whole world was turning on me. Now it turns out it's just some junior superhero league passing messages with their decoder rings. God, I'm such an idiot."

Bing leaned in close over the table. "You think it was a decoder ring that blew up our building yesterday? You think you got those bruises from a junior superhero?"

Ellie turned from him, not wanting to get back into that fearful state of mind. For the first time in weeks, she felt rested and level. Her rage seemed to have been lulled back into submission. She didn't want to climb back up on that treacherous branch. "It was just a misunderstanding. The only reason I got pulled out of the line was because you told me to lie."

"Oh, I get it, sure. The only superhero allowed in your story is Guy 'My-Dick's-As-Big-As-My-Biceps' Roman."

"What exactly is your issue with Guy? Seriously, every time we argue about something you always bring it back to Guy. Have you got a crush on him or something?"

"Have you had some sort of head injury?" Bing asked. "Because the Ellie I knew would have burned the building down if she found out that someone had read her file. She would have fed him his spleen with a grapefruit spoon. The

Ellie I knew wouldn't care how good he was in bed; she'd have—"

"The Ellie you knew is tired of being the Ellie you knew." They both leaned back as Peg returned with a bowl of butter pats and a bottle of syrup. She raised an eyebrow at their heated silence and turned without a word. When she was beyond earshot, Ellie leaned forward on her elbows. "I'm tired, Bing. Yesterday when Guy brought up East Fifth and those early days, and I was staring out at that barrier zone, I just kept thinking, 'This is my life. This is my whole life. This is all I have.' And I realized I've spent half a decade either numb or enraged, and I'm really tired. I'm tired of being so mad; I'm tired of feeling that black dog inside of me."

Bing poured sugar into his coffee. "Do you think it might be the QOL meds? Like maybe they're tranquilizing you?"

"Oh, for fuck's sake, Bing, what next? Think maybe I'm getting my period?"

"Clearly you've gotten over your anger." He stared at her over his cup until she laughed and shook her head. "I know, you hate me."

"I do, seriously, I hate you."

"How long have we known each other, Ellie? Four years? Four and a half?"

She shrugged. "It was cold when we met."

"Yeah, so winter, four years ago. Do you remember what it was like? Do you remember how it was when we first met?"

"To be honest, no." Ellie smoothed out the paper napkin before her. "I was heavily medicated for most of it. The first year or so is kind of a trippy nightmare."

"Well, you didn't miss much. As bad as it might have been in lockdown, it wasn't much better outside. The med center goons busting everybody's heads, the shitty quarters, nobody ever knew what the next day would bring, but everybody knew it would suck."

Ellie nodded. "I have a vague recollection of that sensation."

Bing rested his chin in his hand. "We've seen each other at our worst. You were there when they brought me in. They were pumping my stomach and you threw a chair at the nurse, told them to leave me alone." Ellie laughed. Bing had told her this story many times, filling in the gaps of her drug-clouded memories. "They were wheeling me out when they took you down, and I could hear you roaring. I'd never heard anyone actually roar before."

Peg returned with two plates of pancakes. Ellie cut into hers with her fork and smiled. "And then they let us eat together. It always comes back to food with us, doesn't it?"

Bing talked around a mouthful of pancake. "Do you remember the first thing you said to me that day in the dining room?"

"That I knew you."

He dropped his eyes back to the plate and swallowed. "That's right. I forgot about that. You kept saying that you knew me from somewhere. You said I used to visit you at night."

"That made the guards nervous." Ellie laughed and poured out more syrup. "Those were some serious drugs they were giving us. I was sure of it, though. As soon as I saw you, I knew you. I just knew I could talk to you."

"But do you remember what you said?"

Ellie shook her head. "There were a lot of drugs, remember?"

"I told you about trying to kill myself, and that the first chance I got, I was going to do it again. You reached across the table and, as serious as a heart attack, asked that if I succeeded, could you have my room." Ellie laughed out loud, bits of pancakes landing on the table across from them. Bing grinned. "I knew right then that I wasn't going to kill myself because finally I had found someone in Flowertown who would tell me the truth."

"Well, I was never known for my subtlety."

"But you were always known for your keen aversion to bullshit. That's why I don't understand this thing with Guy."

"Bing…"

"I don't, Ellie, I'm sorry. I mean even if, and this is a big if, if you believe the army has the well-being of the people at heart," he pointed his fork at her, "you said that Guy has signed with Feno, which officially makes him one of the bad guys. He's arrested you and interrogated you; he's read your private files."

"He also tried to warn me."

"Warn you. About what?"

"He didn't say. But when he brought my phone back last night he said—"

"What do you mean last night? Guy came to your room last night?"

"Yeah, I don't know what time it was. You were gone." Ellie watched Bing stab at his pancakes. "Rachel saw him. He brought my phone back to me."

"He came all the way from the compound just to bring you your phone? And you just let him in? No questions asked?"

"He let himself in. Don't look at me like that, Bing. You know we never lock our door, and even if we did, you could break in with a hangnail. He knows where I live, he had my phone, and he brought it to me. And he apologized."

"I bet that was sincere." He rolled his eyes. "Apologized for what? Arresting you or just turning his goons on you?"

Ellie ignored the sarcasm. "He also warned me to be careful." Bing dropped his silverware and fell back in his seat. His cheeks were red, and Ellie recognized the anger in the white line around his lips. "What?"

"What? For four years I've been telling you something is going on and you pass it off as crazy. One word from Guy and you're on full alert."

"Is that what this is about? You think I don't listen to—"

"Four years, Ellie." Bing pushed back from the table. "Four years I've been watching you roll your eyes at me and dismiss me and make fun of me. 'Oh, that's just Crazy Bing.' Now one word from a guy you probably wouldn't even recognize if he had pants on and suddenly you're worried. You know why? Because you're an authority whore."

"Bing, what the hell—"

"You claim to be above it all, too cool for it all, but the truth is, Ellie, you're still waiting for somebody to come in and make it all okay, to come in and take care of it all for you." He jumped up from the table, toppling his chair behind him, jabbing his finger in the air at her. "You're a goddamn follower, Ellie, and I don't know why I waste my time on you."

Ellie could only gape at her friend's outburst. She was used to him flying off the handle, but never so publicly and never so hatefully. She watched as he threw down his napkin and stormed out the door.

Peg came near with the coffee pot. "Everything okay?"

"I have no idea." Ellie rose, her only thought trying to figure out what had just happened. She waved her hand over the table. "Can I get this later? I'll be back. I have to…"

Peg nodded to the door. "Go on. You can't piss off Bing. We need the weed."

Ellie ran out into the street and saw Bing stomping around the corner. She ran after him, calling for him, but he didn't stop. By the time Ellie made it to the corner, he was gone. She stood there, hands on her hips, trying to think where he might have gone and what on earth could have gotten into him. She knew Bing was tightly wound. Their little dustups were frequent, but something about his tone, that furious look in his eyes when she told him Guy had been in her room, made the scene more unpleasant than necessary. She wandered forward, looking in the windows of the buildings, trying to spot her friend.

Two blocks later and she was at the site of the records office explosion. The cordon had been removed from the end of the block and most of the work trucks were gone. It still stank. Ellie wandered through the remaining puddles toward the wreckage. Only the lower half of the framework remained of the building, bare wires and steel bars jutting up from the blackened mess like broken bones. All the desks had been removed, although there were still some bent and blackened office chairs cast aside. Ellie wondered if one of those chairs belonged to Bing.

He was right, she knew. In a lot of ways, he knew her better than she knew herself, mostly because when she looked inside herself, she hated what she saw. There was a part of her, a large part, that did want someone to come and take care of everything. She used to be so independent. When she lived in Chicago, she was the picture of a strong-minded rising executive. It was one of the things that had made her boyfriend, Josh, fall in love with her. She had made the plans for Spain; she had made all the arrangements. It had been her idea to move out of Chicago early, to spend the time with Josh's parents to save money. She was the reason Josh had returned to Iowa. She was the reason Josh was dead.

Ellie closed her eyes, trying to empty her mind of that thought and all thought. She wished she hadn't turned down Bing's offer to smoke earlier. If she hadn't turned it down, she would be high and she wouldn't have started a fight with her best friend and they would be sitting and laughing over pancakes at Crispin's right now. Another thing that was her fault.

No. Ellie opened her eyes. This wasn't her fault. Not Josh, not the fight, not the weed or the anger. This was Feno's fault. Every stinking, filthy second of the past six years was the fault of the greedy, careless bastards at Feno Chemical, with their top-secret compounds and their heavily armed goons. Bing thought she was a follower, that her rebellion was an act, but Bing didn't know she had stolen classified files from the enemy. She knew it was probably the equivalent of throwing a deck chair off the *Titanic,* but she had acted out. She had struck a blow, and Ellie wanted to prove to her friend that he was wrong about her.

She glanced at the runoff grate where she had stashed the bag. A few maintenance workers argued about something at a nearby dumpster, but they didn't seem to be paying any attention. Trying not to be obvious or look like she had a destination, Ellie strolled toward the grate. One of the maintenance men noticed her and she pretended to poke around in the grass as if looking for something. When he turned away from her, she knelt and pulled back the grate.

The bag was filthy, part of it torn away from the debris that had flooded the grate, but the files were intact within it, still wrapped in the newspaper. Ellie tugged them from their spot wedged between the metal plate and a length of pipe. The plastic bag shredded, caught on something hidden within, so she was forced to pull the files and newspapers out uncovered. The oyster cracker box was crushed in one corner of the bag, but Ellie pulled it out and put it on top of the pile. She had no choice; she was going to have to carry the bundle exposed in her arms.

Moving slow enough to not catch the workers' attention, Ellie strolled out of the work zone, looking for all the world as if she belonged there. She listened for someone to yell at her or raise some sort of alarm. She wanted to get the files back to her room, and after two blocks, she began to relax. Nobody had seen her digging in the runoff grate. Nobody had noticed the files. She clutched the bundle to her chest as it occurred to her that these might be the only files that had made it out of the records office. These were the only link to her old job. Her thoughts turned once again to Big Martha, and she decided that, after she had tucked the files away in a safe place, she would head to the care center and ask around for her boss. Hopefully Bing would be home by then and would be over his anger enough to go with her.

When she passed Dingle's Market on the other side of the street, she looked into the window and waved to Annabeth, who stood at the front of the store, picking through the nearly empty produce bins with a customer. Ellie glanced past the other person, catching sight of little more than a ponytail. Then she stopped. She had seen more than a ponytail. Ellie turned back to be sure. There was no pale blue med tech coat, but even from across the street Ellie recognized the large strawberry birthmark. Annabeth Dingle was talking to Olivia, the med tech who had drawn her blood when the med center was supposedly closed.

CHAPTER THIRTEEN

A blaring horn made Ellie jump back from the street. The passenger in the dump truck flipped her off as the truck roared past with debris from the explosion. Ellie hardly noticed the obscenity, intent on getting to Dingle's and confronting Olivia, but when the truck passed and an army truck crossed going the other direction, the window of the market was empty. Ellie hurried across the street, making a Feno truck stop to let her cross, and hurried inside.

"Hi, Ellie." Annabeth waved from behind the toilet paper display. "Glad to see you're okay. When I heard about that explosion you were the first person I thought of. Such a terrible thing. So many people were injured."

"Yeah, I know. It was awful." Ellie didn't want to be rude to the older woman, but she had to find Olivia. She moved quickly past each aisle but saw only two young men and a teenage girl in the store. "Where is that woman you were talking to?"

"Woman?" Annabeth peeked around the endcap.

"A young woman. Dark hair in a ponytail, birthmark on her neck."

Annabeth shook her head. "I don't remember seeing anyone like that. But don't tell the kids, I don't pay that much attention. It's not like there's so much to shoplift anymore."

"No, no, you were just talking to her. Just a second ago." Ellie pointed to the produce bins. "She was standing right there. You all were looking at potatoes or something."

The old woman laughed. "I'd need mighty good eyesight to see a potato in here, Ellie. We haven't had potatoes in two weeks."

"It doesn't matter if it was potatoes. You were talking to her." Ellie noticed one of the young men look down the aisle at her, his attention caught by the rise in her voice. Ellie lowered her voice. "I mean, I don't know what you were talking about. I just wondered if you knew her."

Annabeth headed back to her cash register. "Well, I know just about everyone in Flowertown, it seems. The locals at least. Of course, I guess nowadays we're all locals, aren't we? What's her name, do you know?"

"Olivia." Ellie followed her back, remembering the stitching on the med tech coat. She knew she had seen her, both at the med center that Guy had said was closed and talking to Annabeth, who now said she didn't remember. But she had seen her. She wished she sounded more confident when she spoke. "She's a, um, med tech."

"A med tech? In here?" Annabeth climbed onto her stool. "I doubt that, Ellie. They don't bother with the likes of Dingle's. They have their own commissary, and from what I hear it's pretty sweet. You must have her confused with someone else."

"No, I'm sure it was her. Her name is Olivia and she's local. She said so." She had said so while she drew the blood that couldn't possibly have been drawn. Ellie looked down into the crook of her elbow. The sight of the puncture wound steadied her, but when she looked back at the old woman, she doubted herself once again. Why would Annabeth lie?

"You all right, Ellie? You look a little peaked." Annabeth squinted at her. "Your color's off. Sort of yellow. You need to sit down?"

"No, I'm okay." But her hand went to her forehead to feel the dampness there.

"Honey, you've had a tough go there. I heard about them rounding everybody up. Maybe you're not quite up to snuff, if you know what I mean." Ellie nodded at her soft words. "Here, let me get you a cold drink. On me. It's a Shasta. I always keep a few cold ones back here because sometimes I don't feel like walking all the way up front to the cooler." She bent down under the counter and came up with a can of soda, dripping from the ice water. Popping the top, she passed it across the counter. "Do you need to take your meds?"

Ellie took the can, not meeting her eye. "No, I'm good. Thanks, though." It was Olivia who had instructed her not to take the red pills. At least she thought that's what the note said. She had no note, no proof that she had been to the med center, and now she couldn't even prove that Olivia existed.

"It's important to follow the instructions when you get your meds. God knows I've followed them to the letter and I'm still here." Annabeth settled back on her stool and began leafing through an old gossip magazine. "Make sure you listen every time you go, because the instructions can change and that can throw you off. Did you get any new instructions?"

Ellie stared at Annabeth, at her relaxed shoulders and casual hands leafing through the glossy pages. Then she saw the way the old woman's foot tap-tap-tapped against the bottom of the stool. She knew that move. She did it herself whenever she was nervous or trying to hide something. What the hell, she thought, here goes nothing. "You know, now that you mention it, I did. Maybe that's why I feel so weird. I'm not on the same twice-a-day dosage." Ellie took a deep drink of her root beer and covered her nervousness with a soft belch. "They told me I could take all I want."

Annabeth made a little "huh" sound and flipped the magazine closed, looking up at Ellie with an easy smile. "Well, that's probably what's ailing you. Change can be hard to adjust to sometimes. Takes a little while. You know what might help?"

Ellie glanced around them, wondering if she were going to pull a weapon or a secret clue out from under the counter. Instead the old woman pulled out a copy of "the local," the Flowertown newsletter, and turned it to the back page. "There's a recipe in the back of this issue for a soup that's supposed to fortify your immune system. Carrie Madison put it in there. It's so important this time of year to make sure you're getting your vitamins." She pushed the little paper across to Ellie. "Pretty simple, not sure how it tastes, but it sounds good. Just be sure to follow the instructions. Especially the cooking time. Carrie Madison may be meaner than a raccoon, but she's a whiz in the kitchen. You can count on her timing."

The two young men came to the counter with a basket of groceries, and Annabeth turned to them with a smile. Dismissed, Ellie folded the newsletter up and tucked it between the files and the oyster crackers she still clung to. She grabbed the can of soda and headed for the door. Before she made it out to the street, Annabeth called out to her.

"And Ellie? If I meet anyone named Olivia, I'll tell her you're looking for her."

"Clearly I am losing my mind." Ellie clutched the bundle to her chest and headed for East Fifth. She talked out loud to herself, not worrying how it looked to the few people she passed. That levelness she had felt upon waking was disintegrating fast, and if she couldn't be calm she could at least be high, so she hurried toward the apartment. More than calm, more than weed, what she really wanted was to talk to Bing. This was no time for pride. He was right about her. She wanted him to make this all okay, and she was prepared to beg if she had to.

She waited for a short convoy of army trucks to pass before crossing the final intersection to Fifth Street. Quickening her pace, she made a list of the things she needed to do: get high, text Bing, open the files, get higher, and try to figure out why Annabeth wanted her to read a recipe for soup. Was that everything? Ellie nodded to herself as she climbed the two short steps to East Fifth and then let out a cry.

"Bing!"

He was just rounding the corner from the opposite direction, and for a horrible moment Ellie was afraid he was going to ignore her. She called out his name again and he jumped, snapped from whatever reverie he was lost in. He saw Ellie and held out his hands in supplication. Ellie jumped off the steps and ran to him. They spoke over each other.

"Ellie, God, Ellie, I'm so sorry."

"Bing, I've got to talk to you."

"It's just that what you said about me talking big about the conspiracies when I don't really know what's going on—"

"Listen to me."

"I felt like such a dumbass. I didn't mean those things I said. I just—"

"Bing!" She grabbed him with her free hand. "Stop! It's me, remember? I don't care about that right now. Please, let's go inside. I've got so much to tell you."

"So do I." They headed inside the building and started climbing the stairs. "I felt like such a jackass after I left you. And then I realized you were right and I've been talking out my ass for so long that I went to look for Torrez."

"What for?"

"To see if I could get some more information on the 'all you want' thing."

"That's exactly what I was trying to do."

Bing let Ellie into her room first. "You went looking for Torrez? I didn't see you."

"No, I was in Dingle's."

"Looking for Torrez?"

"Forget Torrez!" Ellie threw her bundle on the bed and flopped down beside it. "I thought I saw someone. It's a long story, but while I was there I thought I'd say something to Annabeth Dingle about 'all you want.'"

"Why would you do that?"

Ellie realized she hadn't told Bing about the bullets she had seen under the curtain in the store. It was too long a story to go into, so she waved it off. "It's not important now. What matters is that she definitely reacted. At least I think she did. I can't tell if she was sending me a message or if I'm just Binging out. No offense."

"None taken." He rested his chin on the wooden back of the wobbly chair he straddled. "Let me guess. She gave you a recipe for soup."

"How did you know?"

He reached into his back pocket and pulled out a folded copy of "the local." "Because Torrez gave me one too."

"Well, that can't be a coincidence."

"No, it can't." Bing unfolded the paper and scanned through it. "It doesn't mean it's an answer, though. Not if we can't figure out what we're looking for."

Ellie slid her copy out from between the box of crackers and the newspaper-wrapped files. She had to tell Bing about the files but decided they would take one problem at a time. "She said something about the soup recipe. Here, on the last page: hearty potato leek soup. Does that mean anything to you?"

"Sounds good. But then according to you I eat ass soup." He looked up at her with a smile. Then she could see in his eyes the memory of the last time they had discussed the foul-smelling soup and the carnage that had followed. "It's probably not about the taste, though."

Ellie climbed back against the wall and crossed her legs beneath her, propping the page up on her crossed ankles.

"When I saw Annabeth, she was at the potato bin. It was empty. She said she hadn't seen a potato in two weeks. Could that be something?"

Bing gnawed on his fingernail. "And maybe leek isn't really leek, like the vegetable, but l-e-a-k, like something leaking out. Like that stupid movie that's opening up about terrorists getting out of Flowertown."

"So what does that mean? Someone's leaking potatoes out of Flowertown?"

"Or maybe leaking them in. Maybe this is about the supplies being cut off."

Ellie leaned over the paper, staring at it, demanding it reveal its secrets. "But what does that tell us? Why would both Annabeth and Torrez give us this if we don't know anything about sneaking things in or out of Flowertown? Annabeth said to pay attention to the cooking instructions. I guess this Carrie Madison is a master chef or something."

"Is that what she said?"

Ellie shrugged. "Something like that."

"Not something like that, Ellie." Bing tapped the pages. "If this is a secret, the details matter. What exactly did she say? You've got to start paying attention."

"I was kind of distracted, thank you. I was trying to break into a secret society. That's your forte, Bing, not mine. And you're so observant, what did Torrez say?"

Bing scratched his head, squinting at the paper. "Somebody was coming up the steps. He just jammed it in my hand and said, 'Time to cook.' Then he left."

"Cooking time. That's what she said." Ellie slapped her hand on her thigh. "She said that Carrie Madison was meaner than a raccoon but a whiz in the kitchen. I think that's what she said. Then she said that you could count on her. Count on her cooking, count on her timing, something like that. What's the cooking time?"

Bing scanned the recipe. "Uh, sauté leeks until soft and semi-transparent, add butter, blah blah blah, potatoes, cream, blah blah blah, cook uncovered thirty-seven minutes. That's pretty specific for potato soup."

They stared at each other, trying to find the answer in the other's face. Neither moved when Rachel slipped between them and lay down on her bed. Ellie nodded with an idea. "Rachel, how long would you cook potato soup?"

"Ugh." Rachel grabbed her stomach and rolled onto her side. "Tell me you're not going to make soup. Please make it somewhere else. I never should have had that chili yesterday."

Bing and Ellie both turned to the girl who, while not as sick as she had been, was definitely under the weather. Bing reached out and rubbed her foot. "I thought you were feeling better. I thought they gave you a shot."

"They did. I guess it's wearing off. I've got to go back tonight and get my final papers. Then I'm outta here!" Her cheer seemed forced as she pulled the pillow tight to her cheek. "What are you guys doing? I didn't know you read 'the local.'"

"Well, we don't usually." Bing met Ellie's glance, asking her to go along with his story. "It's this stupid thing a guy from work is doing. You know, since we have no work for the time being, what with our building blowing up and all. It's some kind of scavenger hunt that he said is hidden in the paper."

Rachel yawned and curled up tighter. "But your place blew up yesterday. 'The local' came out Monday. Next one comes out tomorrow. Is it like an ongoing thing?" Bing nodded, obviously relieved for the out. "Let me see it." He handed her the paper.

"It's got something to do with the cooking time in the soup recipe."

Rachel read the recipe, then pulled herself up to a sitting position and reached over to the crowded nightstand beside her bed. She pulled out a puzzle book and pen. "Thirty-seven minutes. That's the clue? Do you know what you're looking for? Like, a place or a thing or a date, or what?"

"We don't know." Ellie shook her head at Bing. She didn't want to involve Rachel in whatever it was they were getting into. "It's really no big thing. This guy is a total ass."

"No, no, no." Rachel flipped through the pages, her brow furrowed. "I'm really good at things like this. We used to do this at 4-H camp, hide messages in the camp bulletin, use secret codes to sneak out at night." She looked up at them and laughed. "No chance this is a secret code to get us out of here, is there? Ha!" She chewed on the end of the pencil. "Thirty-seven minutes has got to mean something. Is there a map involved? Like coordinates?" Bing and Ellie shook their heads, uncertain, but Rachel wasn't paying attention. "Nah, that's too hard. You'd have to give everyone a map to make it fair. Assuming it's fair, of course. Thirty-seven minutes. Maybe it's a word code, like the thirty-seventh word."

Ellie and Rachel began counting words on the first page. They both tapped along, counting out loud, then looked up and spoke.

"Catalog," Rachel said.

"Every," Ellie said. "Did you count the headline?"

"No. Did you count all the little words like 'a' and 'but'?" She shook her head. "That can't be right anyway. Too complicated. Nobody would want to count that far, not unless the prize really is a ticket out of here. It's got to be something more manageable. I know Mrs. Madison. She's not that smart."

Ellie lifted her gaze from the paper and let it drift to the view outside her window. She didn't have Bing's sweeping view of the street. Her window was just a few feet above the hardware store beside it, and all that was visible was an expanse of oily tarpaper, but Ellie wasn't seeing it. Half of a thought swirled through her mind, looking for form. "She's not that smart." Ellie whispered to herself. "She's not that smart, so maybe…"

She turned back to the paper and scanned through the four pages of the local newsletter until she found what she wanted. "Do you have the last edition, Rachel? The one that came out on Thursday?"

"Yeah." Rachel rifled once more around the crowded nightstand, pulling out a crumpled newsletter like the one she held, only this one had several coffee cup rings on it. "I don't know why you guys don't read this. I mean, I know it's not the *New York Times*, but it is local."

Bing passed the paper to Ellie. "Trust us. We're converted."

Ellie looked back and forth between the papers until she found what she was looking for. She smacked her fingers against the page. "Corrections." She read aloud from the newer edition. "The correct cooking time for Carrie Madison's Pecan Sandies is fifteen minutes, not forty-two as printed on Thursday. We apologize for any inconvenience this error might have caused."

Ellie held the paper out triumphantly. Bing glanced at the equally stumped Rachel. "And this is good news because…?"

"Because," Ellie waved the pages, "Carrie Madison is not responsible for the clue. She puts the right cooking time in. Whoever is sending the message changes the time to send the signal. See, in the last edition, the correction reads, 'The correct cooking time for the Prune Crumble is twenty minutes, not sixty-four as printed.'"

"So they have a lousy proofreader," Bing said. "And what the hell is a prune crumble?"

"No, you're not hearing me. It has to be the incorrect number. The messed-up number is important in every edition." She ran her fingers down the columns of Rachel's stained copy. "Here. Here it is. 'In the last edition the cooking time was mistakenly printed at forty-two minutes.' Here on the second page is an article about Danny Glock's forty-second birthday. Now in this one," she picked up the new edition, "the cooking time is thirty-seven minutes. And here, on the third page, is a fascinating article about Katie McGill's thirty-seven-pound dog."

Bing and Rachel continued to stare at her, waiting for more, until Rachel raised her pencil at her and started pointing. "The clue is in the article. There are all kinds of numbers in the paper. Addresses and times. The cooking time tells you what article to look at." She turned to the correct article and circled it with her pencil. Then her expression darkened again. "But what are we looking for? Is there some connection between Danny Glock and Kelly's ugly dog? By the way, I've seen this dog and it's a flea-bitten mutt. It doesn't weigh thirty-seven pounds soaking wet carrying a cat."

"It doesn't?" Ellie asked. "You've seen the dog?"

"Yeah," Rachel said. "It's not like there are so many dogs left around here. It's a mutt. And last I heard it was on its last legs."

Bing rapped his knuckles on the chair. "But that's the sort of thing only a local would know. Only a local would catch."

"Well, duh," Rachel said, "only locals read this. Why would a Feno-fuck bother?"

"Hey." Bing slapped her foot. "What kind of language is that, young lady? You've been spending too much time with Potty Mouth Cauley over here. You're too pretty to talk that way."

"I'll ignore that." Ellie flattened the paper out on the bed. "So what is it about thirty-seven that makes this article important?"

Rachel ran her fingers along the type quickly. "It's not long enough for it to be the thirty-seventh word. It would be a short message."

Ellie leaned back and squinted at the recipe. "Maybe it's not thirty-seven. Look at the type." The type for "the local" was blurry and mismatched, the lines crooked and awkward. On the cooking instruction line, several letters were blurred. "Look at the numbers. It's not typed thirty-seven. Someone typed it three and seven. Believe me, I've proofed enough ads to know a type space when I see one."

"Three and seven." Rachel took her pencil and began to scan the lines of the article. "Third word and seventh word...uh, gibberish. What about the first word on the third and seventh lines?" She and Ellie marked those as well with no better results. Bing sat quietly, his eyes darting from woman to woman, not wanting to break their impressive concentration. "Wait, Ellie, is this it? Third line, seventh word. 'Wednesday.' Three lines down, seven words in...'seven.' That's weird." She and Rachel continued the pattern, counting three lines down, seven words in, and as Rachel read the emerging message, Ellie and Bing tried not to react.

"Wednesday—seven—evening—church—back—door—food."

Rachel looked to them to see their reactions. "Maybe it means you're supposed to find some food that's left behind the church at the back door. The back door leads down to the cellar of the church where they keep the school lunches, so that makes sense."

"That's probably it." Bing nodded, flashing Ellie a look of caution. "And Wednesday is tonight, so we can just head over there tonight and pick up whatever it is we're supposed to pick up. Rachel, my dear, you are a genius. Who else could have figured that out?"

"Probably lots of people, if they know the game is going on." Rachel held up the paper and pointed to the title bar. "The paper *is* called *Words and Lines*."

"Oh my God." Ellie slapped her forehead at this obvious clue. "Bing, if stupid were a color, we would be its deepest shade."

"This was so fun." Rachel laughed and clapped. "Let's look and see what last week's was." She stepped forward to grab the paper from Ellie and then swayed, staggering into the nightstand. Her knees buckled and she fell to the floor before Bing or Ellie could catch her.

"Are you okay? Rachel?" Bing wrapped his arms around her, pushing the hair off her face. "Did you faint? What's the matter?"

"No, I just…I don't feel so good. I think I'm going to be sick." She let Bing help her to her feet and leaned on him as he led her to the bathrooms. Ellie watched them go, the color of Rachel's skin unnerving her. When she heard her roommate's retching, she picked up the earlier edition of "the local" and found the article on David Glock's forty-second birthday. Counting four lines down, two words in, she pieced together another message.

"Monday—nine—morning—Dingles—guns."

CHAPTER FOURTEEN

Bing slipped back into the room and grabbed Rachel's towel and robe. "She's going to take a shower. I think she's done throwing up. God, how can so much foulness come out of such a pretty little thing?"

"Are you going to help her again?" Ellie asked, eyebrows raised.

"Unfortunately no. She says she's got this. But I'm ready if she needs me." He turned back at the door. "Don't go anywhere. We have got to talk."

"Tell me about it." Ellie slipped the older local paper in the fold of the large newspapers, laying them on top of the hidden files. She had to tell Bing about them. In retrospect, it had been such a stupid thing to do, and now, with the investigation into the bombing underway, the files could be damning evidence. She worried about involving Bing or Rachel in her ill-planned scheme.

When Bing returned, Ellie had slid the files under her pillow and shoved the sheet around them. Her bed was always a mess; nothing looked out of place. He straddled the old chair once more and drummed his fingers on the wooden back.

"I can't believe I'm saying this, Ellie, but are we sure this code thing is real? I mean, doesn't it seem a little Junior Sherlock Holmes to you? A code in a hometown newsletter?"

"I know what you're saying, but if you think about it, it makes sense. Remember, we're not from here. Before the spill, there were less than ten thousand people in the whole county." Ellie knew she was breaking one of the cardinal rules of etiquette by talking about life before the spill, but under the circumstances she really had no choice. "Josh used to talk about what it was like going to school out here. Everybody knew everybody. Well, look at Rachel."

"Gladly." Bing sighed. "I wish I could see her right now in the shower."

"Okay, you're getting a little creepy." Bing nodded and Ellie continued. "She said they used to use codes like this in her 4-H bulletins. How many people in Flowertown do you suppose were in her 4-H camp? These are people who know how to survive. Hell, Rachel could probably trap an animal, cure the meat, and fashion a crude hut from its flesh without even messing up her ponytail. Believe me, I used to live near the Amish. People who grow up on farms know how to take care of themselves and their neighbors."

Bing didn't look convinced. "Even against a multinational chemical company and the U.S. Army and quarantine and poisoning? I think you might be overestimating them."

"Well, that depends on the endgame, doesn't it?" Ellie tried to keep her temper from her voice. They were both outsiders among the locals: she had been here only because of her boyfriend, Josh; Bing had been on his way to a graduate school dig in South Dakota when the spill occurred. It was natural, she figured, for the two of them to always feel a bit like outsiders, neither Iowans nor Feno, but Ellie had come to love and admire the people she met from the area around Penn County, Iowa. It irritated her when Bing spoke down about them.

"What is the endgame? To take over Farmville?"

There was that tone again. "Well, you tell me, Mr. Conspiracy. Maybe they've been stockpiling supplies in case the barrier gets closed—like it is now. Or maybe they're making plans to defend themselves from a breakdown in law in case the army withdraws—as it seems to be doing. You're the one who says Feno is running the Evil Empire, censoring everything. Maybe they're working to keep open communication with the outside world. Did you ever think of that? Or do you think you're the only one smart enough to come up with thoughts like that?"

"I stand corrected." Bing held up his hands in surrender, although Ellie could still hear dismissal in his voice. "So if this intrigue is going on, what's our next step?"

"Well, I guess we go to the church at seven o'clock and see what's happening."

"Shit." Bing pulled his phone from his pocket and scrolled through the screen. "I've got a med check at six thirty. I'll be late, but I'll try to hurry. I hate when they put my appointment at the end of the day. It takes forever to get my meds." He slid the phone back in his pocket and rose. "Look, I'm sorry again about the fight earlier. I guess, you know, I've wanted there to be a conspiracy for so long and now that it seems like there actually is one, I guess I freaked."

"Don't sweat it. Having your building blow up around you will do that to a person. Where are you going?"

"I have a bunch of weed to deliver. My phone's been hot all morning with people from the office. Nothing like a crisis to bring about a spike in profit." He leaned over her to kiss her on the cheek, and Ellie saw his hand on her bed inches from the hidden files. He whispered in her ear. "Be careful tonight. Try to pay attention. Unless of course it's a church dinner, and then just try to steal some food."

"Will do, chief. Hurry back from the med center, though. You know how bad I am at details." She called to him at the door. "Hey, has anyone said anything about Big Martha?"

Bing shook his head. "Well, I'm going to head to the care center and see if I can find her."

She heard him yell good-bye to Rachel as he passed the showers. She had been so worried about not being able to talk to Bing, yet now that he had left her, she was sort of glad. Theirs was a difficult friendship, due in no small part, she knew, to her own thorny personality. Finally with a moment alone, Ellie pulled the files out from under her pillow and unwrapped them. She laid them on her crossed ankles and stared at the plain brown covers. These files could get her into a lot of trouble. Even if they turned out to be old requisitions for toilet paper, the fact that she had stolen them hours before her building exploded made them dangerous.

With a deep breath for courage, Ellie flipped open the first file and began to read. Or tried to. Most of what filled the first page was codes and abbreviations, trains of connected letters that made no sense to her. As she flipped through the pages, she saw notations in ink scribbled on the edges of the paper, large blocks of text blacked out with ribbons of ink, and long lists of dates and times. Nothing made any sense to her, and Ellie was starting to feel very stupid for jeopardizing her safety for such gibberish until she flipped further through the pages and came to a photograph of an old man.

It was a Flowertown ID photo. Everyone within the compound had one on record somewhere, and like this one, most were taken when the occupants were quite ill. The man's color was bad, even in the black and white photo. His eyes were bloodshot and his skin hung loose and papery. The worst to Ellie was the baffled and frightened look in his eyes. She had seen him before. Despite Bing's teasing about her not paying attention, Ellie was quite good with faces. She skimmed over the record. Marvin Delmuth.

She remembered Marvin. He used to run the hardware store right outside her window. Ellie closed her eyes at the memory of leaning against the glass, her restraints finally removed, staring down at the street. Every day for three hours she was allowed to lean against the glass and watch workers building Flowertown around her. At first she would fall asleep where she stood, unable to fight the drugs, but gradually the drugs decreased and the time allowed alone increased, and she liked to spend as much of it as possible watching the people below her. And every day, every single day she stood in that window, the man in the plaid pants would come outside, empty his trash, sweep his sidewalk, and look up at her window and wave.

She didn't wave back for months; she hardly understood what she was seeing. But one day she recognized the gesture and waved back. To this day, even through all the drugs, she could remember the crooked yellow teeth that smiled back at her, sending another wave. When East Fifth was finally unlocked, most of the patients flooded out of the building and headed straight for their families, but Ellie had nowhere to go. Instead she sat on the top step outside of the building and waited for the little man to appear. He emptied his trash, swept his walk, and looked up at her window, and Ellie saw his face fall. Then he looked down and saw her on the step and his smile returned.

"Decided to get a little air, eh? It's a good day for it." That was all he said, no worried looks, no sign that he knew she had been locked up in a loony bin for two years. Just a happy wave and friendly word. That was Marvin Delmuth.

"Oh my God, what's the matter?" Rachel sat on the edge of her bed, her hair wrapped in a towel. "You're crying. Are you okay?"

Ellie hadn't even realized she had started crying. "Yeah, I'm all right. I'm just looking at something that kind of took me by surprise." Rachel cocked her head to see what she was reading, and Ellie realized there would be no hiding the files from her roommate. "I have to tell you something, something kind of serious."

"Oh no." Now Rachel's eyes filled up. "Does it have to do with the blue tag?"

"No, honey. It's nothing like that." Ellie took her hand. She couldn't stand to see Rachel upset. "Besides, you're sick enough for both of us, right? How are you feeling?"

Rachel stuck out her tongue. "I've got to go back to the care center today to get my final round done and to get my papers. I hope they give me another one of those shots. Do you think that since, like, you don't have a job now, you could come with me? I hate to ask, but it's such a drag being over there."

"Of course I will, honey. Besides, I want to see if I can find Big Martha. I don't know what happened to her after the explosion. Hey," Ellie squeezed Rachel's hand, "I didn't know you went to the care center for your detox. I thought that was at the med."

"Oh God," Rachel rolled her eyes and leaned back on Ellie's bed. "It was, originally. And then they moved it because they said the process was too complicated for the med center, that I was fouling up the lines." The med center was where everyone went for their regular testing and maintenance medications. The care center was more accurately a hospital. "You know how this place is. If there's a hard way to do it, they'll find it. I've never seen people more in love with paperwork."

"Funny you should mention that." Ellie tapped the files in her lap. "I'm going to tell you something, and you have to promise me you will never breathe a word of it to anyone, nobody, not even Bing."

"Not even Bing? I thought you told him everything."

"Well, I'm working up to it. This is something really stupid that I did and I just don't know what to do about it. If I should do anything about it." Ellie told an abbreviated version of the theft story, leaving out her torment of Cooper.

"You stole Feno files?"

"Shhh." Ellie looked toward the door, half expecting goons to come bursting in. "It was stupid, I know. I was just mad. I felt like they were accusing me of something, so I figured I would go ahead and do it."

"You might as well be hung for a sheep as for a lamb. My nana used to say that."

"Let's not bring up any sort of hanging, shall we?"

Rachel giggled and pulled the file off of Ellie's legs. "Oh, Mr. Delmuth. I loved him. He was so nice. He used to own the five-and-dime on State Street before he bought the hardware store. He kept rabbits in the window and always let us pick them up and play with them. I was so sad when he died. I got to visit him in the care center when he was in there, right before he died. He remembered me after all that time. He was like that, you know. He always remembered you."

"Yeah, I know." Ellie didn't want to look at the picture. It was probably taken one of the few times in his life he wasn't smiling. "That's nice that you were able to get in and see him. They don't usually let people in who aren't family members."

"I was working there, filing."

"You worked at the care center?"

"Ellie, I've worked everywhere in here. Because I did well on the first round of meds. I was one of the very few who did. They thought it was because I was so young, although a lot of kids in my class didn't make it." She heard Rachel swallow hard as she reached for the other files. "Let's see who else you have. Kevin Denten. I remember him. He went to high school with my sister Lee. He was hot, but they used to whisper that he was gay. Lee never believed it." Rachel looked up at Ellie. "I probably shouldn't say things like that about the dead, should I?"

"He's dead too?"

"Yeah, if I'm not mistaken, he died around the same time Mr. Delmuth did. You probably grabbed the death records

of a certain period. See? Because the next one is Mrs. Den-
ver, and I know she was in the care center at the same time
as Mr. Delmuth. I remember because her daughter was such
a flaming bitch to the nurses that they almost arrested her."

Ellie closed the two files on her lap. "Well, that was a huge
risk for nothing. I mean, it's not like a secret they were dead."

"No, but hey, you did it. And you didn't get caught,
that's kind of cool. Besides," Rachel looked back down at
the open file, "it's nice to see Mr. Delmuth again, although
that's a terrible picture of him. I'd steal it and give it to his
son, but I doubt he'd want to see his dad like that."

"His son still runs the hardware store next door?"

"Yeah, Bradley. He's nice, like his dad. He lost his wife
not long after his father died. That was sad. Annabeth Dingle brought over, like, fifteen gallons of chili." They both
laughed. Annabeth was famous for that canned chili. "That
was less than a year later, I think. Yeah, it was after the fourth
round."

"Fourth round? What do you mean?"

Rachel looked at Ellie as if she had just fallen from the
sky. "The fourth round of meds? Hello? Earth to Ellie. You
do remember the first round of meds, don't you? The ones
they gave us right after the spill."

"I remember them very clearly, thank you." Ellie doubted
anyone would ever forget those first months of containment
and the brutal effects of the decontaminants.

"Well, after that round and all those people died, they
worked up a new round. I was, like, one of the very few who
could handle the first round, so by the second round I was
fine. I mean, as fine as anyone could be in here. That's why
I was working in the care center. That's when they were get-

ting their filing system in place." Rachel put her hand to her mouth, embarrassed. "Oh, that was probably about the time you were…you know."

"Probably." Ellie had told Rachel all about her incarceration. Rachel hadn't cared. She had needed a place to stay after her other apartment building had been commandeered for the army. Ellie waved her hand over the file. "So you know what all this gibberish means?"

"Heck no." Rachel flipped through Mr. Delmuth's file, looking for something. "But one of the women from Barlay told me what part of your Med Tech line means."

"My Med Tech line?"

"Yeah, you know, the thing on your med check receipt."

"We get receipts at med check?"

Rachel made a sound of exasperation. "For crying out loud, do you even live here? Just how high do you and Bing get? You get a receipt every time you leave the med center."

"So sue me. I try not to pay too much attention to people sticking me with needles."

"I'll show you mine." Rachel climbed off the bed, unwrapping her hair from the towel as she went. She tossed the towel over the chair and rifled around the mess on her nightstand.

"Is there anything you don't keep next to your bed?" Ellie asked.

"Here it is." She pulled out a narrow yellow receipt, like a credit card slip, and climbed back on Ellie's bed. "See? You think my name is Rachel Abernathy, but you are incorrect. According to Feno and Barlay Pharma, my name is GrF sixteen E plus slash plus plus plus plus slash two equals Q."

"Very sexy."

"I know. I'm thinking of telling boys to call me Gerf Sixteen."

Ellie laughed. "So you know what all that stuff means?"

"I know what most of it means. It's the filing system. I was sixteen when the spill happened and I was female, so that's the F sixteen." She moved her finger under the row of plus signs. "And see, this means I had a positive reaction to all five rounds of the medications. Every time they fine-tuned the meds, my contamination level reacted well. So I'm, like, an A plus student."

"Show-off."

"I know." Rachel giggled. "And then this part I actually was responsible for organizing. The E plus part. I helped go through all the files to organize them by this part."

"E plus? What does it mean? Super egghead?"

"No," Rachel said, "it means I have a large family outside of Flowertown. If it said just E, it would mean I just had some family. If it said 'I' it would mean I have family internally; I plus means lots of family inside, and IE means I have family in and outside."

"Well, don't most people have family outside of Flowertown? Even people who've lived here for generations? Almost everyone has cousins, don't they?"

"This was for, how did they put it, family of impact. Or something like that." Rachel skimmed through Mr. Delmuth's file. "They only counted family that had to be contacted and that you would maintain a relationship with. You know, next of kin stuff."

"What if you didn't have any family you kept in touch with?"

"Then it would be N, for negative." Rachel found Mr. Delmuth's line. "Here's Mr. Delmuth's. CRnM sixty-three I plus slash minus minus minus. See, he only has three dashes because he must have had a negative reaction to the first three rounds." She ran her fingers over his line, as if it were his hand. "That's sad. He must have been sick the whole time, but he never showed it."

Ellie tried to decipher the line. "So the I plus means he had a large family in the containment zone. What does the CRn mean?"

"I don't know. That's all classified. You know how Feno is. They'd probably shoot us both if they knew we could read this much. Sorry, didn't mean to bring up the execution thing again." Rachel elbowed Ellie and laughed. "This stuff on the end is new, anyway. It's like the code is always growing. Stupid suits trying to make everything more complicated. Mine used to end in the number two, and then about a year ago they added the equals-Q."

"Did you ever ask what it meant?"

"Like they'd tell me. I wish you had yours. We could see what we have in common."

Ellie raised her voice to match Rachel's. "We could be, like, Med Line twins!"

"You wish!" Rachel climbed off the bed, flicking her wet hair over her shoulder. "Remember, I have five plus signs in a row. Yours probably has the code for crazy." Ellie flung her pillow at her roommate, who knew well enough to duck, laughing. It wasn't the first time Rachel had teased Ellie about cracking up, and Ellie figured the young girl was probably the only person on earth who could get away with it.

"Keep running your mouth, Gappy. Maybe the rest of your teeth will fall out."

Rachel dropped her robe and spun around naked. "I'll still be gorgeous!"

"Yeah, yeah, yeah." Ellie laughed. "Get dressed, gorgeous, and let's get over to the care center. Use your considerable influence to help me find Big Martha."

The care center was a two-story building that took up the entire block on the northwest side of Flowertown. It looked and smelled like a hospital with the exception of the heavily armed guards posted at the door. Ellie hesitated when she saw they were scanning tags. If she was a person of interest in the bombing, she might be detained from the secure facility. Working up some sort of bluff, she stayed behind Rachel as they passed through the glass doors.

"There she is!" An enormous man with an equally enormous gun showed at least a hundred teeth as he grinned at Rachel. "How many days is it now? It's got to be close, right?"

"Tomorrow!" Rachel high-fived the guard, and then waved to several other guards around the entryway. "Assuming, of course, I meet all the requirements and pass all the tests."

"You?" the giant scoffed. "Has there been a test you haven't passed yet?"

"Well," Rachel grinned and showed the gap in the front of her mouth, "I failed the dental check. Obviously."

Another burly man leaned over the first guard. "You make it look good, sweetie."

"Thanks, Len." She gestured back to Ellie, who up to now had been invisible. "This is my roommate, Ellie. She wants to be here when I get my final papers. Is that okay?"

"Sure, sweetie. You go right on through." The guards spoke over each other as they buzzed the two women into the secure building. There were shouts of good luck, and Rachel waved to them all before leading Ellie down the hallway, underneath a sign that read, "From this point on, all patients require an escort."

Ellie looked around, peering into rooms filled with files and equipment. "So I take it the escort rule doesn't apply to you?"

"Well, technically you're escorting me." Rachel took her arm and walked with her through a maze of white corridors. "Trust me, I'm here so much they don't even notice me."

"Oh, I think they notice you, honey. Those guards certainly did."

Rachel giggled. "Those guys are always flirting with me. When I used to work here—"

She interrupted herself with a squeal as a group of nurses began to applaud her arrival.

"Speak of the devil and the devil appears!" A woman in dark green scrubs stepped out from behind the station desk, holding a bubble-wrapped package. "Look what just came up from the pharmacy." Rachel jumped up and down, reaching for the bundle, but the woman pulled it back. "Well, first let's make sure this is the right one. We don't want to get this far and screw it up." Rachel handed over her medical tag.

"See, every time I come in for a detox, they send my blood back to the lab," Rachel explained to Ellie. "Then from that test, they formulate the next dosage specifically for me."

"And if we give her the wrong person's dosage," the nurse in green explained, reading the scanner, "then she goes to the infirmary and I use her ticket to Las Vegas." The other women at the station laughed at Rachel's mock outrage. When the scanner beeped, everyone cheered again. "It's all yours. Ready?"

"Ready. Is it all right if my roommate sits with me for the last round?"

The woman looked Ellie over and then nodded. "She can stay for the drip, but I don't think you're going to want her in there for the rest of it, right?" Rachel grimaced and shook her head. "Okay then, this way."

Ellie followed Rachel and the other woman down yet another hallway. Along the way Rachel peeked her head in different doors to wave and say hello. "Is there anyone you don't know, Rachel? You're like a pageant queen."

"I don't think there's anything wrong with being friendly." They stopped two doors from the end of the hall, and the nurse led them into a small, plain room with an examination table and an IV pole. Rachel climbed up on the table and lay down, holding out her left arm for the nurse. Ellie sat on a small stool, the only other seat in the room, and watched as the nurse stuck Rachel's arm with practiced ease, then injected the vial of medication into the IV bag. She waited to be sure the drip was working, then covered Rachel with a thin blanket.

"That feel okay?" Rachel nodded, adjusting the pillow beneath her head. "Then I'll go ahead and leave you to it. I'll be right down the hall, so just call me if you need me. And just think," she touched Rachel's cheek with her fingers, "this could be the last time you're in here."

As the nurse left the room, Rachel's smile faded, replaced by thinly veiled pain.

"Are you all right, honey?"

Rachel nodded and took a deep breath. "This is always the worst part, when the stuff first hits my system. It feels like getting carsick. I get really cold and kind of…blech."

"Is there anything I can do?"

"Just talk to me. If I close my eyes and don't answer, just keep talking. Sometimes I have to fight to keep from spinning."

Ellie watched Rachel's color fade and saw her lips whiten as she lay there. "Let's talk about Las Vegas." Even though her eyes were shut tight, Rachel smiled. Ellie talked about what she remembered of the city, telling her roommate for what had to be the hundredth time about the lights and table games and cocktails and nightclubs. Rachel listened and laughed, and when Ellie couldn't think of another story to tell, they sat together quietly, listening to the women down the hallway going about their business. Someone was complaining about filing and someone else was telling her to suck it up. The exchange was getting heated, and Rachel and Ellie laughed at the snarky comments flying back and forth.

"Thanks for coming with me, Ellie." Rachel's face was pale and her hairline was damp with sweat. "I really appreciate it."

"No problem. I wish I'd known you wanted company. I'd have been here."

"Nah, you were working. And in the beginning this was a lot grosser. The last part is still gross, when they scrub my skin and give me the, you know."

"I know." Somehow Ellie couldn't see Rachel ever saying the word "enema," even though she had already suffered through dozens of them. Ellie watched a tear slide down onto the girl's pillow.

"I can't wait for this to be over. I can't wait to see my mom again."

Ellie blinked back tears from her own eyes. "I bet she can't wait to see you too. She must miss you so much."

"She blames herself." Rachel stared at the ceiling. "My sister said she's been going to therapy because she's been so depressed. Says she thinks it's all her fault, that she should have made me go to the beach with them." Ellie didn't know what to say and so said nothing. She knew only the barest details of how her roommate had come to be in Flowertown alone. It was never discussed. Rachel seemed to be talking to herself, the tears streaming into her hair. "I just want to tell her face-to-face that it was my decision to stay. I know it sounds stupid, but I raised Radishes all by myself. I picked her out of McClusky's litter and I fed her and I cleaned her pen. I loved that pig, and I knew I was going to win that ribbon. I knew it and I wanted to show Patty Samples that she didn't know everything, that she wasn't the only one who knew how to raise a pig. I just wanted—" She threw her arm over her eyes, and Ellie hurried to the bed.

"Don't. Don't do this to yourself."

"Can I tell you something? Something bad?" Ellie nodded, and Rachel glanced at the door to be sure no nurses were nearby. "Sometimes when I think about getting my pass, when I think about being in Las Vegas, I think about running away. Cutting off my anklet and just running, running to Mexico or someplace."

"Of course you do, honey. That's only natural."

Rachel grabbed Ellie's arm and stared hard into her eyes. "But I'd contaminate all those people. I'd make them sick. But when I think about it," her voice broke with a sob, "I don't care. I don't care about them. I don't care about any of them. I just want out of here."

"How you doing, sweetie?" The nurse in green stuck her head in the door, and Rachel and Ellie drew apart. Both of them had tears in their eyes, and the nurse stepped farther into the room. "Is everything okay?" She looked at Ellie as if she were guilty of something.

"We're just talking," Ellie said, leaning back on the stool.

"Uh-huh." The nurse stared at her for another moment and then turned to Rachel with a softer expression. "Looks like you're done here. You know what comes next." Rachel nodded, wiping at her tears, and looked at Ellie.

"Wait for me?"

"Of course. I'll be right outside." She squeezed Rachel's hand and winked at her as the nurse unhooked the IV. As much as she hated hospitals in general and as gruesome as she knew the next steps would be, Ellie had to force herself to leave her young friend's side. She looked back at the doorway as Rachel began undressing. A flicker of helpless rage tickled the base of her spine.

The women at the end of the hallway were still arguing about whatever filing crisis had arisen. A short plug of a woman with badly permed hair was huffing and puffing about how unfair it was that she had to drop everything she had to do to shuffle paperwork. When Ellie came into view, she directed her complaints at the fresh ears, since no one else was listening.

"It's not like we had any kind of warning. We have patients to take care of. Do you think that's the top priority?"

She seemed to be waiting for an answer from Ellie. "No?"

"Of course not. People can just drop where they stand as far as the office is concerned. And is there any point to it?"

"No?"

"Exactly." The little woman bustled past her, her cheeks red with outrage. "And it's not like they're not going to completely revamp it again in six months. Look at this." She gestured to a room full of file cabinets of varying sizes. "It took us over a year to get all the BTM recorded and refiled. That was all they talked about—BTM scores, BTM scores, like it was the freaking holy grail of filing, like it was going to solve the mysteries of the universe. And then six months ago they start talking about the QEH, QEH, and we have to redo everything QEH."

"What's QEH?"

"The new tag, the new test. Aren't you listening?" The woman clearly had no idea Ellie didn't work there. Her tirade carried her along. "And then this week, boom, all these files appear and they expect us, *me*, to drop everything and wave my magic wand over them and file them with the QEH. Well, let me tell you something." She jabbed her pen at Ellie, who leaned back from its point. "They can just kiss my A-S-S. How about that?"

"Sounds good." Ellie could see why her coworkers avoided this little human tsunami. Her puffing breaths and stomping little feet created a hot wave of frustration whenever she passed. Ellie was afraid to step in front of her, and instead slipped out of her way between two file cabinets in

the much-lamented new delivery. The little woman continued to mutter and slam things around, and Ellie was hoping
she could make a break for the hallway soon. She leaned
against one of the shorter cabinets and looked down at a
rough spot under her fingers.

Scorch marks. The pale gray paint had been scorched
in a row of dots. Cigarette burns. Ellie recognized the burns
she had made when this cabinet had been in the records
office.

CHAPTER FIFTEEN

Ellie stared at the cigarette burns trying to convince herself that she was wrong, that those marks could have come from anywhere, that she wasn't the only person on earth who burned marks into a pale gray three-drawer file cabinet, but she wouldn't believe herself. She remembered making those marks, precisely lining up the cigarette ember to scorch in equal-sized dots the length of the cabinet. It couldn't be a coincidence, but how was it possible that this cabinet had moved itself from the records office to the care center without anyone noticing?

When had she last seen the cabinet? Ellie chewed on her lip, trying to sort through the whirlwind that had become her life. Monday. Monday she and Bing had sat on the cabinets in the morning. Bing had gotten mad at her again and stormed out and she had headed to the med center. That was when Mr. Carpenter and his goons had threatened to arrest her. The next morning, Tuesday, was when Cooper appeared, and she knew very well what had happened after that. So when had the file cabinet been moved?

Ellie stared at the drawers, waiting for them to answer her. It had to have been Monday night. There was no other way. Big Martha would have said something if somebody had removed a cabinet as big as this. She had mentioned a messenger bringing in files, but nothing about anything going out. It had to have been after hours on Monday. As logical as the facts sounded, Ellie still had a hard time wrapping her head around it. Had Mr. Carpenter moved all the files out to protect them from her? And if so, why hide it? Why not rub it in?

Ellie hadn't stepped any farther onto the red-painted section of her office than to switch out the file boxes. When she'd seen the file cabinets all lined up against the wall she had assumed they were the same cabinets as always, but clearly that wasn't true. Ellie stepped further into the cluster of newly transferred files. There was a tall, six-drawer cabinet in the grouping, and Ellie craned her neck to see the back of it. In the metal seams sealing the back, she saw the cigarette butts she had been systematically shoving there for months. There could be no doubt. These were the file cabinets from the records office. Ellie leaned on the cabinet, holding her head, trying to think. If they would go through the trouble to switch cabinets, did they also switch out the boxes? Those files she had stolen from the red-taped box— had they been put there after the switch? They'd seemed so unimportant, such a letdown. Was that why Feno had left them unguarded?

But that wasn't right. Feno had guarded them. Unsuccessfully. They had sent Cooper in there to guard those files. Someone had blown that building sky-high, and it seemed the bomb had been in the records area. Had someone

223

been trying to destroy sensitive Feno documents and been thwarted by the switch? Or—and the thought made Ellie sway on her feet, trying to process the ramifications—had the bomb come into the building in the files themselves? She had to find Big Martha.

Ellie hurried down the hall to the nurses' station and heard the angry clerk behind her still complaining about all the filing she had to do. She stopped herself halfway down and cursed. Why hadn't she taken some of those files while she'd had the chance? It wasn't as if she had any moral compunction about stealing at this point. If those files had been spirited away, she wanted to know why. She knew she couldn't just whistle her way out of the building with an armload of files, especially the care center, which was heavily guarded. Acting like she was working a kink out of her neck, Ellie scanned the ceilings for cameras. Every inch of the hallway was covered in surveillance. No doubt the records area was too. Well, Ellie said to herself, where there's a will there's a way. It's probably a bad way, but what the hell.

Turning slowly on her heel, Ellie tried to look like a bored visitor pacing the halls to kill time. She strolled back into the file room where the angry hornet woman was still talking and slamming drawers. Ellie watched her carry armloads of folders that she dumped in a heap on a large table in the back of the room.

"Can I help?"

"Do you know the system?" the little woman snapped at her, both verbally and with her fingers as she passed. "Because I doubt you do and you'll just wind up screwing this up for me and that's exactly the last thing I need right now."

"I could at least help you carry them. Save you a few steps."

The little woman stopped and frowned. "Yes, you could. I would appreciate that. We're starting in the BTM fours. Over there." Ellie had no idea what a BTM 4 meant, but she pulled an armload of files from the half-empty drawer and carried them back. The woman moved to the other side of the table and began organizing the piles of folders, muttering to herself about the goddamn Qs, Es, and Hs and how she had better things to do. Ellie left her to it.

She emptied out the drawer she had started with and then, out of sight of the clerk but in plain sight of the camera overhead, pantomimed being directed to the short cabinet with the scorch marks. She hoped there was no sound on the cameras, because she was miming quite a show, pretending to read the card on the front of the drawers. Nodding for the cameras, she pulled open the top drawer and grabbed an armload of files.

Ellie dropped the files on the end of the table, far from where the clerk was working. She intentionally set them crooked, and the pile instantly slid to the floor in an avalanche of paper. The little clerk let loose a torrent of obscenities that even Ellie thought was excessive.

"Don't worry, I'll get them."

"You sure will. And you'll put them in the right order or you'll get out of my file room." Under the table, out of sight of the cameras, Ellie first flipped off the angry little woman, then opened a file. There was no way she could sneak the whole file out. It was too bulky and she didn't even have the pathetic hiding place she'd had for the other files. Instead Ellie leafed through the pages quickly, trying to find the identity page with the photo. If she couldn't know what she was stealing, she could at least know who. She found the photo page, as well as a stapled med center receipt, and tore it from the file. She grabbed two or three pages behind it as well and jammed the pages down the front of her pants. Closing the folder, she stacked up the spilled files and dumped them before the clerk.

"There you go. That's enough for me today." The little woman gaped at her, taking in a breath for another tirade, but Ellie waved her down. "No need to thank me. Good luck!" She turned and hurried down the hall, catching the tail end of the newest rant as she cleared the nurses' station.

She knew she couldn't just run out. She had to find Big Martha, and she had promised to wait for Rachel. Ellie leaned against the high station desk, both to catch the attention of the woman behind it and to wiggle the papers farther down her pants.

"You waiting for Rachel?" The young girl in pink scrubs smiled up at her. Ellie nodded. "We just love her. I think it's so great that she's doing so well on the detox."

"Me too. She really needs to get out of here."

"Who doesn't?" The girl leaned over her keyboard. "I've been here eighteen months. Ugh. Six more months and I am out of here."

Ellie leaned on her elbows and stared at the girl. "Eighteen months? Really?" The girl realized she was speaking to a local and her faced flushed deep red. She started to fumble through an awkward save that probably would have gotten her deeper in trouble, but Ellie held up her hand to silence her. "I'm looking for somebody." The girl nodded, relieved to be able to recover from her fumble. She put her fingers to the keyboard.

"Name?"

"Logan. Martha Logan."

The girl typed and studied the screen. "Yes, she was brought in yesterday afternoon. Burns, respiratory issues." She studied the screen, scowling. "It says she's in secure quarters."

"What does that mean?"

The girl shrugged. "Could mean she's under arrest. Maybe she's been quarantined. It could just be that someone pulled some strings and got her a private room. It doesn't say."

"Well, can I go see her?"

"Huh-uh." She looked up at Ellie with a worried look. "Unless you have class four Feno clearance. Do you?"

"No." Ellie saw the relief on the girl's face and knew she had just been classified as unimportant. "Can you at least tell me her condition?"

The girl clicked the keys with precision and tipped her head primly. "No."

Ellie closed her eyes. There you are, old friend, she thought to herself. Deep in her spine, firing up from her fingertips, she felt that old, hot rage that she knew so well. It didn't burn as bright as it had in the past, and didn't flicker as fast, but Ellie would know it anywhere. One, two, three breaths and Ellie opened her eyes and smiled.

"Thanks for your help."

Ellie headed back to Rachel's room. It didn't matter how much they smiled and patted Rachel, she knew. To these women, to these "caretakers," Rachel and Ellie and

Marvin Delmuth and his daughter-in-law and all the other good people who had suffered in these halls were nothing more than stained, second-class citizens. They were temporary lists of tasks to be completed while Feno poured money into their bank accounts. Their two-year stints in Flowertown were nothing more than a paragraph in the adventure of their lives, a lucrative anecdote that they could tell again and again after they returned to their real lives, their clean, unstained lives far away from the stinking pit that was Flowertown.

Ellie had to catch herself to not kick open the door to Rachel's room. One, two, three breaths and she knocked softly.

"Come on in. I'm dressed." Rachel sat on the edge of the bed, pale, her hair dark with sweat. Ellie could see her arms were red where the nurse had scrubbed her skin. "Are you totally bored?"

"No. It was fine." Ellie leaned against the wall, her arms folded as the nurse in green scrubs filled out a form.

"Okey dokey, sweet girl." The nurse smiled at Rachel, and it was everything Ellie could do not to kick that stool directly into her abdomen. "The samples are on their way to the lab. Fingers crossed everything comes out A-okay. We will call you later this evening and tell you when you can pick up your paperwork."

"You mean I don't get it now?" Rachel's eyes widened. "You said I got them today."

"No, today was the last day of your detox. You still have to pass the final screening. Then you'll have to get your clearance papers and get fitted for your suit and have your anklet adjusted. Then we have to coordinate our GPS with your itinerary and work out transport."

"But the wedding is Friday morning. You said I'd be out Thursday. Tomorrow. I've only got forty-eight hours once I'm out, and all the arrangements have been made." Rachel's voice began to rise. "They've made all the plans and the rooms are booked!"

The nurse patted Rachel on the arm. "I think our protocols are just a little bit more important than a cocktail party, don't you?"

Ellie experienced that very familiar sensation of tunnel vision as she pushed herself off the wall and came at the woman. Rachel saw her expression and leapt from the table to block her. Ellie could hear her roommate talking her down, but all of her attention was on the patronizing look of the nurse as she signed off on Rachel's form. Clearly blowups in the care center were not unusual.

"Can you at least try to get things to go on schedule?" Rachel asked.

"Of course I will, dear. We're not in the habit of arbitrarily screwing people over." Ellie snorted at that, and the nurse's voice turned to ice. "On the other hand, we are not going to endanger the entire country so that you can go see Wayne Newton."

"I understand." Rachel had to shove to get Ellie to move, and Ellie kept eye contact with the nurse until the door closed behind them.

"Let's get the fuck out of here, Rachel." She grabbed her roommate and hurried down the hall. Several of the nurses at the station started to say good-bye until they saw the black look on Ellie's face. They didn't stop until they were halfway across the street and Rachel began to cry.

"Please slow down, Ellie. I can't run like this." She bent from the waist and threw up in the street. An army truck blew its horn, wanting her to move, and Ellie flipped both middle fingers to the driver. He started to blow the horn again until he saw Rachel heaving. Wiping her mouth, Rachel straightened up and waved an apology to the driver. He waved back as Ellie jerked her out of the way.

"Don't apologize to him, Rachel. He almost ran you over."

"Well, I was blocking the street."

"And he can wait. You're sick. You're more important than whatever he's doing."

"Am I going to get out of here, Ellie?" Rachel started to cry. "Am I?"

Ellie hugged her tight to her chest. "You're getting out of here. Trust me. You will."

Rachel fell into bed while Ellie got her the jug of iced tea from the refrigerator. "Need a glass? Because we don't have any."

"Then I think I'll skip the glass."

"Good choice."

Rachel took a shallow drink from the jug and set it on the floor. "Would you mind sitting with me until I fall asleep? I know I'm a huge pain in the ass."

Ellie made tsk-tsk sounds. "You know how that language upsets Bing. He'll never marry you if you keep it up." Rachel giggled as she climbed under her sheet. Ellie tucked her in and returned to her side of the room. Opening a window, she lit a cigarette and stared out over the hardware storeroom. Part of her was hoping to see Mr. Delmuth on the far corner, sweeping away the dirt and waving to her. Instead she saw another army convoy rolling past the store. Ellie looked away.

The room was dark when she opened her eyes. Ellie started. She had been dreaming about pinning ads to a bulletin board when something snapped her from her dream. She lay on her side, her pillow wet from drool, and it took her several long moments to figure out where she was and about what time it was. Ellie pulled her phone from her pocket. She had gotten two texts from Bing: "Are you there yet?" and "Gonna be late."

"Shit." She jumped from the bed. It was seven fifteen and she was late for the secret meeting. She wasn't even sure exactly where the church was, just that it was on the northeast end of Flowertown. It wasn't a place she frequented. Swearing to herself, Ellie pulled her hair back into the ponytail her sleep had destroyed and ran down the steps. How could she have fallen asleep? She had had her first good night's sleep in weeks last night and she hadn't smoked any weed. That's what clean living will do, she told herself, hurrying down the dark streets.

She was sweating by the time she found the church and took a moment to pull herself together. She didn't know what to expect in this meeting, if that's even what it was, but she figured sweating and panting were not part of the first impression she wanted to make. Ellie bent from the waist, taking in deep breaths as she watched the front of the church.

It was an ordinary-looking building, like most of the suddenly erected structures in Flowertown. This end of the zone was built last and less effort had been made to apply any aesthetics. The buildings lay side by side, with dark, narrow alleys between them for garbage service. Ellie listened for any noise, but there was none. No trucks rumbled by, no security patrols flashed their lights. Maybe that was why they had chosen this location, Flowertown's closest spot to off the grid.

She thought about slipping through the alley between the church and the school, but it was dark down there and Ellie's nerves were high. Instead she jogged around the corner and made her way down the wider alley behind the buildings. As she got closer, the darkness got deeper, and she looked up to see the streetlights were out. It wasn't an unusual sight, but it made her take her steps carefully.

There were trucks in the alley. Again this was nothing extraordinary for Flowertown. Supply trucks and convoys regularly jammed up the alleys during breaks from jobs, but Ellie wished her line of sight to the church was a little clearer. There was the door. The light in the back of the church was out and the area around the small door was full of shadows. With a deep breath, Ellie stepped out from between two trucks and headed for the door, stopping when she realized the shadows were figures.

She stopped in mid-step, still in shadows herself. Were those guards? Was there some sort of password she needed to get into this meeting? Was this even a meeting? For the millionth time, she wished Bing was with her, although her faith in his knowledge of conspiracies had been badly shaken. Still, it would have been nice to have someone by her side. She decided she had come too far to turn back now and stepped once more out of the shadows. She was just getting ready to make her presence known when the back door to the church broke open under the boots of the figures at the door and the night lit up with flares.

Ellie froze as men poured from the darkness and flooded the church. People were screaming and sirens flashed and suddenly the alley was alive with noise. Ellie didn't know what was happening as rough hands jerked her backward, swinging her hard against the side of a truck. A gloved hand covered her mouth, blocking her scream, and she struggled against the arm. She tried to kick up her knee, but her attacker was ready for her and twisted to the right. A gun appeared before her eyes and she grew still.

A radio crackled. "The room is secure, sir. Seven people. No weapons so far, but we're still searching." Another voice broke in. "Front is secure, sir. Situation contained."

Ellie knew before she even turned her head whose voice she would hear next, and she forced herself to relax, defeated, against the familiar form behind her. Guy took his hand from her mouth to grab his walkie-talkie, keeping his eye on her as he spoke. "Secure the prisoners and take them to the compound. Search the premises for evidence and weapons. And watch for booby-traps. I'm right behind you."

Guy dragged her by the arm along the line of trucks. She didn't resist, instead giving herself over to the tingling sensation of rage that flooded her arms and legs. She could feel the growl growing in her throat as her muscles discussed without her permission which limb would strike out first. Ellie had a good feeling it would be her right foot that would get the glory as Guy whipped her around to the back of the last truck. He held his weapon at the ready, but rather than train it on her, he kept it before him as he looked both ways out the end of the alley. Grabbing her hard by the upper arm, he pushed her against the truck, his breath hot in her ear.

"Run."

CHAPTER SIXTEEN

Ellie ran. She tore down the darkened streets while behind her the block came alive with lights and yells as people saw Feno goons dragging out neighbors and friends. She was clearing the third block when she saw a familiar figure hurrying in the opposite direction, his head bent in birdlike concentration.

"Bing!" She cut across the street, dodging a Feno truck, and had to shout again to get her friend's attention.

"What happened?" Bing asked, looking disappointed. "We were wrong, weren't we?"

"Hardly. Or at least Feno didn't think so. The meeting got busted." She held her arm out to steady herself as she caught her breath. "I was late. I overslept. They were kicking down the door as I got there. Said they arrested seven people."

Bing scanned the streets nervously. "Then let's get the hell out of here. How did you get away? Did they see you?" She didn't want to tell him about Guy. She didn't know what to think of his letting her go or what his intentions were, and she didn't want Bing to start one of his rants. She muttered something about hiding in the shadows. Bing dragged her along the street, his long legs making her double-time to keep up with him. "So what are we going to do?"

"What do you mean?"

"I mean, are we going to contact them? Do we keep digging?"

Ellie wrenched her arm free and stood still. "Hell no. Are you kidding me? We don't even know what they're meeting about. We don't even know who these people are. Look, I'm not a fan of Feno, but I'm even less of a fan of the detention center. I spent the first two years in here in lockdown. I'm not going back so Annabeth Dingle can stockpile oyster crackers."

"Are you shitting me, Ellie? I thought those people were your friends."

"They are. It doesn't mean I'm going to jail for them. I don't even know what they're doing. What if they're the ones who blew up the office? What if they've killed people?"

Bing put his hands on his hips. "So what are you going to do? Just go back and act like none of this ever happened? Just get high and look for another job and wait and see how long your liver lasts?"

"No." Ellie jabbed her finger up at him. "You don't get to play that card anymore. All your talk about conspiracies and social uprising—it was all horseshit that you were making up while you sat around in your underwear playing World of Warcraft. You don't give a shit about these people; you have no idea what's going on."

"You don't know anything either."

"No, but I do know that I have a roommate at home who is really sick and really nervous that she's not going to get her pass out of here. She needs me, so I'm going to go back there and take care of her." Ellie turned and started walking down the street. Bing waiting only a second before running to catch up to her.

"Why wouldn't Rachel get her pass out of Flowertown? Didn't she pass the detox?"

"They wouldn't tell her. They're making her jump through all sorts of hoops, letting her hang because they can. Because that's the kind of people they are."

Bing didn't say anything until they crossed onto the next block. "They being Feno, the people who just arrested a group of locals who invited us to a secret meeting."

"Shit." Ellie sighed, trying unsuccessfully to walk faster than the thought. "Shit."

"Shit is right. What are we going to do, Ellie?"

"Well, whatever we're going to do, let's not do it here with Feno trucks half a mile away."

They hurried along in silence, sticking to the darker streets and avoiding people whenever they crossed paths. Ellie could feel Bing's nervousness as he scanned the alleyways and tensed every time a security truck rolled past. By the time they made it to the third floor of East Fifth, Bing looked tense enough to bite through metal. Half of the hallway lights were burned out and the remaining fixtures flickered, a sure sign the power was going to fail again.

"Looks like it's not going to be hard to stay in the shadows." Ellie paused as she passed the toilet closets, catching the familiar sound of retching. She tapped on the door. "Rachel? Is that you?"

"Uh-huh. I'm okay. I'll be out in a little bit. Did you get to your scavenger hunt thing?"

Ellie shot Bing a look. "Not exactly. It was kind of a bust."

"So to speak," Bing whispered, and Ellie pushed him ahead.

"We're going to the room, honey. You need anything right now?"

"Oh," Rachel sighed and Ellie could hear her spit, "a cocktail in Vegas would be nice."

"I'll see what I can rustle up." Ellie tapped on the door again and followed Bing to her room. She couldn't remember where she had left the files or the pages she had ripped out of the care center files and hoped her usual slovenly ways would protect her until she had time to explain to her friend what they were doing there. Bing didn't seem to notice anything as he flopped down on Rachel's slightly neater bed and put his arms behind his head.

"Okay, Ellie, tell me everything that happened tonight. Every detail."

"I told you." The files were peeking out from underneath her pillow, so as Ellie settled in on her bed in the usual spot, she tossed a towel over them. "Feno busted the place."

"No offense, but you are a terrible storyteller. And you'd make an even worse spy. God is in the details, remember? Did you hear anything special? See anyone unusual? Did anyone get out of the building?"

"It didn't look like it. They said it was secure, that they had arrested seven people."

Bing sat up and looked at Ellie over the mess on Rachel's nightstand. "You were close enough to hear their radios and they didn't see you?"

Ellie shrugged, dismissing the question. She didn't want to get into a Guy-bashing session with Bing tonight or any night. She wanted to think. She heard Bing whistling a tuneless whistle, a sure sign that he, too, was working on a thought.

"Okay, I don't want to freak you out." Bing swung his feet to the floor and stared at Ellie, who knew that that was exactly what he was preparing to do. "But do you think it's possible that Annabeth and Torrez set us up? Like they thought we were getting too nosy, so they clued us into a meeting that they knew would get busted?"

"Really?" Ellie pulled a pack of cigarettes off her nightstand. "Even for you, Bing, that's a bit much."

Ellie fanned the smoke from her face and leaned over to open the window. Rachel probably wouldn't appreciate a cigarette funk in the room, considering her condition. The window stuck, as it did when the weather turned damp, and Ellie had to get up on her knees to force the pane up. It was brighter on the street than it was in her room, and Ellie craned her neck to see what the source of the light was. That was when she recognized the telltale yellow flashes of Feno security trucks. Before she could get her head back in the window to tell Bing, her door crashed inward and a team of black-clad goons flooded the room.

"Hands in the air!"

"On the ground!"

Orders were screamed around the room, and Ellie couldn't catch Bing's frightened eyes before one of the goons dragged him off the bed and slammed him hard against the floor. Three guns were trained on her, all of them held by serious-looking men, and Ellie raised her hands above her head.

"On the ground!" The leader of the team yelled at her even though she was less than three feet from him. It had the desired effect because Ellie slid from the bed and joined Bing facedown on the floor. In seconds, her wrists were bound in plastic ties behind her back. She was able to turn her head and look down at Bing, whose head was at her feet. His eyes were huge with fear, and Ellie didn't blame him one bit.

"Where are they?" The leader put his boot on her back and stepped down hard enough to push the air out of her lungs. "Make this easy on yourself."

Bing spoke up, his voice thinner with fear. "We don't know what you're talking about."

"Shut up." Another goon pointed his weapon at Bing's face, and the leader took his foot off of Ellie's spine and crouched down close to her. He grabbed her hair and lifted her head.

"I'm talking to you. Where are they?"

Ellie closed her eyes and swore to herself. "On the bed. Underneath the pillow."

Someone stepped over her, and Ellie saw her clothes fly to the floor. "They're here."

She kept her eyes closed as the leader talked into his radio. "We have the stolen property, sir. We're bringing two suspects in for questioning." Rough hands jerked her to her feet by her bindings, and as they were being dragged out the door, she saw the bewilderment on Bing's face. She shook her head, trying to think of something to tell him that would make sense of the situation, but the guards pulled her along too fast to come up with anything. All along the hallway, doors slammed shut as they approached and then creaked open as they passed. It took every drop of her control to not make eye contact with Rachel, who stood wide-eyed and silent in the bathroom door. She knew Rachel would have enough sense to not step forward. When Feno security came out in force, heroics and loyalty were losing bets.

Riding handcuffed in the back of a paneled Feno security truck was worse than the ride after the bombing, although at least this time she had a pretty good idea where they were going. Bing tried to whisper something to her until the leader slammed his head back against the wall of the truck.

"You can either ride in silence," he said, "or we can wait until you regain consciousness to start the interrogation. Your choice."

The streetlights in the Feno compound burned brightly. There was no power problem down here, Ellie thought, as she squinted against the harsh light. She and Bing were marched at gunpoint past the cinder block building where Guy had first interrogated her, past the row of classrooms that had held her before, and down to a short brick dorm-like building. Two guards held open the doors as their escorts led them down the hall. Bing, who was taller than the guards, had no trouble keeping up, but Ellie was once again half-carried, half-dragged until they got to one of a dozen unmarked doors. The guard holding Bing unlocked this door and shoved them both in hard. Ellie stumbled and would have fallen if she hadn't crashed into Bing, who had crashed into a set of bare metal bunk beds. The door slammed behind them.

"Are you all right?" they said in unison.

"I'm fine." Ellie spoke louder. "You're bleeding." A trickle of blood ran down from a cut on his eyebrow from hitting the bunk bed. "Does it hurt?"

"Yes, it hurts." He blinked the blood back from his eye, his hands still bound and useless. "What the hell is going on?"

"An excellent question, sir." Mr. Carpenter stood at ease in the now-opened door next to an armed guard. "Bring in the chairs." The guard stepped away and returned with two metal folding chairs that he set up before the front wall like desks in a classroom. Ellie doubted they were going to enjoy this lesson. The seats in place, Ellie and Bing were shoved down to sit and Mr. Carpenter leaned against the wall in front of them. He nodded to the guard, who left the room without a word.

"You can't hold us here." Bing's voice shook with either fury or fear, Ellie couldn't tell, but she applauded him for his intensity, however ill-timed. "Who the hell are you?"

"Ask her." Mr. Carpenter smiled that charming smile.

"This is the dreaded Mr. Carpenter, who so thoughtfully rearranged my desk while looking for my Twinkies." Ellie had thought the man was frightening when surrounded by his goons. She was unpleasantly surprised to find him even more unnerving alone in a room.

"Oh, Ellie," Carpenter shook his head, "always making jokes. I like that about you."

"Fuck you."

"Hmm, I don't think that's really an option because, you see," he leaned in close enough for her to smell cinnamon on his breath, "I'm getting ready to fuck you. And believe me, when I fuck you, you will know you have been fucked."

Ellie didn't doubt him, but that didn't mean she had to show it. "Ooh, I'm tingling."

He laughed again and leaned back against the wall. Bing struggled against his restraints.

"Is this the son of a bitch who tore your desk apart? Who accused you of stealing files? Hey, dickhead, ever heard of a search warrant?" Bing leaned forward, spit flying. "How about evidence? Miranda rights? You have no right—"

Carpenter's backhand knocked Bing off his chair, and Ellie could see blood splatter across the linoleum floor. Bing spit and tried to get to his feet, but the other man grabbed him under the arm and yanked him back into his seat. He leaned in close to Bing, his finger jabbing at his face.

"You don't talk. Do you hear me? The smartest thing you can do right now is to keep your big mouth shut. Although I don't think you're very smart. Not if you're running around with the likes of Eleanor Cauley." He turned to Ellie. "Unless of course he's your co-conspirator. Is that it? Is he part of your crew?"

Bing spit blood. "Oh yeah, you caught us. The dreaded Twinkie smuggling ring."

Carpenter made a naughty-naughty sound at Ellie. "You haven't told him, have you?" He smiled at Bing. "It seems your little playmate has been stealing classified Feno files."

"Bullshit." Blood sprayed out from Bing's lip. "Your goons planted whatever it is you think she stole. I've known Ellie for four years, and she doesn't give a shit about your classified little secrets."

"No?" Carpenter pulled out a small digital recorder and pressed a button. Ellie's mouth dropped open when she heard her own voice confessing the theft to Rachel. Carpenter let the audio run up to the point where she said she wasn't going to tell Bing about it. At that, he flipped off the device and slipped it back into his pocket. Bing would not look her way. Carpenter sighed. "This is awkward."

"You've got me on tape confessing to stealing the files. Why don't you let him go?"

"Well, Ellie, I have a couple of reasons. Good reasons, too. For one thing, I don't think you're smart enough to know what to do with stolen files, and so I am positive you have an accomplice. Two," he looked down at the blood on Bing's shirt, "I don't especially like your little buddy. But three, oh, number three is my favorite. Want to know what it is?"

"I'm on the edge of my seat."

Carpenter raised his eyebrows in happy surprise. "What a coincidence. So is he." He swung another backhand, this one even harder, and Bing's head whipped around as he fell to the floor once more. Ellie heard only her own roar as she leaped from her seat, hands bound, and body-slammed Carpenter. Together they crashed into the wall, her knees pounding at him, her feet stomping down, until two guards rushed in and threw her back into the chair.

Carpenter smoothed his clothes, and Ellie could see more than a few of her blows had hit home. She saw he favored his right leg as he stepped over Bing, who remained on the ground. Carpenter smiled and cleared his throat. "As I was saying, number three is my favorite. I'm going to keep your little buddy around, and every time you piss me off, he's going to get another beating. As much as I would enjoy pounding the shit out of you, Ellie, it seems your psychological profile suggests this is a more effective method."

Ellie felt her mouth go dry. "What do you want me to say? I told you I stole them. There's no conspiracy. I was pissed. I stole them." The words tumbled out fast, but Carpenter held up his hand to silence her.

"No reason to get windy now. You've got plenty of time to come up with a good explanation. I'm going to have my men cut your bindings, and you and Gilligan over there can cook up any fish story you like. See this?" He pointed to a jeweled Feno logo pin on his lapel. "This means I own you. You're going to be here for a long, long time."

A heavyset guard held Ellie by the elbows as she lunged uselessly at Carpenter. She could hardly make out the words he was saying. All she could hear was Bing's labored breathing mixing in with the rushing sound of her own blood in her ears. He laughed at her distress and pulled the recorder out once more.

"I don't suppose you'd like to make a statement before I go?"

"I got a statement for you." Carpenter grinned and held the recorder closer to Ellie, who stopped struggling against the guards and spoke very clearly. "Is it recording? Because you're going to want to remember this. Fuck you. Fuck Feno. Fuck Flowertown. I am going to get out of here. Count on it. I will get out of here if it means killing every last person in this compound. I don't care what it costs me, I don't care what happens afterward, but I will get out of here, and when I do, I'm going to find you and I'm going to kill you. You have my word on it. Is that enough of a statement for you?"

Carpenter stared at her for several seconds, his face unreadable. Ellie tensed, waiting for a blow to the face. Instead he laughed, a real laugh, and slipped the recorder into his pocket.

"I couldn't have written it any better myself." He headed to the door and spoke to the guard there. "Cut their restraints, get him some bandages. They might as well be comfortable for the duration of their stay."

Ellie rubbed her wrists when the plastic was cut away and dropped to the floor to get to Bing. His face was bruising and swelling, but he looked more angry than hurt. He shook off her attention, using his shirt to wipe at the blood. Before the guards closed the door, Ellie could hear her voice echoing in the hallway from Carpenter's voice recorder. As the door locked, she could just make out the sound of Carpenter laughing again.

CHAPTER SEVENTEEN

Bing wiped at his lip with the last clean inch of his T-shirt. "I don't suppose there's any happy ending to this part of the story."

"Oh, Bing, I'm so sorry." Ellie knelt beside him, and this time he didn't push her away. "I don't know what to say. Taking those files was a stupid thing to do."

"Agreed."

"There wasn't anything in them except death records of locals. I was just so mad."

"Imagine that."

Ellie sat back on her heels and looked Bing in the eye. "Go ahead. I know you have things to say to me. You might as well do it now."

He shook his head. "What's the point? You don't hear anything, Ellie. You're like some subterranean troll that just covers itself with leaves until someone steps too close, then you lunge up and tear them to shreds. You have two emotions—apathy and rage—and nothing in between." Ellie wanted him to stop, but she could hear the truth in his words. She closed her eyes for his killing blow. "It's like you're not even a person. You're an...organism."

"That's not true." Ellie forced her eyes open. "I am a person. I'm just not good at it."

"Yeah, well, why don't you work on it?"

Ellie sighed and sat back, sliding backward until she rested against the bare metal bunk bed. Bing moved away from her, resting his back against the front wall. They sat in silence, listening to doors opening and closing up and down the hallway until Ellie had to speak.

"I'm going to tell them anything they want. I'm not going to let them hurt you."

Bing looked up at her, his left eye swelling nearly closed. "I just slid my ass through a puddle of my own blood. That can't be a good sign."

"I mean it, Bing."

"I know you do, but it won't make any difference. You really are dense, aren't you?" Ellie started to protest, but he waved her down. "I'm pissed because the troglodyte part of my brain still thinks 'Me man, her woman' and it's somehow my job to protect you. Instead I'm being used as a punching bag because you're so goddamn tough they know I'll break first."

"I'm not going to let that happen."

"What are you going to do to stop it?" Bing swung his hands out, sweeping the room. "We are locked in a room on the Feno compound. There are armed guards outside. Trust me, there's nothing I'd like better than to kill that Mr. Carpenter, and by that I mean let you kill him, but I think we're kind of outnumbered."

"Then let's get out of here."

"And do what? Catch a movie? Go to the beach?"

Ellie got to her feet and surveyed the small room. There was nothing in the room except the beds, which were bolted to the wall, a stack of flattened cardboard boxes, and the two metal folding chairs. "Let's break out of here. I meant what I said, Bing. I am getting out of here. I don't care if I get shot doing it."

"Speak for yourself." But she could see his eyes searching the room, thinking.

"Why on earth would anyone try to escape? Right? Where would you go?" Ellie crouched down in front of Bing. "They've got guards out front, but it's just for show. I'll bet you a can of chili they don't have anyone in the back. It's nothing back there but barrier fencing. All we have to do is stay in the shadows, make it out of the compound and back to town."

"And then what?"

Ellie shrugged. "What difference does it make, Bing? I'm going. I'm not going to stay here and watch them beat you to death because they've got something against me."

"Well, when you put it that way." Bing got to his feet. "Any ideas for how we're going to get out of here? Going to punch your way out?"

"Sort of." Ellie listened at the door and, hearing nothing, gave Bing the thumbs-up. She picked up a flattened cardboard moving box off the pile in the corner. "We'll use this."

"We're going to ship ourselves out of here?"

Ellie laughed, happy to see Bing back to his usual smart-ass self. "Got a better idea?" She carried the box to the window and then stopped, turning back to her friend. "Why is this room empty? All these rooms? This building is almost completely empty."

"I don't know. Off season?"

"I'm serious. Since when are there empty rooms in Flowertown? Even for Feno?" She drummed her fingers against the cardboard. "Like that classroom where they took me before. It was empty. The file cabinets were empty, just old crap left behind. And these boxes. Where is everybody? Are we missing something?"

Bing glanced at the door. "I can tell you where some people are, big people with big guns, including Mr. Carpenter, who looks like he'd be more than happy to show you how crowded this place can be. If we're going to do something, let's do it soon, okay?"

"Yeah, right. Okay. Hold this." She held the cardboard in front of the window. Bing took it from her, pressing the box with both hands against the glass. "You might want to move to the side. Way off to the side."

"What?" Bing looked over his shoulder and saw Ellie hefting a metal chair. "Wait! What the hell?"

"Just hold the box by the edges so it covers the glass. That will help muffle the sound."

"Are you going to hit me with that?"

Ellie grinned. "Trust me, Bing. Chair-slamming is one of my specialties." She swung the metal chair over her head, hoping she had the precision she had promised Bing, and brought it down with all her might. The glass, the cardboard, and the chair flew out of the room. Bing caught Ellie as she nearly sailed along behind them and her right hand scraped along the jagged glass in the bottom of the broken window.

They froze where they stood, listening for any commotion that might arise. Ellie pressed her shirt along the bleeding cut on her right hand and leaned far out the window. She tried to count to twenty but only made it to ten. "There's nobody coming. Let's go." She heard Bing swearing under his breath as she swept the glass away with her wrapped hand and climbed out the window. He folded and unfolded himself through the opening and pressed himself beside her against the building. She could see his eyes widen in the darkness.

"We are going to get shot out here."

Ellie could hear her heart hammering in her chest. "Think we'll do better inside?"

"Not now," Bing hissed. "Now that we've tried to escape."

"Well then, let's not try. Let's escape." She led him along the edge of the building. At the corner, they ducked behind a dumpster loaded with trash and boxes. Ellie peeked inside the metal container, pushing aside some of the cardboard boxes on top.

"What are you doing?"

"Looking for something to use."

"Like what? A car?"

Ellie climbed up and leaned deep into the dumpster, then slid out with a thud. She held two boards from a broken loading pallet and handed one to Bing.

"What's this for?"

"In case somebody tries to stop us." She hefted the board in her hand. The wood was rough, and she could feel splinters in her palms, but it felt solid. At three feet long, it would also give them a little swinging distance. "I told you, Bing, I'm getting out of here no matter what."

They dashed across the narrow opening between buildings, staying low until they had a building at their backs. Bing held onto the wood as if it would turn on him. "I guess I should be glad you didn't find any guns in there. I'd probably shoot myself."

"Don't worry, Bing. I'll do the hitting. You just keep that as backup."

"Great." They ducked beneath the windows of the classroom building. "Any idea where we're going?"

"If memory serves," Ellie peered around the corner to check for guards, "the building where Guy questioned me should be straight ahead. Past that was the picnic area where we waited for the trucks. So that must be the road out of the compound. Shit!" She ducked back, flattening herself against the wall. She and Bing held their breath as footsteps approached. They were farther from the barrier fence and the grounds were well lit. Ellie was counting on their sliver of shadow to conceal them.

A radio crackled and a tinny voice asked a garbled question less than three feet away from where they stood. Ellie drew back the board, ready to swing, then forced herself to exhale as she listened to the guard answer. "Unit Nine checking in. Everything's quiet. Over." She heard static as he turned off the radio. "Of course it's quiet, you dumb piece of shit," he muttered to himself. "It's always quiet in this filthy hellhole." He took a step closer, and Ellie could hear the sound of plastic rustling. The guard was leaning against the wall just around the corner, inches from her face.

A light flared and Ellie could smell the unmistakable smell of a joint catching fire. She risked a glance at Bing, who rolled his eyes in disbelief. Smoke your bone and go, she urged the guard silently. She heard a few soft coughs and a whistling exhalation as a long plume of smoke caught the faint light. There were footsteps and gravel crunching and Ellie started to relax, hoping he was heading away from them. Instead the lighter flared once more, directly in front of them, as the guard stepped around the corner to take another hit.

He saw Ellie half a second after she saw him, dropped the joint, and reached for his weapon. Ellie swung the board around hard, catching him on the ear and jaw before his weapon cleared its holster. He staggered, gripping his head as he hit the wall, and Ellie brought the board down hard on the top of his skull.

She felt like she was moving through mud, and she had no other thought than putting the man down. He fell forward from the blow to his skull, and Ellie brought her knee up hard, smashing into his nose. She had a vague sensation of wetness as she clawed at the back of the guard's shirt. He fell to the side in a heap, and Ellie kicked him hard in the gut, doubling him up. She wanted to stomp him again and again, but Bing pulled her off.

"He's down. Ellie. He's down." He shook her by the shoulders until she focused on him.

"Okay. Let's go."

She had to consciously fight to relax her grip on the bloody board. She didn't plan on leaving it behind, but she knew her grip would tire. She could hear Bing breathing hard behind her as they ran, crouched low, from the classrooms to the freestanding cinder block building. Trucks were rolling close by, and Ellie heard several voices in the picnic area.

"Shit," Bing whispered, peering over her head. "Don't these people ever sleep?"

"They're busy. They've got a long night of arresting people." Ellie spied another squat cinder block building to their right, away from the activity in the picnic area. She and Bing hurried across the shadowed space between buildings and ducked against the wall. Ellie listened for voices or movement. She was getting very good at hearing over the sound of her own heartbeat. Rising up a bit, she peeked in the window of the little building. It, too, was empty.

Bing had crept ahead and rounded the corner of the building. Ellie followed him and saw a row of Feno trucks ahead, their cargo holds open and at varying degrees of fullness. She had no doubts anymore: Feno was on the move. That didn't help them right now, however. Ellie looked around, trying to find a way out.

"There." Bing pointed to a row of smaller trucks lining the road out. "If we can get to them, it doesn't look like there's much activity beyond." Unfortunately, between them and the trucks was fifty feet of open, well-lit space, with a dozen or so black-clad guards running around talking into radios. Bing looked at Ellie. "Do you trust me?"

"Do I have a choice?"

"We are going to stand up and walk right across that field."

Ellie stared at him. "And then what? Shoot ourselves?"

"No, listen to me." Bing grabbed her arm. "These guards are busy, but they're alert. They're going to be looking for anything suspicious. If we creep around in this light, they're going to see us. We need to act like we belong here, like we have all the time in the world to stroll over to those trucks."

Ellie peered out once more at the guards and at their large guns. "I don't think we blend."

"Trust me. These guys respond to authority and smell fear. If we act like we belong, they won't look at us twice."

"Can I bring my board? I'm not going without my board."

Bing nodded. "Yeah, just keep it to your side, out of sight along your leg. Just in case, you know…"

"Yeah, I know."

"Ready? Wait." Bing reached into his pocket and pulled out a bent cigarette pack. "This will make us look more at ease. Like we're not trying to hide." Ellie saw his fingers tremble as he brought the lighter to the tip, but when he exhaled he did look more relaxed. "Okay. Now."

Ellie followed his lead, standing tall and trying to take relaxed steps out into the pool of light. Bing kept his head down, but not too far down, and gestured with his smoking hand as if he were making a point. She felt her neck stiffen up as she resisted the urge to look in every direction. Bing kept his voice low, urging her to relax and slow down, but all Ellie could hear was the alarm she was sure would be raised at any second. The board against her leg reassured her, its splintery thickness solid in her hand. She knew it was an illusion, but the row of trucks seemed to be moving away from them the more steps they took.

And then they were there. Ellie was afraid to breathe as they passed the bumper of the first small truck. The shadows were darker here, but still Bing urged her to stroll. "Just a little further." Two trucks, three trucks, and they could see the road opening up before them. When they were four trucks down, they came to a gap, and Bing blew out a nervous breath.

"Holy shit, I can't believe that worked."

"Now you're uncertain?" Ellie asked, collapsing against a truck. "I'm having a heart attack here."

"Tell me about it." Bing scanned the shadows. "We're not out yet, but I've got to take a piss."

"Are you kidding me? Now?"

"Well excuse me, Mr. T. I'm not used to watching my friend beat a man to death with a board. It's taking its toll on me." Bing turned his back and unzipped his fly.

"I'll skip this part, if you don't mind." Ellie peered into the shadows up the road. A grove of young trees clustered ahead, blocking out the light. "I'm going to look ahead and see if there's any kind of gate. Meet me up there." She could hear Bing relieving himself as she muttered under her breath. "And I didn't kill that guy. I just hit him."

The light from the compound dropped off quickly as Ellie slipped in under the trees. There were still plenty of small Feno trucks parked along this road, and she wondered what they were for. Did every Feno employee get a truck? Crossing the road and slipping into the darker shadows on the other side, Ellie trotted, wanting to clear the compound and put distance between herself and Carpenter. Her fingers were trailing along the bed of a truck as the interior burst into light and two men climbed out of the cab.

Ellie ducked down, bunched small at the tailgate of the truck. She considered climbing under the truck but was afraid she would make too much noise. There was little light out on this stretch of road. It would be noise that gave her away. Holding her breath, Ellie bunched down into as tight a ball as she could manage, breathing softly through her open mouth as the two men grabbed duffels from the bed of the truck. She thought she could feel the wind of one bag as it swung out over her head, but, like the guards in the open area, the two men didn't notice her, talking instead about who would unload what. She waited until their footsteps faded in the darkness before she dared lift her head.

The road was dark once more. "My luck can't hold like this much longer." Her voice, even whispered, reassured her, and when she straightened she was happy to learn her legs didn't tremble as much as she feared they would. She wanted to call out to Bing, to tell him to hurry his ass along, but she was afraid the guards were still within earshot. Instead she slipped to the driver's side of the parked trucks and hurried along in the grass. As the trees grew thicker, the grass lane grew narrower, and Ellie felt safer knowing she could duck into the trees should someone else pop out of a truck.

She just didn't think that someone would pop out of the particular truck she was passing. Once again the cab illuminated just as Ellie cleared the gas tank, only this time she was on damp grass, not asphalt, and her feet slid as she tried to backpedal. She hit the ground hard and tried to crabwalk backward, but the light from the cab flooded the ground and she knew she would be spotted. Ellie grabbed for her board, but the man before her was faster. Unlike the guard behind the classroom, he had his weapon out and trained on her before she even saw his face.

"Aw shit, are you the only person that works here?"

Guy squinted into the darkness, trying to see Ellie's face in the shadows. "Stay where you are."

"I'm on my ass in wet grass."

"Put down your weapon." Ellie sighed and his voice got louder. "Put it down." She threw the board into the light, letting it skitter at Guy's feet. "What are you doing here?"

Ellie climbed slowly to her feet. "I think you know what I'm doing here."

"Carpenter reported you had been picked up."

"Yep, that's about the size of it. That and he tried to beat the shit out of Bing."

With the light from the cab behind him Ellie couldn't read his expression. She could see his gun, though, and could see it never moved an inch. "So what are you doing here?"

"Running away."

"Ellie, I can't let you do this."

"Then you'd better shoot me, because I'm going."

"I shouldn't have let you slide this evening at the bust. I should have taken you in then. I gave you the benefit of the doubt. Don't make me regret that."

"It's a little late for regrets, don't you think?" She took a step toward him, and he raised the gun.

"Stay where you are."

"I can't."

A spring wind whispered through the trees, and part of Ellie's brain wondered at the complete lack of night sounds. When a town was surrounded by three miles of pesticides, crickets were a sound of the past. Instead there was only the rustle of young leaves. Ellie took another step forward, stepping fully into the light, hoping Guy would see her, would know her.

Guy sighed. "I keep telling myself you have no idea what you're getting involved in. You couldn't. You wouldn't."

"I don't know exactly what you're talking about, Guy, but I am getting out of here." She looked over his shoulder into the shadows down the road.

"Ellie, I love you." He slid back the action on the gun, chambering a round, and readjusted his aim. "But if you try to break containment, I will shoot you."

"Containment?"

Before he could explain, Bing stepped out from the darkness behind Guy and brought the board down hard on his skull.

CHAPTER EIGHTEEN

Guy fell to one knee, dropping the gun, and Bing reared back to swing again. Ellie screamed, kicking her foot into Guy's chest, sending him reeling backward. Scrambling to her knees, Ellie grabbed the dropped gun as Guy grabbed for Bing's feet. Bing swung the board, hitting Guy on the back and shoulders, slowing him down but not incapacitating him, and soon both men were on the ground. Ellie saw fists flying and knew Guy was taking the upper hand. She kicked Guy hard in the ribs once and then again, and when he pulled back from a very bloody Bing, she pointed the gun at his chest.

"Stop. Stop hitting him."

Guy was on his knees, palms up. His voice was soft. "Don't do this, Ellie."

"You've got this all wrong. Nobody's trying to break quarantine. Why would I do that?"

"I want to believe you, Ellie, but you have to give me that gun."

"Get off of Bing. Let him get up." Guy kept his hands out before him as he leaned back. Bing rolled to his side, clutching his ribs, and climbed onto unsteady feet. "We're going to go."

Bing leaned on Ellie's shoulder. "Shoot him."

"I'm not going to shoot him, Bing." Guy began to rise to his feet, and she tightened her grip on the gun. "Unless I have to. I'll shoot you if I have to, just like you were going to shoot me. It's an ugly sight, isn't it? A gun pointed at you by someone you supposedly care about?"

"Don't do this. You don't know what you're getting into."

"Shoot him."

"Shut up, Bing."

Bing leaned in close behind her, and she could smell the blood in his mouth. "All he has to do is yell or pick up his radio and every goon in town will be here. You have to do this."

"You don't have to do this, Ellie. You don't have to do what he says."

"I don't have to do what you say either." The breeze blew Ellie's hair into her eyes, and she shook her head to clear her sight. "Where are all the guards? How did we make it this far, Guy? Why are all these trucks lined up? Is Feno pulling out? Where are you going?"

Bing squeezed her shoulder. "Do you think he's going to tell you the truth? He tried to shoot you. He wants to arrest you, both of us, so Carpenter can beat the shit out of me."

Guy looked at Bing. On his knees with his hands held out, he still looked like the calmest person in the group. "If anyone's going to beat the shit out of you, it's me."

"Oh, you're a real tough guy, aren't you?" Bing spit a bloody wad at his feet.

"Tell me the truth, Guy." She heard Bing swear behind her, spitting more blood out of his wounded mouth. "Why would you think I would break quarantine?"

Guy stared at her for a long moment and then shook his head. "We know about the plan, Ellie. We know about tomorrow. We know about Horizon. If you've been told something different, you are being lied to. Listen to me." He put one foot on the ground before him and started to stand slowly. "If you're not involved in this, you need to tell me what you know, because if you think these people are—"

Bing lunged from behind her shoulder and swung the board into the side of Guy's skull. Guy deflected part of the blow, but Bing swung again, this time connecting to his jaw, and Ellie could see Guy had fallen unconscious. Bing moved for another strike, and she charged into his chest, knocking him backward, her arm fumbling for the board.

"What the hell are you doing? He was telling us something!"

"He was telling you bullshit." Bing spit blood into her face, and Ellie saw tears streaking his swollen cheeks. "He was distracting you like he always does so he could grab the gun. For fuck's sake, Ellie, when are you going to learn that you can't trust him?" He struggled to get past her to kick at the unconscious man, but Ellie pushed him back.

"Leave him alone, Bing. He's down. He's out." She wanted to check to see if Guy could breathe facedown like that, but knew Bing would stop her. She knew they were running out of time. "Let's go. We've got to get the hell out of here before someone tries to radio him." Grabbing Bing by the arm, she dragged him after her until they were both jogging, Bing struggling to take in air through his swollen nose.

"How are we going to get past the gate?" He wheezed wet breaths.

"I don't know. Climb it maybe? We could try to…" Ellie slowed her jog, looking around her. The gate enclosing the Feno compound from the rest of Flowertown stood wide open, unattended. She and Bing scanned the edges of the fencing for cameras, but if they were there, they had to be infrared, because the gate area and the road around it were dark.

"Do you think it's a trap?" Bing whispered.

Ellie stared for a moment, listening. "No. I think it's unmanned. I think Feno's down to a skeleton crew."

"Why? Where would they go?"

She shook her head. "Guy said something about Thursday. Something about horizons."

"You'll forgive me if I don't put a lot of stock in that piece of shit." He stepped forward into the darkness, and he and Ellie held their breath as they passed through the open gate.

"That is very weird, Bing."

He nodded. "Weird and good. Now let's get the hell out of here and find someplace to hide for the rest of our lives. Which, considering how my ribs feel, is about three hours." Ellie let him put his arm around her shoulders as they hurried down the darkened streets toward town.

The power was down throughout the southern public end of Flowertown. Whatever power supply Feno used for their compound, they didn't share it with the general population. A wet spring breeze blew down Avenue Four, and everyone who had a window had it open to catch even a whiff of fresh air. Ellie and Bing didn't have to work hard to stay in the shadows. On the ten-block journey they passed only one Feno security truck, and it seemed in a hurry to head back to the compound.

Bing stopped on a corner and held his side. "Where are we going?"

Ellie looked up and down the cross streets. "I don't know. Want to find Torrez?" Bing pointed to the west. "I don't want to go that way," she told him. "That way's the detention center, and I think we should steer as clear of that as we can."

Bing twisted his torso carefully. "My vote is to go anywhere nobody is going to hit me."

Ellie stared down the darkened west street. "Why didn't they take us to the detention center? I mean, why drive us all the way out to the compound when they could have arrested us and kept us in detention? It's closer. It's built to contain people. We sure as hell couldn't have escaped from there."

"I don't know. And to tell you the truth, I don't care. We're out now. Let's get off the street and try to figure out what we're going to do."

"Agreed. How about we go to Dingle's Market?" Ellie squinted at Bing. "Are you in pain or are you making a face?"

"Both. Why Dingle's?"

"Why not? For one thing, I'm starving. I haven't eaten anything but half a pancake today. And another, Annabeth is the one who gave me the newsletter. I want to see what she knows about the meeting. For all we know she could have been arrested. Why are you making that face?"

Bing followed Ellie down the street toward the market. "Annabeth Dingle creeps me out. That no-sleeping thing. It's weird, that's all."

"Seriously, Bing? We just escaped from the Feno goons and are running for our lives in the world's smallest town and you're afraid of an old woman?"

"I didn't say I was afraid of her." Bing shoved his hands in his pockets. "I would just like to get a little weed in me before I have to face her, okay? Let's run by East Fifth."

"Are you kidding me? Why don't we just send up the bat signal? They're going to be looking for us there."

"That's the last place they're going to look for us. Who would be stupid enough to go home when they're on the lam?" He grinned at her as wide as he could with his split lip. "We'll just run up the back steps, grab the weed, and reassess the situation. Besides, I'm covered in blood. I wouldn't mind a clean shirt."

"This is a hell of time to get tidy, Bing."

Ellie insisted they at least circle the block before trying to get into their apartment building. Like the rest of the blocks they had passed, East Fifth was without power. The windows of the hardware store beneath Ellie's window were dark, as were the neighboring apartment buildings. As they turned the corner to cut into the alley in the back, they saw several people on the top floors leaning out the window, shouting to each other. Ellie and Bing ducked down behind a dumpster, watching to see if another raid was taking place.

No trucks came, no lights flashed, and when Ellie looked up, she saw many of the people were pointing to a spot over the rooftops of the next block. Reassured they hadn't been spotted and that no security would descend upon them, she helped Bing out from the cramped spot. No sooner had he stretched to his full height than someone on the sixth floor yelled down to him.

"Hey, Bing. Bing!" A young man waved his arms, trying to get Bing's attention.

"So much for stealth," Ellie said.

"Bing!" The neighbor continued to yell. "Did you see it? A plane flew over."

"What?" Bing shouted back. "Where? When?"

"Just now." The rest of the window-hangers pointed over the rooftops toward the east. "It was a single-engine plane, flew really low, landed on the other side of the barrier."

"That's impossible." Ellie shook her head. "This is a no-fly zone. Always has been."

Bing looked at her. "I don't know about you, but I'm getting the feeling that 'always has been' is getting ready to change."

They hurried to the back door, and Bing searched around behind the garbage cans to find the crowbar that always lay hidden for the residents. The door was unlocked but was made of heavy steel with no handle on the outside, so the residents of East Fifth made a point of keeping some sort of pry bar handy to get in the back door should the need arise. A quick jimmy and he and Ellie were heading up the steps. Bing clutched his side and let Ellie lead the way. At the fourth floor, the emergency stairwell lights were fading fast, and by the sixth floor, Bing had to keep a hand on Ellie to make it through the dark.

"What are you? Half bat?" He banged his hip against the banister and swore.

"Do you know how many times I've climbed up and down these steps in complete darkness? The lights almost never work."

"Yeah, well, I guess I don't spend as much time in the back stairwell as you do. I take my dates to better places."

Ellie snorted. "Like you have dates."

Bing was breathing hard. "Well, if I did they wouldn't spy on me."

"What do you mean by that?"

Bing shushed her when she pulled open the door for the eighth floor. He peered into the darkness and then pulled Ellie in front of him. "Okay, Batgirl, what do you see? Is anyone there?"

"I can't see in the dark, Bing, I just know the layout by heart. If I had my phone I could use it as a flashlight." She remembered leaving her phone on the bed when the goons had come.

"If we had our phones, they'd be tracking us like bloodhounds."

Ellie led them down the black hall. Several steps in and one of the emergency lights flickered briefly, revealing an empty corridor, so she hurried them along to Bing's room. It was unlocked as always.

"Aren't you ever afraid someone's going to steal your weed?"

"If somebody really wants in, a lock won't keep them out." Like Bing, Ellie knew the layout of the apartment by heart and tiptoed through the many pots of plants to the easy chair by the window while Bing rummaged around for a flashlight. "This will have to do." He pulled his lighter out and began lighting a plate full of squat, half-burned candles.

"Were you having a séance or something?"

"I like the ambiance of candlelight. It helps me think." He crouched down beside his coffee table and began searching through boxes.

"What are you looking for?"

Bing opened and closed lids, grabbing small baggies as he went. "Different flavors for different moods. I don't know how long it will be before I can get back here to restock. Plus I've got a purple weed somewhere in here that's better than aspirin. God knows I could use it."

Ellie left him to his search and moved closer to the candles. While she felt safer in the dark, the shadows were making her jumpy. She knelt down and skimmed through Bing's many books as he muttered to himself behind her. She pulled a heavy book from the shelf, holding it up in the dim light to see if she was reading the title correctly. "*The Divisible Flock,*" she whispered, reading aloud. She had to squint to see the subtitle. "*Managing the Human Herd.* Shit, Bing."

"Are you talking to me?" Bing was lying on his back, reaching into the undercarriage of the easy chair for something.

Ellie leafed through the book, unable to read the dense text in the dark. "What did you mean about Guy spying on me?"

Bing grunted as he freed a plastic cylinder from the chair's springs. "You're kidding, right? You heard the recording. How do you think Carpenter got that? Guy obviously planted a bug when he was in your room the other night."

"You don't know that. Any one of those goons could have done it. At any time."

"Come on, Ellie. That's pretty thick denial. Even for you." He opened the cylinder and breathed deep. "Ah, Willy Nilly. A very special blend. Good for what ails you. Want some?"

Ellie shook her head, tracing her fingers over the unbroken binding of the book as Bing crawled over to join her.

"You're not taking the cure or anything, are you? When's the last time you smoked?"

FLOWERTOWN

"I don't know. I just don't feel like it. It's like my mind is trying to pull a thousand different strings together and I don't even know what I'm pulling at."

Bing took the book from her hand and put it back on the shelf. "Heavy reading isn't what you need. You need to face the truth. And this will help." He handed her a burning joint. She hit it, but not very hard. She didn't want to offend her friend; she just wanted a clear head.

"I don't even know where to begin to look for the truth."

"I'll start." He took the joint back from her. "The first truth is you hooked up with a shitty guy who sold you out. Plain and simple." Ellie started to protest, but he talked over her. "I know it hurts and it sucks and it's not fair, but let's face it: he sold out to Feno like a good little corporate drone would. I'm not saying he didn't care about you. He probably did, as much as a jackass can. But when push came to shove, he bugged your room. He turned you in."

"But he's been helping me."

"How?" Bing coughed out a laugh. "By bringing your phone back so he can tap your room? By not taking a rubber hose to you when he interrogated you?"

"He also let me get away when they were busting the secret meeting." Ellie flinched.

"Oh really? You failed to mention that part. Guy was in on that bust?" He snubbed the joint on the bottom of his sneaker. "Well then, that certainly makes him trustworthy."

"Don't start. I don't know what to think."

"You do know what to think, Ellie. You just don't want to think it."

"But why is this happening? What does he think I'm doing?" Ellie lay back on the floor and stared at the dark

269

ceiling. "I've been invisible for almost seven years, and all of a sudden I'm a person of interest. Everyone's watching me."

"I don't know if I'd go that far."

"Really, Bing? Then why did Mr. Carpenter come to my office and try to arrest me? Why did they put a guard on me?" Even the small hit of the joint was making her thoughts jumble and scatter, popping up out of order. "And how did he know I wasn't in the building when the bomb went off?"

"You told him."

"No." She shook her head, feeling the familiar softness of her thoughts. "I told him I was inside. I told the clerk I was inside. You told me to say I was in the building and to lie about my med check."

"Oh, so this is my fault now?"

"That's not what I'm saying, Bing. I'm saying that…" She rubbed her eyes, her thoughts running together. "I don't know what I'm saying. I'm tired."

He braced himself on her shoulder as he unfolded himself from the floor. "I know how you feel. I'm tired too. I'm tired of bleeding and feeling my pulse under my eye, thanks to your boyfriend and his buddies punching on me. I'm tired of having my shirt glued to me with my own blood." He pulled the shirt over his head with effort, and even by candlelight Ellie could see dark bruises coming up on his ribs.

"That looks painful."

"Another keen observation from you." He struggled to pull a black T-shirt over his head. "How do I look now?"

"Stealthy."

"Excellent. How about you? Do you want to change?" He shook his head. "Let me rephrase that. Why don't you change your shirt? You want one of mine?"

"What?" Ellie gave a mock gasp. "And get Ellie funk on it? Never. Let's go."

She led him back down the darkened stairwell, and by the time they made it to the third floor, the power was flickering back on. Down the hallway, people had their doors open to let the breeze blow through their rooms. As they passed, several people saw Ellie and ducked inside. Word of the arrest had traveled quickly. Just before the bathrooms, two teenage boys gawked at her as if she were carrying damning evidence in her arms. They didn't avert their eyes until Ellie stopped and challenged them with a hard glare. Then they turned and found something much more interesting in the toilet closets to discuss.

"Nosy little fuckers." Ellie didn't think to check if anyone was waiting inside her room. She threw open the door with a bang and flipped on the light, hardly noticing Rachel's absence. She was about to continue her opinion of intrusive neighbors when Bing held his hand up to silence her. He pointed to the ceiling and mouthed the word "bug." Ellie nodded, suddenly aware that she was being recorded. She couldn't believe Guy would bug her room, but if they found a bug it would be hard to deny.

Bing ran his fingers along the bed frame and underneath her nightstand. Ellie joined the search, her only knowledge of finding hidden bugs coming from watching cop shows on television. She worked her way across her nightstand, checking under dirty ashtrays and empty cans. She almost hated to search Rachel's nightstand for fear of toppling the impossible pile of papers and magazines. Leaning back against the wall was a broken lamp Rachel insisted on keeping. Ellie turned it up, looking under the base like the cops did on

TV. And just like the cops on TV, she saw a small wire with a microphone on the end.

Ellie ripped the thin wire from the base and showed it to Bing. He held up his hands to say "I told you so" as Ellie crushed the device under an ashtray. Not satisfied with that, she held the frayed wire over her lighter until it began to smoke, then dropped it into a half-empty can of old soda.

"I think you got it," Bing said as she hurled the can out the open window. Ellie gripped the windowsill, feeling her fingers tingle once again with the black rage that never seemed far from the surface. Bing put his hand on her shoulder, and she shook him off.

"What if it wasn't Guy who put that there?"

"Jesus, Ellie, you can't be serious."

"What if it's Rachel?"

Bing stared at her, blinking. "That's impossible."

"Is it? Why is that more impossible than Guy?"

"Because..." He waved his hands, looking for words. "Because Rachel's a kid. Rachel doesn't work for Feno."

"Rachel said it herself—she's worked everywhere in this place. She knew the code for the meeting. She's on the tape with the confession and she didn't get arrested. The wire was under her lamp, a lamp that's never worked, that she insists on keeping." Ellie could feel sweat on her upper lip as the hot logic of this impossible idea took root.

Bing grabbed her by the shoulders. "Listen to yourself, Ellie. You think Rachel is trying to get you arrested? Rachel? Who next? Me? The lady down the hall with the snot-nose kids? Annabeth Dingle? It's Guy, Ellie. It's Guy. It's always been Guy. Face it."

Ellie folded her arms over her chest, not meeting Bing's eyes. "It's just that…I don't know. I mean, why? Why would Guy do that?"

He softened his tone and rubbed his hands over her arms. "I don't know. I don't know what's going on or why he would use you like that, but you have to listen to me. Are you listening?" He lifted her chin until she looked up at him. "Do you trust me?" She nodded. "Something is going on, and you may be in a lot of trouble. I really need you to pull it together."

"I'm together."

"Are you? Are you sure?" He brushed her hair out of her eyes. "I've known you a long time, Ellie. I knew you way back when, remember? I know you don't always like to face things the way they are."

Ellie turned her face from his hands and stepped back. "I'm fine. I told you that. I'm fine. Now shut up and let me find something to wear that doesn't have your blood all over it." She tossed her dirty shirt onto the growing heap of ruined clothes and knelt down beside the bed to find a cleaner one.

"Shit, you still have Guy's gun?"

She pulled another shirt from the pile under the bed and pulled it down over the gun in her waistband. "Hell yes, I do. You think I'm going to give it back to him?"

"No, I think you should get rid of it. I think you should leave it here."

"Why?"

"Because I don't want you getting pissed at me and shooting me."

Ellie stepped up close to Bing. "Then don't piss me off."

CHAPTER NINETEEN

The power was on at Dingle's Market, and Ellie pushed open the door with force. She didn't bother to check if anyone else was in the store. She marched, with Bing in tow, to the back of the store where Annabeth's stool stood empty. Ellie banged on the counter.

"Annabeth? Are you here? It's Ellie Cauley." Bing put his hand on her shoulder to quiet her, but she glared at him and he drew back. "I need to talk with you."

The curtains parted and Annabeth stepped through. "Ellie? And Bing? It's been a long time since I've seen you, Bing. I didn't expect to see you here. What's going on?" Ellie gripped the counter, struggling to find the words to express the enormity of what she was feeling. Before she could utter a sound, the curtain parted again.

"Rachel." Ellie could hardly say the word.

"Oh my gosh, Ellie, are you okay?"

She could feel Bing move in more closely behind her. "Okay is probably not the word I would use," she said. "Did you know our room was bugged?" Rachel said nothing. "Yeah, they have a recording of you and me talking about the stolen files and yet, oddly, Bing and I got arrested. They walked right past you."

"Do you think I—"

"I don't know, Rachel. You tell me. You told us about the code for the meeting and those people all got arrested too. How does that happen?"

Rachel's pale cheeks mottled with red as she stepped up to meet Ellie across the counter. "I don't know, Ellie. I don't know what you think I'm doing, but if you think I have any kind of pull in this shit hole," she spit the profanity out, "you are very, very mistaken. Want proof?"

She slammed a wrinkled sheet of paper on the counter.

When Ellie didn't move, Bing reached past her for the sheet. "What is it?"

"It's my test results." Rachel spoke only to Ellie. "I'm not clear to go."

"That's impossible." Bing scanned the sheet.

Annabeth put her arm around the girl, but she shook her off and leaned in closer to Ellie. "Nope, it's all there. So whatever you think I did to you, however fucked you think you are, I assure you, I am ten times more fucked."

"Don't talk like that," Bing said.

"Shut up, Bing. I can talk any way I want. I can use every fucking dirty word I know, and why not? It's not like I'm ever getting out of this filthy, stinking shit hole. All I have to look forward to now is turning into another greasy, lazy, burned-out stoner nut job like my roommate."

Ellie stepped behind the counter and came close to her. Neither woman spoke. They stared at each other, Rachel bracing herself for whatever Ellie might say, but Ellie didn't speak. She reached out and pulled Rachel tight in her arms, where the younger woman broke into hard, gasping sobs. Ellie cradled her, stroking her hair and whispering in her ear, letting Rachel cling to her until she couldn't cry another tear.

Annabeth waited until they had drawn apart to speak. "I think it's time for all of you to learn what's really going on in the zone. We need to be in this together or none of us will make it. I was just getting ready to show Rachel. Ellie, Bing, from what I'm hearing, I think you need to know as well. Lock the front door and come with me."

Bing hurried to the door and threw the bolt, then slipped through the curtain to join the rest in the crowded storeroom at the back of Dingle's Market. The tiny space was cramped with cardboard boxes and loading pallets. Annabeth waited until Bing pulled the curtain, then headed back behind a wooden shelf holding cleaning supplies. On the floor, at the base of the shelf, was a pallet stacked with plastic-wrapped cases of canned vegetables.

"Through here."

Rachel made a sound of surprise as the old woman lifted the loaded pallet as easily as if it weighed nothing. Annabeth laughed.

"The cans are empty. My son made the hatch." Beneath the pallet were steep, narrow steps to the basement of the market. Annabeth went first, tapping on the side of the step three times before entering. She waited until she heard three taps from within before stepping down. "This way."

The visitors were all wide-eyed as they followed the old woman into the cellar. At first there was nothing to see, just old beams and shelves stacked with more cans of food. Bing had to duck as they stepped through a small door and came out into a wide, low-ceilinged room strewn with cables and car batteries. On one wall hung two televisions, and beside them a young man scrolled through a computer screen. Two walls were covered in large sheets of paper, full of notes and newspaper clippings and photographs, and on the final wall, the wall the door led through, hung gun racks loaded with shotguns and pistols of every size, over boxes of bullets of every caliber.

Annabeth held her hands out toward the scene. "Welcome to All You Want."

The three fanned out, still gaping. Ellie stood before the television sets, which were on with no volume. "What is this?"

The kid at the computer didn't look up from his screen. "This is everything you haven't been seeing in Flowertown for the last three years."

"I told you they were censoring information." Bing punched Ellie's arm as they stared at the screens. "You said I was crazy."

"I stand corrected."

Annabeth stood beside them. "Oh, it's more than censorship. We're being fed quite a show. We don't know how long it's been going on, but we've been onto it for about two and a half years now. Remember when the cable went out for a couple of months and we lost all the upper channels?"

"I remember," Rachel said. "We used to get HBO and Showtime, and then it was nothing but home shopping and sports."

"It wasn't just the movie channels we lost," Annabeth said, and Bing nodded.

"We lost the news channels too."

"That's right, Bing. Nobody thought much of it at the time. But then we couldn't even get the Sioux City news. It started coming in from Fort Dodge. Or so we thought." Annabeth shook her head. "Turns out you can only hold twenty pounds of cow shit in a ten-pound bag for so long. Mistakes started happening. News bulletins would break in with different newspeople than we were seeing on the six o'clock broadcast. Different channel logos would flash on and off. Hell, even some sports scores were wrong." Annabeth put her hand on the shoulders of the boy at the computer.

"You all know my grandson, Matt, right?" He looked up. In his late teens, his eyes immediately went to Rachel. "Well, it was Matt and the Clark twins who figured out what to do. You know that Mindy Clark has never yet met a tree she couldn't climb, and they managed to get up that cable pole and split that signal. They put some kind of gizmo on it that unscrambles the scramble. I never asked them to explain. All I know is that suddenly we're watching a whole different set of newscasts than everybody else in Flowertown."

Bing stared at the boy as if he had become a unicorn. "You knew how to do that?"

The boy shrugged. "Yeah. Wasn't that hard once you knew what to look for. They scramble the signal every couple of months, you know, an automated security feature, but it usually only takes me a couple of hours to unscramble it."

Ellie stared at the screen, watching highlights from a basketball game. "So what is it we weren't seeing? What were they blocking?"

"That was the kicker," Annabeth said, taking a seat on a bench near her grandson. "At first we didn't see anything.

We watched those newscasts side by side, night after night, and there was hardly any difference, except for the reporters, of course, and a few local stories. The commercials were different a lot of the times, but that's to be expected. We thought maybe we had just gotten paranoid. It happens. And then the Senate hearings started."

Bing spoke up. "About the army funding. I saw it online one day in the morning. Of course, the Internet didn't stay on long enough to actually read it."

"People thought it was costing too much to keep the army here. There were hearings, protests, special elections. And we never heard a word about it."

"Wait a minute," Ellie said, holding up her hand. "What about the newspapers? Mr. MacDonald gets all the papers, even the *New York Times*." Matt Dingle snickered, and Annabeth shushed him as she rose to her feet once again.

"You know that chili of mine you like so much, Ellie?" Ellie nodded and followed Annabeth to the first wall of notes and clippings. "Well, I order that special from Culvert's Meats in Council Bluffs. And one day, in one of the boxes, I see that the packers lined the carton with a *USA Today*. I didn't recognize the headline, and I read all the papers whenever I get a chance. Turns out this particular edition was one that didn't get delivered to Mr. MacDonald."

"And? So we didn't get a paper one day."

"Not just one day, Ellie. And not just one paper. This paper had a story in it about Feno Chemical coming close to filing bankruptcy. Well, I asked the folks at Culvert's Meat real nicely if they wouldn't mind to keep packing the chili the way they did, and wouldn't you know, every time we got a paper in a carton that we hadn't gotten at the newsstand, there was some sort of story about Feno or Barlay or the protests about the army being in Flowertown."

Bing nodded. "They're controlling the information we get about the zone."

"But why?" Ellie asked. "It's not like we can do anything about it. No matter what happens, we're stuck here."

"That's not entirely true," Annabeth said. "We started stockpiling supplies. Of course, most of us hadn't turned over all of our weapons. You know how it is on a farm, Rachel. There's usually a secret stash of the necessities under the floorboards, right?" Rachel nodded. "And we all took to being very careful in our communications with each other and with our families on the outside. It stood to reason that if the news was being censored, our mail was being read."

Bing punched Ellie once more on the arm in triumph. Her complaint was shushed when they heard the door to the cellar opening. Annabeth's grandson reached for the pistol sitting beside the computer until they all heard three soft raps. Everyone relaxed as Matt tapped three times on the floor, then someone came down the steps. Annabeth smiled when she saw who it was.

"Ellie, I believe you know Olivia." The med tech with the strawberry birthmark cleared the low door and stopped at the sight of the small crowd. Annabeth made introductions.

Olivia didn't bother with a greeting. "You haven't been taking the pills, have you?"

Ellie shook her head, too surprised to speak, and Bing nudged her. "You're not taking your meds? Since when?"

"Since my med check yesterday. The one that got me arrested." Ellie pointed at Olivia. "The one that happened when the med center was closed. What was that?"

Olivia moved past them to the wall of notes and tacked a set of prescription pages to the board. "I had to get a blood sample from you. I couldn't do it through the regular channels, so I paged you using another tech's code, one of Feno's boys. We had to contact all of you, to see if the H had changed. Oh, and Marianne wanted me to apologize to you for being such a bitch. It's the easiest way to tell if you've got it."

Ellie stared at her. "Am I supposed to understand what you're talking about?"

Olivia turned to Annabeth. "I've only got about fifteen minutes before I've got to get back. The timetable has been moved up. They're making an announcement about the release. It's the Es, just like I thought."

Annabeth folded her arms, a worried line on her forehead. "Could we be wrong about this? If it's the Es, that's an awful lot of people."

Olivia nodded. "It's sixty-five percent of the locals. Ninety-eight percent of Feno. That doesn't leave a lot of people behind. I think we've been right all along."

Rachel stepped closer to Olivia. "Are you talking QEH? The file codes? I'm a Q; what does that mean?"

Olivia and Annabeth shared a serious look. "It means you're staying here with the rest of us. The word is Saturday Feno is releasing everyone on the E with a clean bill of health."

Bing's eyes grew wide as Olivia spoke. "You said 'on the E.' What does that mean?"

"The E program. Equilibrium. It's the name of the third phase of medications. Obviously the most successful." She looked at Rachel. "You're on Quantum, along with about sixteen percent of us, including me, Annabeth, and Matt. There are only a few Hs."

"Like me, right?" Ellie asked, and Olivia nodded. "Let me guess. Horizon."

"How did you know?"

Ellie looked at Bing. "A very reliable source told me. He also mentioned that something is going down tomorrow, not Saturday."

"That's the press conference." Annabeth looked at a calendar taped to the wall. "In the clean rooms. They're bringing in the national media. Now we know why, to announce the release of the Es."

"Well, according to Guy, something is going to happen on Thursday, and it sounded more serious than a press conference. And it sounded like I was going to be involved. Why would Horizon be singled out?"

Olivia pulled out her phone and started texting while she spoke. "I'm going to be late. I'm calling in. I need to know everything you heard about tomorrow and I'll tell you what I can." She slid the phone back in her pocket and headed to the second wall of notes. She pulled a box out from a pile and rifled through looking for a folder.

"How much do you know about the BTM scale?"

"I'm a two," Rachel said, and Olivia cracked her first smile.

"Why doesn't that surprise me? What about you?"

Bing answered quickly. "Four."

"Me too."

Ellie looked around the group. "What am I?" Olivia looked at her in disbelief.

Rachel shook her head. "Ellie never pays attention to anything."

"Well, you'd better pay attention to this." Olivia opened the file. "You're a six on the BTM scale, Ellie. That's a scale of one to seven. None of us knew exactly what that meant when we got classified, and we still don't know everything. It was a psychological profiling tool named after Byrd, Tabor, and Marcum, the three doctors Feno brought in when quarantine turned long-term."

"Classifying people by their psychological profiles," Bing said. "Like they do in hostage situations or prisoner of war interrogations. I've read about this."

"Exactly." Olivia flipped through the file, looking for something. "It didn't seem that important at the time. I mean, hell, they were running forty tests a week on us. What difference did another one make? The doctors were working undercover as lab techs and file clerks, just mixed in the general population. Then Dr. Tabor, the T in BTM, apparently changed his mind about the program and tried to contact the federal government. He said their findings were being used unethically, and he wanted a full-scale investigation."

She pulled a picture out of the folder. "Unfortunately, he waited too long to make his request. By then the censors were in place and the complaint never got filed. Or if it did, it got buried. He knew he'd been found out and started sneaking information to local techs like me and Marianne. It wasn't much, but he told us to watch the changes in medications. That they were tailoring the new rounds of meds not just to your physical requirements, but to your psych profile too. He said it was all very aboveboard except that he and his team had hand-selected a group of people to be what Feno referred to as their 'fail-safe' should anything go wrong."

Ellie seemed to be the only person in the room not understanding what she was hearing. "Why are you telling us this?"

Olivia held the photo to her chest. "As far as we can tell, the BTM breaks people down into three groups. Ones and twos are classified as docile, obedient even. People who don't struggle under changes in authority."

"I'm not docile," Rachel said. "Am I?"

Bing smiled at her as Olivia continued. "The majority of the population is three through five: moderately civil, frustrated, but generally working at a functioning level."

"And now we get to my tribe, right?" Ellie folded her arms. "The dreaded sixes and sevens. Tell me what fun surprises we have for the team."

"Sixes and sevens are at the extreme end of the spectrum. Tendencies to violence, anger issues, compulsive behavior. Generally antisocial." Olivia was the only one looking at Ellie. She could feel her throat tighten as she asked the next question.

"So should I assume we were the subject of Dr. Tabor's concern?"

Olivia nodded. "It took us a while to cross-reference everything. All of the files are kept on paper, not on any computer we could find. Feno is paranoid about being hacked, and for good reason. Matt's already been in their personnel records twice. We began to notice, when the QEH meds were assigned, that most of the H meds were given to sixes and sevens. The doses were always changing and the blood tests were classified. Then, about six months ago, we saw another trend. Sixes and sevens in the H class were being blue-tagged. Just about every one of you is."

Bing put his arm around Ellie, who had grown very pale. "What are you saying to her? That she's being poisoned? That Horizon is killing her?"

"No—at least we don't think so. We think Horizon contains certain psychotropic compounds that might exacerbate preexisting tendencies."

Ellie gripped Bing's arm. "Want to try that in English for the rest of us?"

Olivia nodded. "We think they might be chemically inciting you to violence. That once the majority of residents have been cleared, H-sixes and H-sevens will react violently enough that Feno will be justified in clamping down on us in a stronger and more permanent fashion."

Annabeth sighed. "We think if the remaining group is small enough, when the world thinks enough people have been saved, Feno will move those of us they can't cure to a more contained area, maybe even just a compound, until they can dispose of us and make Flowertown disappear."

"And they think they're going to blame that on me?" Ellie asked. "That I'm just going to do what they say? I wasn't handpicked by anybody. I don't care how they classify me."

Olivia turned over the photograph and Bing closed his eyes, pulling Ellie closer. "Do you know this man?" Ellie shook her head.

"What are you saying, Ellie?" Bing looked down at her.

"I've never seen that man in my life. I swear."

Bing sighed. "I have. He was a doctor in East Fifth. He was your doctor, Ellie."

CHAPTER TWENTY

Ellie pulled away from Bing and found herself in the center of the group. She tried to laugh but felt short of breath. "So what are you saying? That I'm some sort of ninja death sleeper agent? That I'm going to be activated or something?" Bing reached out his hand, but she pulled back, folding her arms tightly across her body. "I'm telling you I have no memory of that man."

"You were on a lot of drugs. I know. I was there too."

She knew the more she argued the crazier she sounded, but she couldn't stop herself. "I'm telling you, I'm good with faces. I may not remember names or how I know you, but I always remember faces."

"Yeah," Bing said, "you're a real people person."

"There are symptoms of Horizon psychotropics." Olivia kept her voice neutral, like a doctor delivering a bad diagnosis. "Deep flushing on your face, numbness and tingling in your extremities, difficulty swallowing, constricting of airways."

"All right, all right, I get it." Ellie paced to the back of the room. "I think we've all got the picture. But I'm not taking the meds anymore, so it's not really a problem, is it?" She could read the answer on Olivia's face and held up her hands to block it. "You know what? Let's not worry about me right now, okay? I'm fine. I'm here. I'm aware of what's happening. There are other things we should be worried about, right? Guy said something was going down Thursday night."

Bing shoved his hands in his pockets. "I think he meant you."

"You don't know that." Ellie kept pacing.

"I know this," Olivia said. "I've got to get back to the med center. I'm late and they're going to miss me. We're trying to get some kind of evidence against Feno together to give to somebody who's getting out Saturday. We've got to find Es who are willing to help."

Bing's voice cracked. "I'm an E. I am." Rachel's mouth hung open in surprise, and Ellie had to bend from the waist to catch her breath. Bing was leaving her. She could feel the blood rushing to her head. Bing didn't seem to notice her distress. "I can help. I can take whatever you want."

"It won't be that easy." Olivia headed for the stairs. "They're probably going to give you new clothes from the skin out and do a final cleaning. They're not going to let anything get out of here easily."

"Don't worry about that," Bing said. "I'm very good at subterfuge. You get me whatever evidence you can and I'll get it out of here."

Olivia smiled and pointed to his face. "You going hide it under your cheekbones?"

Bing touched his bruised face. "This is a little gift from Ellie's 'source' that I plan on paying back in kind."

"Well, however you get it out, we appreciate the help."

Ellie heard the hatch door close as she circled the room. One-two-three calming breaths and she felt her throat opening. She let her mind wander around the image of Dr. Tabor, but nothing about him raised any memory. She didn't care what Bing said. She'd remember a doctor, wouldn't she? Ellie stopped in front of one of the paper-covered walls.

"I've seen this before."

Bing glanced at what she was staring at. "I should hope so. It's our country."

Ellie threw him a dagger of a look. "Not just the map, these dots. I saw these." She closed her eyes and thought, not wanting to admit that she didn't trust her memory. "At the Feno compound, when I was locked in that classroom. This was on the news."

Matt looked over his shoulder to see what she meant. "Yeah, I think they keep the real news feed on in some rooms at Feno. That's the map of their 'discoveries.'" He held his fingers up for air quotations and then turned back to his computer. Annabeth came over to the wall.

"These are the locations Feno claims that contaminees have been found. Red pins are confirmed sites, blue are rumored." She pointed to pushpins in various states on the map.

Ellie touched the pins in disbelief. "So people have broken quarantine?"

Annabeth scratched her head. "In a manner of speaking, I guess. See this one?" She pointed to a pin in southwest Georgia. "That was where they found my neighbor, Paul Collins, on February eleventh of last year. Which is really interesting when you consider that Paul died on February ninth, two days before his 'escape.'" Bing and Rachel looked over her shoulder.

"And see this one? Up here near Pierre? That was Davis Chowith. You remember him, don't you, Rachel? Went to school with your sister Elaine?"

"Yeah." Rachel stared at the map as if she would see him posted there. "He's dead too."

"That's right. Just before that Thanksgiving two years ago. They found his body frozen in a car in South Dakota on the Saturday after. Claimed he was the first escapee." Annabeth's voice got tight as she spoke. "There were a bunch in South Dakota, right around the holidays, mostly older folks. Some good friends, good people, who just couldn't make it through another winter in here." Rachel reached out and took her hand. "Maybe the meds were too much or their hearts just couldn't take it anymore. I was with some of them in the care center when they passed. Never even got to give them a burial."

Behind them, Matt typed furiously. "We've got another one. A breaking story. Looks like another discovery." He typed harder. "Damn it. They're scrambling it again."

"Language, young man."

"Sorry, Grandma." He typed in a few more lines and waited. "This is going to take a minute, but I'll get it."

Annabeth smiled at her grandson. "He's a good boy. And very talented."

Ellie wasn't listening. She stared at the map of the United States with her head tilted. "Have they ever found anybody alive?"

"No. I've never heard of anyone escaping. Or even trying. It's impossible." Annabeth shook her head. "And why would they? These were good people. They would never risk contaminating anyone else."

"And they've never found any sign of contamination at these sites?"

Bing stared at the map. "What are you thinking, Ellie?"

"Do you know what order these were found in, Annabeth?"

The older woman tapped her finger against her lip. "Oh, let me think. It's written under the pictures. I know Davis was first, and Sandra Sammons might have been second, or maybe she was after—"

"No," Ellie paced before the map. "Not by person. By state. Do you know the order of the states that were threatened with contamination?" She looked at Annabeth. "Or better yet, let me tell you. First was South Dakota. A bunch, all close together, you said. Then Oklahoma, right? A rural spot, not too close to any big cities?"

"That's right. How did you know that?"

"Then the rumors started about Kansas and Mississippi." Ellie pointed to the two blue pins. "But it wasn't until Georgia that they confirmed another body. That's right, isn't it?"

"Yes," Annabeth said, her eyes wide. "Just this January."

"It was in the South, not too close to Atlanta. Closer to Florida, closer to where they found the next body. Central Florida. Not Miami or St. Petersburg. Nothing on the coast, nothing touristy, but close." Ellie was talking to herself at this point. "Then there was a gap. I'd say, a month? A month and a half? That's when the rumors started about a body in Ohio, where?" She looked closer at the blue pin. "Just south of Columbus, the capital. Close, but that's a pretty rural area, isn't it? Mostly farms, but close to the capital city."

"That's right. How did you know that? They're all rural locations." Annabeth stepped closer to the map, next to Ellie. "That's why we think they're going to relocate us. We think maybe they're scouting locations that will work, that can be contained." The older woman's voice rose as she spoke. "We think maybe they're taking soil samples or maybe testing the viability of the areas. Or maybe even, God forbid, testing another pesticide." Rachel took the old woman's hand again, trying to comfort her in what was obviously a frightening train of thought, but Ellie didn't look away from the map.

"I don't think so, Annabeth. I don't think that's it."

Bing watched Ellie's hand trace the path of discovery. "What are you thinking?"

"It's got to be Feno, right? I mean, who else could get a body out of Flowertown?"

He shrugged. "The army?"

"Yeah, but why would they? What would be the gain of creating a scare of contamination across the country?"

"Maybe to keep the funding, more money for the military."

Ellie scrunched up her face and then shook her head. "They wouldn't need to go through all that to make that argument. Think of the risks. They could create the illusion of a crisis right here with just a few well-placed disruptions. Or even just reports of them."

Bing stared at her. "You mean, like, explosions? Hello."

"No." Ellie waved him off, staring at the map like the answer was emerging from the faded ink itself. "Those just started. This has been going on for two years. At regular intervals in a sort of spiral. See? It's moving away from Iowa but not in a direct line. Radiating outward. Never in an urban area, but always getting closer to one. Moving out of the center of the country toward the coasts. Toward the East Coast." Ellie pressed her fingers to her forehead. "Did you say there was another one, Matt?"

"Yeah, I'm trying to unscramble it right now. It's running through the program."

Ellie's voice was a whisper. "I know where it's going to be."

Bing moved in. "Where? How can you know where it's going to be?"

"Here." She pointed to Washington, D.C. "Not here exactly. Not in the District, but nearby. Within driving distance, less than two hours, I'd say. In a rural area but affluent. Maybe Virginia. Suburban Maryland."

"Why do you say that?"

Ellie smiled at Bing. "Because that's where I'd put it."

"Got it!" Matt pounded on the desk. "Breaking news, PennCo contaminee discovered, woman, deceased, come on, tell me where. Here. Just outside of Falls Church, Virginia."

"You were right." Annabeth sounded impressed.

"Oh shit." Ellie put both hands on her head, trying to absorb the implications of being right. "I am right. That's what they're doing."

Annabeth put her hand on Ellie's shoulder. "Honey, if you know something about where they're taking us, you'd better start talking."

"This has got nothing to do with us going anywhere. This has got nothing to do with us period. At least, not directly. Didn't you say Feno was going bankrupt?" Annabeth nodded. "How's Barlay Pharma doing? Matt, can you check their stock prices?"

"I do it every day." He spoke over his shoulder, keeping his eye on his screen. "They've been going up slowly, but rose pretty sharply last month."

Ellie nodded. "They've spread the rumors to the investors. It's happening."

"What's happening?" Bing grabbed her arm. "What are you seeing?"

"This!" She banged on the map. "This is not an accident. They didn't place those bodies randomly. And they're not researching anything. They don't need bodies for that. This isn't an investigation." She turned and looked at the bewildered faces before her. "It's a campaign."

Nobody spoke for several seconds until Rachel whispered, "For what?"

"For fear. Or more precisely, concern. Not terror. They don't want panic. They want concern, awareness. They are slowly and carefully bringing awareness of Flowertown back into the forefront of the American consciousness."

Bing shook his head. "But why? What's the benefit of that?"

"They've got a vaccine."

Annabeth cocked her head to the side. "Well of course they've got a vaccine. What do you think we've been taking all these years?"

"No, not for us. We've been taking treatments. Barlay is marketing a vaccine for the rest of the country. They're banking on fear of contamination to market their vaccine. And I'd bet they're not playing small potatoes. They're going for a government contract. A big one. Nationwide.

Maybe even global. How else could they possibly recover the money they've lost?"

Bing nodded several times. "That makes sense." Rachel bit her lip, a gesture Ellie knew meant she was uncertain. Before she could say anything, Matt let out a sigh.

"Oh shit."

Annabeth marched over to his seat. "What have I told you about language like that?" She caught her breath. "Oh shit."

"What is it?" Rachel hurried over to them and saw what was on Matt's screen. When she looked back at Bing and Ellie, her eyes were filling up. "They've identified the woman in Virginia. Oh Ellie, I'm so sorry."

"What? Who is it?" She stepped close enough to look over Matt's shoulder, and he rolled away to give her a clear view. On the screen, in an enlarged ID photo, was Big Martha.

Bing stepped up behind her, but Ellie pushed past him, hurrying to the other side of the room. She didn't breathe until she pressed her forehead against the bulletin board, and when the jagged sob broke free it rustled papers all around her face. Ellie pushed her fists into her stomach, trying to hold back the howl that wanted to rip out of her. She didn't want to turn around and see the soft eyes of the others in the room. She didn't want to see the map of Feno's marketing strategy. She didn't want to see the tough, thick face of her boss being spread across the national news as a domestic terrorist. Ellie raised her head. She did want to see it.

"Bring that picture back up."

"Ellie, don't do this to yourself."

She pushed past Bing again and pounded on Matt's desk. "Can you bring the picture back up? Full screen?" Matt nodded, checking with his grandmother before scrolling back through the story to find the photo. He clicked on the photo and Big Martha's face filled the screen again. Ellie jabbed at the print underneath the photo. "Look at that. Look what that says."

Rachel leaned in to read. "It's her med tag."

"Yeah, look at the end. Big Martha was an H just like me. Only she was an H seven."

"Big Martha?" Bing looked to make sure. "Wow, I wouldn't have guessed that. If I'd have known I would have been more careful about bringing that stinky soup up." He looked at Ellie and they both laughed, even with tears in their eyes. "I'm really sorry. I know you liked her a lot. And she liked you too."

Ellie let Bing pull her to his chest. She felt his shirt get damp against her cheek and breathed in the smell of clean laundry. She knew it had to be killing him, letting her wrap her arms around his bruised ribs, but he said nothing.

"What are the odds of two dangerous psychos like Martha and me getting jobs in the same office?"

Bing laughed and rubbed her back. "Maybe they thought they could bore you into submission."

Ellie drew her head back from Bing's chest. "But you know, really, what *are* the odds? Isn't that weird? It was supposed to be a secure facility, and they put two people who are supposed to be so dangerous in the same space?"

"Don't start down that road, Ellie. The situation is weird enough without getting paranoid." Bing stepped away. "You were assigned that job after the BTM scale was assigned, but

Martha was probably there from the beginning. It's just a coincidence."

Ellie nodded, unconvinced. "It's kind of hard not to get paranoid, though. If Feno brought in a team of psychiatrists to profile us, they obviously put some stock in that sort of thing. And the records office was the only classified building to blow up. The other places were all storage facilities. I can't help but wonder if whoever set the bomb might have known about my and Martha's classification. You know, if they knew about the plan to have the H-sixes and H-sevens become violent."

"If that's even the plan." Bing took her by the shoulders and looked into her eyes. "No offense to anyone in this room, but this is all a bunch of supposition. We have no proof there is any kind of plan."

"But Olivia said the Horizon meds have psychotropic compounds to make us violent."

"No, she said they think the meds have them." He dropped his voice to speak to her alone. "Not to point out the obvious, but you were in lockdown before they even came up with Horizon. If those meds are doing anything, I think they're making you paranoid."

"I wasn't being paranoid when they put a guard on me because they thought I was stealing classified files."

"You did steal classified files."

"Yeah, afterward." Ellie dropped her gaze. She felt an odd sense of shame and embarrassment, as if the revelation of her medical class had revealed her to be unworthy. Everything she said sounded stupid and desperate to her ears. She couldn't stand what she saw in Bing's eyes. She pushed him away, hating how juvenile she sounded. "What difference does it make to you? You're getting out of here on Saturday."

"Ellie…"

Ellie walked away, relieved when Matt announced he had unscrambled the evening news feed. She joined Rachel and Annabeth before the big screen and waited for the headlines. The news program began with the usual serious drone and the flash of the logo, then the screen filled with an alert of a special bulletin. Annabeth shook her head.

"These are never good."

The camera cut to the news anchor sitting at his desk. Behind him, a specially designed graphic flashed: PennCo Crisis.

"Do we have sound?" Rachel asked, and Matt nodded.

"It's going to take a second. It may not be all clear."

Despite the broken audio track, they were able to piece together the gist of the anchor's story. He talked about something jeopardizing the announcement to be made Friday morning in Flowertown. The screen behind him cut to images of news crews from around the world assembling at the eastern gate of the containment area, awaiting clearance to set up in the clean rooms. The audio cleared enough to hear the news anchor deliver his lead.

"Our sources have just confirmed that the following video was sent from within the PennCo Containment Area to the security offices of Feno Chemical. The identity of the individual is being withheld until further investigation, but we are being told that the threat is being taken with utmost seriousness and that security forces are on high alert. They assure us that at this time the press conference will continue as scheduled, although no confirmation has been received as to the exact reason for the conference." The newsman softened his voice, succeeding in achieving that tone unique to news anchors, a perfect mix of sadness, authority, and enthusiasm. "Of course we are well aware of the rumors that have been growing on the Internet, as well as the hope that has lived in all of our hearts, that the announcement will pertain to the release of the many, many souls quarantined and isolated from their loved ones for so many years. Which makes this video, if it is indeed a viable threat, that much more terrible and tragic."

The graphic behind the anchor grew to fill the screen. A brief test pattern flashed, then static, then the image faded in to a tight shot of enraged eyes. It took a moment for all of them watching to recognize the face as Ellie's. The shot was grainy and jumpy and the audio was unclear, so the television station ran a subscript beneath the image. Ellie didn't need to read it. She remembered every word. Her mouth fell open as she saw herself as the rest of the country would, crazed and dangerous. The words filled the space beneath the images.

"F**k you. F**k Feno. F**k Flowertown. I am going to get out of here. Count on it. I will get out of here if it means killing every last person." The screen jumped as Ellie saw their edit to her tirade. "I don't care what it costs me. I don't care what happens afterward, but I will get out of here." Static cut the image off and the camera shot returned to the anchor.

"Turn it off."

Matt looked at his grandmother, who nodded. Ellie staggered backward until she let herself sit down on the floor, her legs splayed before her. Bing stood slack-jawed, his arms hanging uselessly at his sides, staring at the blank screen. The rest of the room waited for one of them to say something.

Ellie could hardly make her mouth work. "That pin. Remember that pin Carpenter showed me? With the Feno logo? It must have had a camera in it. It must have. And that recorder." She lay on her back, the floor cold and hard against her skin. She thought of her parents and her sisters and her nieces and nephews and friends seeing that video, seeing her so enraged and dangerous and saying those awful, terrifying things. "No wonder Carpenter laughed. He said he couldn't have written it any better himself."

She was an H6. A bunch of stupid letters and numbers on the end of a medical tag she never read about medicines she took without question. And now she was a weapon.

She closed her eyes, unable to move. "Still think I'm paranoid, Bing?"

CHAPTER TWENTY-ONE

They left Ellie lying on the floor. She heard Bing whispering to them, no doubt telling them that it was probably best not to bother her. She had become one of "those people," people who needed special handling. That wasn't exactly right, was it? She had returned to being one of those people, people who got locked up in small rooms with large pills. As Bing had so helpfully reminded her, she had been one of those people before Feno had ever started with the Horizon regimen. They didn't give her Horizon to make her crazy; they gave it to her because she was crazy. She was crazy and dangerous and they planned on using that for whatever plan they had laid. Ellie took a deep breath and felt the butt of the gun dig into her skin. Fuck that.

She sat straight up and uttered her thoughts aloud. "Fuck that." Everyone in the room turned to her as she got to her feet and dusted herself off. "Feno thinks I'm so dangerous they can use me as some kind of weapon? Fuck that. We need a plan."

Bing grinned. "There's my Ellie. I knew you wouldn't take this lying down."

"Glad to have you on board." Annabeth nodded to her. "Olivia gets off from the med center in about an hour. It looks like we're going to be up all night working out some details. Who wants chili?" Rachel laughed and Annabeth play-punched her arm. "Laugh all you want, little missy. An army runs on its stomach, and nobody can be brave and hungry. Bing, have you ever had my chili?"

"Yes ma'am." Bing put his arm around Ellie. "It's Ellie's favorite."

"Well, I know that. She buys it by the case, but you never come in my store." Annabeth pointed her finger at him. "Don't bother lying about it. I know you shop at the Walmart even though they don't carry it."

"I get my fix from Ellie."

"Yeah, he steals it from me." Ellie nudged him softly in his bruised ribs. "Don't bother trying to deny that either."

Bing jerked his arm away from her to cradle his side. "I think we have some slightly more important things to worry about, don't you? I'll send you a case next week after I get the hell out of here." Both Annabeth and Rachel stared at him with a look of shock, and he shoved his hands deep into his pockets. "Sorry. That was shitty. I just…aw hell. Just ignore me. Let's get to what we need to do. What kind of evidence was Olivia talking about sneaking out?"

Annabeth spoke over her shoulder as she led them through a curtained door into another large room, this one lined with well-stocked shelves, huge vats of water, and a kitchenette. "She's not sure what we'll be able to get our hands on or even what it will prove. In the strictest sense, we don't know that Feno has done anything illegal or unethical. If we could find some sort of evidence of the death records of those folks who were taken out, that would help, but it's going to be hard to prove they're not faked."

"How can you say they haven't been unethical?" Ellie climbed up on a stool beside a high counter. "What about the Horizon drugs? What if they contain those mind-melting chemicals? Surely that would be evidence, right?"

Annabeth began opening a can of chili. "If we can prove it. We're going to need to get our hands on some of those pills and find a way to get them out of here. Plus Olivia says the pills alone won't be enough because Feno might be able to claim that the pills were manufactured illegally by locals as a recreational drug. We all know the lax policy about drugs in here, don't we, Bing?"

Bing shrugged, and Ellie interrupted his answer. "There's a big difference between baggies of pot and hard-core psychotropic chemicals. What else does she think we'll need?"

"The medical records of an H. At least, something with the dosing records. Olivia says the paper records keep track of what levels of the compounds were given. If we have a record of a dose and the pills to corroborate it, it might be damning enough."

Rachel took the can opener from the old woman and helped open another can. "We can't use the records Ellie stole because Feno took them back. Plus they were before the Horizon meds were even given. Where would we find more records?"

Ellie thought of the stolen sheets she had torn out of the files in the care center. She was pretty certain they had been stuffed into the files Feno had confiscated. Still, she knew where the cabinet was. "Rachel, do you think you could get back into the care center? There are a lot of files in there. Medical files. The clerk in there was complaining about having to refile them according to QEH."

"I could go with you if you want, Rachel," Bing said. "Maybe I could go in for treatment, you know, for my bruised ribs." He shot Ellie a look that said he blamed her for them.

"We could try it." Rachel dumped the chili into a large pot. "I could go to the back like I want to see everyone again to complain about not getting my pass and create a distraction so you can sneak back and steal some files."

Annabeth held her hands up. "That's very brave of you, but why don't we wait until Olivia gets back and talk it over with her. She knows the med and care centers better than anyone, and she may already have a plan. I was hoping we'd get to talk with Nick tonight."

"Nick Torrez?" Rachel asked.

Bing raised his eyebrows. "You know Nick Torrez? Big guy? With the scary tattoos?"

"Nick worked for my dad. Fixed our tractors."

Annabeth began setting out bowls. "Nick works on the north wall maintaining the tamping drones now."

"Really?" Ellie asked. "I just saw my first one the other day when I was at the Feno compound. I thought they never stopped, just rolled on and on."

"No, they run circuits," Rachel explained. "There are thirty-five altogether, fifteen on the field at all times and fifteen being refilled and refueled, and five as backups. Nick's one of the guys who gets them in and out of the gate."

Annabeth grabbed a handful of spoons. "He said he's been called in to change the rotation of the drones. They want the barrier at the east gate tamped and dried before dawn."

"Did he say why?" Bing asked.

"He thinks it has something to do with the press conference in the morning. The convoy is coming in on the east barrier road. They don't want the tamping drones near the road. I guess they don't want the reporters to discuss the smell. Plus the CEO of Feno is coming in and he's probably allergic to the dust."

Rachel snickered. "Poor little lamb."

Bing rested his chin in his palm, chewing on a fingernail. "David Pattern is going to be here? Is he heading up the press conference? I thought he was persona non grata. After all, he was at the helm when Feno spilled HF-sixteen. He's been in exile for years."

"Still on the payroll, though," Annabeth said. "He's still the CEO, still gets the private jet and the big paycheck. I guess that kind of money takes the sting out of shame."

"But if Barlay really has made a vaccine," Bing said, tapping his lip with his finger, "I would think the CEO of Barlay Pharma would be here, not Feno. I would think their head honcho would be here to take the credit, or at least share the limelight."

Ellie shook her head. "No, it makes sense. Feno is taking the fall for this, as they should. They're smart to distance themselves from Barlay Pharma right now. Barlay is on the brink of recouping a ton of money from the government. They don't want to be associated with Flowertown. They want people to see them as a separate and distinct entity, a solution to the problem that is Feno."

Annabeth reached past Rachel for a ladle and then put her hand to the girl's head. "Honey, are you okay?"

Rachel had turned an unpleasant shade of pale. She fanned her face with her hands. "Maybe it's just the smell of chili. I think I really need some air." Bing pulled out a chair for her to sit on as Matt stuck his head through the curtain.

"Grandma? Just got a message from Olivia. She says she's not getting out of the care center tonight. Something's going on, and she says whatever we're going to do, we've got to do it now. She says she's heard six of nine are out of play."

Annabeth swore under her breath.

"What does that mean?" Ellie asked. "Six of nine are out of play?"

"We had nine people lined up who were willing and able to sneak evidence out if they were called with a clean bill of health," Annabeth said. "Mostly folks who had gotten copies of their medical records or maybe had samples of old meds they hadn't finished. Any concrete evidence that suggests Feno and Barlay have been experimenting unethically."

"You don't know for sure what they have?" Bing perked up, perched on the stool, birdlike.

"No, we thought it best to keep information separate, you know, not have anybody able to tell everything." Annabeth stirred the chili, her mind elsewhere. "This way if anybody gets caught, they can't give away anyone else's identity."

"But you know who the nine are?"

"No, Ellie, we've kept in touch with e-mails and drop points, messages in 'the local.' It just seemed safer that way."

"Am I one of the nine," Bing asked, "or am I a happy accident?"

Annabeth set a bowl of chili before him. "I christen you number ten."

"So that makes four of us that you know of who can and will try to get evidence out. Since there are so few of us, maybe we should get together, pool our resources." He looked to Ellie for support. "Because I'll tell you right now, hell itself won't keep me from getting out of here, and if I can help build a case against Feno, I'll stash evidence in any orifice I can reach."

"Well, like we said, we don't know all the names. I don't know who Olivia meant when she said six were out. I know one of the Es on the list was Marianne, works with her in the med center and the care center. According to Marianne, a lot of sensitive records are kept on the computer system at the care center." Annabeth pointed her chili-stained ladle at Bing. "And if you tell anyone that, I will have to kill you." Ellie didn't think she was kidding.

Bing got to his feet. "Then that's where we need to go. Rachel, you want to get a little air and come with me to the care center? I do believe these battered ribs of mine need some tending right away." Rachel jumped to her feet, the pallor on her cheeks making the perkiness seem a touch fake.

"What about me?" Ellie asked. "I want to do something."

Bing shrugged. "It might look funny, a crowd of us heading into the care center. Maybe you could wait for us outside?"

Annabeth pointed at Ellie. "You said you weren't taking your meds. Do you still have them? That would be some handy evidence, actual samples of Horizon."

What had she done with them? Mentally retracing her steps over the last frantic days, she groaned when she remembered. "I had them. I had them in a bag with the stolen files that I hid." She thought back to fishing the bag out and couldn't remember seeing the pills in the dark shadows of the runoff grate. "They might still be there. I can check and I'll meet you two at the care center. I'll wait for you out front."

Annabeth turned down the heat beneath the pot of chili. "Looks like I'll be keeping this warm for a while." She smiled. "Let's hope we're all being overly pessimistic." They looked one to the other, none of them believing it.

Ellie stayed with Rachel and Bing for a few blocks, until they had to head north toward the care center. The power was off on the blocks leading to the ruins of the records office, and Ellie tried not to let the midnight silence spook her. She told herself to relax, that the darkness was her ally. In one of the apartments she passed, two people argued at top volume and she narrowly escaped being hit by a sneaker hurled into the night. It seemed she wasn't the only person tense in Flowertown tonight. At the site of the records office, the police tape had been removed but dumpsters still lined the area, loaded with debris. Emergency entry lights flickered from across the street, making the shadows between the garbage bins darker.

"It's almost one o'clock in the morning, Ellie." She spoke loudly enough that the sound of her voice would reassure her. "There is nobody out here. Really." Almost convinced, Ellie stayed in the darkest of the shadows and searched for the runoff grate where she had stashed her bag. The shadows along the narrow patch of grass played tricks with her vision, and twice she reached down only to touch broken boards or discarded bricks. Finally her fingers found the grate and pulled back the heavy iron grille.

Taking one more useless look around in the darkness, Ellie lowered herself to her stomach and reached into the hole. She braced herself on the rim with one hand while she held up her lighter with the other. Saying a silent prayer there were no flammable gases in the drain, she flicked the lighter and could just make out the rack of pipe ends into which she had stuffed the bag. The light from the small flame only made the shadows darker, so she let the flame die. Ellie stuck the lighter in her mouth and reached into the blackness. There was a sheet of plastic; she could feel it slip between her fingers. That had to be the bag, still stuck on whatever bolt she had jammed it over.

Scooting farther into the hole, Ellie felt her stomach burning as it held her weight on the rim of the drain. Grunting, she pushed herself several inches deeper, her hips now taking the punishment, her balance pushed to its limits. She felt slime and damp plastic and sediment as she drew what was left of the bag closer to her and dared to breathe a sigh of hope when she thought she heard the rattle of pills inside a bottle. She knew she had to pull the bag slowly. If it tore, the pills would be unreachable, but she felt her legs and back struggling with the awkward position. She nearly bit through the lighter in her teeth as the bottom of the bag got closer and closer.

One gentle tug and the plastic came loose from the pipe. Ellie heard something rattling against plastic and swore to herself when she realized the bottle was not in the bag. The bag was now nothing more than a shredded sheet of plastic. Trying not to panic, Ellie reached her fingertips once more into the pipe and could feel something plastic roll from her touch. The pill bottle. Her shoulder felt as if it were being dislocated as she forced her reach even farther. Two fingernails just caught the lid of the bottle, and she prayed she could keep her hold. The bottle slid though whatever mucked up the pipe end, building up a nice coating of slime on itself, but finally it was close enough for Ellie to wrap her fingers around.

With a grunt, she inchwormed her body back out of the hole. Her stomach once again held her weight as she pulled her shoulders clear of the drain. Before she could get a handhold, however, the air whooshed out of her body as a something incredibly heavy smashed into the small of her back, pinning her to the metal drain. She couldn't even cry out as the lighter flew from her lips and the pill bottle squirted from her fingers, both disappearing in the darkness below her. Stars exploded before her eyes as blood rushed to her head and pain flooded her mind, but the only thought she could understand was the need to gasp for air as rough hands lifted her out of the hole and slammed her down on her back on the concrete.

Heaviness fell upon her again, this time on her hips, pinning her to the ground. Her ears rang with the concussion of her skull against the pavement, and she swung her hands uselessly into the blackness before her. There was a face, difficult to see over the mountain of black that pinned her to the ground, cutting off her air. Ellie struggled to squirm free, but a thick hand clamped down over her mouth and the face came into clear view in the darkness.

"Make a sound and I'll break your neck, do you understand?" Fletcher, Guy's overweight partner, leaned in close enough for her to smell his breath. His hand was hot and sweat dripped from his forehead onto hers. "Nod if you understand me." Ellie nodded as best she could, the weight of his hand making the gravel beneath her skull grate into her skin. In his free hand, he held a gun. "I'm going to take my hand away. If you scream, you'll regret it."

Ellie gulped in air as Fletcher lifted his weight slightly from her body. He kept the gun trained on her as he pulled his radio from his belt. Rather than speak, however, he pressed the talk button several times for different lengths of time, his eyes flickering from her to the darkness around them. In a moment, the radio sparked in short bursts of static, someone pressing the talk button as well, answering him in a code of static. The message received, Fletcher leaned once more into her face, whispering.

"How much did you put down there?"

"I didn't put anything down there."

He brought the gun to her forehead. "We don't have time for this shit. Where is the C-4?"

"What?" Ellie's breath came in pants as the gun cut into her skin. "C-4? Like explosives? I don't have anything to do with that. I didn't set that bomb."

Fletcher shushed her as the sound of a truck engine rumbled closer. Moving quickly despite his bulk, he jumped to his feet and jerked Ellie up with him, pinning her to him with his hand over her mouth once more. The truck approached down the avenue. Fletcher quickly and silently dragged her into the darkest shadows between dumpsters, pressing her with him against the metal bin.

Ellie struggled to breathe over his rough fingers, and it was only the gun pressing into her temple that kept her from stomping his foot with her own. Instead she stood silently, waiting, as a Feno security truck rolled slowly through the explosion site, headlights off, nearly invisible. Within the truck, two Feno guards scanned the area, peering into shadows, while two more with machine guns rode in the truck bed. Ellie felt Fletcher stiffen behind her, not relaxing until the truck was long out of earshot. He let the gun drop from her temple as he stuck his head out from between the dumpsters and scanned the scene.

"Fletcher?" Ellie whispered, not wanting his fat hand clamped over her mouth again.

"Shut up." He pulled her closer to him.

"Fletcher, it's me, Ellie. Guy's friend, Ellie."

"I know who you are." He ducked back in, not looking at her. "Now shut up and stay still or I'll coldcock you, understand?" It was a pretty simple command to comprehend, and Ellie nodded. She tried to put some distance between her back and the heat of Fletcher's chest, but he pulled her tightly to him again. She hoped he couldn't feel Guy's stolen gun still tucked in the back of her jeans.

Several long moments passed, and the fatigue from her wasted effort at the drain left Ellie no choice but to lean heavily against Fletcher's large frame. He didn't seem to notice the burden, keeping her tucked under his arm, his attention on the darkness of the avenue. Somewhere to the left, another argument broke out, maybe the same couple still at it, and glass shattered on the street. Fletcher didn't move, didn't shift his position until something metallic pinged on a nearby dumpster. He stiffened again, tightening his grip on her, and leaned out toward the sound. In a moment, three quick pings sounded to the right and Fletcher exhaled. Using the butt of his gun, he tapped the dumpster behind him twice, paused, then twice again. Seconds later, soft footsteps hurried toward their location.

It was hard to see faces in the shadows, but Ellie recognized Porter, another of Guy's army buddies, slipping into the space between dumpsters, followed by two other men and one woman, none of whom she recognized. Nobody spoke. Nobody looked at her. They crowded into the narrow space, looking out onto the street until the unmistakable figure of Guy moved out of the shadows and joined them.

"What have you got?" he whispered to Fletcher.

"Something you should have taken care of." Fletcher grabbed Ellie by the back of the neck and pushed her forward. "Found her crawling out of a runoff drain."

Guy swore under his breath. Ellie started to explain, but Fletcher jerked her back by her hair and hissed in her ear. "Shut up. Keep your goddamn voice down." A word from Guy and he released her once more. Guy pulled Ellie toward him, too close, as he always did, although this time Ellie doubted he wanted her to massage him. In the faint light from across the street, she could see a dark stain on the side of his face, no doubt from Bing's board.

"I didn't put anything in that drain," she whispered. "I was looking for something."

Guy stared at her for a moment and then turned to Fletcher. "Did you search the hole?" Fletcher's silence was his answer. Guy looked to the much taller and slimmer Porter. "Get out there and search the drain." Porter slipped into the shadows as Fletcher sputtered.

"What the hell else would she be doing in a runoff drain?"

"Let's ask her. Ellie?"

Finally given the chance to talk, Ellie feared words would fail her. She turned her back on the other soldiers and whispered only to Guy. "I left meds in there. Red pills."

Fletcher snorted. "In the runoff drain. That makes sense."

Ellie ignored him. "It's a long story, but I needed those pills for..." She didn't want to tell him who was involved. "I just needed the pills. I stashed them there after the explosion." She grimaced, knowing how that must sound. "It's a long story, Guy, but you've got to trust me."

"I don't need to trust you, Ellie." He looked out into the shadows. "I need there to be no C-4 in that runoff drain."

"There isn't! At least I didn't put any there. Why would I?"

Guy turned back to her. "We've dismantled six loads of explosives tonight. They were all set with remote triggers, and they were all big enough to blow everyone in this compound to hell and back. If you know anything about this—"

"I swear to God I don't. I swear. Nobody has said anything about blowing the zone up. Why would they?"

"You tell me." He squeezed her arm. "Don't deny you're working with All You Want. I know the locals have contacted you. You have to tell them the plan is not going to work. They cannot blow their way out of Flowertown."

"What are you talking about?" Ellie squirmed in his grip. "They don't want to blow anything up. They don't want to break containment. These are decent people who don't want Feno to make them disappear." His grip loosened just a touch. "Guy, they've heard that a bunch of people are getting released, a huge group. They're afraid that Feno plans on moving the people who are left to a hidden compound or even a testing facility."

"Why would they think that?"

"The locals think Feno is scouting out new locations. They're worried that if the world sees a huge crowd being released, they'll forget about the people who weren't cured and Feno will try to erase them as unfixable mistakes. They're planning on taking a stand, on staying in Flowertown. They don't have explosives; they've got stores of food and guns to protect themselves."

"And what do you think?"

"I think something bigger is going on, something worse." She looked at the silent group around her. "Why else would you all be hiding from your own company?" The group shared a look, nobody offering an explanation. Porter broke the silence by slipping back into the group.

"The hole's clean." He wiped his hands on his black pants. "There's nothing down there, no explosives, no triggers. Just garbage and whatever shit's been running through there."

The radio on Guy's belt crackled with wordless static, a series of short bursts. Ellie seemed to be the only one who couldn't understand the code. "That's Marshall at the north med center. Fletcher, did you sweep the rest of this area?" The heavyset man nodded. "Okay, you all head up there, check in with Marshall, then wait for my go."

"You're not coming?" Porter asked.

"In a second." Guy stared down a look of disapproval from Fletcher as the group slipped out into the shadows. When everyone was out of earshot, Guy took Ellie's hand.

"Are you going to explain to me what you and Fletcher and the rest of your group are doing sneaking around, hiding from Feno?" Guy shook his head. "Let me guess. It's classified."

"It is. And it's complicated."

"I bet. This is a complicated night."

Guy sighed and leaned back against the dumpster. "When we signed with Feno, they handed me the reins of security awfully quick. My team and I went from army outsiders to top dogs just like that, and overnight we're expected to investigate threats of violence from the locals, attempts to break containment, plots to destroy Flowertown. The evidence has been strong. We know there's an underground. We've found the C-4. Supplies are being destroyed. Fletcher, Porter, and I started thinking we were being set up to take the fall for a security breach that they had let happen."

"I'm telling you, Guy, the locals are not behind the bombs."

"If what you say is true, if you believe these people, then that means someone else is setting the explosives. Why would they do that? How does Feno gain from being responsible for the deaths of hundreds of people?"

"It's not the death. It's the chaos. They're banking on Barlay to bail them out of their financial sinkhole with a vaccine they're marketing. They release the majority of the population as cured, then plant a few crazies like me in the crowd to blame for blowing the remaining people to smithereens. Domestic terrorists, a terrible tragedy, and the book is closed on Flowertown." Ellie leaned back against the other dumpster, facing Guy. "And if the explosives are as big as you say, there won't be bodies to identify. Then they can keep the threat of escapees and contamination alive and keep selling the vaccine."

"You haven't seen these explosives, Ellie." Guy looked out into the shadows. "If we don't find the rest of them and figure out what's going on, nobody's getting out of here alive."

CHAPTER TWENTY-TWO

His radio crackled with coded static once again. Whatever the message, it made Guy swear under his breath. He held his hand up, motioning Ellie to silence, and leaned out from between the dumpsters. Ellie heard no sounds in the night, no arguments, no vehicles, no night noises. Guy stood still and tense, and then he motioned for Ellie to follow him. She hurried behind him and followed him away from the explosion site, down the avenue. He began to head north, but she grabbed his hand.

"Wait," she whispered. "I've got to go to my apartment."

"What?" Guy spun on her. "Don't you know what those trucks we've been avoiding are doing? They're either raiding locations or evacuating them under the pretense of security. My team wasn't informed of it, but we've seen it all night long. They're gathering everyone. We've dismantled explosives in three of the gathering locations. Ellie, I think we're in a deep pile of shit here. If they get their convoy out before we get these explosives cleared, we're going to have a big problem."

Ellie pulled him by the hand. "I've got to find my pills, and I'm almost positive I left some in my pocket." She heard Guy start to protest. "It's a long story. Just trust me. What's this convoy you're talking about?"

He hurried along beside her. "Fletcher picked up intel that a VIP convoy is being shuttled out tonight before the press conference. Feno officials, the psych team, the chemists. The official word is that they're sending a team out to prepare for the press, but that sounds unlikely, all things considered."

Ellie led them down the alley a block from East Fifth. The power was out as far as she could see, and they ran through the shadows. "So these guys doing the raids, you think they're trying to kill everybody? Even the people who were supposed to be released? That's their plan?"

"I don't think so. I know these guys. I know what they're being told. They think they're doing the right thing."

"You'll excuse me if I don't share your faith in Feno goons." She fished around in the dark for the crowbar to pry open the back door.

Guy put his hand on her shoulder and let her lead him up the dark stairwell. "These are regular guys, not mercs. They have no reason to doubt what they've been told."

"And you do?"

"Hell yes, I do. But I have alternate sources of information." He grabbed her ass as they entered the third-floor hallway. "Like my crazy, drugged girlfriend."

"I'm not exactly CNN, am I?"

He pulled her close to him in the dark. "You'll do." He kissed her neck and whispered in her ear. "Now tell me what the hell we're doing here."

319

Ellie pulled away, still holding him with her right hand and, with her left, feeling her way down the black hall. "I need to get evidence of what Feno's doing. Bing and Rachel are at the care center trying to get records. They want to try to sneak some evidence out with Bing."

"Bing? You're going to trust your evidence with that idiot?" He followed her into her room and closed the door behind him.

"What is it with you two?" Ellie began feeling her way through the heap of dirty clothes.

"For one thing, he smashed my face with a club."

Ellie sighed. "Yeah, I guess there's that. But I kicked you and you still like me. Besides, he was trying to help us get away. He was scared."

"I don't trust him."

"The feeling is mutual. Have you ever even spoken to him?"

"I don't like people with secrets. He's lucky, and I don't like lucky. I don't trust it." He looked out the window as she searched. "There are trucks out front."

"Lucky?" Ellie felt something hard in a pocket of a pair of jeans. "How exactly do you consider Bing lucky?"

"He doesn't just stay under the radar; he stays off it. He wasn't marked as a person of interest even though he deals marijuana, works in a classified position, and is a known channel of communication for All You Want."

"No, he isn't. They don't know him at all. He didn't even know their code."

"What code?"

Ellie sighed when she realized what she had found— Rachel's tooth. She couldn't leave it behind. She shoved it in her pocket and kept searching. "I'm telling you, Bing knew nothing about the locals' plans."

"And I'm telling you we've been monitoring his mail and his computer and we've found coded messages. What we could decipher has been pretty interesting."

"Oh, I get those flyers too. I sent him one last week. They don't mean anything. And who the hell gets e-mail around here?"

"He does. He gets a lot. And it's encrypted."

Before he could say more, harsh light seeped in under the door and a bullhorn voice yelled. "This is Feno security. This building is being evacuated for security purposes." Heavy footsteps could be heard both in the hallway and overhead.

Ellie swore and pawed through the clothes. Finally she felt a tumble of pills in the pocket of another pair of jeans and scrambled to reach them.

"We've got to get out of here, Ellie."

"The window." She stuffed the handful of pills into the pocket that now held Rachel's tooth and climbed over her bed. She swung one leg out the window and peered down at the tarpaper roof of the hardware store several feet below. "We can make this jump."

"We don't have a choice. Go."

Ellie let her body slip off the sill and kept her knees bent as she collapsed on the roof below. Guy tumbled beside her seconds later and they lay flat, listening to shouts and thuds from the building above. Guy turned to her, but Ellie was smiling up at the sky. The yellow lights of the security trucks flashed below them.

"Are you all right?"

She laughed. "Do you know how many times I dreamed of doing that when I was in lockdown? I used to dream about it every night, just slipping out the window and running away. And then when they finally unbolted the window, I never did it. There was never any point."

"You've got a good reason tonight. Let's lie low until the trucks pull away." He reached out and took her hand.

"So you monitored Bing's mail. Did you monitor mine?"

Guy sighed. "I didn't, but it was in your file. It was in Bing's too, but it didn't get flagged. He's either dirty, stupid, or lucky, and I don't like any of those."

Ellie heard shouts and complaints from the people filing out of East Fifth and rolled over, pressing into Guy's body. It was ridiculous. Flowertown was blowing up around them and all she could think about was the taste of his neck on her lips. Guy pulled her close, one hand around her waist, the other buried in her hair, guiding her face to his. The kiss was long and wet, and Ellie kept her eyes closed as Guy's hands moved over her body.

"Is that my gun?"

She ground her hips into his. "I was going to ask that same question."

He pulled the gun from the back of her waistband. "Is this my gun?"

Ellie let out a long breath and tried to pull away, but Guy held her close, bringing the gun to her shoulder. "Yes, that's your gun."

"Do you know how to use it?" She nodded. "Good." He checked the clip and then slipped the weapon back into her jeans. "Keep it. Use it if you have to. Don't hesitate. If you draw that weapon, you fire it. Ellie, I don't know what's going to happen tonight…"

She closed her eyes, not wanting to see the emotion in his eyes. "Guy, don't."

"Listen to me." He put his hands on her face. "I don't care what they say; I don't care what the plan is. Dr. Byrd and his crew can kiss my ass. You are not a weapon. You are not a pawn. Whatever happens tonight, they did it. Not you. Not the locals. I know that now. And if it takes my last breath, I'm going to expose them and their crazy manifesto."

She put her forehead against his. "Manifesto?"

"It's all starting to make sense now. I never thought of the vaccine. All this crazy shit we found when Porter hacked the system."

"Oh, you mean the wacko drugs? Making me flip out? Too late, I guess."

Guy pulled away. "It's too late to use you, but they've got to have others in place. People who fit their profiles."

"Whose profiles?"

"Byrd, Tabor, and Marcum," Guy said. "The psych team."

"The BTM scale." Ellie rubbed her eyes, trying to remember what Olivia had told her. "Tabor was the doctor who tipped the locals off to what was going on. Told them about Horizon. Apparently he wasn't comfortable with what they were doing."

"Which would explain why Dr. Tabor is dead. He's the only one we have an ID on. Rumor is Marcum is already out. But we've read their files, their data. Porter went deeper and read some of their older work. These guys are wack jobs. Byrd has a complete agenda for orchestrating a massive disaster; he's written books on it. His works are what tipped us off to the Horizon plan, that psychotropic drugs were being used. It seemed impossible that Feno would try to put one of his plans into action, but that was before we found dozens of packets of C-4 buried in civilian buildings."

"But if you can find all the explosives, they can't blow the place up. If word gets out that they've planted the bombs—"

"If word gets out. If we get out. We only know about the explosives in the buildings." Guy stared up at the sky. "There's a total communication blackout with the outside until nine this morning when the press conference gets set up. We know about Horizon, but we don't know how many people they're planning on using. We don't know how many Hs there are or if that's the only weapon. You didn't read this guy's stuff, Ellie. These are sick people, and if Feno plans on implementing even a fraction of what he proposes, we've got a real problem."

Ellie put her hands over her face, trying to collect her thoughts. "Look, they've got a limited pool of people to choose from, right? We know they're planning on pinning the violence on me and the other Hs. I saw the newscast. It looks like I'm the prime suspect. You've read this Dr. Byrd's stuff. What else does he need for his event?"

Guy ticked them off on his fingers. "He says to maximize the effect of a disaster, you need three things: victims, heroes, and villains. He also says to really seal the deal and cement the effect, you need irony."

"Irony? Who is this guy, my high school English teacher?"

"Hardly. Part of his irony is that the majority of your characters be dead and your villains be misinformed. Those were his words, not mine. We wrote this stuff off as insanity, but if someone in Feno is setting off these bombs, it's going to be hard to find many survivors."

"But misinformed how? What does he mean by misinformed?"

"It was so crazy, Ellie, I didn't pay that much attention," Guy said. "He said you could manipulate certain types, put them where you needed them, make them believe anything to create any effect you wanted. He had profiles of who makes good villains—prone to rage, antisocial, substance abuse."

"Shit, did he put my picture in there too?"

"That wasn't all. There was another type—paranoid, gullible, obsessive. He said they made good visible targets, were easily coerced to make grand gestures and could be used—"

"Oh my God." Ellie sat up straight. "Paranoid, gullible, and obsessive? Guy, they're going to use Bing. I've got to get to the care center."

She was halfway over the edge of the building before Guy caught her. He grabbed her arm and let it slip through his hands as she dropped onto a dumpster below. She heard him swear as he followed to the dumpster and then to the street, keeping step with her as she ran. How could she have been so stupid? Bing was totally paranoid and obsessed with Rachel. He'd do anything to keep her safe. Of course Feno would use him to trigger some kind of incident, or trip a bomb or something. Why else had they been allowed to just stroll out of the Feno compound?

"You can't just charge into the care center." Guy pulled her back, slowing her down. "Look." Ahead they could see three Feno trucks parked before the care center. The power hadn't gone out on this block, and light flooded the streets where the doors were held open. "If you go running in there during a raid, you're going to be detained, I assure you."

"What are we going to do? I've got to get in there."

Guy watched the guards evacuating the building. "You're under arrest."

"What?"

"Give me your hands." She pulled her hands away, but Guy was faster. "If you're already in my custody, they can't take you." He pulled a zip-tie restraint from his belt and wrapped it around her wrists loosely.

"Don't bind my hands."

"You can get them out. Just keep them together. Oh, and try to look pissed."

She flipped her middle finger at him as he led her up the steps to the care center. Uniformed workers and patients filed out in crowded lines, hurried by Feno guards. Guy pushed through the throng, jerking Ellie along by the elbow. A young guard with a face full of freckles jumped to attention.

"Mr. Roman, what are you doing here? Is something wrong?"

Guy pushed Ellie to the side. "Everything under control?"

"Yes sir. We're moving the personnel to the auditorium. Medical has been set up for the patients, but there's nobody critical. Um," he looked down the crowded hallway toward the treatment rooms, "the other team is here too. At the nurses' station."

Guy nodded and clapped the young man on the shoulder. "Good work." He pulled Ellie along, shouldering through the people making their way out. Ellie tried to keep up.

"What other team?"

"This is an evacuation. If there's another team, they're arresting people."

"Guy, that's where Bing and Rachel were headed, down past the nurses' station. That's where the records were kept." At the end of the hallway, where it branched off to the treatment rooms in which Rachel had received her detox, two armed guards stood ready. Guy dragged Ellie along, but when he went to move between them, one of the guards held out his arm.

"Sir, I can't let you go through there."

Guy turned on the guard with a sharp look. "You can and you will."

"Sorry, sir." The guard was much taller than Guy, but seemed cowed. "I have orders."

"Yeah, I gave them." He pulled Ellie between them. "Don't let anyone pass."

"Yes sir."

Ellie caught up to Guy as he ducked his head into the first room. "Aren't you a bad motherfucker? One word from you and they jump."

"One word from whoever's running this raid and we're screwed. Hide in here." Ellie tried to protest, but he pushed her into an empty room and pulled the door almost closed. She could hear voices down the hallway barking orders. "No matter what happens, you stay in here." He whispered through the crack in the door. "If anything happens, get out and head to the north med center. My team is there."

"Where are you going?"

He ignored her and headed down the hall. She heard a woman swear loudly and the sound of something metal clattering to the floor. In a few moments, soldiers headed Ellie's way dragging several nurses in handcuffs along with them. Ellie withdrew farther into the room as she watched the procession. One of the nurses was bleeding, another fought the guards without success. Ellie tried to see through the throng of soldiers to find out if Rachel or Bing were in the group but couldn't tell. A loud stream of obscenities echoed up the hallway and Ellie saw Olivia being shoved along in cuffs. She twisted in the grip of her guard, wresting herself free of his grasp, but before she could run, the guard slammed the butt of his machine gun into her back, sending her sprawling across the floor, her shoulder slamming into the wall just outside of Ellie's door.

Ellie crouched down, hating the sound of Olivia's body hitting so hard. Before the guard could haul her to her feet, Olivia looked up directly into Ellie's shadowed face. Her eyes widened in recognition, and as she was lifted bodily, she flicked her gaze over her shoulder and mouthed one word: Bing. Ellie ducked back into the shadows, forcing herself to remain silent as she saw Rachel being carried out unconscious behind Olivia. More guards moved through as a voice at the end of the hallway called out.

"This section is clear, sir."

"All right, move out." Guy spoke in a calm voice, not looking into the room where he knew she hid.

"Sir," the guard stood before Guy, "I have orders to clear the area."

"It's clear."

"My orders said to be the last person out of the area. That includes you, sir."

Guy nodded, his face dark, and walked down the hall. As he passed, his eyes flickered toward Ellie's hideaway but his face showed nothing. The guard walked behind him, gun held at the ready, pulling doors closed as he went. His hand was inches from Ellie's face as he pulled her door closed as well.

She waited in the dark until she could hear nothing. It was hard to tell if everyone was gone; her heart banged in her chest so loud she was certain someone else could hear it. Finally, summoning all her courage, she turned the knob and eased the door open. The lights were off in the hallway, but a glow of lamplight shone from somewhere behind the nurses' station. Olivia had mouthed Bing's name. Maybe that meant that Bing had made it back here, that he had somehow managed to avoid capture. She had to find him.

Crouching low and staying close to the wall, Ellie hurried down the hall and ducked behind the high desk of the nurses' station. The light came from a file room behind a large cabinet, and she crept as quietly as she could to the doorway. Pulling the gun from her waistband, Ellie peered through the crack. She couldn't see anything except a tall shelf of medical supplies. Ducking low, Ellie gripped the door and pushed it open. She crept along with it, hoping to stay low enough to go unseen by anyone who might be inside.

As the room came into view, she saw file cabinets and an old metal desk. Before she could move toward them, she heard a keyboard clicking. Freezing behind the door, Ellie held her breath until she heard Bing swear softly.

"Son of a bitch, hurry up."

"Bing?" Ellie stuck her head around the door, and Bing jumped where he stood.

"Ellie?" His face was pale with shock.

She pushed the door closed behind her and hurried to the desk. "What are you doing?" She kept her voice a whisper. "How did you get back here? They've arrested everybody."

"I know." Bing stared at her as if she had just dropped from the sky. "How did you get back here?"

"I snuck in with Guy. I hid."

"Shit, Guy is here?" His eyes moved wildly about the room.

"No, they made him leave. What are you doing?" She looked at the cable running from the computer tower to a small plastic box the size of a deck of cards.

Bing blew out a deep breath. "I broke into the medical mainframe. Rachel covered for me so I could sneak back here. I'm downloading medical records onto an external drive. How did you know I was back here?"

"Olivia told me. When they were dragging her out she told me to find you."

Bing stared at her. "What did she say exactly?"

Ellie made a sound of exasperation. "She didn't really have time to get into it, Bing. She was being dragged out by Feno goons. She looked back here and said 'Bing.'"

He shook his head and looked back to the computer. "You really need to start paying more attention to details, Ellie. I don't think she was telling you to save me. I think she was warning you." He moved the computer mouse and clicked on more files.

"What? Warning me about what?"

Before he could answer, they heard footsteps, and Ellie spun around. Mr. Carpenter stood in the doorway. Ellie raised the gun and stepped in front of Bing. "Don't move." She hoped he couldn't see her tremble.

Carpenter raised his hands, his eyes wide. He looked from her to Bing. "We had a report of a breach in the mainframe. I should have known it would be you."

Ellie took a step closer, keeping the gun level. "Yeah, well, you knew you couldn't trust me. Bing, are the files loaded?" She risked a look over her shoulder as he unplugged the drive and slipped it into his pocket.

"Yep, all the evidence we need to make sure Feno keeps up their end of the bargain."

"What do you mean?" Ellie looked at him and then spun around as Carpenter lowered his hands. "Stay where you are!"

"No." Carpenter leaned against the doorframe and smiled at Bing. "The convoy is ready whenever you are, Dr. Byrd."

CHAPTER TWENTY-THREE

Ellie knew she had misheard him. She kept the gun trained on Carpenter despite the whooshing sensation of impossibility flooding over her. She looked to Bing as she always did, for answers, for a reality check, and he smiled at her. Turning to Carpenter, he tipped his head in her direction.

"See that expression, Carpenter? We call that 'fracturing of reality.'"

"It's very interesting, Doctor."

"It never gets old, no matter how many times I see it."

"Bing?" Her voice caught in her throat.

"Yes?" He smiled at her again, a calm and patient smile, then turned back to Carpenter. "Are we still exiting through the east gate?"

"Yes sir. You know, they've noticed the file download. They're not going to let you leave with that external drive."

"You don't think so?" Bing drew his brows together. "Why don't I tell them you did it? After all, you do owe me for the bruises on my face. Overplayed your role a bit." Carpenter's mouth opened in surprise, and Bing looked back at Ellie. "I think that's only fair, don't you?"

Without waiting for the answer, he reached out to the gun in her hand. She jerked it away, but he gripped the hand around the weapon. He didn't try to take it from her; rather, he wrapped his hands over hers and twisted it to one side. Three quick squeezes of the trigger and Carpenter fell back into the hallway. Bing released her hands, and Ellie nearly dropped the gun from her trembling fingers. She heard a sound like a panting animal, and she knew the sounds came from her throat.

Her arms shook badly and her shoulders ached as she raised the gun at Bing. She wanted to scream at him, to demand answers, but her throat failed her and she could only gasp at air that would not go into her lungs. Bing glanced back at the computer and then at her. He saw the weapon and her struggle to form words and he laughed.

"Don't even bother, Ellie. You're not going to shoot me." He pulled out the chair to sit and then stopped. "Trust me. I spent four years making sure you can't raise a hand to me. Don't believe me? Go on. Pull the trigger." He stepped closer to her and grinned. "Do it. Kill me."

Ellie blinked hard, her focus failing as she stared into the face of her best friend. Her fingers burned on the weapon and her muscles trembled with the effort, but her body would not obey the command her brain screamed. Bing. Bing. Bing. One word pounded through her brain, obscuring all logic and thought. She gritted her teeth, hearing her breath whistling.

"See? Four years of smoking you up with the right combo of meds and you're quite the docile pet. You're going to hyperventilate if you keep gasping like that. Not that it matters."

She forced a word out. "Why?"

Bing laughed again. "Why? Could you be a little more specific? You mean, why did I offer my services to Feno? That's easy. An assload of cash. And proof that my theories on psychological manipulation worked." He slapped his forehead in comic despair. "Oh, man, I thought you had me on that. I thought for sure even you weren't so fucking stupid that you would miss it." Ellie only blinked, struggling to understand the words he was saying.

He grabbed her by the shoulders, the gun pressing against his chest, forgotten. "The book? In my room? You had it in your hands—*The Divisible Flock*. I wrote that. It's my fucking masterpiece. It got me kicked out of Stanford on an ethics violation, but do you think I give a shit about that now?" Ellie drew her body in tight as he shook her. "It got published and got me invited to Feno to fix their little problem. And you had it in your hands and still couldn't figure it out." He pushed her away and she staggered backward, still drawn into herself.

He turned back and leaned over to bang on the keyboard. "For the love of God, how long does it take to launch a virus?" A few more keystrokes and he drummed his fingers on the desk. "You can put that gun down, Ellie. You're not going to use it. On me, at least. Save your strength. You've got a long night ahead of you."

Ellie raised the backs of her hands to her face, the gun pointing toward the ceiling. She couldn't understand how she was still on her feet or why the ceiling hadn't come down or why the walls weren't melting. All she could hear was a blurry roar, and her mouth tasted like copper. She heard Bing approach her, and she didn't resist when he lowered her hands. She heard herself sob when his thumb gently wiped at the tears she couldn't feel on her cheeks.

"Oh, Ellie." His voice and his eyes were soft. "You're such an authority whore."

Her throat tore as she whispered through her tears. "Please don't do this."

"No? How about I do this?" He brought his arm around in a hard backhand across her face, slamming Ellie into the file cabinet. She cried out as she hit the metal, and Bing let out a loud sigh. "Oh, God, I have wanted to do that for so long. You have no idea."

Ellie's stomach cramped and she bent forward, gasping. Bing leaned down to look into her face.

"What's that you're saying? Please? Please what? Please shoot you? Please take care of every fucking thing so you can sit around and get high? Is that what you want? Speak up."

"We were friends!" The words blew out of Ellie's mouth in a spray. Bing grabbed her roughly by the hair and dragged her up.

"You want to know why we were friends? You want to know why?" He yanked her hair to make her nod. "Because there's only one person on this whole planet who has more contempt for you than I do. You know who that is? Huh?" He dragged her across the office and pushed her in front of a wall. Ellie screamed, trying to pull herself free, but he twisted her arm behind her and forced her head back. "There she is."

She saw herself in the mirror. Blood smeared from her nose, and her lip had begun to swell from Bing's blow. He held her back to his chest, her hair pulled back tight, and hissed in her ear.

"Nobody could possibly ever hate you as much as you hate yourself, Ellie. You let this happen. You made it easy because you are so goddamn pathetic." She tried to turn her head away from the sight of her sweating face and panicked eyes, but he held her fast. "Would it have killed you to ever give a shit about anything? Or anyone? Hell, would it have killed you to take a fucking shower once in a while? Look at you. Look what you have made of yourself."

"No." She saw blood and saliva spatter on the mirror and wished she could make herself go blind. "You did this. You did this with your drugs."

"No, Ellie, you did this. The drugs just made it easier."

The pain from his grip on her hair gave her mind a point of focus, and Ellie struggled for control. She gritted her teeth and glared at Bing's reflection.

"Fuck you."

Bing's eyes widened in surprise. "Fuck me? Fuck you." He slammed her forehead into the mirror. Ellie gasped and swore again. Again he pounded her forehead into the glass. She saw their image fractured. In the many shards, she saw Bing, and when he brought her face to the glass again, this time hard enough to make the glass fly to the floor, she saw him in her mind as she had seen him so many times.

"Bird."

Bing banged her head once more against the glass, and Ellie could feel her legs tremble beneath her as blood began to run down the wall.

"Bird," she said again.

"What are you saying?" Bing yanked her head back.

"Bird. You look like a bird." The light over his head blurred as she blinked blood out of her swelling eyes. "I know you." Bing let her go and she swayed on her feet, her speech slurred. She forgot about the blood and chased her thoughts through the fog. "You looked like a bird. In the hospital. I knew you. I didn't know Dr. Tabor. I knew you."

She tried to focus on Bing as he sat back against the desk and watched her sway. "I look different without my beard, don't I?"

It took a moment for the words to get through to her. She had to think what a beard was, and slowly her memory put the ideas together. In her mind she saw the face of her best friend in a thick, dark beard. And in her mind he transformed into that hated shadow-face of her nightmares, the face that had loomed out of the drug-thick soup of those long nights in East Fifth in the early years of Flowertown.

"You were my doctor." The words slipped from her lips like smoke.

"Duh."

The breath that tore up from her lungs was hot. "You fuck."

He rolled his eyes. "Such elegant last words. You really are a piece of trash. It took me all of three sessions to know you would be a perfect event catalyst."

"Why me?"

"Don't kid yourself, Ellie. It wasn't personal. You're not that important." He moved back around to the computer. "You're just convenient. You were handy, but if you hadn't worked out, there were half a dozen others I could have used. Big Martha would have been a fantastic face for a suicide bomber, but the sheer amount of meds it took to get into her head just wasn't cost-efficient. Big bodies, big doses. You were a cheaper choice." He looked over at her, running his eyes down the length of her body. "I mean that in every way."

Ellie spit a bloody wad onto the floor. "Guy is going to stop you."

He leaned over the keyboard. "Guy is going to run around like GI Joe and get himself blown up. His psych eval makes him a perfect candidate for one of our heroes. Brave, handsome, loyal, and stupid enough to fuck the one piece of ass that tries to blow the whole place sky-high. I love it."

She wanted to move. The back of his head tempted her to raise a chair and smash it into him, but her body would not obey her wishes. "Is that the irony you were looking for?"

Bing looked over at her, eyebrows raised. "Now you've decided to pay attention? How did you know about the irony factor? It's a huge selling point to cement tragedy in a media-covered event. People lap it up. But no, that wasn't the intended irony. Like your incredibly malleable mind, it was just a bonus." He looked back at the screen, typed in a few more keystrokes, and swore as the computer beeped. "Don't think I'm not appreciating the irony right here in front of us as my brilliant escape is being held hostage by the very computer that is going to cover my tracks."

Ellie took a step forward to look over his shoulder. "Do you know what a smart bomb is, Ellie?" He didn't bother to see if she answered. "I have a virus hidden in my own medical file—well, Ian Billingsly's medical file. There are only a handful of people who know my alias. After what happened to Tabor, I decided not to take any chances. If anything had happened to me and someone tried to delete my file or mark me as 'deceased,' I hid a worm that would be activated to corrupt every bit of data on file. If I disappeared, so did their vaccine research. Now that I'm leaving, I'm detonating that little rascal. I've got all the research here on my external drive. This is going to ensure that Feno keeps up their financial end of the bargain—and doesn't decide to grow a conscience once their stock goes back up."

"I'm not going to blow anything up for you." Ellie tried to make her voice strong, but the blood running down the back of her throat made her whisper. "You can't make me, no matter what you do."

"Oh, honey, you really are dense, aren't you?" Bing sat back against the desk and folded his arms. "Did you really think I would put the success of my venture on your lame stoner ass? I don't expect you to do anything but flail about helplessly like the crazy person the world thinks you are. My team is setting off the explosions. My team is getting me out of here."

"Guy's team is finding them before you can set them off."

"When we're done here, Guy won't be able to find his dick with both hands. We have provisions for all eventualities. The best-case scenario is that I get out, the press comes in, and before the whole world, bombs with your name on them blow this shit hole right back to hell. Then, as we read off the names of the hundreds of lives you took, the CEO of Barlay Pharma breaks in with the heartbreaking and, yes, ironic revelation that you mistakenly believed nobody was getting out of Flowertown when, in truth, everyone was being released. The world will shake their collective heads at the senseless tragedy and cruel irony."

"That's a lie."

"Which part? The bombs with your name? Yeah, but you already knew that. Oh!" Bing let his mouth hang open in mock surprise. "You mean the part about being released? No, that's true. Well, it would be true if that wouldn't bring down the shit storm of all time onto Feno and Barlay Pharma. Believe me, the celebration of the cure would be quickly overshadowed by the first autopsy. Whew."

Ellie heard herself begin to pant again, her heart hammering in her ears as she tried to absorb what he was saying. "Who's cured?"

"Everybody. Q, E, H, they all work. They've worked for over a year, closer to two." Bing spoke casually, as if he were discussing a baseball game. "We had to be sure, of course. You know, cure, reinfect. Cure, reinfect. Bring in Feno newbies for some clean slates. Side effects, fatalities, they took forever to straighten out. Turns out Equilibrium has the fewest side effects in the short run and can actually be adapted to a spray to neutralize the chemical should it get into the soil again."

"What are you saying?" Blood flew from her lips as she lurched forward. "Why aren't you letting everybody go? Why aren't you letting us out?"

"Are you kidding me? Do you have any idea what the months of reinfection have done to your livers? Your bones? Hell, your tooth enamel is enough to make this place look like the Island of Dr. Moreau. No, the most important thing we need at this point is to make sure no bodies get out. That's why incineration is the best-case scenario."

"I'll kill you."

"No, you won't." He didn't sound concerned as the computer beeped. "The virus is launching, so all my tracks are covered. Don't bother scheming, Ellie. Trust me. I'm smarter than you. Even if Guy and his little band of heroes get most of the bombs dismantled, at the first explosion, when the press is here, Flowertown is going to be locked down tighter than ever. Plan B. Nobody will ever see the outside world again." He checked his watch. "The absolute best ending you can hope for is to spend the rest of your miserable life tied to a bed in a very white room being pumped with mind-altering medications." He grinned as her jaw went slack. "Sounds like something from a nightmare, doesn't it? Oh, wait, it is something from a nightmare. Your nightmare. The white room. White, white, white. Am I right?"

"Fuck you."

He shook his head. "Poetry. Where the hell is my team? We'll just sit tight until they get here. Then I can show them what you did to poor Mr. Carpenter. You're so violent."

Ellie fought back a scream. She hated Bing, or Dr. Byrd, or whoever the hell he had become. She hated her inability to act. Of all the helplessness she had felt over the years of containment, this was a fresh slice of hell that burned her skin. She wanted so badly to blow a bullet through his brain, but she knew her hands would not obey. Breathing in hard through gritted teeth, she closed her eyes. Bullets weren't the only weapon she had.

"Rachel always told me you were a sick fucker."

"She did not. She is far too smart to think that and way too classy to talk like you."

Ellie snorted. "Are you kidding? We used to laugh our asses off about you and your little flirtations. She used to call you The Beak."

"Nice try." Bing shook his head and looked away, but Ellie could see the tendons in his neck stretch as he tried to calm himself. "But since you couldn't even pay enough attention to change your underwear every day, I doubt very seriously you could even comprehend the subtle nuances of a lovely girl like Rachel."

"Subtle nuances?" Ellie laughed out loud. "She was a fucking farm girl. She wasn't the Virgin Mary. She wasn't even a virgin. I think you were just about the only guy in Flowertown she didn't fuck, or at least blow."

"You shut your mouth. You have no right to talk about her like that."

"And you do? You're going to blow her ass up. Of course, I guess that's the closest you're ever going to get to doing anything to her ass…"

"Hey!" Bing jabbed his finger at her. "I tried to get her out of here. I tried to get her cleared on the detox. There was no reason she had to suffer like that. I was the one that got her the Equilibrium shot. I was the one that got her a chance to leave. What the hell did you do?"

"You didn't do shit." Ellie knew how much this snarky tone of voice got under Bing's skin. "All you ever did was fawn over her and bother her."

"I blew up the goddamn records office for her!"

"For her? You think Rachel wanted people blown up?"

Bing leapt to his feet and barked into Ellie's face. "Rachel wanted out and I was making it happen. They were supposed to give her enough Equilibrium to cancel out the detox. But those stupid fucking monkeys in the lab got it wrong and now she's blue-tagged while you're still dragging your useless ass around as healthy as a horse. She was supposed to be outside the zone when all of this went down. You were supposed to be up there in the records office, you stupid bitch. Big Martha lied and said you'd gone out for cigarettes. She said you'd be right back. I guess I can't trust any of you psychopaths."

"You set the bomb? You killed those people?"

Bing smiled a hard smile at her, his tone that of a naughty child. "You know what else I did? I stole your fucking chili. Right out of your desk. I didn't even think about it. I just took it so I could have something for Rachel that night, thinking she'd be better. Thinking we could mourn your pathetic life. Stupidly, I worried later that you might realize that I never go to Dingle's to get that shit and then I thought, 'Like Ellie is going to put anything together.'" He slapped his head for emphasis.

He was trying to be sarcastic and taunt her, but Ellie could see his temper fraying. She knew a little something about that. Bing thought he was a master manipulator, but Ellie was familiar with button-pushing herself. She smirked at him. "Ever wonder why I used to spend so much time up in your room?"

He laughed. "To get away from your wide circle of friends?"

"To get away from the porn shoot that was always going on in Rachel's bed."

"You suck as a liar, Ellie." His face did not look so certain.

"All kidding aside, I think you might be the only guy in Flowertown that hasn't put it to her." It was childish, and what she was saying was untrue, but Ellie wanted to see the pain it drove into Bing's brain. "You know Tito, that Mexican kid who works at the library? I came in one day after work and they were going at it. I'm no anatomy major, but I'm pretty sure they weren't doing it the way God intended."

Ellie laughed, hearing Bing's breathing get hard. "She used to tell me that getting it in the ass—"

She looked up in time to see the white skin of Bing's elbow as it crashed into her face. She heard nothing but a crunching sound as she collapsed to the floor, clutching her face, blood pouring out between her fingers. Above her, Bing screamed, but the sounds around her had vanished. The feel of blood evaporated, replaced by the familiar tingling in her hands and feet.

Ellie felt her throat closing off and hot, mottled spots rising on her skin as rage flooded her body like ecstasy. In one short blow, she was no longer kneeling on the floor of the care center. She was back to the early days, on her knees, gushing blood in the medical tents where all the people around her were dying in puddles of their own filth. Only this time she hadn't been vomiting for days. This time she was well fed and her legs were strong. This time she wouldn't need a box cutter to take down the man before her.

She saw Bing's eyes widen as she lunged from the floor, her hands like claws tearing into him as an inhuman howl tore from her throat. Whatever control he thought he had over her evaporated as her mind went back to the blackest of the black rage that had consumed her. Ellie punched and tore, clinging to the body before her, the impact of her lunge pinning him to the desk beneath her. Bing pulled at her, screaming, but she was too close and held on too tightly.

Her hands dug at his skin, sometime tearing, sometimes punching. She didn't feel the bruising of her bones against his skull or the scrapes of his teeth breaking against her knuckles. He tried to flip her off of him and they tumbled to the floor together, Ellie clinging to his clothes and skin like a creature from hell. He punched at her, but she was beyond feeling. He tried to smash her head against the floor, but she craned forward and bit down hard on his lower lip, his blood pouring as his skin gave way with a thick, popping sound. There was nothing to see on his face but blood, and still Ellie clawed and screamed and bit, not thinking of escape or rescue, thinking only of violence and the sounds of his pain.

She didn't register the sounds of gunfire until a piece of ceiling tile rained down on her like glitter. Bing was keening, his lip pierced between her teeth, and she could just see his eyes wild through the blood. She heard heavy boots in the doorway and bullets flew very near them. Ellie released her hold on Bing's face, and she had to turn away to keep from inhaling the river of blood he poured down on her.

"Shoot her!" Bing screamed, his words garbled by the damage done to his face. Two guards stepped forward, their guns out, but Ellie was quicker and kicked Bing off of her toward them. The closest guard jumped back to avoid being splattered by blood, and Bing lurched in a puddle of wetness beneath him. The second guard fired into the crowded room as Ellie launched herself under the metal desk. Lying flat on her stomach, she squeezed herself under the back of the heavy furniture and slithered out into the open space between two file cabinets.

It was bedlam behind her as Bing screamed unintelligible commands, and Ellie used the confusion to risk getting to her feet and running. Bullets tore through the doorframe over her head and she was down the back hall. The hall was dark, but Ellie's eyes were sharp with fear, and as angry shouts and heavy footsteps filled the hall behind her, she saw the emergency exit light ahead.

She didn't slow down, knowing if the doors were locked it wouldn't matter if she knocked herself out. It would be preferable to what she would encounter at the hands of Bing's team. Like the bullets heading her way, Ellie smashed into the emergency door and tumbled into the darkness of the alley. She jumped over a pile of trash and pounded into the darkness. Her hands were slick with blood and sweat, and she felt what she held in her left hand trying to slip away. In a pool of light from the streetlamp, she was surprised to see what she held. It wasn't the gun. That was gone. Instead she clutched the small plastic case that held Bing's external hard drive.

CHAPTER TWENTY-FOUR

The electric light on the block made Ellie feel vulnerable, so she ducked back into the alley behind the buildings. She had to get to the north med center. She had to find Guy. She knew Bing's men would be looking for her; Bing needed the external drive she carried. He could get out without it, but after that virus he had released, this held the only records of the testing Feno had done. That meant it must also hold the proof that they were no longer contaminated, and that meant she needed it more. Ellie jammed the small plastic case deep into her pocket, not trusting her sweaty and blood-slick hands to hold it while she ran.

She wished she still had the gun. As she moved through the shadows, she watched for movement around the back doors of the buildings. Most of this block was storage and maintenance, but one taller building looked like apartments. Ellie slowed down as she neared the door and saw it was a heavy steel door like the one on her own apartment building. Plastic trash bins lined up on either side of it, and Ellie took a chance and stopped. Maybe the people in this apartment, like East Fifth, used the back door as well. If so, maybe they had also hidden a pry bar of some sort under the trash cans. It wasn't a gun, but Ellie knew she would feel better with something metal in her hands.

She pushed away the first can and reached around in the darkness. She found a brick, which she considered as a backup, but it felt heavy and unwieldy in her hands. There was nothing to the right of the door. To the left, she had to dig around underneath a paper-recycling bin. Her fingers left smears of blood on the sides of the bin, and the rough plastic made her wince. Then she felt something cold. Sticking her arm deep into the bin, she pulled out a long, tapered iron crowbar. That would do nicely.

Hefting the crowbar, Ellie began to run again, trying not to think about the throbbing ache in her face. She had to breathe noisily through her mouth, and it took focus to not let the sound of her panting panic her. The realization that she was clean filled her with energy, and Bing's image of being tied to a bed kept the wind at her back. She had to move.

The blood staining her face and her clothes helped her blend into the shadows. She moved from alley to alley, ducking to hide from Feno trucks that crisscrossed the roadways, some with their lights on, a few without. She couldn't take any chances. She had to assume they were on Bing's team. She headed east, off the main avenue, closer to the eastern barrier, where the traffic seemed a little lighter and the buildings a little darker. Two blocks ahead, the power was definitely on because the block was flooded with streetlights and floodlights and every window glowed with overhead lights. It was what they all called the "Public Building," where the clean rooms were, where the few visitors who ventured in

were taken. It was also the site of the upcoming press conference and, according to the guard at the care center, where a
large group of residents had been evacuated. Armed guards
strolled the edges of the block while a dozen or so civilians
milled about in the light, smoking and talking.

Ellie's first thought was to put as much distance between
her and the guarded building as quickly as possible. Then
she saw a familiar figure leaning against a light post, fishing
a flask out of his tweed jacket. It was Mr. MacDonald, the
newspaper vendor, looking for all the world like the professor he had been in his previous life. He was the first person
to have suggested she read the local paper. In his own gruff
way, he had always been nice to Ellie. If this was one of the
buildings Bing's men planned on blowing up, she had to
warn him. At the very least, she had to let him know he and
the people being held were clean.

A pair of guards walked very close to where she crouched
between a dumpster and the corner of the building. She
dared not crouch down farther in case she made any noise.
Everyone was on full alert. When the guards had passed, she
fished around in the darkness at her feet for a stone or piece
of debris she could toss into the light to get MacDonald's
attention, but with the strict recycling laws, there was little
to no garbage anywhere except in the clamped, closed garbage bins. She couldn't risk a whistle or a shout; she could
see another pair of guards turning the far corner.

She pulled at the plastic lid of the dumpster hiding her.
Thankfully it didn't creak. She bit back a gasp of pain as
she lifted herself over the rim of the bin, her bruised ribs
sending white sparks to her eyes, and fished around in the
top bag of garbage. She felt old food and something furry

that she prayed wasn't a deceased pet. Her fingers felt something powdery with little bits of spongy paper. She knew this, someone had emptied an ashtray. Grabbing a handful of butts, Ellie slipped out of the dumpster and crept closer to the opening of the alley.

The approaching guards stopped at Mr. MacDonald, and she heard them urging him to go back inside. True to form, the old man took umbrage at their suggestion, and she could make out what sounded like a cutting lecture on his opinion of their suggestion. One guard waved a finger in his face, and MacDonald dismissed him with a wave. Rolling their eyes, the guards moved on to the end of the block, again coming very close to where Ellie crouched hidden.

She launched the first cigarette butt, then a second. He paid no mind. The third hit him in the shoulder and fell unnoticed, but the fourth bounced off his hand. He looked up to see what had fallen, then fished in his pocket for a cigarette of his own. Ellie checked her palm. She had six butts left. Risking a step to the very edge of the shadow, she flicked two butts in quick succession, one of them pinging the old man on the cheek. He looked annoyed and pushed off the light post, his brow dark. Ellie waved to him from the shadow and his eyes widened. She put her fingers to her lips and he got her meaning. Taking a casual stance, he strolled down the curb and made his way to her hiding place.

Keeping his back to her, he leaned against the building and spoke softly. "Do I want to know why you're hiding in an alley covered in blood?"

"There isn't time to explain. You've got to get away from this building."

"That's funny. That's exactly what the guards who brought me here told me at my apartment. Can you give a better explanation than they did?"

"I think the building has a bomb in it."

"Hmm, that's what they said about my apartment." He blew out a plume of smoke. "I am more inclined, however, to believe you. A bloody face is very convincing."

"Mr. MacDonald, please listen to me. There isn't much time. You can't be near this building or the press conference tomorrow morning. Feno has a plan that is..." She hesitated to tell him the details, wondering if she could even tell him he was not infected. If Bing's plan worked, if this building blew up and these people were killed, was it a kindness or a cruelty for them to know they died uninfected?

"We're becoming more and more aware of Feno's plan." He pulled his flask out and passed it into the shadows where she hid. "You're going to need this when I tell you what Olivia has learned. It seems we are clean."

"You know." She took a sip of the bourbon, liking the burning on her cut lips.

"Yes. Some people think this gathering of the population into several crowded locations is a good sign. I am not one of those people."

"You're right. Listen to me. You have to get as many people as you can away from this building. Do whatever you have to do. They don't plan on letting any of us out of here."

MacDonald chuckled. "The very words they are ascribing to you, young lady."

"I've got to get to the north med center. There are soldiers there who are—"

"Don't bother. It's been evacuated. They dropped off a dozen or so people here and are taking the rest to the clearinghouse at the east gate." He reached for the flask and took a drink. "It cannot be a coincidence that they are gathering us in a tidy line, easily viewed by the world press gathered on the other side of the east barrier."

Ellie looked to the east as if she could see the plan unfolding there. "Shit."

"Shit is right, Ellie. Listen to me very carefully." He turned his head and she could see his profile against the streetlight. The light caught the glassiness of his eyes, and she wondered if he was just a little bit drunk. She didn't blame him. "It is very probable that I and most of us here are not going to make it out of this purgatory alive."

"No, there's got to be a way—"

He held up his hand to silence her. "This isn't the time for false optimism. We are being detained. You are not. You are in the unenviable position of being able to do something, and do something you must. What is your full name, child?"

"Eleanor Marie Cauley." All at once she felt as if she were in fourth grade.

"Eleanor Marie Cauley, we have been held in the clutches of evil for nearly seven years." She heard the slur in his voice. Drunk or not, she hung on his words. "We are outnumbered and outgunned and have every reason to despair. But it is exactly these odds that cause Fortune to smile upon those of us stupid enough to fight to defend what is decent and what is right. They cannot be allowed to silence the cries of the lives they have taken. You know what you need to do."

Ellie choked back a sob. "I don't."

"You do. You have got to get out of this zone, no matter what it takes. You have got to tell the world what has been happening in here."

"There's a team of soldiers who are trying to get word out—"

He turned to face her fully. "You can't count on that. You have to do this."

"How?" Tears cut through the blood on her cheeks. "I can't just bust out of here."

He put his hand on her shoulder. "A man much wiser than I once said, 'If not you, who? If not now, when?'" He pulled her closer and kissed her forehead. "I have all the faith in the world in you, Eleanor Marie Cauley. Thank you for letting an old professor give one last lecture. Now go. I'll do what I can here."

Ellie watched him head back into the building. She felt the plastic hard drive in her pocket dig at her hip. She had to get it to Guy. Mr. MacDonald might have all the faith in the world in her, but Ellie knew she was nobody's hero. Slipping through the shadows, she ducked between two parked Feno trucks as another black truck rolled by. She headed east. If Guy had been at the north med center, he would know that's where they were headed.

She didn't know this far edge of Flowertown. Seven years and she had never had cause to come to the clearinghouse where deliveries in and out had to be cleared. It was a large, beige metal building with enormous rolling doors. Around it, several small two-story buildings sat back on narrow roads that branched off of the main road. Ellie hid behind a paneled truck and looked down the road toward the clearinghouse. The asphalt was black under the halogen lights, and the road was in perfect condition. It widened here to three times the width of the roads within the zone, and the length of it was lit all the way to a heavy chain-link gate. She stared at the gate and the guards posted on either side of it. This was the east gate. This was the road out of Flowertown.

Somewhere in the shadows off to her right, she heard a scuffle and the sound of guns being cocked. She ducked down as far as she could get, peering out from beneath the truck to see who was there, but whatever was happening was behind the cinder block building on the corner. She couldn't risk crossing the main road here, under the lights, with all the guards around. She had to get into the shadows behind the cinder block building. Gripping the crowbar like a club, she ran in a crouch across the pool of light above her and flattened herself against the back wall. She heard radios crackle.

"Gate building four secure, sir."

A staticky voice answered, "What's the count?"

"Seven, sir. From north med. Plus two army."

"Sanitize the scene. Do not, repeat, do not call in security."

"Understood, sir."

More static. "The convoy is en route."

The convoy. Ellie blew out a silent breath. Bing was on his way out of the compound. If he got out of the zone before Guy's team, he would blow the buildings. Even if everyone wasn't killed, Ellie knew the lockdown protocols would be unbreakable. Checking her grip on the crowbar, she risked a peek around the corner of the building. Two black-clad guards adjusted their weapons and, looking to see they weren't being watched, slipped through the door.

Ellie heard a dull thud come from inside the building, then another.

She crouched down below the high window and argued with herself about looking. She had to find Guy. She had to get away from this area, but she couldn't stop herself from straightening her legs and peering over the ledge into the bright room. At first she didn't understand what she was seeing. It looked like the guards were examining piles of laundry. Then she saw a muzzle flash and saw one of the piles collapse onto itself. They were people in hospital scrubs on their knees, facing the wall, their heads covered in pillowcases. One by one, the guards moved behind them and fired their silenced guns into their brains, letting the bodies topple forward.

Ellie caught her scream and dropped to the ground. She had to cover her face with her hands, the crowbar pressing into her bruised forehead. Her ears rang with terror, and she was sure her heartbeat would give her away. The metal bar grew slick in her sweating hands, and she nearly dropped it when the door to the building swung open and light flooded the area around the corner from where she hid. She had to fight to silence her harsh breath as the guards passed less than five feet from where she crouched. They opened the tailgate of a black Feno truck and pulled out two bound figures.

The radio crackled once more. "Black Team, convoy is on the move, ETA three minutes. Secure gate, weapons ready. Escort vehicle in position on my mark."

One of the guards picked up his radio. "Black Team is approaching position." He slipped the radio back onto his belt along with his gun. He nodded to the two figures kneeling before his partner. "You got this? I'm riding in the back of the lead vehicle."

"Yeah, go ahead." The second guard nodded. "I'll set the explosives on these two and follow in this truck. Make sure the gate is clear and nobody tries to stop us. I heard Byrd on the radio earlier. He's having some kind of meltdown. This has got to go off without a hitch." His partner headed off toward the gate. As he stepped away, the light fell on the two people on the ground. Ellie squinted, trying to make out the figures, and bit down on her lip when she saw them. It was Guy and Porter, on their knees, hands bound behind their backs. The guard checked his clip.

Her palms filled with sweat as the guard pointed the gun at the back of Guy's head. Not giving herself time to think, Ellie charged from the shadows, crowbar held high, and threw herself onto the black-clad man. A foot taller than her, he staggered rather than fell, and his bullet blew into the dirt beside Guy. Guy and Porter leapt to their feet, their hands still bound, as Ellie silenced the guard with one crushing blow of the iron bar to the side of his skull. The man twitched, his mouth moving, but he didn't make a sound.

Ellie raised the bar again, ready to pulverize him should he recover, but Guy ran to her. She nearly swung the club at him until she realized what was happening. She ripped away the duct tape covering his mouth.

"He's got a knife on his belt," Guy whispered, nodding to the dead guard. "Cut our ties." Ellie turned the guard over, not looking at the mess of blood and bone on his head, and found the utility knife on his belt. Her hands trembled as she cut the heavy plastic ties that bound Guy and Porter.

"It's Bing." She and Guy spoke in unison.

"I know," they answered together, and Guy pulled her to him in a tight hug.

Ellie pulled back, looking through the shadows to the main road. "The convoy is coming. Bing is going to get out of here and give the orders to blow the rest of the buildings. Did you find all the explosives?"

"There's no way to know. We've got a man outside on the barrier we've been trying to contact." He knelt down and searched the guard's pocket until he found a set of keys. "We're taking this truck out of here and across that barrier before Byrd's men get him out and he activates the protocol."

"How are we going to do that?"

Guy put his hands on her shoulders. "You can't go." He silenced her protests with a squeeze to her shoulders. "Listen to me, Ellie. There are going to be guns and soldiers and they're going to be shooting at us and we're going to have to shoot back. It's too dangerous. You have to stay here, find a place to hole up away from the buildings."

"Guy, I can't just stay here."

He put his hands on her cheeks, being careful not to hurt her. "Enough people have died, Ellie. I can't let you be one of them. You can do more here. If we don't get out, if something happens to us, you have to keep working to get the word out."

"If something happens to you, we're all dead. All of us."

He kissed her forehead and grinned at her. "Then I'd better be as good as I think I am."

He and Porter disappeared into the shadows before she had a chance to realize she hadn't given him the hard drive. She swore under her breath and swung the crowbar uselessly in the dark. What the hell was she supposed to do now? She couldn't go back up the main road. To get back to the Public Building meant crossing the same busy streets and shadows she had barely made it across the first time. Ellie felt her fingers tingling and took one-two-three deep breaths to control herself.

She had to hide. Guy told her to hide away from the buildings that might blow, but Flowertown was nothing but buildings. Buildings and fences. She moved quickly away from the main road, closer to the barrier fence, figuring the last place Feno would place a bomb would be along the fence line. As she slipped between the trucks parked against a low cinder block building, she heard the heavy rumble of a motor and the rattle of chain-link fence. Was Bing already at the gate?

Not caring if she was spotted, Ellie ran out of the shadows and looked down the service alley toward the main gate. Guards were running around the gate and the guard shack, but the gate itself remained closed. A black-clad guard approached the man at the control panel of the main gate and she saw another muzzle flash. The goon dragged the body out of the control room and tossed it aside. In a moment the main gate began to open.

Ducking back into the shadows, Ellie ran along the length of the building until she turned the corner toward the fence. Less than twenty feet ahead, another large section of the gate was rolling to the side. The motor sound grew deeper, and Ellie ran forward as a tamping drone rolled slowly through the barrier. Up close, she was surprised to see it wasn't much larger than a VW Bug.

She watched it, her mouth open. She couldn't do this. It was impossible. She thought of Mr. MacDonald and his earnest speech and knew she wasn't one of those heroes Fortune smiled upon. She never had been. But she had the evidence in her pocket to bring down Feno. She remembered Bing and his threats and the feeling of being tied to a bed in a very white room, and she ran.

The drone moved slowly and Ellie caught up to it before it even cleared the first gate. She dropped the crowbar and trotted alongside the machine, trying to figure out how she could hide herself on the simple metal machine. Since it was unmanned, there was no seat, no cab in which to hide. There was only the axle with two heavy tires around a long spraying pipe attached to a heavy steel drum. The entire mechanism was shielded in metal plates with half a dozen valve openings scattered across the surface. She heard the sound of the outer gate opening, and for the first time in almost seven years, Ellie was within touching distance of earth that was not contained within Flowertown.

She knew she would be spotted running alongside the drone, and so she jumped up against the side of the machine, bracing herself over the drum cover, until she could find hand- and footholds in the open valves from which to hang. She pressed her face to the cool metal, her bloodied fingers fighting for purchase on the oily valves, her toes trembling in their precarious position, and she felt sweat slip between her and the metal as the drone slipped through the final gate.

Behind her, a radio crackled. "Drone seven clear, gate clear."

She almost relaxed until a loud siren blared and lights flooded the fence line as far as she could see. Ellie nearly lost her grip as she craned her head around to look. A worker in a jumpsuit ran toward the drone gate, waving his arms, and then crumpled. Ellie gasped, not understanding what had happened until she saw a dark-haired man step into the light. Torrez held her crowbar. He nodded at her and pulled the gate closed.

The lights that lined the barrier road shone over her head, the drone keeping her in shadows as it began its route along the highway. Ellie heard a whirring sound within the metal casing and nearly fell off as the pesticide/herbicide mixture sprayed out inches in front of her face. Fumes from the noxious chemicals burned her eyes, and her lungs ached to take a breath. She turned her head away and could see, just over the heavy drum behind her, the east gate of Flowertown come to life with activity. Sirens flashed and searchlights flooded the gate area. Ellie nearly lost her grip once more as she lifted herself high enough to see the road beside her.

Two black Feno trucks raced along the barrier road. Tears streamed from her eyes from the chemical fumes, obscuring her view, but she could make out muzzle flashes. Over the heavy rumble of the drone, she could hear the scrape of metal on metal as the two trucks clashed. She knew one truck was Bing's; she prayed the other was Guy's. The drone rolled along the dead earth of the barrier zone parallel to the road, well ahead of the trucks. The chemicals burned the open wounds on her face, and she pressed her cheek against the metal. Guy would make it. He would stop Bing.

The drone slowed and she heard gears shifting. Pulling her face back, she cried out as she saw the road to her left getting farther away. The drone was turning. It was running its circuit. It was heading back to the barrier gate. She trusted Guy and knew his team would make it, but the plastic case of the external hard drive still dug into her hip. She had the evidence. She had everything she needed to bring Feno down. Ellie knew she could not go back to Flowertown.

Pushing off with her knees, Ellie dropped and rolled away from the tamping drone. It finished its slow turn and with relentless precision began its course back to the gate. Ellie stood alone, exposed, on the gray ash of the barrier zone. On the highway less than twenty yards to her left, sparks flew as the trucks collided side by side, and ahead, spotlights exploded. Straight ahead Ellie could see TV trucks with high, mounted halogen lights and a wall of brightly colored media vans, police cars, and army trucks. There were no fences on this side of the barrier. And she knew that if she could see them, they could see her. She began to run to them.

The barren soil of the barrier crumbled under her pounding feet, and Ellie felt her muscles burning with the effort. Tears streamed from her eyes, her vision blurry from the chemical burns, and she tasted blood in her mouth as she worked to push her lungs. She was less than half a mile from the end of the barrier zone, the outside world, when she heard the gunshots. Daring a look to the left, she saw one of the Feno trucks skidding as its tires exploded. The other truck tore down the highway, racing toward the crowd.

She could see faces now and knew they could see her. People pointed and lights were turned on her, nearly blinding her, and still she ran. She pounded across the soft dirt, not thinking, not feeling, just running, one word screaming from her lips.

"Clean! Clean!"

From the corner of her eye, she saw the truck pass her and saw a figure in black watching her too. Not just watching—pointing a gun at her.

When the bullet punched through her shoulder, Ellie Cauley experienced many things in a matter of seconds. She felt herself lifted off the ground and knew an odd coldness in her shoulder. As she spun, her feet flying out before her, she saw the truck racing out of her line of sight and, behind it, a figure running hard down the road. She heard another shot and saw the figure fall as she herself crashed into the soft, dead earth of the barrier. She heard a loud thud as her skull collided with the ground, and before she lost consciousness, she saw a blaze of light as buildings in the distance exploded. Then everything was darkness.

CHAPTER TWENTY-FIVE

Ellie felt herself coming up from a deep hole. The first thought she had was that she was impossibly thirsty. She tried to pull open her eyelids, but they weighed a hundred pounds and seemed to be glued shut. She heard her breath whistling through her nose and felt something lying on her face.

With a superhuman effort, Ellie forced her lids apart and stared at the whiteness before her. She blinked, her focus blurry, and ran her dry tongue over her rough lips. It hurt to swallow. Taking a deep breath, she tried to move. Her left shoulder ached with a dull, drumming pain, and she couldn't turn her head in that direction. She tried to pull her right hand up but felt something pull at her wrist. The sound of metal rattling at the effort brought Ellie out of her sleep with a panicked rush. She tried to sit up and failed against the restraints. Above her head, an IV bag dripped clear liquids down a tube. As the room came into focus she saw a television mounted on the wall on the other side of the room. A cartoon pig danced to a silent song. Ellie fell back against the pillow.

She could smell flowers.

The room was white. The white room. White, white, white.

The door opened and a middle-aged woman in scrubs came to her bedside to check the IV bag. She smiled at Ellie. "You're awake. How are you feeling?"

A scream ripped out of Ellie's throat as she arched her back, tears flooding her eyes. The nurse put her hands on her shoulders, forcing her back into the bed as Ellie's screams became a chant: "Fuck you! Fuck you! Fuck you!"

She burst into hard, jagged sobs as an armed soldier burst through the door. The nurse struggled to hold her still, and Ellie heard voices at the door. She didn't care. Let them shoot her. She screamed and kicked, the thin hospital blankets flying to the floor around her. Another woman ran into the room, syringe in hand, and injected it into the IV port. Immediately Ellie felt warmth in her muscles and fell back against the bed.

The nurse holding her relaxed her grip. "Are you in pain?"

"Fuck you."

The woman took a deep breath and tried again. "Are you in pain?"

"Fuck you!"

"Okay." She stepped back. "I think you'll live."

The door opened once more and Ellie heard a man's voice. "Oh, she'll live. She's too mean to die from just a bullet." The nurses stepped away from the bed and Guy swung into view, balancing on crutches. Ellie stopped screaming, her breath frozen in her throat. Guy leaned against the foot of her bed.

"We've given her a sedative."

Guy smiled. "That's probably a good idea."

"Tell me about it." The nurse shot Ellie a look as she followed the other woman out of the room. Guy waited until the door closed before hopping up toward the right side of the bed. Ellie could hear herself panting as panic and confusion flooded over her.

"Guy?" He brushed the hair off her forehead. "Untie me."

"Untie you?"

She pulled at the restraint on her right wrist and heard the metal rattle again. Guy frowned and looked closer at her arm.

"You're just twisted in the sheets." He unwrapped a thick length of hospital linen tangled around her wrist where it stuck out between the bars of the bed guard. "Unclench your fist." He put his hand on hers and gently unfolded her fingers. "Do you know where you are?"

Ellie began to cry. "In the care center."

"No. This is the Walter Reed Medical Center." His voice was soft. "In Maryland."

Ellie couldn't let herself believe it. "Then how come I smell flowers?"

Guy pointed to the other side of the bed. Ellie had to strain to turn her head that far. On the nightstand sat a vase with an enormous flower arrangement, including a dozen stargazer lilies. "Sorry about that. They're from your family. They insisted."

Ellie squeezed her eyes shut. "My family?"

She felt him kiss her fingertips. "They've been here for two days waiting for you to wake up. You lost a lot of blood.

You were in isolation until the chemical burns started to heal." He ran his fingers lightly over the gauze on her cheeks. "Do you want me to call them in?"

Ellie shook her head, knocking loose tears that dampened the bandages. "Not yet. I just...I need... The drive! Did the hard drive get out?"

Guy nodded. "They found it a few feet away from you. The FBI has it and none of the data was corrupted. They found the red pills. Did you know you had a tooth in your pocket? I can only imagine how that got there." He squeezed her hand. "You're under full protection until you're able to testify to the grand jury."

"You were shot."

"Yeah, I guess I wasn't as good as I thought I was. It turns out Fat Ass Fletcher was the only one who won the footrace to the gate. How's that for irony?"

Ellie stared out at the patch of blue sky she could see through the blinds. It was her first non-Iowa view in almost seven years. The enormity of that overwhelmed her, and she looked away.

"Why isn't it on the news?"

Guy looked up at the dancing pig on the television. "Do you know how hard they had to look to find a channel that wasn't covering it? The doctors didn't want you waking up and seeing it on the news." He smirked. "They thought it might upset you."

"I hate doctors."

"So do I." Guy reached across her bed to the far nightstand for the remote, pushing his body close, too close, the way he always did. The way she loved it. She tipped her head forward until her cheek brushed the warm muscle of his shoulder. He shifted, not breaking contact with her body, moving his face until his breath was hot on her ear. "Want sound?"

Ellie shook her head, pressing her face into the warmth of his neck. She kissed the soft spot beneath his jaw, feeling his pulse on her lips. Behind him, she could see the television filled with images of burning buildings and smoke-filled skies. She closed her eyes as the medication in the IV began to settle over her.

"Rachel?"

Guy pulled his head up, careful not to disturb the gauze on her cheek, and pressed his forehead to hers. "They said she wouldn't leave the building until everybody got out. She wouldn't leave the old women on the second floor. She didn't make it out of the Public Building."

"Stupid farm girl." Ellie's voice cracked. Before she could speak again, Guy placed his lips against hers. It wasn't a kiss. It was contact, breath, and she let herself drift on the sensation.

"Ellie," Guy whispered against her lips. "When I saw you…when you were shot…" He leaned back to look at her, his hand stroking her hair. The muscles in his jaw worked to say the words. "I thought…"

Her hand felt heavy as she lifted it to his cheek. She shook her head, not making him say the rest. Her thumb caught a tear in the corner of his eye and she smiled.

"Tough guy."

He laughed and kissed her palm. "Stoner."

"I'll say." She sank back into the pillow.

"I told them to give you the good stuff," Guy said, straightening out her sheet and tucking her into the bed. "I told them you had a high tolerance."

She felt her eyelids sliding down but wasn't ready to let Guy leave. Her hand found his and he wrapped her fingers in his own. "What's going to happen now?"

"Now you're going to sleep."

"No." She could hear the thickness in her own voice. "I mean, what happens with Bing and Feno? What's going to happen?"

"Sleep, Ellie."

Something in his tone made her struggle to open her eyes, and she grabbed his hand before he could pull it away. "What? What are you not telling me?"

"Ellie, you need to sleep."

"I need to know what happened. What's going to happen."

Guy stared down at her hand squeezing his. The tension had returned to his face, and she could see him struggle for words. "They didn't get him, Ellie."

She felt the breath rush from her lungs as if she'd been punched.

"In the confusion, in all the explosions and the chaos, he, um…" Guy wouldn't meet her eyes. "His whereabouts have not been confirmed. Several Feno guards have testified that he never made it out of the barrier zone."

"You know that's not true."

His hand clenched into a fist in her grip. "It's complicated, Ellie. My orders. The people involved. This investigation is…complicated."

"Complicated?" Shock and pain medication were winning and she fell back against the pillow. "What's complicated about it? He's out there."

Guy finally looked her in the eye, his voice low and raw. "I know. And I'm going to find him. I don't care what my orders are. I'm going to find him and I'm going to make him pay."

She couldn't speak; her lips were numb. There was nothing to say anyway. She could only stare, struggling to stay awake, fighting to keep her eyes on Guy. She wanted to burn the image of his face on her brain, but as her body drifted into the pit of sleep, she knew the nightmare that waited for her, the birdlike face in the darkness. But she wasn't afraid. Not anymore. If Guy promised to get him, he would.

Unless she got him first.

ACKNOWLEDGMENTS

There is no way I can close this book without expressing my deepest gratitude, appreciation, and love to the many people who helped bring this story to life: to my friend, agent, and whip-cracker Christine Witthohn for never giving up; to Terry Goodman and the Amazon team for taking a chance; to my development editor David Downing, whose skills are nothing short of magical; to Judy Jennings and my radio family who helped me make that scary leap; to Mary, Monica, and Matthew and all my family who keep on loving me no matter how weird I get; special thanks to my best friend Gina Milum and all the Book Thugs—Christy Smith, Debra Burge, Tenna Rusk, Debra McDanald, Angela Jackson, Alisha Jackson, Alecia Cole, and Tina Dayhaw—the smartest, toughest readers I know; and finally to Gordon Ramey for too many reasons to count.

J

OCEAN
LIFE UP
CLOSE

Walruses

by Kari Schuetz

BLASTOFF!
3
READERS

BELLWETHER MEDIA • MINNEAPOLIS, MN

Note to Librarians, Teachers, and Parents:

Blastoff! Readers are carefully developed by literacy experts and combine standards-based content with developmentally appropriate text.

Level 1 provides the most support through repetition of high-frequency words, light text, predictable sentence patterns, and strong visual support.

Level 2 offers early readers a bit more challenge through varied simple sentences, increased text load, and less repetition of high-frequency words.

Level 3 advances early-fluent readers toward fluency through increased text and concept load, less reliance on visuals, longer sentences, and more literary language.

Level 4 builds reading stamina by providing more text per page, increased use of punctuation, greater variation in sentence patterns, and increasingly challenging vocabulary.

Level 5 encourages children to move from "learning to read" to "reading to learn" by providing even more text, varied writing styles, and less familiar topics.

Whichever book is right for your reader, Blastoff! Readers are the perfect books to build confidence and encourage a love of reading that will last a lifetime!

This edition first published in 2017 by Bellwether Media, Inc.

No part of this publication may be reproduced in whole or in part without written permission of the publisher. For information regarding permission, write to Bellwether Media, Inc., Attention: Permissions Department, 5357 Penn Avenue South, Minneapolis, MN 55419.

Library of Congress Cataloging-in-Publication Data

Names: Schuetz, Kari, author.
Title: Walruses / by Kari Schuetz.
Description: Minneapolis, MN : Bellwether Media, Inc., [2017] | Series:
    Blastoff! Readers. Ocean Life Up Close | Audience: Age 5-8. | Audience:
    Grade K to grade 3. | Includes bibliographical references and index.
Identifiers: LCCN 2015051072 | ISBN 9781626174245 (hardcover : alk. paper)
Subjects: LCSH: Walrus–Juvenile literature.
Classification: LCC QL737.P62 S38 2017 | DDC 599.79/9–dc23
LC record available at http://lccn.loc.gov/2015051072

Printed in the United States of America, North Mankato, MN.

Table of Contents

tusks

Walruses are **mammals** with mustaches. Two huge teeth called **tusks** stick out of their mouths.

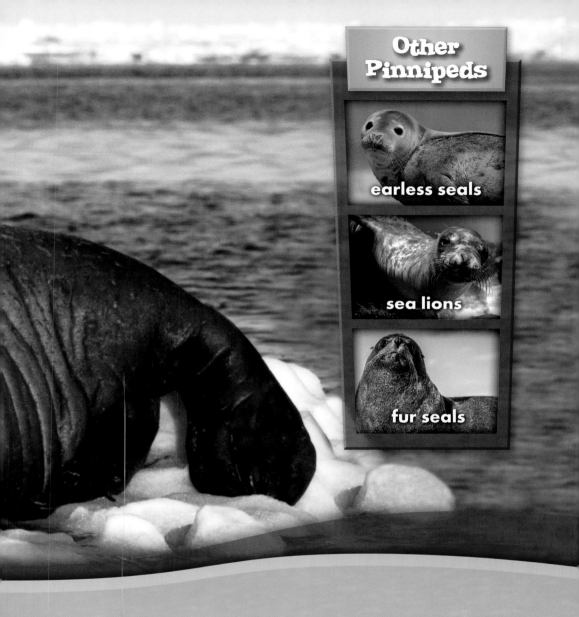

earless seals

sea lions

fur seals

Like other **pinnipeds**, walruses
have **flippers** for feet. Flippers
help them move underwater and
on ice.

These mammals are found in the **Arctic**. They mainly live in the cold, northern waters of the Pacific and Atlantic Oceans.

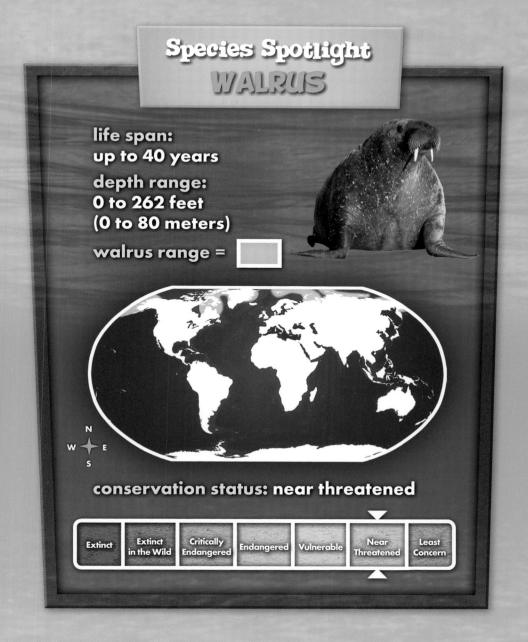

Species Spotlight
WALRUS

life span:
up to 40 years

depth range:
**0 to 262 feet
(0 to 80 meters)**

walrus range =

conservation status: **near threatened**

Extinct	Extinct in the Wild	Critically Endangered	Endangered	Vulnerable	Near Threatened	Least Concern

The large animals rest on land and floating ice.

Blubber and Whiskers

Walruses are huge in size. The biggest males can be 12 feet (3.6 meters) long and more than 3,000 pounds (1,361 kilograms)!

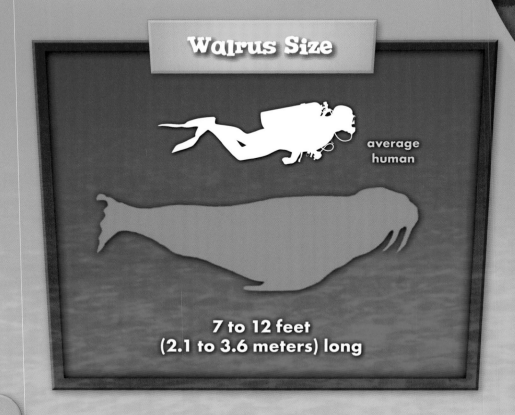

Walrus Size

average human

7 to 12 feet
(2.1 to 3.6 meters) long

Part of their weight is thick
blubber. This layer of fat under
their skin keeps them warm.

Walruses' tough skin is wrinkled. It is usually gray or brown in the cold water. But it can turn pinkish on land.

Walruses usually suck up **prey** from the ocean floor. Whiskers help them feel for food.

Catch of the Day

soft-shell clams

Pacific razor clams

Baltic clams

whiskers

Front flippers work
like paddles in water.
They guide turns.
Back flippers power
walruses forward.

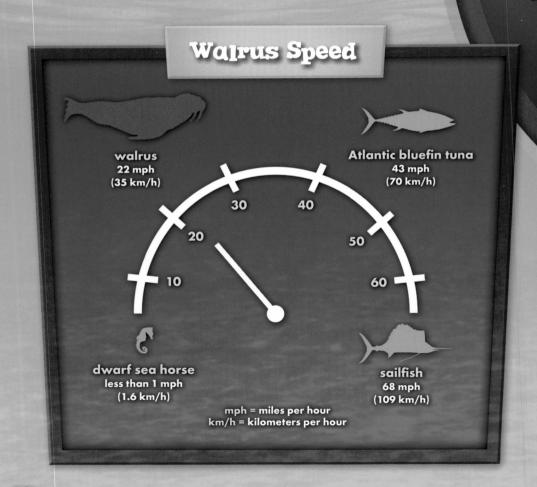

Walrus Speed

walrus
22 mph
(35 km/h)

Atlantic bluefin tuna
43 mph
(70 km/h)

30   40

20

50

10   60

dwarf sea horse
less than 1 mph
(1.6 km/h)

sailfish
68 mph
(109 km/h)

mph = miles per hour
km/h = kilometers per hour

front
flipper

back
flipper

Walruses also use flippers to flop
on land. Rough bottoms keep the
flippers from slipping on ice.

Tough Tusks

Up to 3 feet (1 meter) long, walrus tusks are strong tools. They can chip at ice to make holes for breathing.

Identify a Walrus

thick mustache

long tusks

flat flippers

Walruses also use tusks like ice picks. These teeth help lift walruses out of the water!

Males have longer tusks than females. They show them off in **threat displays**.

Sometimes the tusks become
weapons to fight other males.
The animals fight over **territory**
and females.

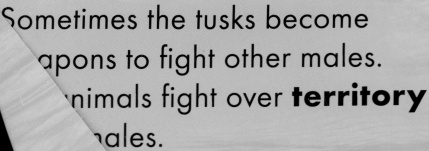

In the Herd

Hundreds of walruses can make up a **herd**. Male and female walruses spend most of the year in separate herds.

herd

18

Pups grow up with females. The moms look after the pups for up to three years.

Male walruses always make sure
they are heard. They often growl
when they fight.

To charm females, males make bell-like sounds underwater. To do this, pouches on their necks swell with air!

Glossary

Arctic—the cold region around the North Pole

blubber—the fat of walruses

flippers—flat, wide body parts that are used for swimming

herd—a group of walruses

mammals—warm-blooded animals that have backbones and feed their young milk

pinnipeds—ocean mammals with four flippers; sea lions, seals, and walruses are pinnipeds.

prey—animals that are hunted by other animals for food

pups—baby walruses

territory—the area where an animal lives

threat displays—behaviors that animals perform to show strength

tusks—long, curved teeth

To Learn More

AT THE LIBRARY

Kaufmann, Carol. *Polar: A Photicular Book.* New York, N.Y.: Workman Publishing, 2015.

Miller, Sara Swan. *Walruses of the Arctic.* New York, N.Y.: PowerKids Press, 2009.

Person, Stephen. *Walrus: Tusk, Tusk.* New York, N.Y.: Bearport Pub., 2011.

ON THE WEB

Learning more about walruses is as easy as 1, 2, 3.

1. Go to www.factsurfer.com.

2. Enter "walruses" into the search box.

3. Click the "Surf" button and you will see a list of related web sites.

With factsurfer.com, finding more information is just a click away.

Index

The images in this book are reproduced through the courtesy of: Vladimir Melnik, front cover, pp. 3, 7, 15 (bottom); Louise Murray/ Age Fotostock/ SuperStock, pp. 4-5; Marco Rolleman, p. 5 (top); Longjourneys, p. 5 (center); SkyLynx, p. 5 (bottom); SuperStock/ Glow Images, p. 6; Michael Nolan/ robertharding/ SuperStock, p. 9; Yuriy Kvach/ Wikipedia, p. 11 (top left); RazorClam23/ Wikipedia, p. 11 (top center); Sandy Rae/ Wikipedia, p. 11 (top right); Rebecca Jackrel/ Age Fotostock/ SuperStock, p. 11 (bottom); Paul Souders/ Corbis, pp. 13, 16; Kenneth Canning, p. 14; SasinT, p. 15 (top left); tryton2011, p. 15 (top center); Hal Brindley, p. 15 (top right); Juniors Bildarchiv GmbH/ Alamy, p. 17; Maximilian Buzun, p. 18; tryton2011, p. 19; BMJ, p. 20; Fabrice Simon/ Corbis, p. 21.